MAGGIE ALMOND AND THE MASKED WOMAN

JENNY BOND

Cover design DAMONZA.COM

ISBN: 9780645345964

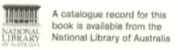 A catalogue record for this book is available from the National Library of Australia

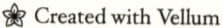 Created with Vellum

CHAPTER 1

Durham, North East England
Mid-September 1880

THE DOOR to the cottage thrust open and Maggie charged through it like a dragoon. Throwing her bag on the table, she sat and tore off her hat as though it were on fire. She ran her fingers through her hair and pins, discharging like shrapnel, scattered across the surrounding floor. Finally, she took a deep breath and was still. She slumped her head in her hands. William, who was working at the table, calmly placed the cap on his fountain pen, twisting it slowly until it was secure. He had witnessed Maggie's displays of temper many times before, but this was different, more intense, more inflammable. She was small but mighty.

A minute later, Grace Dodd entered through the front door and offered her son a pitying shake of her head, an action he read as 'Don't try speaking to her yet.' Silently, the older woman moved to Maggie and squeezed her shoulder, then pressed her lips to the crown of her head. Maggie touched Grace's hand in gratitude. Grace smiled and bid the pair goodnight.

William rose and moved to the cooker.

'Don't make tea,' Maggie said firmly. 'Please, don't make tea.'

'Something stronger?'

She nodded. Maggie had discovered in the twelve months she had been living in County Durham that there were few beverages stronger than Geordie tea, but this was definitely an occasion for one of them.

William hastily snatched a bottle of whiskey from the shelf along with two glasses. He filled them both. He raised his in her direction.

Maggie drank half of hers in one swig.

'Tell me,' William prompted.

Maggie looked into his earnest hazel eyes for a moment and sighed. *Where do I even begin?* she thought.

It had been the Eleventh Congress of the Durham National Society for Women's Suffrage, an organisation founded by Maggie shortly after her arrival in Durham. As usual, she held it in the kitchen of William's sister. Beth, a midwife, was well liked – sensible, straight talking and wise, with a wry sense of humour the weary women of Durham appreciated. The men, too. Her home was on the High Street, in the centre of town. She, her husband Jack Littlefair and their four children lived above her husband's shop. He was a blacksmith and ironmonger.

Maggie had chosen Beth's kitchen as the venue for the meetings over the town hall and St Bede's because it seemed to be the most accommodating spot. She had ruled out the Dodd's cottage immediately. Many of the women whom Maggie had hoped would attend the meetings lived in the township; she'd not wanted the inconvenience of a thirty-minute trek along the river to dampen their enthusiasm for the cause. She had also assumed a clandestine venue would suit any attendee who would not want their husband knowing they were at a women's suffrage meeting. Most of the men in Durham (William excluded) were as freethinking as whelks.

'You're overthinking the situation,' William said when they had discussed the location. 'I'll collect the ladies myself in the cart and ferry them from town to home again.'

Maggie stood aghast at the suggestion. 'This isn't one of your union meetings!'

'Tell me, what's the difference?' he replied, raising an eyebrow. 'Your wee meeting is all about justice and equality, is it not?'

She both loathed and loved him when he grew facetious.

At the commencement of this most recent meeting, Maggie had lifted her fountain pen and set to the task of listing the attendees in her register. Grace, William's mother. Beth, William's sister – obviously. It was her kitchen, after all. Beth's daughters, Agnes, Betty and Jane, sat on a rug in the corner playing with their dolls. Although Maggie included their names on the roll of attendance, she had to admit that the girls, aged seven, five and three, were less than engaged in the proceedings. Missus Regina Hartley, the butcher's wife, who could cure and smoke an extremely fine pork belly, sat beside Grace with an expression as sour as pickling liquid. Enid Winship, Missus Hartley's widowed sister, was also in attendance. Cheerier than Regina but less radically minded, it was clear to Maggie that Enid was only present to offer moral support to her sibling. There were several other women there as well – a mix of pitmen's and storemen's wives – and one face she had not seen at any of the previous meetings.

'Welcome,' Maggie said, looking directly at the unknown young woman in what she hoped was an encouraging way. 'I don't think I've seen you here before.'

In fact, Maggie had to delve deep into her mind to recall

seeing the woman anywhere in Durham. Although town growth had ceased since the collapse of the Stanley Pit, Durham was a sizeable district of almost 10,000 people. Still, Maggie's memory was a steel trap and if she had seen the woman before, even once, she would surely recognise her. Her gaze lingered on the woman and then she had it – she'd seen her once or twice in town. She had appeared anxious each time Maggie had passed her on the High Street, averting her eyes as though she were a sheep wary of being stalked by wolves.

'Lucy Owen, Miss,' the young woman said, pushing a lock of blonde hair behind her ear. 'Missus Hartley mentioned your meetings the last time I was in the shop.'

Maggie smiled and added the name to her list, then glanced at Regina Hartley who nodded in a way Maggie could only describe as pompous.

Once the administrative tasks were dealt with, she began.

'Welcome to the Eleventh Congress of the Durham National Society for Women's Suffrage. As President, I would like to begin by thanking you all for coming.'

Maggie paused and smiled again. Grace and Beth both looked at her supportively.

'Now, I realise at our last meeting we resolved to pen a petition regarding the installation of a women's lavatory in the town hall.'

The attendees nodded and murmured, recalling the resolution.

'However, I would like to delay this item until our next meeting in October,' Maggie said, looking pointedly at Grace, who was taking the minutes.

Grace nodded. 'Are we all in agreement?' she asked the gathering.

A series of 'ayes' echoed around the kitchen.

'Thank you, ladies,' Maggie said, before going on. 'Very well, then. The first order of business I wish to raise concerns the education of girls in Durham.' Maggie glanced at Beth's three daughters. 'Despite the passing of the recent Education Act legislating the compulsory education of all children aged between five and ten, parents rarely enrol their daughters in school – or what passes as a school here in Durham. I checked the numbers with Reverend Cald—'

'You're saying it's the law for mothers and fathers to send their girl children to school?' Missus Hartley interrupted, astonished.

'Indeed.'

'My Alma is nine. She's needed in the shop.'

'That may well be, Missus Hartley, but the law states—'

A loud, dismissive scoff silenced Maggie.

Regina Hartley folded her arms defiantly. 'I'd like to see them try to enforce it.'

Maggie drew in a bolstering breath. The idea to help educate the next generation had come to her a few weeks after she had moved to Durham. The number of school-aged children working on their family's farm or in their father's store was shocking. More shocking was the fact that girls far outnumbered boys in these occupations. While most of the male children sat in the schoolroom at St Bede's, parents sent their female children to work. The girls had no opportunity to learn their letters or numbers.

Recently, a more specific idea had picked up steam in Maggie's mind: she had begun to envisage a school for girls. Although she was loath to admit it, after ten meetings of the Durham National Society for Women's Suffrage, she had achieved nothing. Maggie realised she needed to target girls, not grown women who were reluctant to see change. Most women refused to recognise change as a positive force –

sticking with tradition was one of the few constants in their lives over which they had some control.

'It is not a matter of enforcing the law,' Maggie continued. 'Parents need to understand that if children receive a basic education, even one of the most rudimentary kind, then they will have greater choices in life. Missus Hartley, do you wish to see Alma working in a butcher's shop her entire life?'

Missus Hartley laughed, quite heartily, at the suggestion. 'Don't be daft, lass. Only until she marries and has bairns of her own.'

Maggie released an inner groan. It appeared Regina Hartley was a suffragette only when it was convenient.

'A ladies' lav in the town hall would be a blessing,' Maggie recalled her saying with an anticipatory sigh of relief at the last meeting. 'Men don't know how hard it is to sit through one of the mayor's meetings. My legs are locked as tight as an oyster by the time he's done.'

'Maggie, the girls who are enrolled at school are instructed only in the boys' curriculum,' Grace put in reasonably. 'Reverend Calder will have it no other way. He knows nothing about cooking or sewing or raising a bairn. Parents see no value in their daughters learning mathematics and science when they're destined to be homemakers.'

'I see. But don't you agree this is a question of choice? Girls *should* be able to study maths, science and literature, as well as sewing, if that is what they desire.'

'When did women ever get a choice in anything?' she heard a voice mutter.

Maggie sensed her blood rising, a familiar flush rushing from chest to cheeks.

They're nothing but narrow minded ... Maggie wanted to scream. *Stay calm.*

'Unable to read or even understand the most basic mathematical problem, a lack of education will forever restrict girls to live as a wife and mother, or worse. What's more, a basic knowledge of numbers would give a woman more say at her home. I have seen too many women surrendering control of their family's finances to their husband. And what if they don't wed?' Maggie said, her voice rising in concern. 'What remains for them? A life underground in the mines? Surely, girls should have a choice between marriage and a career. Perhaps they may even choose both!'

Maggie observed the Mmes Hartley and Winship pondering the connotations of such a word as 'career'. There was silence among the group. All of them had witnessed Maggie's temper flare before, but never at such close quarters. They all watched her expectantly. It was as though Vesuvius was in their midst.

'It makes sense, doesn't it?' Lucy Owen put in quietly.

Missus Hartley shot her a hard look.

'What Miss Almond is saying, I mean.'

Maggie was grateful for the young woman's words. Knowing she had one supporter in the room tempered her rage.

'It's worth considering,' Beth said. 'I would like to imagine my three girls will have a choice in the life they lead. I only want them to be happy, after all.'

Grace nodded, considering Lucy's point. 'All of yer here know I've recently taken up studying at the university. I don't regret a day of my life with Archie and our children, but I can't help but think how my life could have panned out if my mam and fatha had let me stay at school a wee bit longer.'

Grace's appeal did nothing to lighten the atmosphere in the room. Most of the women gazed at her, perplexed, as though she were speaking gibberish. Nevertheless, Maggie was grateful for her efforts. Grace's return to school only a few weeks ago, and the joy she had discovered in her learning, had helped cement Maggie's idea.

After a few seconds, good natured Missis Winship attempted to break the wall of tension that had so quickly risen. 'More tea, anyone?' she said, rising and reaching for the teapot.

Once Missus Winship had successfully topped up all the teacups, Maggie went on.

'What I am proposing is the establishment of a girl's school in Durham, one that could provide a suitable education that offers your female children a choice between a home and family or a career. All I am asking for is your support at the next Town Hall meeting.'

Although modest, Maggie's request seemed only to infuriate a few of the women further still.

'When are *you* planning to wed and have bairns, Maggie Almond?' Missus Hartley asked, as her sister resumed her place beside her. 'Or have you *chosen* not to?'

All eyes turned to Maggie.

How dare she use my name in that way? she thought, infuriated. *She makes me sound as though I were renowned throughout England for deviancy!*

Yet despite her indignation, the question did not surprise Maggie. In fact, she wondered why someone hadn't asked it sooner. She had been living with William in Durham for over a year, and people still regarded her choices as completely unfathomable. To them, she was as strange as a sailor on horseback.

'I'm uncertain,' Maggie replied, raising her chin. 'Perhaps I will never marry.'

All she wanted at that moment was to upset Regina Hartley's equilibrium, but then she saw Grace's brow pucker into a frown. Maggie immediately regretted uttering the words. Although Grace had never broached the topic, it was obvious to Maggie that she longed for William and her to be married. The recent loss of her husband and sons had left Grace with an insatiable need to shore up her family with weddings and births.

'Has anyone told Willie that?' Missus Hartley asked rather snidely, or so Maggie thought.

The other women stared into their teacups.

The discussion never returned to the subject of a girl's school. Maggie's confession had only led the women to comment on the upcoming wedding of Maude Watts, Magnus John's eldest. As Beth collected the cups and the women began on the tidying, Missus Hartley had steered the conversation back to the subject of a ladies' privy in the town hall. It seemed her urinary relief was far more urgent than her daughter's education.

Now, as Maggie sat opposite William sipping whiskey and gradually calming, she knew she couldn't divulge all of the evening's events – her admission about marriage would crush him – but she could tell him some.

'I broached the idea of a school for girls. William, it was as though I suggested we all should fly to the moon on broomsticks.'

William laughed and shook his head in astonishment. He looked at her so kindly, Maggie sensed a wave of cold, hard regret regarding the words she had let fly at the meeting cool the warming effects of the whiskey. Still laughing, he lifted her to her feet.

'Well, you have successfully bewitched me, Maggie Almond, and I often wonder at what further magic you're capable.'

He could always make her smile. No matter the situation, William could find humour in it. The only area that was out of bounds to his light-heartedness was the pit. After the collapse of the Stanley Pit the year before that saw the death of his father and brothers, William treated the subject of mine safety with the seriousness of a judge.

'Maybe you're aiming too high,' he said as they readied for bed.

'How can a basic education possibly be too high?'

'Perhaps if the women of Durham saw you as more ...'

'Chaste?' Maggie offered, ruefully.

'Domestic,' William grinned. 'Perhaps then your ideas might become more palatable to them.'

Over the twelve months that had passed since her arrival in town, people had called Maggie many things to her face – indecent, reaching, ambitious, idealistic, hysterical and foolish. She knew that many of the local women viewed her as wanton, although it wasn't the first time she had been thought a harlot. Her position as the only female employee of the *Illustrated London News* and the events of last year – her breaking her engagement to Raymond, her relationship with William and her eventual discharge from the publication – had damaged her reputation irreparably. Maggie's 'wanton ways' had ostracised friends, family and employers.

When William had asked her to follow him to Durham, she had agreed willingly. She loved him and would follow him anywhere. But over the past year she had come to realise that part of her motivation for leaving London had been to escape. She had wanted to flee all the terrible experiences that had occurred over the summer, particularly the tragedy of her friend Claire Clairmont's death. Having written Clairmont's story – a story that England needed to read, whatever scandal it might cause – Maggie had been dismissed from the publication mere hours after learning of Clairmont's passing. Devastated, she had hoped to begin again in the North with William.

She had thought that in a new town, she could be a new woman, build a new life. She had hoped to make new friends as well. Ironically, just the opposite had happened. Apart from William's family, she had made no friends, despite her best efforts. Although Maggie had been in Durham for a year, most women still steered clear of her.

Now, musing on William's words, Maggie considered how she might better engage with the woman of the town.

'Perhaps I could begin a reading group?' she suggested enthusiastically.

William grimaced. 'Women around here have little time for novels and the like. They've got their hands full running the household, feeding bairns, cooking.'

Then Maggie hit on it. 'Sewing! What about a sewing circle?' Despite her inadequate skills, she thought it was an excellent idea.

'I've never seen you with a needle and thread in hand,' William said as she removed her stockings. He gazed at her legs.

'I could say the same of you,' she countered.

He smiled and took her in his arms. Reaching beneath her chemise, William felt the warm, smooth skin of her buttocks and thighs. He kissed her, and her disappointment and frustration over the evening's events vanished. Maggie believed she would never tire of his lips pressed against hers or his hands on her body.

One evening not long after Maggie had arrived, Grace had spoken to them both about their living arrangements. Maggie could sense she had given quite some thought to the situation.

'I give you both my blessing. You are both adults who know your own minds. Don't fash about the gossip. No one will say anything to my face ... and if they do, they'll think twice about doing it a second time.'

The following day, Grace had vacated her bedroom, the one she had shared with her husband, and offered it to Maggie and William. It was the biggest bedroom in the cottage, with a large picture window overlooking the dales, the hedgerows and the fields with flocks of sheep moving across them like clouds.

From that day to this, they had lived as a married couple. Apart from the absence of a wedding band, Maggie was devoted to William and he to her. It was a disappointment to Maggie that to alter others' perception of her or, it appeared, to change the community, she needed to marry. Marriage was too serious a circumstance to be forced into under the pressure of acceptance.

William peppered her neck with kisses as soft as feathers. How she relished these moments when it was just the two of them. His caresses in the dark, his moans and sighs; after more than a year together, they knew each other's bodies intimately. A gentle nibble on his ear could drive him to rapture. The softest of kisses on her neck filled her with fire. Yet, in many ways, they were still getting to know one another. William could still astound her with his turn of phrase and his seemingly infinite well of kindness and support.

She sat astride him, looking down at his dark curls and muscled chest, still bronzed from the summer. He was exquisite. On the hottest days during the summer just past, he would swim in the River Wear, in a bend near an old mill. The water was deep and cold. It was where he had swum as a boy, with his brothers and schoolfriends.

Maggie would watch him peel off his clothes. He'd then dive into the water from the mill's short jetty and disappear for a moment, leaving Maggie holding her breath until he surfaced. As she readied to bathe, he would watch her from the water with only his eyes and nose above the waterline, like a crocodile. Maggie was less daring with her entry. Once free of all her clothes, she would wade in cautiously from the bank.

'Come on, Maggie,' he had called on one occasion. 'Dive in. You're a brave lass.'

So, she had. Shocked by the cold, she came up spluttering and he had pulled her into his arms and laughed. Then they played and chatted in the cool, cold water of the Wear, touching each other and giggling like children.

'What if someone should see us?' Maggie asked the first time she joined him.

'No one comes here anymore, not since the mill closed.'

Occasionally, still slick and cold from the river, they would make love on the bank as the sunlight glinted off William shoulders and dried his back. Once, they had even fallen asleep, naked and twined. That evening, Maggie noticed wide bands of pink around her torso. William's arm and leg had created a stencil for the sun. He anointed her body with a cotton swab dipped in cold tea. Then he had kissed the burns. Roving her body with his tongue, he had nudged open her legs and explored. Clutching his shoulders, she had never felt such pleasure. Finally, a crash, a crescendo. It felt like diving into the Wear all over again, swathed in bubbles and turquoise light.

Now they locked eyes and, as she moved against him, she marvelled at her good fortune. Handsome, ardent and caring, William gazed at her in similar wonder through his lovely hazel eyes.

Once their desire had been sated, William drew her into the crook of his arm and sighed. 'I love you, Maggie Almond,' he whispered. 'I sometimes believe the two of us were simply meant to be, despite our differences.'

Maggie felt exactly the same. A life without William was unimaginable, yet a life with him occasionally made her fret.

'What do you want in the future, William?' she asked into the dark.

'You, a home of our own ...' he began, then paused.

'Children?' She positioned herself so she could see his expression in the dim light.

He nodded solemnly. 'And you?'

Maggie was silent. She wasn't certain what she wanted. But she had fired a shell into the room and, with the most subtle of nods, William had lit the fuse.

'Perhaps.'

CHAPTER 2

MAGGIE WAS in the sitting room practising her needlework on a piece of cross-stitch Grace had discovered in the bottom of her sewing basket. It was the piece her granddaughters practised on. All three girls were more advanced than Maggie, even Jane, and she was only three. Maggie sighed.

Grace had departed early for her lectures. At Maggie's urging, she had enrolled at the university a few months ago. Grace was an intelligent woman; Maggie had argued that there was nothing stopping her from furthering her education. In fact, Grace Dodd had just as much right as any person, male or female, to gain knowledge. Maggie was thrilled when Grace finally agreed. Now she was busy with her studies in the Natural Science Department, leaving Maggie at home with a needle and thread.

The irony of the situation never ceased to amaze Maggie.

When she heard wheels growling along the gravel road outside the cottage, she placed the fabric and thread back into the basket and pulled a curtain aside. Jack, Beth's husband, had arrived in the clarence. It was rare for him to take the clarence out. Typically, if he had an errand to run for Beth, he'd simply ride.

Today, Jack had several bags of seed strapped to the roof in an improvised style, even though the fancy carriage wasn't designed to carry cargo or baggage. *He must have passengers, too*, Maggie thought. Jack had several vehicles in his blacksmith yard – he was a 'collector', he liked to joke, 'in more ways than one.' In his stable were a brougham and landau, as well as a handsome hansom he had purchased from a cabbie in Edinburgh not long before the pit collapse.

Maggie admired Jack and Beth immensely. They made a wonderful team. Beth operated the ironmongery, taking time out to birth a baby or two when needed, and Jack ran his smithy in the yard behind their home on the High Street. They were deeply in love, and their daughters and youngest child, an infant also named Jack, whom everyone called 'Little Jack', were delightful. Maggie was instantly reminded of her conversation with William the night before. If she wanted it, they could have Beth and Jack's life in a second.

But is it what I want? she thought, suddenly anxious.

William had departed at sunrise. Working two jobs did not seem to exhaust him as it would other men. By day, he wrote for the *Durham County Advertiser*, a position he gained when he resigned from Mister Latey's employ at the *Illustrated London News*. Most evenings he devoted to the union. Since the collapse of the Stanley Pit, William was determined to bring change to the collieries in the North East, particularly the assurance of safer working conditions and the eradication of haphazard practices. Unfortunately, he was met with quite a sizeable amount of resistance, mainly from the union members themselves.

Following the disaster, the colliery had remained closed. It was due to reopen in a fortnight and the improvements the union had recommended had already begun. The new owner, who had made his fortune in cotton, had recently sent an open letter to the *Advertiser* informing the town of the progress of the improvements and of his impending arrival.

Ever since they had been made aware of the sale of the mine, the colliers of Durham had been champing at the bit to return to work. While the union was providing members with a pension, it was a pittance compared to their usual salary. It was the reason Jack had been acting as the town's collector; business had slowed considerably in the wake of unemployment caused by the collapse. Ferrying people to and fro in his various carriages helped keep food on the table.

The miners resented the union for slowing their return to the mine; it seemed as though they wanted to work with or without the upgrades. Maggie could see that it was a situation that baffled William. The pitmen were hurting, but if the new owner did not improve the mine before it opened, further death and heartache were inevitable.

Through the window, Maggie watched Jack hop down from the driver's seat. He was as thin as a scarecrow, but his movements had an ease and a music to them. She slung her shawl around her shoulders and ventured outside to meet him. When he saw her, he tipped his cap.

'Good morning, Mags,' he said merrily.

To Jack, Maggie was always 'Mags' or 'Meggie', sometimes 'Magpie' and occasionally 'Maggie Pie'. *He should have been a writer of fiction*, Maggie thought with a laugh then waved. Jack seemed to possess too much imagination for a smithy.

She moved forward, wondering who the honoured guests were who rode in the clarence. Jack opened the door and Mister Latey alighted. Maggie stopped on the path. There had been minimal correspondence between them since she had departed London, and certainly nothing that would indicate he was intending to visit. She was aware he now ran the London office of the leftist newspaper, the *Manchester*

Guardian. C.P. Scott had hand-picked him. Scott, the editor, had been impressed with Maggie's Clairmont series and William's moving account of the mine disaster, both of which Latey had encouraged them to write.

Latey had written to her at the beginning of the year, asking if she might consider a return to the capital. He'd informed her there was a position open for her at the *Guardian*, if she wanted it, complete with her own office and by-line. Maggie had refused. At that stage, she had only been in Durham for a few months. Not wanting William to doubt her commitment to their new life together, she had chosen not to tell him about the proposition. What's more, Latey's proposal had arrived too soon; her dismissal from the *Illustrated London News* still smarted. At the time, she had not been willing to return to the world of big-city journalism.

'Almond,' Latey said by way of a greeting. He approached and reached out a hand.

'You should have told me you were coming,' Maggie said, taking his hand firmly in hers. 'I would have arranged—'

'Our travel plans evolved rather quickly. There wasn't time.'

'Our?'

Latey nodded as he snipped the tip off a cigar. A second man stepped from the clarence. He was tall, well-built, red-headed and red-bearded, and dressed in a remarkably well-tailored suit, the likes of which Maggie had not laid eyes on since she left London. The man caught Maggie's eye and nodded, then stood by the carriage door momentarily. His hand seemed to float in air as he waited for the third occupant to alight. A woman, Maggie assumed, judging by the hand and the length of the wait. When she eventually stepped from the carriage, the woman swept the black lace mantilla from her face and her eyes panned her surrounds.

Maggie's heart temporarily stopped beating (or so she

informed William later). She would recognise this woman anywhere. In fact, she had imagined her in many situations, but she had never imagined her among the dales of North East England. In Maggie's mind, she was the very definition of London – intelligent, unswerving, spirited and original.

The woman was George Eliot.

⚜

WHILE MAGGIE MADE TEA, she attempted to compose herself. She would not describe herself as obsessive or easily excited, but in the presence of her literary hero, Maggie found herself quite flustered. Her heart (which had started up again) beat wildly in her chest and, despite the chill in the air, she sensed the uncomfortable stickiness of perspiration under her arms. Latey was speaking, but his words seemed to evaporate into mist as Maggie examined the woman – the goddess – seated before her.

Since her arrival, the authoress had spoken only a few words in greeting. Reticent to meet Maggie's gaze and seated stiffly, it appeared that George Eliot was shy. The observation surprised Maggie. The authoress was dressed simply in a dark-grey suit, but the fine lace and beading around the collar, cuffs and hem leant her ensemble a certain exquisiteness. Latey introduced her as 'Missus Cross'.

Maggie had read in the newspaper a few months ago that at sixty, George Eliot had finally married – to a man twenty years her junior. This was John Cross, the distinguished gentleman who now conversed with Jack in an easy, affable way that belied his elegant appearance. He seemed entirely comfortable speaking with a blacksmith, fascinated by the details of the profession. Fortunately, Jack possessed not an inkling of George Eliot's renown. He stood blithely chatting to Mister Cross about the variety of goods he manufactured, from gates to grills and, most recently, a chalice for St Bede's. Jack's ignorance went some way towards normalising the situation for Maggie. Finally, Jack concocted an excuse about watering the horses and left the party to their business.

'So, Almond,' Latey continued, smoothing his hand across his bald pate as though wishing to draw attention to it. 'We would like you to write the series.'

Maggie blinked. 'Series?'

'Missus Cross's story, a memoir of sorts, in the same style as Clairmont's,' Latey added, puffing away on his cigar. The odour was so familiar. Maggie breathed in deeply. While she had been in Latey's employ, she had despised the stench of those cigars. Now, she found their smell as sweet as a newly bloomed rose.

Maggie seemed to awaken from a long slumber and stared at Latey, confused. She realised she had not heard a word he'd uttered, and, judging from the disturbed look in his eyes, he must have spoken at considerable length. Fearing George Eliot think her an absolute ninny, she decided the best course of action was honesty.

'I am extremely sorry, Mister Latey, I have missed everything you have said.' She turned to her hero. 'Missus Cross, I must inform you I am one of your greatest admirers. Your writing and your ideals have shaped my life. To have you here, before me now, is tantamount to a dream. Please excuse my momentary loss of focus.'

The writer looked at the young woman. Her gentle blue-grey eyes eased Maggie's perturbation.

'Thank you for saying so. I receive an extraordinary amount of praise from my readers, but those words, coming from a writer of your calibre, thrill me.'

To Maggie, her voice was low and warm, as though kissed by the sun. She could barely focus on the words it carried.

'Miss Almond, I would like you to write my life story in a

series of articles for the *Manchester Guardian*.' She paused and waited for Maggie to take in the request.

A small 'Oh' issued from Maggie's lips.

Satisfied, Missus Cross continued. 'I thoroughly enjoyed your Clairmont series. The articles were moving and humorous and so provoking. I know you are a woman who shares my ideals regarding certain matters.' She paused again.

Despite the awe she felt in the presence of the great author, it was clear to Maggie that the person before her was familiar with having her every word waited on.

'The "woman question", I mean.' Those blue-grey eyes flashed with mischief for an instant. 'When Mister Latey informed me that Claire Clairmont bequeathed the infamous diaries to you, I was amazed. Those journals have become literary folklore. To be frank, I doubted their existence.' Missus Cross threw Maggie a quizzical look. 'Sadly, I never had the good fortune to meet Claire Clairmont, or Mary Shelley. I am, however, a great admirer of Mary's work, as I am of her mother's, and our lives and careers have taken similar journeys.'

Maggie was silent. A year later and those journals were still as real to her as the stars. From the time when she had first become aware of their existence, Maggie had coveted the journals of Clairmont and her sisters, Mary Shelley and Fanny Godwin. In Maggie's mind, those notebooks possessed the power and mystique of the Holy Grail and the recollection of them still stung. They were now six feet below the earth at the Cimitero Monumentale Della Misericordia, Antella in Florence, in the arms of their protector for over fifty years. When the merchant's men had taken Clairmont and her beloved chronicles away, Maggie had written to the Sisters with whom Clairmont had lived and worked for so long. They promised they would lay Clairmont to rest in holy ground. No one would touch the journals, they assured her. In death, the old lady had finally received the kindness that had so long eluded her in life.

Maggie touched the wristwatch that lay flat and cold against her skin. It had been gifted to Fanny by Mary and Percy, and bequeathed to her decades later by Clairmont. It was her most treasured possession.

'What ever became of those journals, Almond?' Latey asked.

Maggie started from her reverie. 'They are in very safe hands,' she replied, hoping to avoid further questions on the matter.

'Miss Almond, on my wife's recommendation, I read your Clairmont series as well,' Mister Cross put in, leaning slightly towards her across the chipped and marked table.

He was more handsome than Maggie had first believed. His eyes were dark blue and his hair an immensely becoming shade of auburn. When he had helped Jack unload the bags of seed, he had removed his coat and folded it neatly. It was now hanging on the back of his chair. Maggie stared at his cuff-links for a moment. She wondered if they were real rubies.

'What struck me primarily about your writing,' he continued, 'was its honesty.'

'My honesty cost me my job, Mister Cross, and Mister Latey's as well.'

'That won't happen at the *Guardian*,' Latey said. 'Mister Scott is a more zealous suffragist than even Missus Ingram.'

Maggie smiled. The trio were flattering her and it was working. However, she remained mildly traumatised by her experience at the *News*. She had trusted Missus Ingram, the owner, and she had felt betrayed when dismissed from her post. That betrayal still haunted her.

Snippets of what she knew of George Eliot intruded on her thoughts. In many ways, Eliot's life was even more scandalous than Claire Clairmont's ... She looked at Latey. Could he really guarantee that revealing Eliot's truth wouldn't lead to another professional humiliation?

She frowned, then glanced at Missus Cross. She was disturbed to find she was being observed by her.

'I believe you are in a moral quandary, Miss Almond,' Missus Cross said kindly. She spread her slender fingers on the table. 'My husband and I are staying in Durham for a day or two. I was born in Warwickshire and then moved to London. While my travels abroad have been vast, I have seen very little of the British North East. Durham is a place I would like to know better.'

As soon as she rose, her husband followed, then Latey.

'In other words, Almond,' Latey added as they approached the door, 'sleep on it.'

CHAPTER 3

WHEN LATEY and the Crosses departed, Maggie fell into a state of deep contemplation. She had been unsatisfied with how her life in London had ended and remained so to this day. She had lost her job, a fiancée and a close friendship with an amusing milliner's girl from the East End. She had also lost her relationship with her mother. These losses melded with her grief over Clairmont's death, a surprising woman whom she had grown to love during the course of writing the articles, and together, they became an unyielding ache in her chest. That time had been so emotionally fraught, so very difficult.

While Maggie was confident she could trust Latey, could she trust C.P. Scott? Newspaper men (and women) spun with the wind. And, if her experiences during the summer of 1879 had taught her anything, a person could be easily betrayed by another.

She departed the cottage and walked towards town. Her purpose was not clear. All she knew was that she needed to think … she needed space and air to think. She felt that once she had those, surely the pieces of her future would fall into place.

Thoughts tumbled through her mind like leaves in a gust. When she reached the River Wear, the stillness of the water, a glistening pane of glass, struck her. Bubbles broke the limpid surface and Maggie looked hard to find the fish responsible. When she could not, she walked on towards Prebends Bridge.

Her father had taught her not to be foolhardy, that to blindly rush into any situation was misguided. 'Research the context and the conditions' had always been his advice, based on his years of experience in the army; 'Be completely fore-warned before heading into any precarious situation.' Yet she had rushed to Durham with William. Although she didn't regret her decision (a life without William was an unbearable notion), she often wondered how the past year might have evolved had she stayed in London.

She would have probably accepted Latey's earlier offer of a position at the *Manchester Guardian*. Despite rejecting it at the time, the hunger to be a renowned female journalist who wrote serious stories still clawed at her like a lion. In the capital, she would have continued the fight for equality in a location more conducive to radical ideas. The notion of a school for girls would not be disturbing in London. The bitter taste of Briar's decep-tion – a woman she'd trusted but who turned out not to be a milliner's girl, but a private detective hired by her mother – had not diluted in the slightest, yet her opinion of the canny young woman had softened somewhat over recent months. Briar had taught her to be bold, to take risks when female equality was at stake ... and to never hide in the face of adversity.

Maggie sighed and stopped on the bridge. Hiding was exactly what she had been doing for the past year. She looked beneath her into the water and felt the sun on her neck. It was autumn, yet the summer heat lingered like an unrequited love. She gripped the cool stone.

The opportunities Latey's new offer presented were huge. Maggie would have a once-in-a-lifetime chance to work closely with a legendary woman and writer she had admired since she was a girl. She could still vividly recall the evening Dorothea had suggested *Middlemarch* as a suitable book for her to read. The moment occurred in the common room of Cheltenham, by the hearth, when Maggie was fourteen. The book was a birthday gift.

Looking back on those days, Maggie believed Dorothea had sensed something in her student. *Here is a girl I can mould*, she imagined her thinking. Maggie had been so receptive to any learning, precocious, a dry sponge in need of water. Her father Henry had enrolled her at the college when her governess at Chester Square had reached the limits of her expertise. The young woman had complained, 'There is nothing more I can teach her!'

Maggie's mother Lydia had rejected Henry's first idea of employing a male tutor to instruct Maggie in Latin and Greek, citing it would be 'unseemly'. Cheltenham Ladies' College was a compromise with which both parents could live. When Maggie arrived at the school at the age of eleven, she was an empty vessel, eager to be filled.

A few years later, Maggie examined the book Miss Beale gifted her. 'A male author?' Maggie had queried, confused. Miss Beale made a very particular point of supporting the works of female writers through her curriculum.

Dorothea had smiled. 'Read the book. Once you have, I would like you to return and share with me your opinion of George Eliot.'

In every spare minute, Maggie read, becoming thoroughly absorbed in the town of Middlemarch and its inhabitants. The story of Dorothea Brooke touched her; she was a young woman not unlike herself, with an insatiable desire for knowledge. In order to expand her mind, she marries a learned man over twenty years her senior, but their union fails. He is mean spirited and jealous, and stubbornly refuses to recognise the inner beauty of his young wife. Dorothea Brooke's fate disappointed Maggie, while the journey of Rosamond Vincy filled her with anger. She, too, marries a learned man, an ambitious young doctor, but not for his mind. It is his status and means she finds appealing, but her vacuous, material goals prevent him from acting on his true calling. Maggie had noticed that several of her classmates were as shallow as Rosamond. Dorothea Beale's progressive style of education was entirely wasted on them.

'George Eliot is a very fine author,' she told Dorothea once she had finished the book. 'He has such an intimate knowledge of the feminine spirit. Surely, he must have many sisters.'

Dorothea had laughed at the observation and Maggie was both surprised and unsurprised when Dorothea revealed George Eliot's real name was Mary Anne Evans.

'Miss Evans must use a male pseudonym in order to be published. The male establishment does not approve of her ideas or lifestyle.'

It seemed bitterly unjust to Maggie that a man, even an imaginary one, was receiving credit and praise for such a magnificent book.

'What a terrible situation for Miss Evans to endure,' she said, aware of exactly how she would feel in the same situation.

Maggie greedily read the rest of Eliot's books and was exceedingly impressed. However, her favourite remained *Middlemarch*. As the first Eliot novel she read, it had the most profound effect on her. It was not only Dorothea Brooke's journey in which she found comfort, but also in the authoress's shrewd observations of human behaviour. Maggie had always been mildly ashamed of her penchant for observing visitors to Chester Square or strangers on the street. Lydia would vehemently admonish her for staring at others. After reading *Middlemarch*, she felt validated in her actions.

In hindsight, Maggie realised the novel was most likely the reason she pursued journalism as a career … so to be offered the opportunity to work with George Eliot and refuse seemed unthinkable. However, Maggie knew that chronicling Missus Cross's life in full would shock many readers. Would C.P. Scott, despite his suffragist ideals, be willing to withstand the backlash from his readership and advertisers?

More importantly, would she?

'Aareet, lass,' William called, heading towards her across the bridge.

When he reached her, they kissed, and Maggie leant her head against his shoulder.

'You're coming home early,' she remarked.

'Not so early. It's half five. Drummond arrives tomorrow.'

'The new colliery owner?

William nodded. 'I want to work on my questions in the quiet.'

Maggie looked into the sky. The sun had lowered and the crisp blue of early afternoon had given way to shades of pansy and topaz. She wondered how long she had been standing there.

'Your hands are as cold as a frog,' William remarked, rubbing them between his. Then he removed his coat and placed it around her shoulders. 'Remember that evening on Fleet Street? I discovered you, a lost soul, outside the office of the *News*. You were so beautiful, but sad, too. Do you recall?'

Maggie nodded. Only an hour before that meeting, she

had broken her engagement to Raymond and had run from her home in a tempest of emotions. Directionless and feeling incredibly alone, as though no one in the world knew her experience, she had found herself standing on the footpath outside the *News*, wondering what she had sacrificed for her career. William had gently threaded her arms through his jacket and walked her home, listening gravely to her sorry tale.

Now he lifted her chin with his finger and gazed into her brown eyes. 'What's troubling you, lass?'

Maggie told William everything that had occurred that morning. 'Missus Cross wants me to write her story,' she said. '*Me.*'

'Then you'd better accept. To be honest, I'm not exactly certain why you didn't leap at Latey's offer in the first place. George Eliot ...' He shook his head, baffled 'She's your idol.'

'It's fear, I suppose.'

William made a noise, a low *humph*. He frowned, then nodded as though Maggie's words confirmed what he already knew.

'You've been away from London and your work for too long. You're letting fear get the better of you. Sometimes I worry ...'

He seemed unable to voice his concern. Maggie gave him a questioning look.

'I worry that provincial life doesn't suit you.'

Maggie immediately embraced him, squeezing his muscled torso as hard as she was able, attempting to prove to him how mistaken he was. But she also felt she needed to be honest.

'I admit to feeling frustrated lately,' she said when they broke apart. 'Especially after the bitter response to my idea of a girls' school. Regina Hartley, for one, was clearly unimpressed.'

Regina's comments about her marital status haunted Maggie. They had been cruel and had made her feel entirely outcast. She pushed the memory aside and took William's hand.

'But I would never leave. While Durham is your home, it's mine as well.'

Now it was William's turn to squeeze Maggie. 'In that case, this might be exactly what you need. Latey has brought a part of London to you. And as for Regina Hartley ... she was an unpleasant little girl who turned into a nasty woman.'

'You knew her when she was a girl?'

'We're of a similar age. She'd chase me round the school yard, singing *Wee Willie Winkie*, trying to snatch my cap. It would drive me barking.'

'Really?' Maggie asked, finally hitting on why Regina Hartley had been so unnecessarily hostile to her. 'You know, William, little girls typically torment the boy they like the most,' she said, smiling playfully.

CHAPTER 4

MAGGIE ACCOMPANIED William into town the next morning. Matthew Drummond was due to arrive at ten o'clock and the mayor had hired Jack to meet him at Newcastle Station. It was a journey Maggie had taken for the first time on the evening of the pit collapse over a year ago. Now she and William stood waiting by the post office in the centre of town. When Maggie spied Regina Hartley peeping through the butcher's window at the activity on the High Street, she nudged William and raised an eyebrow. 'Haddaway, woman,' he said under his breath, scowling. Maggie laughed, drawing the attention of people on the surrounding street.

After the Stanley Pit tragedy, the managers had departed Durham before rescuers had pulled the last body from the rubble. The owner of the mine lived in London. He made no apologies for the collapse. In the telegram he sent to the union, he even suggested the miners themselves were to blame. 'In my experience,' he had written, 'haste has been a consistent failing of miners. Their chief priority is to remove the coal in the timeliest manner possible. They pay no heed to safety.' William could not argue with the observation. His father was forever complaining about the young miners, who had never lived through a collapse, taking monumental risks where safety was concerned in order to earn more money.

However, it was the responsibility of those managing the site to ensure the correct practices were being adhered to. 'It is a consistent failing of colliery owners,' William had written in one of his first articles for the *Advertiser*, 'to be more concerned with removing as much coal as possible from the ground as quickly as possible than with mine safety. They do not want the extra expense and delay of digging adequate ventilation shafts and shoring up the seams already mined.'

Maggie didn't know how William could be so reasonable, so measured in his response. When one day, through various means and connections, he had discovered the London address of the owner, Maggie had been unable to fathom how he had not hurried to the capital, forced a confrontation and demanded accountability.

'And what good would that do, lass?' he remarked when she suggested such a response. 'I'd wind up in gaol. It's better I stand apart, making change that will last.'

It had taken many months to sell the pit. The frustration of the miners mounted rapidly each day, their sense of purpose plummeting at the same rate. But today, the new owner was arriving in Durham and Maggie could taste the hope in the air.

The crowd parted, allowing for the passage of Tommy Fellowes, the head of the Durham Miners' Association. Tommy required a wide berth. Working in the narrow seams for thirty years had caused his legs to bow dramatically to the point that walking was a painful and ungainly chore. Tommy lurched left to right with such an unsteady gait that Maggie feared he would topple over. When she observed the men around Durham, it was easy to discern those who were, or had been, pitmen. Each time she saw a man whose occupation had crippled him, she thanked God William's height and size made him so obviously unsuited to pit work.

When Tommy's legs grew too painful to work underground, he found himself a position at the union. His amiable presence and calm negotiating skills soon saw him rise through the ranks. When William's unsuitability as a collier became clear, it was Tommy who brought him into the union.

'Aareet.' Fellowes shook William's hand and doffed his cap at Maggie. 'Quite a day,' he said, thoughtfully. 'The Stanley Pit will soon be open again and all these men can go back to work. Quite a day, indeed.'

'Aye,' William returned. 'A decent wage coming in and decent food on the table. It's been a long time coming.'

Fellowes agreed with a reflective nod.

Maggie had met Tommy Fellowes frequently since she arrived in Durham. He and William's father had started at the pit together. They had been childhood friends, inseparable. They had reared their families alongside one another. As William's godfather and a close friend of Grace's, Tommy made it a habit of visiting once a week, always offering Grace a shilling. She politely declined the gift each time, despite her circumstances. The union paid her a widow's pension. It was a pittance, but she claimed it was enough.

As a hansom rounded the corner into the High Street, the crowd that had gathered cheered with excitement. *The entire community has their hopes pinned on the man in that cab*, Maggie thought, looking around her at the expectant faces of every man, woman and child. She hoped Matthew Drummond wouldn't disappoint.

When the cab stopped, Drummond did not wait for Jack to jump from his seat and open the door. The carriage door flung open and Durham's newest resident leapt to the ground, waving merrily at the awaiting spectators.

'Good morning, people of Durham!' he called.

The crowd cheered. Drummond was younger than Maggie expected. Perhaps a similar age to Mister Cross, although his dark hair had turned silver at the temples. It was an aspect that lent him a rather majestic appearance.

'Thank you for your warm welcome,' he went on.

Maggie glanced at William. He was eyeing the newcomer dubiously.

'I'm pleased to be here, and I'm thrilled to be reopening the Stanley Pit!'

Another round of applause.

His accent suggested Manchester, but the coarse edge had been buffed away. Since arriving in Durham, Maggie's ear had grown quite attuned to sounds of the North. She wondered what public school he attended. *There must be family money*, she mused.

'And it is my absolute pleasure to become part of this community. Finally, I wish to assure you of my intention to make the Stanley Pit safe again. For so long, too many high-risk practices have been part and parcel of the mining industry. I intend to change that. Pitman safety is my priority.'

A cheer rippled through the crowd.

'He's certainly voicing all the appropriate sentiments,' Maggie said into William's ear. She noticed him frown; he was clearly troubled by the man.

Drummond moved towards the throng, then seemed to be swept up by it. Attempting to see over their heads, Maggie spotted Mister Cross standing a few yards away, observing the proceedings. She wondered where his wife was.

Fellowes ventured into the crowd and withdrew Drummond from the well-wishers.

'Have they met before?' Maggie asked William.

He nodded. 'Tommy delivered the union's demands when the sale occurred. Drummond agreed to them all on the spot, apparently.'

'You seem doubtful.'

'Let's just say, he'd be the first colliery owner in history to make safety a priority.' He kissed Maggie on the cheek. 'Will you be alright? I must go. I'm meeting Drummond at the pit.'

'Of course. I see Mister Cross over there ... I'll go and wish him a good day.'

⚜

'MISTER DODD OF THE *ADVERTISER*, I assume,' Drummond said when he opened the door of the colliery office in answer to William's knock.

'Aye.' The men shook hands. 'I'm pleased to meet you.'

'Take a seat.' Drummond gestured to a chair. As Drummond walked back to the seat behind his desk, William examined the man's attire. Drummond's jacket was made from a fabric much like his own. His trousers were moleskin and, to William's surprise, he wore sturdy workman's boots.

'Excuse the dust and general untidiness. As you well know, the previous owner vacated rather swiftly. This place has been unoccupied for a disturbing amount of time,' Drummond said, as removed his bowler hat and placed it on the desk.

William noticed that the brim was frayed.

'Disturbing?'

'For the men of Durham, of course. The closing of the Stanley Pit affected their livelihood considerably.'

'Aye, it has. The Stanley Pit alone employs over 300 men.'

'Of that fact, I am aware, Mister Dodd.'

The men locked eyes for a moment. William was uncertain whether Drummond's tone suggested he was affronted by William's remark or outraged at the length of the closure. He was unable to read the man's expression.

Averting his gaze, William removed a notepad and pencil from his coat pocket.

'So, tell me, Mister Drummond, what possessed a Mancunian such as yourself to purchase a Durham colliery?'

Drummond sat back in his chair and thought. William took him to be a man who did not like to be rushed. After a moment of meditation, he began.

'My great-grandfather was originally a lowly spinner in Salford.' Drummond paused, frowned, then cast his gaze through the window, as though whatever thought had entered his mind was a sad one. In an instant, he seemed restored. 'But he possessed an entrepreneur's spirit. After many years in his trade, he realised there must be a more efficient way of making yarn. So he invented a mechanical spinner. Such was the novelty of his machine that the Duke of Shrewsbury soon patronised the contraption. Eventually, fifty mills in Salford purchased his machines and the rest, as they say, is history.'

A rags to riches tale as old as time, William thought as he scribbled notes. Drummond's words flowed smoothly. No pauses or gaps, no *ums* or *ahs*. William wondered if it was confidence or if Drummond had rehearsed his tale.

Looking up and meeting Drummond's blue eyes again, he remarked, 'And the Drummond empire spread from there.'

'That's correct. Until the America Civil War erupted, that is. The war proved to us that relying on imports was entirely ... well, unreliable. Our mills suffered and, although we have recovered since, the experience stressed to us the need to diversify our assets into an industry where the raw material lies on British soil.'

'Or under British soil, as the case may be.'

'Exactly, Mister Dodd.' Drummond spun in his chair to face the window.

William took a moment to observe the man unnoticed. Drummond was well-educated with a polished turn of phrase. His family had wealth. *Why, then is he dressed as a pitman and not an owner?* William mused.

He looked beyond Drummond, at the scene through the glass. Several of the town's mine workers – former hewers and hurriers, thrusters and getters – had been re-employed to ready the pit's above-ground area for the opening. *And,* William thought, *if the safety measures have been taken in the shafts, they will soon return to their work below.*

He found it strange to see such activity in the place. Life had ceased at the pit following the collapse. Even the hillocks of rocks and dirt William had worked so hard to remove from the shaft following the disaster had been left untouched until a few weeks ago. They had flattened slightly and been pitted by rain, but remained as constant reminders of his loss.

William was drawn back to the present by Drummond's voice.

'Now that this belongs to me,' the man said, turning to face him, 'I plan to make Durham prosperous again.'

❧

TOMMY FELLOWES ARRIVED at the cottage at five o'clock.

'What do you make of Drummond?' he asked William, following a minimal amount of small talk.

While Maggie had to admit polite conversation was often meaningless, the Northern male's lack of expertise in the area never ceased to amaze her. After an 'Aareet' and 'Fine day', it was straight down to business.

William was seated at the table, examining his notes with Maggie. Grace moved around the kitchen, preparing the evening meal. Despite the burdens life had thrust upon her, Grace was remarkably elegant in her movements. She might have been a ballerina in another world, Maggie often mused.

'Will yer be staying for tea, Tommy?' Grace asked, lifting the plates from the hutch.

'Aye. Ta for the offer.'

Tommy's wife had died some years ago and although his three daughters had remained in the North, they no longer lived in Durham. As a result, Tommy was always grateful for a home-cooked meal. He drew a chair out from the table and repeated his query to his godson.

'So, what do you think of Drummond?'

William shrugged. 'He seems genuine. But there's something out of kilter with him,' he said, recalling Matthew Drummond's clothing and the sense his answers had been prepared. There was something about his manner, too, which William couldn't put his finger on. The man was as inscrutable as the sea.

A slight raise of his bushy eyebrows showed Tommy wanted to know more.

'If he's to be believed, there are generations of wealth running through his veins, yet he dresses like a pitman.'

'Perhaps he wants to fit in?' Grace suggested, pushing her dark curls from her brow.

'Or perhaps he is attempting too hard to fit in?' Maggie added pointedly. 'That could also explain the practised answers. It makes sense for him to prepare in an uncertain environment or situation, especially one where he wishes to make a good impression. After all, William, you were there representing the press.'

William made a noise, a low *humph*.

'How old are yer now, Willie?' Tommy asked affably. 'Twenty-eight, nine? Far too young to be so cynical. Give the poor man the benefit of the doubt. He's signed our agreement. It's more than any other owner in the last twenty years has done.'

William nodded warily. Maggie squeezed his hand, sensing his dilemma. Trust was a risky proposition in Durham. Trusting Drummond could lead to the death and injury of another two hundred men.

CHAPTER 5

THE WOMEN TOOK a seat on Palace Green. The reality of the situation had not quite struck Maggie yet. To be seated next to George Eliot was the stuff of daydreams.

She could not stop herself from stealing glances of the authoress's face from time to time, or what she could see of it. Her visage was long and her jaw masculine; Maggie wondered whether the authoress wore the mantilla in mourning or disguise. George Eliot's unattractiveness had never been disputed, but she was also slender and strong. *And*, Maggie thought, *her nose isn't large, it is noble*. She could well imagine the authoress's striking profile appearing on a postage stamp.

When Maggie was younger, she had often fantasised about receiving an invitation to one of Eliot's Sunday-afternoon salons. They were renowned, and by invitation only. Despite her father's military and political associates, and her mother's raft of society acquaintances, there was not one literary connection to be found among the intricate webbing of their combined networks. Her mentor Dorothea Beale, as the head of a leading girls' school and recognised suffragist, had been invited once. Maggie was sick with jealousy. Afterwards, Dorothea informed her that Missus Lewes (as Eliot preferred to be known at the time) had sat on high, commanding proceedings, while her guests and 'husband' scurried like courtiers around her, hanging on her every word.

Dorothea was shocked to note there was even a young lady present who asked Missus Lewes if she might kiss her feet. The authoress refused, but Dorothea remarked, 'It was not the request so much that surprised me as Missus Lewes's refusal. To be honest, for a country girl from humble beginnings, she was behaving in such an insufferably supercilious manner that I expected her to welcome the gesture.' However, Dorothea's report did nothing to tarnish Maggie's idolisation of the writer; she was used to her mentor dismissing even the most accidental displays of haughtiness as arrogance.

Besides, in Maggie's opinion, George Eliot had every right to be queenly.

She followed the authoress's gaze. Missus Cross appeared intrigued by the location of their meeting. The vast stretch of manicured grass before them that constituted the green was partially surrounded by the majestic colleges of Durham University.

'This was once the site of a market,' Maggie said, remembering Missus Cross had mentioned she had never visited Durham. 'Until the twelfth century, that is, when Bishop Flambard decided "the church should neither be endangered by fire nor polluted by filth".'

The authoress examined the scene before her. Couples promenaded on the manicured grass and students scuttled like ducks to their studies. Her eyes squinted into the distance, as though she was attempting to imagine the green as it was hundreds of years ago – a bustling, raucous marketplace.

'Do you enjoy studying history, Miss Almond?' she asked.

'I do,' Maggie replied. 'Especially military history.'

'That is so much of our past, isn't it? Powerful men wanting more, forcing nations to war.'

'Sadly, you are correct, Missus Cross,' Maggie said. 'Some might think me callous, but I enjoy studying the subject. I find that the tactics of these powerful men help me understand non-military people more completely.'

Maggie did not feel the need to elaborate, and Missus Cross accepted her response without further enquiry.

The truth was that Maggie had found herself with a great deal of time on her hands over the past twelve months in which to study history and much more. She had visited every historic site in Durham more than once, hoping that by becoming familiar with her new home, she might grow to feel more accepted by it. She could now speak at length about the castle and the cathedral, the university and the pilgrim trails, of which she had walked three; the first with Grace, the second with William and the third, known as 'The Way of Life,' she trod alone. Maggie had tramped a combined total of 280 miles. She had even sipped the healing, sulphurous waters of Gainsford Spa in an attempt to halt her spiritual decline. In the duration of a year, her life had drastically altered and she had steadily lost sight of the confident woman she thought she had become. She had done everything she could – had appealed to both God and nature – to resurrect something she had lost, to regain herself again.

However, as she sat beside George Eliot on the edges of Palace Green, she began to view her companion as a far more reliable deity.

'I would like you to call me Marian,' the older woman said after a few moments of silent contemplation. 'And I shall call you Maggie. Titles are so tedious.'

Maggie nodded in agreement. She liked the directness of

Marian Cross. Yet while pleasant, she was also rather intimidating. It had taken Maggie hours to dress for their meeting. The image Dorothea had described of 'Missus Lewes' had stuck in her mind like a leech, sucking her dry of all her confidence. Now, she realised the promenading gown she was wearing probably was unnecessarily grand, although when she had donned it earlier, she had gained a new sense of purpose. While the commission was hers for the taking, Maggie hoped her attire would convince Marian of her suitability for the role. She wanted to impress Missus Cross.

As she was dressing that morning, Maggie recalled the last time she had worn the ensemble. It had been at the beginning of summer at Chester Square. Before Clairmont, before William ... Raymond had taken her to Kensington Gardens. She could recall the heat of the sun on her skin, and Raymond's steady hand on her lower back as he guided her towards the kiosk. He had bought a strawberry-flavoured ice for her and a ginger and lemon one for himself, remarking, 'The first of the season. The first of many.' They had knocked their paper cups together, as though toasting their future happiness and longevity.

Recalling the past, Maggie became pensive. *How suddenly the course of one's life can change*, she thought. Not long after she had left London, Raymond had married Vera, a young woman a little older than Maggie, and started a family. By all accounts, his daughter Adelaide was a beautiful child and Raymond a doting father. After a whirlwind romance, he had proposed to Vera at the opera. The location of the proposal had amused Maggie; when she and Raymond were engaged, he had avoided the opera like the plague. It was clear that his desire to make Vera happy surpassed his own aversion to that particular entertainment. Maggie saw this as a sign he had finally met a woman he could love wholeheartedly.

Examining her reflection in the looking glass, she noted

the gown's narrow, ruched skirt and short train of mint green. The bodice was made from striped, pink silk with long side panels draped to below the knee. It was extravagant for Durham, but Maggie had seen the mayor's wife wearing a similar style; it was one of the reasons she had chosen it.

When she was finally dressed, she turned in a circle to allow William to take in her appearance.

'Very nice,' he commented. 'Very nice, indeed.' Then he frowned. 'But the arse bows?'

The back of the gown was decorated with three bows that sat in a crescent slightly above her buttocks.

'William!'

'Bum bows, then. They seem a wee bit impractical.'

'Whoever claimed high fashion was practical?'

Maggie had left the cottage in a flurry. With her button hook nowhere to be found, the tiny buttons of her corset cover, bodice and boots exhausted much of the morning, even with Grace's unruffled assistance.

Yet as elegant as it was, Marian did not seem to notice Maggie's attire. *I could be wearing a dirndl and she wouldn't give it a second glance*, Maggie thought, mildly amused. Marian was wearing a skirt and coat in charcoal, and a white lace mantilla that covered the top half of her face.

'I'm rather surprised no one has recognised me,' Marian remarked when a gentleman caught her eye and nodded good day, then walked on. 'Poor, John. My fame was the bane of our honeymoon in Venice. We could venture nowhere without admirers accosting me. Eventually, we rarely left our hotel. It made our time together extremely trying.'

Maggie sensed her companion's mood alter. She glanced at Marian's profile and wondered what expression the mantilla concealed. Reflective? Regretful? Boastful? What had occurred in Venice to warrant Marian's sombre recollection of her honeymoon?

'I don't believe you will experience the same problem here,' Maggie said, to lighten the mood. 'On the whole, Geordies are an extremely pleasant bunch, but I doubt they are familiar with the Eliot canon.' She smiled to ensure Marian of her good spirits.

When Marian, still contemplative, did not react, Maggie went on. 'I'm afraid that apart from the extremely well-off, very few people in the community have received a substantial education, or even see the value in one, especially where female children are concerned.' A reminder of Missus Hartley's attitude threatened to smother her cheerfulness. She hastily shook it away. 'Trust me, your identity is safe in Durham.'

Marian laughed, a gentle, melodic sound that bubbled from her chest like a spring.

'Of course, my ...' Maggie paused. She had still not discovered an adequate way to define William. 'My beau is the exception. In fact, he was educated here, at the University of Durham,' she said, gesturing to the grand colleges across the green.

Marian nodded. 'Yes, I know. I must confess, I had John do a great deal of investigation into your life before I approached Mister Latey with my idea. By nature, I am distrustful of people.'

Maggie's breath caught in her throat. *How much does she know about me? Surely a woman of her experience couldn't be horrified by my past?*

'I know your father is a military hero from the Crimean War and you were engaged to a wealthy and handsome doctor, one Raymond Turn—'

'Why not write your story yourself?' Maggie interrupted, before her idol could reveal the more sordid aspects of her findings. 'Clairmont needed a ghost writer because, despite her bloodline, she had no talent in the field. But you are one of the greatest English writers of modern times.'

'That is true, but how can I write objectively? How can I ignore my feelings, the pain and disappointments I have experienced, so they do not taint my words?' Marian paused for a moment. 'I want you to write about my life because I am confident you will be compassionate towards the subject but not subjective. There are hundreds of journalists in London who would sell their grandmothers for this commission. But your recent past echoes my life in so many ways ... Therefore, I believe only you can write my story.'

Maggie knew that Marian was referring to the love affairs of her youth and her relationship with George Lewes. They had lived together as husband and wife for a quarter of a century without marrying. Initially, the arrangement forced the couple out of London and then out of the country.

'Why have you chosen to marry now?' Maggie asked. Although she had not given formal confirmation, in her heart she had already accepted Latey's proposal. This question had been nagging at her since Marian arrived with her husband and Latey at the cottage.

'It is nothing to do with my ideals, I can assure you. The men with whom I fell in love before simply did not love me in return. George was the exception, of course, but he was already married. It was extremely poor timing on both our counts ... I would have married him in a heartbeat, but it was not possible. With John, he was free to ask me and I was free to accept.'

Maggie nodded.

'But, oh, the scandal my arrangement with George caused ...' Marian shook her head despairingly at the memory. 'I lived in hiding for many years until my celebrity made my presence in society desirable.'

Maggie nodded, although she doubted whether her own

presence would ever be desirable anywhere in Durham. She was an outcast, and she dreaded to imagine how her reputation was faring in London.

'Shall we explore the cathedral?' Maggie suggested, needing to shift her thoughts.

Marian rose. As the women were about to begin their walk across the green, Matthew Drummond approached them at a trot, grinning, playful as a rabbit. He removed his hat, the same tattered bowler Maggie had seen him wearing the day before.

'Maggie Almond, I presume?' he said, extending his hand.

The enthusiasm for that greeting seems to have reached the North rather late, Maggie thought. She shook Drummond's hand politely, then introduced Marian as Missus Cross, 'a friend from London'.

'I believe it was your ... ah, husband? ... whom I spent some time with yesterday, Miss Almond.'

Maggie shot him a look and nodded. 'Are you sightseeing, Mister Drummond?'

'Indeed. I want to get acquainted with Durham and everyone in it. It's my home now, after all. I have taken a house on South Bailey.'

The previous colliery owner had never lived in Durham. Maggie remembered that William doubted the man had ever stepped foot in the North East. She supposed that taking a house was Drummond's means of proving to the community he intended to be a hands-on owner.

'Then you must have brought a large family with you,' she remarked. South Bailey was where the mayor and town aldermen lived, as well as the wealthy landowners who desired a town house.

'On the contrary. I'm here alone,' he said, his gaze lingering longer on Maggie more than she liked. 'Quite alone.'

'I see,' she said, feeling a blush rise in her cheeks. She

took Marian's arm. 'It's a wonder you have time for sight-seeing then, Mister Drummond, with only two weeks to ready the pit for the reopening.'

Feeling mildly affronted by his attention, she felt it only right to point out Drummond's neglect of his duties.

Drummond laughed. 'Perhaps I should be off then! I hope we meet again soon, Miss Almond,' he said, tipping his hat. 'And it was lovely meeting you, Missus Cross.'

They watched him stroll away, seemingly unconcerned with anything more serious than enjoying the day. The women looked at each other, bemused, then made their way towards the cathedral.

'For what he lacks in subtlety,' Marian whispered to Maggie, 'he certainly makes up for in allure. Your new colliery owner is an exceptionally attractive man.'

CHAPTER 6

WHEN MAGGIE ARRIVED home in the mid-afternoon, she discovered Grace and her father sharing a pot of tea at the table like old friends, as though they were country neighbours. Their laughter instantly stopped when she walked through the door. Grace lowered her green eyes. Henry cleared his throat, then rose in greeting. Maggie rushed to him, throwing her arms around his neck. Then the tears came ... tears of joy. She had missed her father greatly.

'Why didn't you write and tell me you were coming?' Maggie said once she had composed herself.

'The element of surprise,' he laughed, flashing Grace a look, an expression Maggie had never seen before. It was the context, Maggie assumed. She had never seen her father standing in a collier's cottage.

'If my father hasn't informed you, he was in the army for over thirty years,' Maggie said excitedly. She was still giddy from her morning with Marian. 'Now retired, he attempts to relive those days whenever he can in his civilian life.'

'You look well,' Henry said, holding his daughter at arm's

length to examine her. 'Lovely. Grace let slip you were meeting a potential client.'

Maggie offered Grace a grateful smile. It was extremely clever of her to word Maggie's whereabouts so subtlety.

Latey's contract had arrived by messenger the night before. Maggie was to be paid £100 to ghost write the series of twelve articles.

'A hundred pounds!' William had said, astonished. 'Obviously, your talent is worth it, but £100 ... My salary at the *News*, a London newspaper, was only £90 a year.'

Maggie snorted. Her annual salary while at the same paper had been £15 less.

While the salary Latey had promised was more than pleasing – enough to buy a home of their own, William pointed out – she had requested several caveats be included in the contract before she signed, the foremost being a guarantee the newspaper would protect her anonymity. No one, apart from those directly involved, was to know she was the true writer of the series. Maggie had not failed to notice the irony involved. For years she had been battling for a by-line, now she was fighting for exactly the opposite. Despite Latey's reassurances, she simply could not face another backlash against herself or her work. If that were to happen, she felt that what little confidence she might regain by writing the articles would evaporate into thin air.

'Why did you come?' Maggie enquired, hurriedly. 'Mother? Is she with you?'

Henry broke away and cleared his throat again. 'No, she's not well. Nothing serious, just a chill, but you know how she likes to take to her bed and have Beatrice pamper her.'

Maggie had not communicated with her mother since their last confrontation at Chester Square. She still had not forgotten her maliciousness. Attempting to manipulate her own daughter out of a career and into an unsuitable marriage had seemed unforgivable, but now, Maggie felt she might just be ready to absolve Lydia.

'I am here on my own. I wanted to spend time with my daughter. Does a father need any other excuse?'

❧

AFTER TEA, Grace left Maggie and her father alone. Grace was repairing the family's baptism gown for Little Jack. It had been the gown she had worn herself as a babe, and it was becoming a little frayed at the edges. 'It's tradition,' she explained. 'For every baby in the family to wear it. William and his brothers had their turn, as did Beth's daughters. I like to keep it ready for every bairn that comes along.'

Maggie immediately assumed Grace had directed the comment at her. But it would be unlike Grace to be so cutting. Maggie had been overly sensitive since the suffrage meeting.

There was a pamphlet William had to write for the union, so he retreated to the sitting room. Once mother and son departed, Henry took his daughter's hand.

'I worry about you, up here alone, Maggie. It's been over a year since you left London and you've not written a word professionally.'

'That's not entirely true. I'm not alone and while I've not written a word for a newspaper, I have written.'

The corners of Henry's mouth turned down. He seemed doubtful.

'Descriptions of the countryside, the dales and the river,' she added.

'Fiction?'

'Not quite. I wouldn't call them stories yet, and I haven't shown them to anyone. To be honest, I'm just keeping my hand in, I suppose.'

'For a woman as ambitious as you, I can't imagine that is satisfying.'

She looked questioningly at her father.

'Merely "keeping your hand in", I mean.'

Halfway to the sitting room, William realised he had left his notepad in the kitchen. He turned back in time to hear the last of Henry's observations.

'Papa, I would be lying if I denied my career hadn't stagnated somewhat since I moved to Durham. My career in journalism has halted, and the ladies of Durham have trampled, quite mercilessly, upon my zeal for the women's movement. But my experience last summer was more distressing than you may realise.'

William continued to listen, knowing to do so was wrong. He had never eavesdropped before. It was the habit of a coward. *Why am I doing it now?* he asked himself. He knew he should make his presence known, but curiosity had rooted his feet to the floor.

'You're speaking of your mother?' Henry asked quietly.

Maggie nodded solemnly, unwilling to say more. She wasn't certain how much Henry knew of Lydia's plotting.

'Not only that. Being discharged from the newspaper left me adrift, completely rudderless. What would I have done if I had remained in London? I ask myself this question a hundred times a day. Moving to Durham with William gave me a direction.'

William smiled.

'But in doing so, you lost your purpose, Maggie.'

His smile quickly faded.

'I prefer to believe that I have merely neglected my purpose for a while,' she said. 'But I am hoping the new client Grace spoke of might provide a focus for my art and my energy. Also, I believe I may have hit on a new purpose.'

Henry looked at her, interested.

'I want to start a school for girls.'

⁂

WILLIAM TIPTOED BACK to the sitting room, which was a challenge for a man of his size wearing heavy leather boots. He slumped into his father's armchair and placed his head in his hands. *Is there any way to hold her here?* he wondered. The Eliot commission had given him a moment of reprieve, perhaps two or three months, but after that, he wasn't certain. 'Ambitious', 'driven', 'tenacious' were all words he had used more than once to describe Maggie. *Durham will never be big enough for her*, he thought with a sigh. Maggie's calling and her desires often seemed too great for one woman to manage alone.

William realised he had been holding his breath since Maggie arrived with him in Durham. He knew as she stepped from Jack's cab on that first day that she didn't belong. Not because there was anything remiss with Maggie (in his eyes she was perfect) but he was sure a woman like Maggie could never be content in a backwater like Durham. The worst of it was that while her career had 'stagnated', his had flourished. The editor at the *Advertiser*, Mister Armstrong, was speaking of promotion, and the satisfaction he received from working at the union was immense. In Durham, William knew his function in the world. He was safely anchored but it was clear that the woman he loved was adrift.

William wondered how long it would take for her to float away entirely.

Marriage would keep her here, he knew, then hated himself for the thought. Maggie saw marriage as a prison; she had told him so numerous times, although she had never directed the comments at a marriage with him. Instead, they were more offhand observations when she noticed an injustice or inequality – a woman struggling with too many bairns, a young girl being taken out of school to add the tuppence she might earn to her household's purse. How many times had Maggie mentioned the young women who were forced to marry from necessity, from lack of choice? A hundred? A thousand? William had longed to propose on so many occasions. He had rehearsed the words in his head a dozen or more times, like an actor preparing for the stage. Yet each time, something had stopped him.

It was the certainty that she would deny him. Maggie wasn't ready to be proposed to, even though she had been engaged once. He wondered what sort of fly Raymond Turner had used to hook her. Because Maggie was like a Wear trout – glistening, colourful, intelligent and just as difficult to catch. William was a patient man, but what would he do if she got away?

❦

WHEN WILLIAM CAME up to bed, Maggie was buried beneath the bedclothes, rolled up like a hedgehog. The evenings were getting colder and while Grace had made a fire for Henry's bedroom, William told his mother he and Maggie did not yet need one.

Maggie poked her head out from beneath the covers as he approached the bed. He was a holding a wooden box in his hands.

'Is that walnut?' Maggie asked. 'What's in it?'

She sat up eagerly and threw back the covers, then moved to the foot of the bed, her body warming with anticipation.

'It's a gift for you, lass. I collected it this afternoon. I was intending to save it for Christmas, but now your father has arrived, I thought you might like to use it with him.'

William handed her the box and she examined the

surface. Her initials, 'M.L.A.', were engraved in the wood. The thoughtful detail reminded her of Mary Shelley's writing slope, the one Clairmont had left her. Certain William intended the engraved initials to do just that, she glided her fingertips over the letters.

She looked at William. He could tell what she was thinking.

'You loved that writing slope. When you gave it over, it was as though you were giving away a child.'

Maggie had donated Clairmont's treasure to the Ashmolean Museum, minus the journals, of course. It was when they were travelling to Durham that they had stopped in Oxford for the night. 'You don't have to donate it,' he had said as they entered the museum. 'No one'll ever be the wiser.' He'd seen the tears forming behind her eyes and hated to watch her hurting. 'I must,' she had replied. 'Mary's writing slope is a national treasure. I cannot keep it to myself, although there is nothing I wish for more right now than to hold onto it forever.' Maggie had breathed in deeply, wiped her eyes, and ventured through the doors. William mused that there was no mistaking her as the offspring of a war hero.

'I wanted you to have a possession like Mary's writing slope,' William said to her now. 'A treasure you can keep and pass on ...' They locked eyes. William swallowed. 'Perhaps this will wind up in the Ashmolean one day as well. There's not a doubt in my mind you'll end up as renowned as Mary Shelley.'

Maggie opened the small silver clasp to reveal the contents. It was a chess set ... a beautiful, delicately carved chess set.

'Did you make this?'

William laughed and held up his hands, thick fingers spread wide. 'With these?'

She laughed, too.

'It was Old Barney.' Barney Wilks was a joiner and cabinetmaker. 'He carved the pieces himself from ebony and boxwood.'

'Ebony?' Maggie asked, intrigued a joiner in Durham would have access to such a rich and exotic wood.

'It was the remains from a previous commission. An alderman who lives on South Bailey had a hope chest made for his daughter.'

'It's exquisite,' Maggie murmured, touching the pieces. Removing each one from its snug, velvet hollow, she examined the fine detail.

'I described your old chess set, the one you sold, and the box that housed it. He did a canny job, did he not?'

'Right canny,' Maggie echoed, as though in a dream. 'I love it,' she uttered, closing the lid softly. 'And I love you.'

'Do you want to play a match?' he suggested. 'You haven't played in a year. I might actually have a chance of winning ...'

'Not tonight,' Maggie said, placing the box gently on the dresser. She took William's hand. 'I'd rather you come to bed and keep me warm.'

CHAPTER 7

The Manchester Guardian
Wednesday, October 6, 1880

Dear Reader,

OVER THE NEXT three months leading up to Christmas, I intend to write to you weekly. If you do not wish to read my musings, or are too busy with the season's chores or Yuletide merriment, do not concern yourself. But once you become engulfed in the story of my life, I believe that the task of bedecking your house with radiant evergreen, candles, sweets and fruit will pale in comparison. Do you think me overbearing? In truth, I am – my experiences have taught me to be so. As I have never entirely discovered my place in the world, I have learnt to push and squeeze, force and propel myself forth until I am sated with comfort.

I will not write my story in a chronological manner for I do not view my history chronologically. Rather, I see my life as a series of experiences and relationships that have shaped me into the various women I have been at one time or another. Having said that, surely all stories must begin at the beginning.

My Aunt Elizabeth informed me when I was a girl that I slipped into the world with remarkable ease, as though I already knew my place in it. She was a minister, a lay preacher if you will, who sermonised outdoors to her congregation. I admired Aunt Elizabeth greatly and, in my eyes at least, she was imbued with the authority of the Almighty. I believed her every word. It was not until I was an adolescent, questioning and curious, that I doubted her belief in me. At that time, I often asked myself where I belonged; the certainty of my place in the world which had been so clear in early childhood completely deserted me.

Following the birth of my twin brothers, my mother Christiana took to her bed for they arrived too soon and died only ten days later. It was a difficult birth. I was told this by Aunt Elizabeth, although I was only five years old myself at the time. Afterwards, I was never certain whether the ailment that had sent my mother prematurely to her bed was a physical malady or one of the spirit; to this day, my strongest memory of her is as an invalid. She was a beautiful woman.

My older sister Chrissy, who was named for my mother, inherited her blonde curls and pert nose – the Pearson nose. Unfortunately, I inherited the Evans' nose and jaw of my father Robert, as did my older brother Isaac. The powerful, determined features suited the men in the family, making them extremely handsome. I, on the other hand, felt cursed by my rather masculine countenance.

Doctors visited the house regularly. My father loved his wife dearly and wanted her to be well again. Despite her confinement, her fussy and particular ways made Christiana a voluble presence in the house, and when we children visited her in her chamber, she was always flattening a curl or fixing a frill.

When Chrissy departed Griff House for boarding school, Father and Isaac dominated my life; they made up the entirety of my small world. And Warwickshire was an incredibly small world, although I did not realise it then.

My Warwickshire consisted of windmills, canals, endless roads, and farms and fields that stretched to the horizon. The railroad had not yet arrived. It was a world of market towns and cottage industries, although some, such as the handloom weavers, were seeing their livelihoods devoured by the beast of Industrialisation. It was the 1820s, and an entirely different time. Why, a Hanoverian monarch still occupied the throne! Is it even possible to imagine there was a period in Great Britain when Queen Victoria did not reign?

By trade, my father was a carpenter. However, he was an ambitious man and before long – before he had even married my mother – he had lifted himself above the status of a common tradesman to the rank of yeoman farmer. The township saw my family at church each Sunday. Public worship, you see, was a means by which Father could display his rank and respectability. It was not until later in life that he realised he might also find spiritual comfort behind the oak doors of Saint James's.

Our dairy farm was profitable, although not prosperous. Father soon earned the role of bailiff and became a local consultant to the landowners in the county. One might label Robert Evans a jack-of-all-trades, but he would have loathed such a common-sounding moniker.

Griff House was my home until I was twenty. Darling Old Griff still smiles at me when I open my mind's door to it. My favourite place was the attic. I would climb the stairs and take a position among the boxes and dust and stare through the window for hours. The view was of infinity. I remember flower-filled gardens, fir trees and a wide, tree-shaded lawn … although perhaps I have romanticised my remembrance. My early childhood was coloured deeply by the immense happiness I found within Griff's red-brick walls.

I travelled a great deal with Father when he visited the local farms. Often, he would let me drive the cart. I would stand between his legs and grip the reins and he would tell me about everything we saw. His vast knowledge of the countryside astounded me. He could name any tree to which I pointed. He would know when rain was imminent by studying the behaviour of the cows. He could tell a farmer when a field should lie fallow and when it should be sowed. Robert Evans was always correct.

I believed then that my true place in the world was to be driving the cart with my father and discussing the day we had shared together …

❧

MAGGIE LAY DOWN HER PEN. The first interview with Marian had gone exceedingly well. Interviewing Clairmont, initially, had been a battle of wills. Even once they had become friends, Maggie had suspected that the old woman was constantly holding back. Her instinct proved correct once she had read the journals. But Marian was open and, Maggie believed, completely honest. The authoress wanted the truth and nothing but the truth to be printed. Mary Anne Evans, Marian Lewes, Missus Cross and George Eliot finally desired to reveal her true self to the world.

'But my childhood was not ideal,' Marian had confessed to

her during the interview. 'I wanted for a mother's physical love. Failing that, I wanted companionship. My poor brother ... I clung to Isaac mercilessly, desperately. I was lonely, and he was my only friend.'

'And school?' Maggie enquired, raising her cup to her lips and sipping the tea. *It's not a patch on Millie's brew*, she thought, feeling a momentary flash of nostalgia for Clairmont's sour-faced girl.

Earlier that day, Maggie had visited the town house the Crosses had taken next to Framwellgate Bridge. Durham Castle loomed over the narrow residence, blocking the morning sun and leaving the sitting room, where she sat talking with Marian, in the shade. Although Durham was enjoying the final glorious days of warmth before winter cast the North East in white, the Cross's sitting room was chilly and a fire had been lit in the grate. Marian wore a thick shawl, the colour of which matched her eyes.

'At Miss Latham's, my first school, I was constantly homesick. Because of this, the other girls saw me as weak and I was bullied relentlessly. My sister Chrissy, five years older, did her best to protect me and offer me friendship, but I was a needy, whining child. When I was fourteen, my father sent me to Missus Wallington's School in Nuneaton. There, opinion of me did not improve, unfortunately, although I eventually made one or two good friends. By then, my educational experience had transformed me into a solemn, grave child. I read widely, shone at painting and I was an expert at English composition and French. I translated Maria Edgeworth's novels into French when I was just thirteen years old! But my peers viewed me as eccentric.'

Maggie wrote quickly. She had never met a woman as accomplished. She wondered if Marian suffered so due to the jealousy of the other students.

'My piano playing was also outstanding. I had an insatiable desire for the esteem of my peers, but the more time I dedicated to my studies and the harder I attempted to win their friendship, the more they viewed me as strange. So, I tried even harder. I became devoted to my intellect.'

Maggie nodded as she finished the sentence. *For Marian, intellect took the place of friendship*, she thought as she looked up from her notepad.

'You were a prodigy.'

'Yes. But the only way in which I saw myself was alone,' Marian said. 'So, I reimagined myself.'

Maggie frowned sympathetically. Had she ever felt the same way, entirely alone? Maggie was a precocious child, but never a prodigy. Her academic gifts never surpassed those of her peers to the point where they considered her odd. During the events of her last summer in London, when society had shunned her, she'd still had her father and Dorothea, then William on her side. And Briar, at least for a time. Even Latey had been an ally. And now, when Maggie was feeling sorry for herself and imagined nobody understood her or experienced life's hardships as deeply, she could return home to William and Grace. Beth and Jack, too, were always ready to offer support. Although her social circle had narrowed and her connections had dwindled, Maggie had never truly been alone.

'You reimagined yourself? Who as? *What* as?'

'An evangelical,' Marian stated.

Maggie wrote the word in the centre of a page, followed by a double question mark. Unlike Clairmont, Maggie imagined Marian understood shorthand, so she crossed her legs and rested her notebook on an angle to prevent her interviewee from deciphering her notes.

'The headmistress of Missus Wallington's was a warm and gentle Irish woman, Maria Lewis. She was young and, in my eyes, quite brilliant. She often saved me from my loneliness and the scolding of the other girls by summoning me to her office to carry out a task, or inviting me to tea on Sunday afternoons. I formed an extremely strong attachment to her. Eventually, Maria grew to be a mother, sister and friend to me. I aped her gestures and accent, even her beliefs. I adopted her Calvinistic principles. Thanks to Maria, my spiritual fervour grew to be as large as my intellect,' she smiled. 'I denounced all pleasure. I am embarrassed to admit that I even condemned imaginative literature.'

Maggie lifted her gaze to the woman sitting opposite. The greatest of all British female writers, if not the greatest British writer since Shakespeare, condemning imagination? This was more shocking to Maggie than Clairmont's affair with Lord Byron at sixteen years of age. Marian noticed Maggie's astonishment and sought to provide greater context.

'On a trip to London with my brother, I refused to join him at the theatre, decrying it as frivolous. I also criticised his desire to sightsee in the capital.' Marian shook her head in wonder at the girl she once was, as though that person was someone else entirely. 'I even protested when he wanted to go shopping, and berated him on crowded Regent Street! He called me "holier-than-thou".'

'You were Casaubon!' Maggie announced, referring to the pompous and ineffectual religious scholar in *Middlemarch*. How she had loathed Edward Casaubon when she had first read the novel. His selfishness had made vibrant young Dorothea, her favourite character, miserable.

'Far, far worse, I'm afraid,' Marian laughed quietly, clearly embarrassed by her past self. 'Can you believe I even began a great work to rival Casaubon's *The Key to All Mythologies*? I spent six months labouring on a chart of ecclesiastical history!'

The women laughed. *How wonderful*, Maggie thought, *to be at the point in life where one can reflect on past failings, flaws and mistakes and view them humorously*. That place seemed far beyond Maggie's reach at her current stage of life.

At that moment, Mister Cross entered the sitting room. The women looked up at him. Maggie smiled and closed her notebook.

'Is everything going well?' he asked.

'Quite well,' his wife replied. Mister Cross checked his pocket watch.

'I expect we shan't be much longer.'

He nodded and touched his wife's shoulder. '*La mia madonna*,' he said before walking away, closing the door behind him. Marian and Maggie exchanged a glance.

'It was a name George often called me. He used "Polly" mostly, but occasionally "*La mia madonna*",' Marian explained.

Maggie frowned, making mental note of Marian's comment. How unusual for a man to use another man's term of endearment for the same woman. She opened her notebook again, ready to continue the interview. A smile formed on her lips as she recalled the anecdote they had shared before Mister Cross's interruption.

'Seriously, Marian, how could you, even as an adolescent, condemn the imagination?'

'I have asked myself the same question many times,' the older woman said. 'I had a boundless imagination but I have come to the conclusion that I was afraid to use it. I became ashamed of it, believing it to be a fault rather than my greatest asset.'

Maggie gazed at her, confused.

'You see, Maggie, I did not grow up in a home crammed with books. I was not Jane Austen or one of the Brontë sisters. I was not born into a family of scholars and learned men. You are well familiar with Mary Shelley's birthright and her upbringing; that was not mine. I did not have the advantage of a bookish home. In his heart, my father was a simple farmer. To me, being a writer was not my logical place in the world.'

Now, as Maggie worked on her article and marvelled at Marian's admission, she wondered how any individual could change so vastly. Remembering how she had transformed over one summer, Maggie realised that life was a continual metamorphosis. With this new understanding, she stretched her fingers on the edge of the desk, picked up her pen, and continued to write.

ॐ

ONCE MAGGIE HAD DEPARTED, John emerged from the upstairs. He was always there when she needed him, like an extremely good butler. John had been there to greet Maggie at the door, as was the custom – Marian never opened the door herself – and had shown their guest into the sitting room. He had instructed the maid to make tea and to serve it with the lavender cookies the maid had baked that morning from a recipe he had written out for her himself. John was a considerate and tirelessly attentive husband. Of this, Marian was grateful.

Now he had returned to her, keen to know what had transpired in the interview.

'Did it go well?' John asked, taking a seat opposite his wife on the Chesterfield Maggie had occupied earlier.

'Exceptionally. She is a bright girl. I am glad we chose her.'

'Were you able to be honest?' he asked. 'I know how very much you long to be honest with the world.'

Marian nodded. She could see he was curious.

'Johnny, I am tired and a little sore from being seated for so long. Will you help me to the bedroom?'

He rose hastily and took his wife by the arm. 'Of course. Should I ask Julia to draw you a bath?'

While warm baths helped with the pain she regularly experienced from an affliction of the kidneys, she shook her head.

'A small tincture of laudanum and water? You've already had a dose this morning so we must be careful.'

'It makes me dream, John. Rest is what I need. A dreamless sleep.'

'Of course. Life has been quite hectic since we married.'

Marian turned her face towards his and smiled. His expression was full of concern for her.

'We should use our time in Durham as a period of rest,' he said. 'Once we return to London and you begin your next work, we will not have the opportunity to relax.'

She nodded. Then John led her upstairs and guided her to the bed. He removed her shoes, placing them neatly on the floor with the toes tucked beneath the bed frame. When he pulled the covers over her body, he kissed her lightly on the forehead. She was asleep in an instant.

Or so she hoped to make him believe.

When she heard the door close, Marian opened her eyes. She had not wanted to talk anymore, and she worried she had said too much to Maggie. Staring at the canopy above her bed (maroon chintz flecked with gold) her mind was a hurly-burly of the past, images and memories rushing forth, then disappearing just as quickly. Not one would fix in her consciousness even for a second. Eventually, her lids fell closed and sleep claimed her at last.

Griff House
Warwickshire

June 16, 1836

Dearest Maria,

I hope this letter finds you well. While it is a comfort to be back at Old Griff (its familiarity bolsters my spirt) I feel there is a fathomless distance forming between you and me. It was a piteous sight to see you waving to me from the steps as Isaac drove the wagon away along the cobble drive. I watched you grow smaller and smaller until you were but a pinprick in the distance. The diminishing image brought tears to my eyes. Somehow, I was diminishing, too. I realised then I would never return to Missus Wallington's. Then I turned and focused on the road ahead.

'Why am I leaving school?' I asked my brother.

'You are sixteen now. Surely, you have been educated enough,' he answered without a shred of remorse. 'Besides, Chrissy is getting married in the spring and Mother and Father will need you at Griff.'

I examined my brother's grave countenance. There was something he wasn't telling me. We had spent enough time together as children for me to realise that. We had been inseparable once.

I pressed, demanding a more adequate response.

'Your bate in Birmingham did you no favours.'

Isaac's harsh reminder of my behaviour silenced me and I looked in the opposite direction, hoping my brother would not notice the colour rise in my cheeks. I have not shared this episode with you, but now I must in the hope it will ease my conscience and soothe my shame. Giving voice to a humiliation somehow buffs its rough edges.

In September last, I accompanied Isaac to Birmingham to attend the annual classical music festival. I had wanted to go since I was a child and Isaac finally relented to my pleas. It was when we arrived at the Theatre Royal for a performance of Mendelssohn's Italian Symphony that I discovered the true reason he had agreed to accompany me. Waiting by the doors was Miss Sarah Rawlins, a lady from Edgbaston, who, until that moment, I had not known was Isaac's fiancée.

I sat through the performance tight-lipped, barely able to hear the swelling music that filled the theatre. Isaac had purchased a box, an extravagance uncharacteristic of him. He seated himself between his fiancée and me. I noted the many instances he whispered in Sarah Rawlins's ear throughout the performance: seventeen. I counted. He leant my way only twice.

You will find fault with me for my behaviour. You will label me sensitive and neurotic, I know, and I am certain your assessment would be correct. I find that I cannot always control my behaviour.

Had Isaac told me of his engagement, I might have been more amenable. However, following the symphony, when Isaac suggested 'a spot of dancing' at the Assembly Rooms (Isaac never dances), I could barely contain my rage. 'Be a good sport, Mary Anne,' Miss Rawlins laughed. 'We'll be sisters soon and there'll be quite a few eligible gentlemen in attendance.' At the time, I assumed she was making fun of me. You, of all people, understand how painfully aware I am of my plainness.

While Isaac and Miss Rawlins danced, I stood by the wall feeling ashamed. Not a single man approached me, and I backed further and further into the shadows. It was while the couple were dancing a rousing Viennese waltz that I was overcome. The combination of the wheeling figures on the dance floor, the music (Strauss, played much too boisterously) and the cloying scent of a myriad of colognes undid me. Before long I was sobbing, then screaming, then I had fallen to my knees in a wild and uncontrollable frenzy which I could not halt, even though it was exactly what I strove to do.

Isaac was unaware of my distress until the music stopped. Then he must have heard my moans and cries. He told me later that he turned towards the ruckus and the crowd parted. He was shocked to find his sister was the one making a spectacle of herself.

What is wrong with me, Maria? Too clever, too ugly, too temperamental ... Where do I belong in this heartless world?

I thank you, dear friend and teacher, for reading of my failings and my missteps and I would value your counsel. I will endeavour to write to you weekly, if not daily, with news of my life at Old Griff.

Yours ashamed,

Mary Anne Evans

☙❦☙

IN DURHAM, Marian opened her eyes with a start. The light in the room had altered. She took in the canopy's luxurious chintz and recalled where she was.

Perhaps she should not have shared that particular memory with Maggie Almond.

CHAPTER 8

MAGGIE TAPPED her fountain pen against the desk, thinking. Henry was due to leave Durham in three days. She was dividing her time carefully between her work and her father, although her father seemed quite content to do not very much at all except help Grace with her household work and escort her to and from her classes at the university. Maggie had never seen Henry Almond lift a finger at Chester Square. Then again, the family employed the services of three maids and a footman. His conservatory of exotic plants was different; he could toil there for hours.

His favourite time of the year was summer when the family would retreat to their country house in Hampshire. It was a place where he could indulge two of his favourite pastimes: target shooting and riding. She had thought it odd, however, that her father had engaged in neither of these activities since arriving in Durham, even though she had suggested both. Rather than enjoying the sight of Henry galloping across the dales, Maggie had observed him each morning hauling water from the well. Instead of firing a rifle at clay pigeons, he had split wood for the hearth. She supposed as an open-minded style of man, he was simply taking enjoyment in such domestic novelties so different to the duties of his own daily life.

Still, it was odd.

The foursome would sit by the hearth of an evening, comfortable in each other's company. Usually, Maggie and her father would stage a chess tournament. If William was not involved, he would pen a pamphlet or petition for the union while Grace read one of her textbooks or knitted booties and bonnets for Little Jack in preparation for the coming winter. One evening, the familiarity of the scene struck Maggie. A memory came to her of both sets of her grandparents playing bridge together at Christmas. Her mother's and father's parents did not come together often, but each year at Christmas, they enjoyed a relaxed camaraderie as heads of the family. When the children became boisterous, they would demand silence, and they expected their sherry glasses refilled without having to ask.

Maggie had shuddered as she stared at the pieces on the board. She was only twenty-five. She wondered who she was becoming.

Now, Maggie looked down at her interview notes. She had informed Marian the first two or three articles would take the longest to complete, explaining that she would undertake many revisions while she was finding her footing in Marian's world and discovering the authoress's voice. At present, achieving that seemed to be a far simpler task than discovering the voice of Claire Clairmont. Maggie placed her fountain pen on the desk as she remembered the difficulty she'd had in writing the first instalment of her first series. No matter how hard she had tried, she had been unable to find purchase in Clairmont's world, one so removed from her own. Latey had advised her to find a new approach, and so had William. With their encouragement, she kept trying until she just seemed to slip into character. And what a character it was!

Maggie sighed and felt tears prickle behind her eyes. She had grown close to Clairmont, closer than she had expected. She still missed her friendship, lively conversation and the challenges she presented. The old woman had become friend, mentor and mother during a time when Maggie needed all three.

The light faded. It was October, soon to be Christmas, and the days were growing shorter. Maggie rose to turn on the lamp in the sitting room and caught sight of her father and Grace in the garden, choosing the vegetables for tea. Maggie frowned. The pair were so companionable. Henry reached to the ground to pull a carrot from the earth. It was more difficult than he assumed, and the effort involved almost caused him to topple. The couple laughed.

Couple? Maggie thought. *Surely not!*

Maggie nibbled the end of her pen as she viewed them. Papa had been in Durham a week, and he had not sent a single telegram to Chester Square to check on his wife's health. Even if it was a mere 'chill', it was unlike her father to be so remiss. Maggie kept sight of the pair as they examined the vegetables. Papa was animated, alive in a way she had never witnessed before. Then Grace looked towards the horizon and across the dales, sweeping her hand in a wide arc, clearly describing perhaps a walk they might do together or a trip to the seaside. She was extremely becoming, Maggie realised. Her dark hair, green eyes and petite figure made her resemble a far younger woman. Finally, after more conversation, the pair walked away from the garden. Grace led the way towards the house, Henry's hand resting gently on the small of her back.

Maggie watched as they met William coming home from

work. After a few words of greeting, the three of them ventured back to the cottage together.

'IT's a week until the pit opens,' William said during tea. 'I'm hearing discouraging rumours that Drummond has made no significant improvements. Admittedly, they're only rumours. Apart from a chosen few, no one has descended into the seams yet.'

'When I saw Drummond,' Maggie began, adjusting her serviette, 'he was occupied with sightseeing. When I reminded him of the work that needed doing, he seemed completely unconcerned. In fact, his behaviour was rather off-putting.'

Maggie had thought of their strange meeting often. However, she had put his attitude down to the immense pressure he must be experiencing. After all, so many lives depended on the man.

William looked at her, puzzled. 'When did you see him?'

'At the beginning of last week, at Palace Green when I met Marian.' Maggie loved referring to her favourite writer in this way, as though she were her most dear friend. 'He was ...' Maggie searched her mind for an appropriate description. 'Frolicking.'

'Frolicking?' William and Henry questioned in unison.

She nodded. 'He was extremely happy. Seemingly without a care in the world. Looking back, it *was* a particularly splendid morning.'

'I'm pleased Durham has taken his fancy.' William said dryly.

Maggie did not mention how forward Drummond had been with her. There was no telling what William would do if he knew. At the very least, he would grow even more doubtful of Drummond's intentions. If she allowed him, William would attempt to protect her from the world. Yet Maggie had received worse slights.

'Tommy says he has it on trustworthy account that Drummond has hired labourers from Yorkshire, men experienced in meeting the requirements set by unions. They've done the same job a dozen times, he says.'

'Really? Where are they staying?' Maggie asked, surprised. 'I've seen no strangers in town, and Jack hasn't mentioned seeing anyone new about. Surely, they would need tools mended or sharpened?'

William considered Maggie's observation. 'Tommy reckons they're sleeping at the pit. I went out and checked. I did see tents from the road, but I couldn't see any workers.'

'I suppose until he proves otherwise, we'll have to hope Drummond does what he says he will.'

'Drummond, you say?' Henry asked.

'Yes, Matthew Drummond. When I interviewed him, he told me his family made their fortune in Manchester. They started in cotton mills.'

Henry placed his cutlery on his plate and closed his eyes for a moment, attempting to recall what he knew about the family.

'They had a rough go of it, from memory. There was a time when the Drummond mills outfitted the regiments of the British army for the subcontinent and West Indies. But the American Civil War took its toll on the company.'

'Aye. Drummond told me as much, but I wasn't under the impression the mills suffered greatly. After that, they diversified.'

'Mister Drummond certainly doesn't dress like a rich and powerful mill owner,' Grace put in.

'Perhaps his style of dress has little to do with his wealth, and more to do with his desire to be accepted by the Durham community?' Maggie suggested.

'Well, I'd have more faith in him if he dressed like an owner and not a hewer,' Grace added.

'Your mother makes a good point, William,' Henry said after some thought. 'In the army, officers are uniformed, so they are recognisable as officers, leaders. For the troops, that uniform is partly what instils the confidence they need to have in their officer's ability to lead.'

'The man is a puzzle,' Maggie said as she cleared the plates. Her father rose to help. She shot him a sideways glance. Although she was appreciative, the sight of her father stacking plates was still incredibly foreign to her.

'So, what is our appraisal of Matthew Drummond so far?' Maggie asked once the dishes were in the sink. 'Is he to be trusted?'

The four glanced at one another uncertainly. It appeared they could come to no definitive answer that night.

❦

'YOU'RE READING *MIDDLEMARCH*?' Maggie asked when William withdrew his book from the nightstand.

'Aye,' he replied without missing a beat. 'If it's your favourite novel, I think I should read it, too.'

Maggie smiled mischievously and removed the pins from her hair. 'I don't think it will be half as engaging as the last book you read.'

She was referring to *The Coal Question: An Inquiry Concerning the Progress of the Nation, and the Probable Exhaustion of Our Coal Mines.*

He narrowed his eyes. 'You've got a wicked sense of humour, lass.'

She sat beside him on the bed and pressed her cheek to his. 'Thank you,' she whispered.

He cupped her head gently and inhaled. 'Think nothing of it.'

'Are you enjoying it?'

He nodded. 'Very much so. But I'd like to warn Lydgate to steer clear of Rosamond Vincy's sticky web.'

Maggie laughed.

'The man is capable of doing so much good in the world.'

'He is blinded by beauty.'

William kissed her. 'Well, I can't blame the man for that.'

When they drew apart, Maggie took up her hairbrush. 'The Crosses seem to have an unusual relationship,' she commented as she brushed out her hair.

William placed the book against his chest and waited for her to continue.

'Mister Cross interrupted the interview to check we were well. Then as he was leaving, he touched her shoulder and called her "*mia madonna*". It was a term of endearment used by her first husband. I swear I saw Marian flinch.'

'Odd,' William agreed. 'Perhaps he's trying too hard to fill another man's boots, so to speak.'

Maggie gazed at him in interest. *To come second would always be difficult*, she mused, *especially to a man such as Lewes.*

'Or maybe she doesn't like public displays of affection,' he added.

Maggie shrugged, then noticed a light flicker outside, drawing her attention to a far more vexing relationship. She drew the bedroom curtain aside and peered into the dark, attempting to locate the pinprick of light.

Grace and her father were standing by the road. Henry was carrying a miner's lamp, the flame of which he soon turned out. All Maggie could detect was Grace's butter-coloured shawl and the white of her father's collar.

'Turn down the lamps, William,' Maggie said hurriedly in a whisper, as though the subjects of her interest might hear her.

He looked at her, confused.

'Hurry!'

William did as instructed, then joined her at the window. Maggie's observations of the couple in the vegetable garden that afternoon had ignited a spark of curiosity in her mind. There was more to their relationship than companionship, Maggie could tell by how they held each other's gaze for longer than necessary. She recalled her father's hand on the small of Grace's back and instantly remembered the moment in the offices of the *Illustrated London News* when she and William had first shaken hands. Such an innocent gesture, but one charged with passion.

Grace was a widow, a free woman. But Henry wasn't free. While Maggie still struggled to elicit any kindness or sympathy for her mother, she did not long to watch Lydia betrayed. But her father wasn't that type of man. Although he may have discovered Lydia's secret – her long-ago engagement to Raymond, her determination to ruin her own daughter's happiness – he would never betray her.

In the room's dark, they watched Henry and Grace stare at the sky, star gazing. Her father knew a good deal about astronomy and it was the first subject Grace had studied as part of her course. Maggie discerned from her father's gestures that he was pointing out the constellations to his new friend. Maggie and William looked at each other, both concerned and bemused.

'You were speaking about public displays of affection,' Maggie remarked.

They continued to watch Grace and Henry until the older couple were swallowed by the velvet night.

Determined not to dwell on the ramifications of Henry and Grace's friendship, Maggie instead focused her thoughts on Drummond and helping William discover whether any of the agreed-to improvements were occurring at the mine. William was determined to ensure that when the Stanley Pit opened in a week's time, it would be safe. The experience of losing his father and brothers had made him single-minded in this regard.

'I can't watch another pit collapse, Maggie,' he said as they lay in bed. It was when he was the most honest with her. Lying side by side, fingers twined in the dark, was when he could tell her anything. 'If Drummond has Tommy's faith, why am I filled with such doubt about the man?'

Maggie lay silent, contemplating what she should counsel. It would devastate William all over again if men were to die in the pit and he believed he could have prevented another disaster.

'Tommy assures me Drummond has agreed to having the pit inspected by the union before it opens. What more can I ask?' he said, then sighed. 'Still, there's no means of policing it and if the union doesn't witness the changes ... If I don't see them with ...'

William stopped, unable to fully voice his concern. Maggie squeezed his hand, sifting through her mind for a solution. It was highly unlikely Drummond would allow William, a journalist from the *Durham County Advertiser*, to descend into the shaft to witness proof of the improvements, although it would make good sense.

'I spent over an hour and a half with the man and ...' He shook his head.

'And?'

'I have not an ounce of confidence in him. But I can't put my finger on why.'

'Your father and brothers died in a preventable tragedy. Would you have confidence in any owner after what happened?'

Yet she knew he needed to have confidence. The tragedy of the collapse had cut him more deeply, perhaps, than Maggie realised. If he couldn't see the improvements with his own eyes then for him, they had not occurred. William needed proof.

William made a noise – part groan, part sigh – a sign of his frustration at his ineffectualness.

'Your feelings are entirely understandable.' She squeezed his hand tighter and moved a little closer.

'I need to trust Drummond, Maggie,' he said grimly. 'The future of Durham, not to mention my sanity, depends upon it.'

Maggie listened to William's breathing as she stared at the ceiling. Nothing she could say would allay his fears.

'I've got it,' Maggie whispered into the dark after some minutes. 'What you need is a spy. I know a person who is quite expert at the art of subterfuge. Also, she owes me a favour.'

❧

THE FOLLOWING morning Maggie bumped (quite literally) into Matthew Drummond as she was leaving the post office. Her mind was still occupied with the wording of her telegram. Neither in nor out of the store and wondering if she should return to the counter and alter the sentiment, she had stumbled inelegantly into the man. There was a rather awkward moment, with Drummond clutching her arms to prevent her from toppling off the front step. Finally regaining her footing, she looked up into his eyes. They were pale blue and extremely clear, as though she were gazing into shallow water. Maggie apologised, righting herself and straightening her hat.

'You're in a hurry, Miss Almond?' Drummond asked.

'No, I'm not really ... for a change,' she said. 'It seems that matters more important than walking in a straight line have taken my mind hostage.'

He smiled in a bashful, childlike way that touched Maggie's heart.

'Would you allow me to accompany you to wherever it is you're heading? I'd loathe to learn you had stumbled into peril.'

It was Maggie's turn to smile. He was charming in a modest way, as though he wasn't aware of his charisma.

'I'm not going very far – just to the cathedral – but your offer of a supporting arm might be just what I need this morning.'

Maggie placed her arm lightly on his and they walked together towards the bridge.

'You're a newcomer to Durham, Miss Almond, like myself,' he began once they were away from the High Street and heading down to the river. 'Would you mind sharing with me any tips you might have regarding fitting in?'

Maggie's laughter surprised him. 'Oh, Mister Drummond! I am not a newcomer at all, although I feel like one. I arrived in Durham a year ago and all my efforts to find my place in this community have failed dismally. Denying my religious views, I have attended church. Despite my abhorrent culinary skills, I have baked treats for fairs and fetes. And now, regardless of my lack of finesse with a needle and thread, I have suggested the idea of a sewing circle, which, as of this very moment, comprises me and no other. So, if you have any urge at all to improve your crochet or embroidery skills ...'

'I see, I see ...' he said with a laugh. 'Clearly, it is no straightforward task being accepted in this town.'

'You shouldn't concern yourself, Mister Drummond. Geordies suspect all newcomers, but as you're providing employment for over 300 men, I'm sure you'll find acceptance much sooner than I, a woman living in—'

'Sin?' he suggested, entirely without malice.

'Equality,' Maggie responded calmly, quite astounded at not only the sentiment but the tone of complete ingenuousness in which the word was uttered.

Drummond bowed his head, seemingly ashamed of his clumsy turn of phrase.

They walked on in silence for a time. Despite his graceless comment, Maggie found herself softening towards the man. For all his charisma and 'allure', as Marian might have termed it, Drummond seemed to lack the ability to contain and modify his thoughts before they escaped his mouth as utterances. She supposed it wasn't such an awful flaw. Many would argue her own faults were far more distressing.

When they reached the bridge, Drummond stopped and turned to face her.

'I apologise for my carelessness, Miss Almond. I by no means believe your living arrangements are sinful. I was merely completing—'

'A well-known expression,' Maggie finished with a smile.

'Indeed,' he said. 'And it pained me during our walk that I might have destroyed our chances of friendship with one careless phrase.'

He uttered the thought so pityingly, Maggie could not help but respond in a light and positive manner.

'Please don't trouble yourself any longer,' she said as she held out her hand. 'If you have no greater success in your efforts to be accepted in Durham, now that we are acquainted you'll at least know you are not alone in trying.'

CHAPTER 9

THE FOLLOWING WEEKEND, William attended a union meeting in Ryton. Knowing he would depart early with Tommy Fellowes, a plan had formulated in Maggie's mind. That morning, she took her chess set and headed into town. Although she hadn't told William of her destination, she was positive there was nothing untoward in her intentions. Besides, she didn't want his concern to stop her. She was keen to learn more about Drummond and had wondered whether a woman, rather than a man, might encourage him to reveal more about his purpose in Durham. Despite his somewhat odd nature, she had come to hold a certain sympathy for him. If someone, anyone, had reached out a hospitable hand to her in the twelve months she had been in town, she might have been more satisfied with her new life in the North East.

Besides, chess was the perfect occupation for such a grey and gloomy day.

At half ten in the morning, she knocked on the door of Matthew Drummond's South Bailey residence. It was a lovely home with a baroque facade. A footman opened the door a minute later. A minute after that, as Maggie was explaining who she was, Drummond appeared.

'Miss Almond! How lovely to see you,' he said, greeting her eagerly. 'To what do I owe this pleasure?'

The footman offered her a dignified bow before retreating.

Maggie lifted her chess set. 'I was wondering if you might enjoy a game of chess. If you don't play, I am quite equipped to instruct you.'

'I play! Oh, yes, I do!' Drummond rubbed his hands together, readying for the battle, and allowed Maggie to enter his home.

The footman served them hot chocolate – Belgian hot chocolate, no less – a treat Maggie had not supped on since she lived at Chester Square. The Geordie palate did not extend to luxuries such as the finest hot chocolate in Britain. Maggie sipped it with relish as she examined her surrounds. The sitting room had a delightful view of the river. It was a vantage point she had never seen before. Drummond's home was built on a bend in the Wear, and from the sitting-room window, a unique vista, featuring both north and south forks of the waterway, was on show. As Maggie observed the scenery, it struck her that it was a lonely view as well, especially on a cloudy Saturday morning. Each time she glanced at it, there was a choice to make. Maggie decided that most times all one wanted was certainty.

After sipping her chocolate for a time, she set up the board. Drummond immediately admired the pieces.

'William had it crafted for me locally. Chess is a passion of mine, and I ... lost my set last year.' She recalled the moment when she sold the precious set she'd had since her final year at Cheltenham. She had done so to fund Clairmont's burial. A small wave of grief went through her, but she quickly recovered herself. 'It is so lovely to play with such exquisite pieces once again.'

'Mister Dodd is a thoughtful partner to you, Miss Almond.'

'Indeed,' she replied. She did not want conversation to stray towards William. Maggie did not wish Drummond to associate her with William and the *Advertiser*. 'Please, call me Maggie. Miss Almond is much too formal.'

Maggie wanted to be as sociable as possible. She wanted Drummond to trust her; he would need to if she were to find out more about the mine.

'Of course. And I am Matthew.'

The pair shook hands once more on a slightly different footing.

'It has been a few days since our chat,' Maggie went on, studying Drummond's playing style. He was an extremely competent player. 'Have you made any friends since we last spoke?'

He shook his head. 'Unfortunately, not. I don't wish to appear affected, but there are so few suitable men. The pitmen are amusing but limited, and Mayor Hardy and the aldermen are pompous without reason.'

Maggie smiled and examined the playing field. She moved a rook across the board.

'Is there any good reason to be pompous?' she queried.

She hoped to make Drummond aware that, despite the claim he was not affected, he certainly sounded as though he were.

He laughed at her comment. 'Forgive me. It is a failing of mine to speak too quickly.'

'I have noticed.'

Their eyes met briefly, then Maggie returned her gaze to the board. She took another sip of her chocolate. Licking her lips, she scrutinised the pieces.

'I must say,' Maggie said as she touched her knight's muzzle lightly with her finger. 'I am surprised you've not planned a gala to celebrate the opening of the colliery.'

Drummond watched closely as she relocated her knight. 'To be honest, I considered it. However, I believe the community would prefer to see my money spent on the pit and the workers rather than a lavish event.'

Maggie sensed a rebuke and she looked up. Drummond was watching her, but without malice. She smiled.

'I agree. The pit and the workers are a far more worthy cause.'

Over the course of an hour and a half, they played three games. Maggie won them all. They had chatted easily, although he had said no more to her about the pit than he had to William. As she was readying to depart, Drummond suggested they play one more game. Maggie checked her watch. It was nearing one o'clock. There was still time, she supposed, and she *was* having an extremely agreeable visit. Drummond was a charming host and from his kitchen, hot chocolate seemed to flow like the Amazon.

More importantly, he had shared a personal tale, a story of a young woman called Irena, to whom he had been engaged. The relationship had ended suddenly when she left him without warning. Heartbroken, he decided he needed a change of scene. Love lost is the reason he purchased the Stanley Pit.

'I'm so sorry,' she had replied earnestly. 'But it is probably for the best if her devotion was so unsteady.'

When Drummond nodded rather ruefully, Maggie experienced a twinge of sympathy for the man. The end of a relationship was never simple. There was always pain on both sides.

She thought on his revelation as Drummond set up the pieces for their fourth match. He had offered something of himself. If she was to gain his trust and friendship, she would need to offer a little of herself in return. So, she shared the tale of her engagement with Raymond and its aftermath. Matthew's story echoed her own in so many ways.

'It was a terrible situation, but he has married since our parting. His wife gave birth to a beautiful daughter recently. I'm sure you will find happiness as well.'

She spoke what she was certain to be the truth. From where Maggie was sitting, she could see no reason the opposite sex would ignore a successful and charming man such as Matthew Drummond. In fact, she wondered why he had not already been snapped up. Women could be extremely predatory when an eligible and handsome bachelor was on the loose.

'It sometimes just takes patience for the perfect person to walk into our lives,' she added.

They played in silence for a moment before Drummond asked, 'Is Mister Dodd the perfect person for you?'

Maggie looked at him, mildly surprised by the question. 'I believe so.'

He nodded and made a sound. It was neither a snort nor a *humph*. It was the noise of disbelief.

She stared at him for a moment. 'Do we not seem well matched?'

'It is none of my business, Maggie,' he replied lightheartedly, pushing his dark hair from his forehead.

When Maggie looked down at the board, something had changed. She scrutinised it closely. Then she saw it. Her knight had disappeared from the board, yet it had not been taken during the course of play. Maggie replayed the game in her mind backwards, counting each move and the fallen soldiers that sat on opposite sides of the board.

Drummond had cheated.

She looked at him in surprise. He stared ingenuously at

the board. Although she loathed to accuse the man of such an abominable offence, Maggie was certain of it. He had distracted her with questions about William and snatched her knight. She was amazed at such sleight of hand. When his eyes met hers, there was nothing in their pale blue shallows that revealed his treachery. Maggie took the last sip of her chocolate and lost the game.

WHEN SHE DEPARTED, she thanked Matthew Drummond for his hospitality. He gripped her hand in both of his and thanked her profusely for her visit. Maggie walked away, confounded. She wasn't angry in the way she had been when Briar had defeated her in only four moves. On this occasion, Drummond's actions saddened her. Despite the ire she knew her visit would raise in William, she hoped a sign of friendship might assist Matthew Drummond to ease into the community and, in turn, he would then genuinely grow to care about the wellbeing of his neighbours. She wanted to believe that he meant well for the town, for Durham certainly needed something, or someone, to bring it hope.

She also wanted to believe in Drummond for William's sake.

After a few minutes, when she was feeling more herself, she stopped by Prebends Bridge to consider the event further. Had she been too bold in the game? Should she have allowed him to win at least one?

Men's egos are so ridiculously fragile, she thought with an inner *tssk*.

As she was assessing her role in his misdeed, she heard a voice calling her name. She turned. Matthew was running towards her.

He was panting by the time he reached the bridge. It took

him a moment to catch his breath. When he did, he spoke quickly and with emotion.

'I cheated. I apologise. I am such a fool.'

Relief flooded her body. She clutched his hand. 'Oh, I am so happy you admitted to it!'

'You knew?'

'Of course.'

Drummond leant against the stone wall of the ancient medieval bridge for support. He was still a little puffed from his exertions. 'Why didn't you confront me? I do not take you for a shrinking violet.'

Maggie leant beside him. They both stared into the water as Maggie framed her response.

'At first, it surprised me you would be so underhanded. After that, I suppose I didn't want to embarrass you.'

Drummond stared at her for a moment. 'You have an enormous heart, Maggie, to be able to show mercy in that way.'

'Why did you do it?' she asked. 'Was it because you were being beaten by a woman?'

'Not in the slightest!' He seemed stunned she would believe that was the case. 'The truth of it is, I didn't want you to think me stupid, an unsophisticated Mancunian who doesn't know how to organise an opening gala or win a game of chess.'

'Those thoughts never entered my mind, I can assure you.' She smiled and touched his arm. 'And I believe your decision against an opening celebration is quite ... honourable, especially considering those who lost their lives not so long ago. Besides, I am an exceptionally skilful player. Perhaps I should have admitted this before we began, but to do so always makes me sound rather, well ...'

'Affected and pompous?'

'Exactly,' she laughed. 'Now, if we are to be friends, we must promise to be honest with one another from now on.'

He smiled and held out his hand. Maggie took it firmly, and they shook on the agreement.

◈❀◉

MARIAN HAD BEEN RAISED a country girl in Warwickshire, so it seemed unnatural to Maggie that the authoress would be so uncomfortable at the cottage in the company of herself, William, Grace and Henry. Arrogance was not the correct word for her demeanour, but she was certainly aloof.

Maggie observed Marian's discomfort. She recalled that Robert Evans had worked hard to rise in the world. Perhaps his daughter shared similar yearnings? Or perhaps it was merely a case of being too long in the company of intellectuals and literary types, and she had lost her ease with common people ... *Although Henry Almond, Eighth Earl of Wessex is hardly common*, Maggie thought.

However, Mister Cross seemed a far more adaptable personality than Marian. He chatted companionably to both Henry and William, although he had offered her father a small bow of respect appropriate to Henry's rank when they were introduced.

Maggie believed the party assembled around the hearth was a diverting group. She had briefly considered inviting Matthew but William's opinion of the man had given her pause, leading her to reject the idea. Thinking on it now, she was sure she had made the right decision.

Grace served sherry and William offered their guests an amusing anecdote about the current story he was working on for the *Advertiser*: 'Dognappers at large in Sherburn Hill'.

When the laughter died, Maggie sprang to her feet.

'Voila,' she said, producing a copy of the *Manchester*

Guardian from behind her chair and placing it in Marian's hands.

It was the reason Maggie had arranged the dinner. She wanted to make a show of the first published instalment of the new series, which she had dubbed 'The Many Faces of George Eliot'. It had taken only a few days to arrive. Latey was good to his word and posted the edition featuring the first article, along with an encouraging note regarding his admiration for Maggie's talent. 'My edits', he had written, 'were minimal.'

Clairmont had relished the experience of having Maggie read each article aloud to her. Following this, the pair would scrutinise the illustration and ponder its many meanings. Although Marian would not require Maggie's services to read the article – she was considerably younger than Clairmont had been and wore silver-rimmed spectacles for reading – she hoped sharing the first instalment with her would provide some of the joy she had shared with Clairmont. While the *Guardian* had none of the illustrative flair of her former employer's paper, Latey had included a single likeness of Marian. It was the flattering François D'Albert Durade portrait of the writer.

The article appeared on page twelve, the section allotted, Latey explained in his brief note, to the newspaper's human-interest stories and serials. Maggie was pleased, recalling the angst the placement of her Clairmont series had caused her last year. Mister Cross edged closer to his wife as she unfolded the newspaper. He was the epitome of a mother hen, scanning the article a few lines of print ahead of his wife, hoping to alert her to any offences ... or so Maggie imagined. She glanced at Henry. He flicked his eyebrows skywards.

While Marian silently read the article, the rest of the gathering sipped their sherry in wait. She made no comment, gave nothing away. Marian's reaction disappointed Maggie.

She had envisaged her hero reading the article aloud to the entire gathering. What a boon that would have been! For Maggie to have her words flow like sweet syrup from the mouth of George Eliot would have been not only memorable, but momentous.

When Marian had finally finished reading, she looked up.

'Do I sound like that, Maggie?'

Her voice was level, entirely reasonable. Maggie wasn't certain whether the question was a criticism or merely an observation. The gathering looked at her, waiting for a response.

'Like what?'

'Witty, intelligent, wry, a tad world-weary but optimistic at the same time?'

Maggie nodded. 'I believe so.'

'Wonderful,' she remarked quietly. 'I appreciate your efforts to make me appear so ... erudite and realistic.'

At least, thought Maggie, it was praise of a kind.

❦

OVER SUPPER, and after a second glass of wine, Marian became more loquacious with her admiration. In particular, she admired the format of the article.

'I have written so many letters in my life. It just always seemed the most natural form of writing to me. Penning a correspondence to a friend is no effort at all. Often, I write as though the person is in the room with me and I am speaking to them, so having the article written in this way feels particularly appropriate.'

As the others continued to chat, Marian leant closer towards Maggie's ear. Lowering her voice, she said, 'George would often laugh at the emotion I'd pour into my correspondence. But for a long time, letters were my only connection to the outside world. While I have begun journals periodically over the years, reflective writing always seems so self-indulgent to me. I would give up after only a few weeks.'

Maggie imagined Marian's no-nonsense, presbyterian father uttering something similar.

'I must agree, Marian, yet journals can become a valuable chronicle of one's life – a record of the people we once were and have become,' she said wistfully, recalling Clairmont's bequest. 'But to adopt a regular practise requires a great deal of discipline. Miss Clairmont told me William Godwin had his daughters journaling from the time they were young children, mere babes in arms. At least that what she led me to believe.'

Marian laughed quietly, gently, a soft zephyr of sound.

Maggie could not believe she was discussing writing techniques with George Eliot. How many times had she dreamt of this moment? She inhaled, her chest swelling. As she did so, she caught William's eye. He winked and offered her a nod in deference.

While she could speak with Marian all evening, Maggie turned her attention to Mister Cross. She knew so very little about the man. Apart from his physical appeal, surely he must also be interesting and intelligent for Marian to have accepted his proposal.

'I believe you have written for the *Times*, Mister Cross,' Maggie remarked. 'I discovered several of your articles in the archived copies of the university library. You contributed to the correspondence column frequently?'

John Cross laid down his knife and fork and touched his serviette to the corners of his mouth. 'Indeed, Miss Almond.'

Despite her protestations he should call her Maggie, the man would not relent in his rigid formality.

'The editor seemed to value my opinion on a number of

matters, from finance to the Battle of Five Forks. And it was an excellent means of occupying my idle hours.'

He doesn't seem like a member of the idle rich, Maggie thought, remembering the way he had helped Jack with the bags of seed on the day he and Marian had arrived at the cottage.

'You're an accountant by profession, are you not?'

'That's how we met, Maggie,' Marian interjected. 'Well, that's not entirely true. We met in Rome.'

Marian stopped talking and John began. Maggie guessed that the couple had related this story several times. This was Mister Cross's part to tell.

'My mother and I lodged at the same pensione as Marian and her first husband, Mister Lewes,' Cross went on. 'We met them one evening for dinner. While I conversed with Mister Lewes on financial matters, my mother and Marian spoke of art and literature. Oh, how I longed to be a part of the other conversation!'

Maggie laughed. It seemed he had been enchanted by Marian even then.

'George and I so enjoyed the company of John and his mother that we travelled on to Naples with them,' Marian continued. 'Once we returned to England, we asked John to manage our finances. George had been responsible for them in the past but ... Well, let's just say John was better equipped in that regard.'

Through her research, Maggie discovered that George Henry Lewes had an immense intellect and was a talented writer, but made a meagre income from his work. The small amount he earnt went to the upkeep of his rather unconventional family – his wife Agnes and his children, three of whom he had not fathered. In contrast, George Eliot was famously one of the wealthiest writers in England. Only Charles Dickens surpassed her, and not by much. Maggie discovered Marian received £7000 when her novel *Romola* was published seventeen years ago, enough to live on comfortably for a lifetime. Since then, she had penned four more novels, including *Middlemarch*, her most successful. It was no wonder she needed an advisor of John Cross's calibre to manage her riches, neither was it surprising that she married him. He was attractive, intelligent and, having retired from business at just thirty years of age, clearly a man of independent wealth. Maggie had concluded Marian could trust that her new husband loved her for herself and not for her fortune.

'Johnny was also a wonderful companion to us both,' Marian went on. Mister Cross had absented himself from the conversation by now. 'Johnny taught George and I to play tennis, you know. George, of course, later insisted on constructing our own court on the lawns of The Heights, our home in Witley, Surrey.' She smiled at the memory. 'He always refused to wear the customary white cotton trousers and shirt. Instead, he'd take to the court wearing his dark woollen suit or tweed. Within minutes, he would be sweating freely. We had so much fun together, didn't we, Johnny?'

Mister Cross agreed with a courtier's nod.

'Those were wonderful times,' Marian said, smiling.

CHAPTER 10

The Manchester Guardian
Wednesday, October 13, 1880

DEAR READER,

I hope you have fared well since our last correspondence. No doubt that wherever you are on this great island, you will be savouring the brilliant ambers and russets of the season, and enjoying the delights autumn brings with it. Perhaps you have been collecting conkers and pinecones, apple picking or gazing at the Hunter's moon?

As a child, a beloved event for me was the Nuneaton Harvest Festival. Saturday's harvest supper preceded Sunday's harvest sermon at Saint James. I close my eyes now and I see splashes of crimson, orange, raisin and wine. They are burnt into my memory. How I loved filling baskets with squash, apples, plums, blackberries and spice biscuits, and proudly heaving my colourful bounty to the altar.

It was those moments that remained vivid in my mind during the otherwise frustrating years following my return to Griff House. As you may have gathered from the first instalment of my story, I was a lonely and solitary child. Ostracised and mocked, I drew inwards and kept to myself. Little did I know what I discovered during that time would one day become my dearest companion. However, at such a young age, I was not yet ready or able to befriend what I had found within.

Imagination can be a terrifying concept for a child. Well, it certainly was for me! Venturing into that world was akin to walking into a lion's den; power, unpredictability and a ferocity that could not be controlled was what lay in wait. I backed away cautiously and did not drift inside again for quite some years. Instead, I endeavoured to build a wall around that part of my myself, that part of my mind, to ensure my terrible and much-feared imagination would never escape. I planned to keep it a silent captive forever. Fortified with knowledge, my mind became a fortress.

Fortunately, my father agreed I should carry on my education away from Missus Wallington's school. When I was not caring for my ailing mother, churning butter or pickling vegetables, I was busy teaching myself Latin and Greek. As I was coping so well with my duties, Father even agreed to my request that he hire a languages tutor to instruct me in German and Italian. In addition, when we travelled to Arbury Hall each month to visit with Sir Charles Newdegate, the owner of the estate on which we lived, the kind man gave me complete and glorious access to the Hall's remarkable library. What a stroke of luck! Of course, I limited myself to biblical texts at that time.

One day I was lured by the title *An Inquiry Concerning the Origin of Christianity*. The book immediately caught my attention and, despite the seditious nature of the words on the pages, I could not help but read it. The author, Charles Hennell, had somehow knocked a stone from my fortress, but I was not yet ready to fully grasp what that meant for me.

A few months following this encounter, my mother died a terrible death of cancer of the breast. I was seventeen. Father and I grieved, but he was wretched and remained so for years after her death. When I was twenty years old, my brother Isaac married Sarah. You must remember Sarah, ever-so-devoted Reader, the handsome lady whom I so shocked and distressed with my 'performance' at the Birmingham Festival? Once, she had called me 'sister'. After Birmingham, she knew me as 'Isaac's eccentric sister'. Such was my peculiarity, she required distance. Much distance. It was a gap I could never bridge. If not sisters, I spent much time wondering if we could be friends. I discovered years later that this was not to be.

Once Isaac married Sarah, my brother took Griff House as his own. He asked Father and me to leave. My father took no offence at Isaac's request, but I argued that Old Griff was large enough to accommodate all of us. How I did not want to leave the safety of those red-brick walls! Yet as the plain, bookish youngest child – and as a female – I had no say in the matter. Isaac had been groomed by our father as his successor at Arbury Hall Estate since he was a boy.

Father and I moved to Bird Grove, on the outskirts of Coventry, just ten miles away. Although I experienced real sorrow on leaving Griff, I slowly became confident that I could build a new life for myself among the evangelical community, to whom Maria Lewis had taken lengths to introduce me.

But then I met the Brays and my cloistered, confined and critical perception swelled in an instant, like the chest of a man set free.

The Bray family were ribbon manufacturers. When I met Charles, the eldest son, he had only recently inherited his father's successful company. I remember the encounter so clearly, as if it were yesterday; it was in the gardens of Rosehill, Charles's home. Sitting under the boughs of a glorious purple beech tree, I began to bloom.

MAGGIE WAS WRITING in the university library. The scholarly air inspired the words to flow. Clearly attracted to one another, Henry and Grace were proving quite a distraction to her work. Henry had decided to stay on for a little longer, claiming the 'fresh air' was doing him good. When Maggie was at the cottage, she couldn't help but constantly strain to hear their conversations.

Whenever she heard the door close, she would rush to the window to spy and interpret their actions and behaviour. Furthermore, her exchange with Drummond only days ago troubled her. Yes, he had cheated ... but he had also apologised. Because of that, she felt that Drummond deserved a second chance. Yet William was so intent on finding fault with the man. *How am I to convince him that he might be mistaken without feeling like Judas Iscariot?* she wondered. Attempting to focus, she rested the end of her pen between her lips and breathed in the scholarly air, hoping the application of the students and tutors around her might be contagious.

She returned her attention to Charles and Caroline Bray.

Along with Caroline's sister Sara Hennell, these freethinkers became the centre of Marian's world. The coincidence that Sara and Caroline (or 'Cara', as Marian referred to her) were siblings to Charles Hennell, author of the book that shook Marian's world, had not escaped her notice.

She tapped her fountain pen against the polished oak of the table, attracting the attention of several students. She whispered an apology, then lowered her eyes, ashamed. Maggie had never attended university, but she enjoyed being around the students now, even if she could not be as still and silent. Looking back over her notes, she realised it was the Bray family that was the key to unlocking Marian's mind and soul.

Evangelicalism led Marian to the Brays; Charles Bray had once been as devout as Marian. However, over the years he had taken on other philosophies which had softened and rounded out his Calvinist extremes. By the time Maria Lewis introduced Marian to the family in 1841, Charles had transformed into a free-thinking radical.

'Maria Lewis scolded me when she came to visit,' Marian had told Maggie during their interview. The women had conversed in the cathedral's shadow. With a chill in the air, Marian had offered Maggie the second shawl she had brought with her. Johnny had insisted she bring it, she said. Maggie refused her offer. Speaking with a subject at length tended to raise her temperature. It was the intense concentration needed, she believed.

'Knowing Maria was such a significant person in my life, Charles and Cara invited her to Rosehill for the afternoon. Charles – a married man – and I walked across the lawn arm in arm to greet her. I could see she was quite shocked, not to mention furious. Once we were alone, she informed me I was inviting scandal.'

Maggie nodded. Charles Bray *was* rather scandalous. His

ideas regarding sexual freedom were as avant-garde as Percy Bysshe Shelley's. Charles and Cara had an open relationship, Maggie had learnt. The couple even adopted Charles's two children by another woman.

'Maria's censure did not bother me,' Marian went on, taking in a deep, full breath. 'What I gained from being at Rosehill with Charles, Cara and Sara, far outweighed my fear of controversy.'

'And what did you gain?'

'My soul, Maggie,' the authoress said gravely. 'I was reborn. I was truly and fully alive for the first time in my life.'

Maggie smiled. She knew something of that feeling. She shifted on the bench on which they sat and turned her face towards the sky. Cloudless.

'My world suddenly opened like a blossoming rose,' Marian continued. 'We would spend hours each week in serious discussion over philosophical matters. We were constantly speculating ...'

Maggie noticed a bittersweet tone colour Marian's recollections.

'It was because of Charles and Cara that I met the likes of John Conolly and Ralph Waldo Emerson. They even introduced me to George Sand.'

'George Sand?' Maggie looked up from her notes. 'Meeting a female writer of her calibre, were you not inspired to ...?'

'No, no, not then. I was not yet ready. Besides, I was engaged in a number of charitable works that kept me occupied. I also volunteered at Sara Hennell's school for infants.'

'A school?' Maggie asked, her interest piqued. Marian had not mentioned this before. Maggie wondered if the authoress's experience might shed light on her own ambitions.

Marian nodded. 'When Charles took over his father's

business, he was so shocked by the lives of the factory workers that he opened a school for their children. Sara and Cara staffed it and, when my father did not need me, I helped as well. They were all such wonderful, charitable individuals. Charles genuinely cared for the welfare of his employees. The residents of Rosehill engrossed my soul.'

Marian's face was aglow with the memory of the Brays and their home. Maggie's thoughts turned to Matthew Drummond. She wondered if he would prove similarly philanthropic.

'My adherence to the Bible as the one and only source of truth fell away,' Marian went on. 'I became unglued from God, but I had discovered something far greater. Charles Hennell was Cara and Sara's brother. I had read his book quite by accident in the Arbury Hall library. Although I did not realise it at the time, that book had caused a very fine fracture in my values and beliefs, allowing the Brays to penetrate my heart and mind.'

'Tell me about this book,' Maggie said. 'I've never read it. I don't believe I've even heard of it.'

'In it, Charles Hennell argues the Bible is a mass of inconsistencies. While he does not deny the existence of Jesus, Charles concludes the miraculous events we read about in the Bible could be explained by natural phenomena. He claimed that Jesus was a man and nothing more.'

'And your father's reaction to this? I remember you remarking he was devoted to his worship.'

Marian lowered her eyes and examined her slender fingers.

'He was furious. One evening over supper, I informed him I could no longer accompany him to church. Religion had become detrimental to me; the thought of attending church suddenly sickened me.'

How father and daughter must have struggled, Maggie

thought. Mary Anne was precocious and unconventional, growing more so each day she spent in the company of the Brays. Robert Evans was a conventional country artisan who had always yearned to be more, constantly striving for status and respectability. Maggie gave silent thanks for her own father's encouragement. He had always supported her choices.

'Poor Father. His shame fuelled his anger,' Marian said. 'He had endeavoured his entire life for respectability. Suddenly, his position was hampered by a daughter who refused to behave in a proper and marriageable manner.'

'What did you do?'

'My father simply would not soften. He even threatened to leave Coventry and abandon me. Faced with the prospect of life as a governess, I relented and agreed to a compromise. I would attend Sunday service like an obedient and dutiful daughter, but I refused to alter my views.'

Maggie looked at the authoress. 'You chose to do so for his sake?'

'We disagreed on so many issues, but I loved him very much. When he died, it felt as though I was shrinking. I had nightmares frequently. Once, I dreamt I was a geometrical equation, decreasing to a point of nonexistence.'

Confounded by the analogy, Maggie nodded uncertainly. She wondered if the death of Robert Evans offered the young Mary Anne a release in some way. *Could it have been this momentous event that allowed her to explore her creativity?*

'Was it at this point you started writing?' she asked.

'Yes, but not fiction. I wrote articles for the *Coventry Herald*, the newspaper owned by Charles Bray. I also completed an English translation of Strauss's *Das Leben Jesu* which Charles Hennell's wife, Rufa Brabant, started before their marriage. Poor Rufa. She was forced to give up translation work when they wed …'

Maggie was not familiar with that text either. Or work with Rufa. She never felt as undereducated as she did when she was with Marian, the woman who dreamt in mathematical metaphors.

'Continuing her work was harrowing, to say the least. After reading Charles Hennell's book, I viewed Jesus as a man as opposed to a mythological being, therefore the scenes of the crucifixion … they haunted me day and night. I couldn't eat or sleep, and I fell into the deepest melancholy. My head burned as though it was I who wore the crown of thorns. Sara stayed with me for weeks and nursed me back to health. She was a kind woman who did not view my irrational moods as hysteria. It was at this time we became close.'

Maggie remembered that melancholy and depression had plagued Mary Shelley as well. She noted the similarity.

'You must have valued Sara's friendship very much.'

Marian nodded. 'She showed me patience and kindness. Sara understood me intimately. She provided gentle encouragement when I most needed it. Still, it took some years before I garnered the courage to write fiction.'

Maggie was puzzled by Marian's admission. The progressive environment at Rosehill appeared to have been a lush ground for inspiration and she had friends there who supported her endeavours.

'Do you mean that even under the Bray's influence you were still not brave enough to set your imagination free?' Maggie asked, astonished.

Marian shook her head. 'That was a very slow process.'

Maggie put down her pen and stretched her fingers. She took a moment to observe the students seated around her as she contemplated Marian Cross's early life. Young men and a few women around her studied, although Maggie knew the women would not be rewarded with degrees when their labours concluded. Reading furiously, writing frantically, the scratch of their fountain pens echoed in the silence.

Maggie could not believe George Eliot had so struggled to discover her creative spirit. It made her appreciate the authoress's novels even more. The knowledge that their birth was so hard fought made their existence even more wonderful.

Maggie's imagination, in contrast, was so free it was dangerous. Was the romance between Henry and Grace a fiction she'd created born from boredom? Was the friendship she'd seeded with Drummond merely the fruit of a reckless mind? Was the establishment of a girls' school in a town such as Durham pure fantasy? While she had only ever dabbled in prose in the past, Maggie was certain that if she ever did decide to turn her hand to fiction, she would release a floodgate of creative speculation. Perhaps that was what was holding her back – once released, would she ever be able to close it again?

Maggie looked once more at her notes. Robert Evans left Marian a small legacy which allowed her to travel throughout Britain and Europe with her new circle of friends. She had told Maggie that she was 'remade in Geneva'. Maggie exhaled with an audible sigh and the students raised their heads once more. It was in Geneva that the lives of Mary Shelley and Claire Clairmont had also been changed for ever. She wondered for a brief moment what it was about that city that was so transformative. Then she turned back to the task at hand.

❦

THE INTERVIEW with Maggie had gone longer than expected. Marian could not blame the young woman. She was so interested and alert; she never let a single line of enquiry go untethered. Marian had not spent so long in the outdoors since George, not since their many walks, coastal and forested. Fresh air and sunshine had exhausted her even then. Now, any outdoor experience was positively gruelling.

During her honeymoon with John, she was always falling behind. 'Keep up,' he'd cry, striding ahead on his young, long limbs. She and George had always naturally fallen in step with one another ... Maggie, like John, never seemed to tire. Throughout their time together, she remained sharp. 'As smart as sixpence', as Dickens might have written. Marian had to admit that while tiring, the outdoors was conducive to debate and ideas, just as it had been under the Bray's purple beech.

By the time Maggie had walked her back to the house and they farewelled, it was suppertime. Standing on the bridge, she and Maggie had admired the sunset and the way the colours were reflected in the river's waters. Fanned in the breeze, they resembled an Impressionist painting. It had reminded her of Venice.

Marian entered the house on her toes as quietly as a mouse, or so she imagined a mouse might enter. John heard her entrance and burst through the sitting-room door, surprising her on the stairs.

Standing on the third step, she gazed down at him.

'I am exhausted, darling. Will you be so kind as to ask Julia to save my supper? You know my appetite has a habit of striking at all manner of odd hour.'

Marian watched as his expression flickered between disappointment and concern. He reluctantly agreed. What else could he do? She climbed another step, then another.

'Do you need help to undress? I can send Julia up?'

'Please, don't bother her. I can manage.' Her last words trailed down the staircase. George would always help her undress, but now she preferred to do so on her own.

Her lower back was aflame, but she had not wanted to tell John. He would have insisted on laudanum and a warm bath when all she wanted was rest. Once she was in bed, her fatigue brought sleep to her within moments.

Bird Grove
Coventry

SEPTEMBER 2, 1849

Dear Chrissy,

I write to you to explain my choices and decisions, realising neither you nor Isaac will ever understand them. However, I wish to make it clear to you, dear sister, that the choices I have made are beyond my control. I feel my life is forever evolving and adapting. Life's hardships and joys strengthen me.

In May, I was disconsolate. I could not imagine life without Father. It was as though a part of me was gone. My moral fibre had vanished with his last breath.

On the eve of his funeral, I suffered a mortifying nightmare. I had transformed into a creature from hell, wanton and proud. I wandered about the coach roads like a demon. It was a sign, I believed, of my displacement and the moral void that threatened to engulf me without his guiding hand.

Both you and Isaac barely acknowledged me at the service. I had longed to share our grief, but it appears my choices have made me untouchable. For the weeks after Father's death, I was inconsolable. Tell me, has another person ever shed so many tears? Sara, Charles and Cara were deeply concerned for me. They feared I might cry myself away, pool and puddle, and disappear forever.

Since then, they have proved themselves to be truly wonderful friends, Heaven sent. They stepped in when you and Isaac chose to step away. They organised a trip and insisted I join them ... but when I read the itinerary – the Lakes District, Scotland, Paris, Milan, Como, then finally Geneva –my heart stopped.

I informed them my inheritance would not stretch that far. But Sara said, 'You need not worry, dear friend. Your health is all that matters.' My tears flowed anew.

I gradually put myself back together over the course of our travels. Then in Geneva, I was courageous enough to sit for a portrait. It was Sara's idea. The artist, Francois d'Albert Durade, was a funny little man; extremely engrossing, but inflicted with a hunch back. His garret studio was a haven for him, as it became for me during the four days I sat for him.

Staring at the portrait when it was complete, my first instinct was to fall into a depression. The image was too glowing, too engaging, the eyes too blue. Durade noticed my expression and rummaged among the rags before finally producing a looking glass. When I examined myself, I instantly saw what he had seen. There was colour in my cheeks and my eyes were clear and intelligent. You know, dear Chrissy, no one will ever consider me a beauty, but there was a radiance about me which Durade captured that I had never glimpsed before.

When I returned to England a fortnight ago, I went first to Griff to visit Isaac. While Isaac and Sarah allowed me leave to stay for dinner, they told me plainly I was welcome no more at my childhood home. I had seen Sarah flush when I spoke of my friends, those who filled my sails after Father's death. I am saddened to inform you that the entire experience was dismal.

When I departed, I became determined to sell everything in my possession and transform completely, to fully embrace the person I had become in Geneva.

I am Mary Anne no more.

I know I can be honest with you, darling Chrissy, and while you may not understand my evolution, you will not exile me.

Yours reborn,
Marian Evans

CHAPTER 11

'WHY ARE YOU HERE, PAPA?' Maggie asked as she cast her line. The soft *plop* of the sinker echoed in the quiet. Casting was the only aspect of fishing Maggie enjoyed. It was an act so filled with expectation, such surety that within an instant a glistening pink trout would dangle from the end of the line. But fishing was nothing like that at all. The initial expectation would quickly vanish and dissipate into languor.

Henry glanced at her, then gently tugged on his line. 'To be with you, Maggie.'

'I see.' She stared into the crisp water of the Wear.

The morning was still. There was not a wisp of breeze to break the surface of the river. Trout as silky and shadowy as a dream were visible beneath the glossy veneer. Maggie attempted to count them, but they were too quick and canny. Because she struggled to enjoy the sport, Maggie would invent challenges for herself, such as counting the fish or mentally reciting the Saint Crispin's Day speech from *Henry V.* Such efforts, although small, distracted her from the tedium. Fishing required patience, a quality Maggie possessed in extremely short supply. William told her she should view trout fishing as a battle, just like she viewed chess ... Just like all those wars she knew so much about.

'Do you think the Greeks would have lost patience in their efforts to invade Troy?' he had asked her once as they stood knee-deep in the water. 'Building a wooden horse would require weeks of patience, I imagine. I'm asking only a couple of hours from you.'

'There was more at stake for the Greeks,' she argued. 'What's more, I'd receive more satisfaction from outwitting the entire Trojan army than one poor fish.'

How was she going to lure her father into speaking to her honestly now? Maggie had orchestrated the outing in order to catch him alone. Dressed in breeks and a pair of waders which had once belonged to William's youngest brother, Maggie considered which fly she should use next. Since her father arrived in Durham, it had been difficult to speak to him in private. The fishing expedition was an opportunity to discover the truth regarding his visit.

'Have you been taking care of my bonsai?' she asked, hoping to hook him into conversation. Bonsai was another pastime that required patience. It was one, however, that Maggie found far more satisfying than fishing. While there was nothing or no one to corner or catch, at the conclusion of her time with the secateurs, there would always be a transformation for her to witness. An image that had begun in her mind would, on tending to the miniature trees, manifest in a physical reality before her eyes.

'Hush, Maggie. You'll scare away the fish.'

'To be honest, you're scaring me.'

Henry reeled in his line.

The bait had been taken.

'I know in the time you've been here something has sparked between you and Grace Dodd,' Maggie said. She had never imagined she would be speaking to her father about his romantic liaisons. 'I'm beyond certain Mother hasn't caught a chill. Please view me as an adult. Surely, I must be considered the world expert on tricky romantic entanglements by now.'

Henry smiled. 'How did I ever believe I could hide something from you, my clever girl?'

Somehow, he seemed proud and relieved Maggie had uncovered his secret. He walked to her and took her in his arms. As he did so, Maggie felt a tug on her line. She gasped, wriggled out of her father's embrace and reeled in the line. She had never caught a trout before. Typically, she would give up before reaching this immense climax. After a moment's frantic effort, a sheeny, spotty brown trout was hanging from her line.

◈

FATHER AND DAUGHTER sat on the bank eating lunch. It comprised bread Grace had baked earlier that morning, a wedge of Cotherstone cheese procured from a neighbour in return for two pounds of potatoes, and a pot of mustard pickles Maggie had made herself. Labelled 'September 1879', they were one of the first domestic tasks she had undertaken when she had arrived in Durham. Grace had guided her through the picking and preparation of the vegetables, the cooking and the bottling. After her disappointments in London, Maggie felt she had accomplished something rather extraordinary as she lined a shelf in the cellar with her golden jars.

Maggie had released the trout she'd caught earlier. After Henry had scooped the fish into a net, Maggie carefully removed the hook from the corner of its tensible mouth. Gazing into its sorrow-filled black eyes, a wave of guilt like she had never felt before forced her to place it back into the water and let the slippery wee creature loose.

'We will disappoint William,' Henry said. 'Grace, too.'

Both had joked they wanted at least six fat trout for tea seeing as Beth, Jack and the children were joining them.

'What is it between you and Grace?' Maggie said as she retrieved an apple from the basket.

'I'm none too sure.' Henry shrugged, admitting to the attraction. 'The moment I met her, it was as though we had been friends for years. She is so unlike your mother.'

'Two women could not be more different!' Maggie said, laughing. 'But you've always been so in love with mother. Besotted, even. I wouldn't have thought there was another woman in the world who could turn your head.'

Henry examined the bread in his hand, then placed it back into the basket. He gazed at his daughter seriously, ruefully.

'When you departed London so suddenly, I didn't understand what had led you to such a finite act. You were so terribly distressed on the evening you visited me in the conservatory. I sensed it was more than William's imminent departure and Clairmont's death. To me, whatever it might be seemed even more catastrophic than losing your position at the *News*. I knew there was something you were holding back from me.'

Maggie squeezed her father's hand. He knew her so well.

'I believed your mother knew the truth, but she refused to speak a word about it. She refused to speak of you. And she hardened. I couldn't understand ...' Henry frowned, contemplating that time. 'The weeks, the months wore on and her unusual behaviour grew to become normal. Her remoteness, her irritability became a part of her nature.

'Then recently, I found her in your bedroom. Lying on your bed, with her head on your pillow, she was weeping. Sobbing. I went to her and held her, and she told me everything.'

Maggie looked at him, surprised. He nodded sadly.

'I believe it was the first time in our twenty-five years of marriage that your mother was entirely honest with me.'

What a shattering realisation. Maggie's heart reached out to her father and instantly she understood his attraction to a woman like Grace. With Grace Dodd, there was no dissembling.

'Learning of Lydia's schemes stunned me beyond comprehension. To force you into a marriage that was not your desire, and her past affection for Raymond Turner ...' He shook his head in dismay.

'And Mother?'

'Finally relieved of her burden, she apologised. She vowed that the experience had changed her. She hopes to reconcile with you, which I support, of course. However, the truth of the matter is, she hurt me. I am a man scorned and ... I need time apart.'

'Do you love her?'

Henry sighed. 'Of course I do. But differently. Lydia is not the woman I believed her to be. And I can't carry on as though she is.'

'And this attachment to Grace?' Maggie asked hesitantly.

'Our relationship is chaste, I assure you,' Henry declared, straightening.

Maggie forced herself to keep listening.

'We have a great deal in common, although we must appear to be entirely different.' He looked at his hands. 'Also, I like the way she smiles, how the lines gather around the corners of her eyes and mouth. And she laughs so freely, without hesitation or embarrassment, as though she has not a care in the world, when not so long ago she lost her husband and sons. I feel an intense attraction to her, yet we are worlds apart.'

Maggie understood her father's words more than he could

know. London society had shunned her for pursuing a relationship with a miner's son. However, if after her refusal to be Raymond's wife she had become his mistress instead, society would have turned a blind eye.

'Were we born into the wrong class, Papa?' she asked eventually.

'If we lived in a better world, Maggie, you would not need to ask that question.'

☙❧

THERE WERE no fat trout for supper. William and Jack taunted Maggie endlessly for her lack of fortitude and fishing finesse. Fortunately, William knew Maggie well enough to know she wouldn't harm a fly. He had stopped by the butcher on the way home and purchased two pounds of sausages. When Maggie learnt this, it became her turn to taunt him about the affections of Regina Hartley. William soon quieted, desperate for Jack not to learn of his schoolyard secret.

The atmosphere at dinner was merry. Jack and Beth's daughters were good-natured, cooperative children who listened to the conversation of the adults attentively, laughing when appropriate and seeing to their baby brother who was asleep upstairs when needed.

Maggie was busy observing her father and Grace. The blush and shy smile when they caught each other's eye. That flush of longing and excitement ... Maggie knew what they were feeling so well. She still felt it when William arrived home from work each day. It was why she usually met him at Prebends Bridge; she wanted to experience the sensation sooner. They had been living together as husband and wife for more than a year, yet to her, there was still something illicit in their relationship. Perhaps that's what made it exciting. *What if we were to marry?* she wondered. *Would our relationship transform into something pedestrian? Would our passion become routine?* Maggie frowned, then rose from the table.

'Will you excuse me? I must finish my article. I have to post it by tomorrow.'

'Go on,' the gathering cried in unison. They were merry from the whiskey Henry had brought with him from London. He had been saving it for such an occasion.

After a few moments, William tapped on the bedroom door and entered.

'It's not like you to leave a party early,' he said. 'Deadline or no.'

She slumped onto the bed and revealed everything her father had divulged during their fishing expedition.

'It's no wonder you had no luck with the trout then,' William said finally, joining her on the bed.

Maggie smiled. William could always see the lighter side of a situation she thought too grave to even contemplate.

'I just want Mam to be happy,' he said.

'But with my father?' Maggie gasped.

William raised his eyebrows. 'Aye, I see what you mean.'

'And there's still my mother. Were she and father to divorce, one of them would have to admit fault ...' Maggie shook her head as she considered the ramifications of such an action. 'For the Earl and Countess of Wessex to divorce ...'

'The scandal!' William said, his hand clutched to his chest.

Maggie raised an eyebrow. 'You can make fun, but it would be a scandal, one that would devastate them both.'

'I'm sorry, lass,' William said contritely, placing his arm around her shoulders. His eye caught on a document on the writing table. 'What's that you're working on there? It's not your article.'

'It's the prospectus for my school. I'm presenting it at the town meeting on Monday night.'

William rose and wandered to the table. He read the first page.

'It's good, Maggie, but tread lightly. To call Mayor Hardy conventional is an understatement.'

'Nothing I'm intending to present is going to be controversial. I'm merely calling for funding for a school for girls.'

'Just tread lightly,' he reminded her before returning to the party.

⚜

WHEN BETH and Jack departed and William retired, Grace and Henry finished washing the dishes. After Henry had polished the last glass to a shine, they sat. Grace took his hand and sighed.

'You're leaving the day after tomorrow.'

Henry nodded. 'To be honest, I wish I weren't.'

He squeezed her hand, and Grace smiled shyly. He gazed at her for a moment and pushed a loose strand of her hair behind her ear. She was delightful.

'I know I've told yer before, but you shouldn't worry about Maggie. She will find her way. She helped me find mine.'

Henry gazed at her as he gently stroked her knuckles.

'When she arrived here, I was at a loss ... Archie and Willie's brothers were gone. I was so accustomed to taking care of a house full of men, I didn't know what to do with myself. To be honest, I spent half the day weeping and the other half finding fault with myself for being so weak.' Grace paused and stared at their hands clasped on the table. 'Maggie saw immediately that I needed a new purpose. She took me to the university and together we met the dean of the College of Science. The very thought of meeting such a distinguished and scholarly gentleman terrified me, but Maggie spoke to him as an equal. She acted as though it was the most reasonable, the most natural thing in the world for me to enrol at university.' Grace smiled at the memory. 'She was at my side that same night, helping me write my application.

'When we were choosing the course of study I should take, I remember her saying, "Well, you're clearly an expert in the domestic sciences, surely the Natural Sciences can't be that different".'

They both laughed. 'That's my girl,' Henry said, smiling.

'Don't fret over her, is all I'm saying,' Grace finished.

'I am forever grateful Maggie has you in her life. Her own mother can be a difficult woman.'

They were silent for a time as they held hands, listening to the sounds of the early evening drifting to them through the half-open window.

After a moment Henry closed his eyes. 'Crickets,' he murmured. 'Maggie thinks it's riding and shooting I love about the country. But it's the chirp of crickets I miss most when I'm not in Hampshire.'

'The crickets will be gone soon, as will you.' Grace eased her hand from his. 'Whatever we have here, Henry, can go no further. That's no to say I don't like yer because I do. Very much.' Her cheeks flushed. 'When Archie died, I believed there'd be no one else for me. I'm forty-seven, and I accepted that part of my life as done with. I planned to devote myself to my grandchildren and, later, my studies. Then you arrived ... and from the very instant we met, I knew there was something between us.'

Henry nodded his agreement.

'But you are a married man, and I cannot see the Eighth Earl of Wessex divorcing his spouse and setting up house in County Durham with a widowed collier's wife.'

Silently, Henry rose and drew Grace to her feet. He scanned her face closely, as though committing it to memory.

Clutching her hands, he leaned in and kissed her softly on the mouth.

'I know,' he murmured when they broke apart.

'This affection we share, you and I,' Grace said, 'doesn't have life outside of this place. To take it further would mean ruin for us both.'

'I know,' Henry repeated, smiling ruefully. Then he kissed Grace once more, lingering a while longer, breathing her in.

'But I haven't departed yet.'

CHAPTER 12

ON THE DAY of Henry's departure, he and Grace spoke a hushed farewell to one another. Grace nodded gravely, then offered the merest of smiles. Maggie wondered what they were saying. Just how deep did their attachment run? Henry appeared stoic, as though he were heading to the battlefield. Maggie supposed he was, in a fashion. Who knew what Lydia had in store for him on his return?

Henry stepped into Jack's cab and offered the party a final truncated wave, then closed the door. When Grace turned, Maggie noticed the wash of restrained tears in her green eyes. Maggie led William into the cottage so he would not notice. She wondered what her father would tell Lydia of his time in the North East.

The following day, Jack and his cab arrived again. This time, he was ferrying another new arrival to Durham. Maggie emerged from the cottage and Jack called a jolly, 'Good morning to yer, Miss Magnolia.' Jack's pet names for her were becoming more obtuse each day.

'Good morning, Jack,' Maggie replied. 'Who have you got there?'

Before he could answer, the passenger flung open the door and stepped from the cab, waving away Jack's helping hand.

It was Briar Haines.

The women took each other in for a time lengthy enough for Jack to glance at them in confusion. It had been over a year since the two had seen each other. Whenever Maggie remembered their final meeting by the Thames, Briar's betrayal still stung. Yet during the time they spent together, Briar had become Maggie's friend, her closest friend, she'd believed at the time. Maggie had been certain their friendship was real. Now, she was determined to focus on that and not on the pain of Briar's deception.

In fact, it amazed Maggie just how much could be forgiven with enough time and space. Standing by the gate as Jack readied to unload Briar's many trunks and cases, Maggie found the familiar, freckled face of her one-time comrade most welcome. When she thought of London now, she most often thought of Briar and the adventure it had been to be part of her world.

'Miss Magnolia, are we now?' Briar said by way of greeting, adding a mischievous wink. 'You'll be gettin' airs before long.'

The women clutched hands and offered each other a light peck on the cheek. Maggie couldn't help but warm to her immediately. Briar was wearing another absurd hat – a violet toque adorned with a nest of amber feathers. At the crown sat a tiny finch.

'Jack is my brother-in-law,' she whispered in Briar's ear. 'He takes immense pleasure from the nicknames he invents for me. I believe it's a sign he has accepted me into the family, so I daren't object.'

Briar broke away and called to Jack as he was climbing onto the cab's roof to retrieve her plentiful luggage.

'Jack-be-nimble, you shall be, Sir.'

He gave Briar a questioning look.

'You scale that cab with the sure-footedness of a mountain goat.'

Taken aback by his passenger's bold statement, Jack replied seriously, 'I've had a fair bit of practise, Miss. But I must get on. I told the mayor I'd collect him by half eleven and have him to the station by one.'

'Perhaps "Jack-be-quick" would be more suitable, then?' Briar suggested as she smoothed the skirt of her travelling ensemble.

Maggie noticed the outfit was lovely; a grey wool skirt and bodice featuring intricate gold detailing that gave the effect of a breastplate. Briar was always battle ready.

Jack frowned, utterly perplexed. He lowered the bags to the ground, then leapt from the back of the cab, landing without a wobble.

'And Jack jumped over the candlestick,' Briar added for her own amusement.

Poor Jack did not know what to make of the young woman.

'Miss Haines is teasing you, Jack,' Maggie said. 'She thought your name for me was brilliant and she's attempting to best you.'

Briar reached into her bag and produced a shiny guinea. Jack examined it, amazed.

'For your troubles, Sir,' Briar said, offering Jack a demure curtsey.

The gesture confused the poor man even further. When he eventually drove away, Maggie wondered what he would tell Beth of 'Maggie's unusual friend' from London. She looped her arm through Briar's and led the way into the cottage.

Maggie made tea, glancing at Briar's headwear as she placed the pot on the table.

'Don't worry, the bird's not real,' Briar said, turning the pot. 'All your speeches about the plume industry ...' She shook her head. 'How could I ignore them?'

It pleased Maggie her sermons on the unfortunate use of real feathers in millinery had had an effect.

'The feathers are fake and the finch,' she patted the little bird's head, 'is a pretender. He's simply for show.'

Although her hat was ridiculous (it would certainly turn heads on Durham's High Street), the sight of it and Briar made Maggie miss London more than she cared to acknowledge. It wasn't only the hat and Briar's glorious outfit, it was Briar's spirit, the boldness of her attitude. Maggie believed she had lost a little of her own spirit since arriving in Durham. She had felt it trickling away and drying up like a stream in the summer. Marian's arrival had helped to stopper the leak, but now she hoped that Briar's pluck would be contagious. It had certainly been last year. Maggie recalled casting a rock through a staid parliamentarian's window following encouragement from Briar. While the small action of protest for the suffragette cause had later horrified her, she now looked back on that evening in Wimbledon fondly as a symbol of the woman she used to be and could become once more.

As Maggie poured the tea, she could feel Briar's eyes on her movements.

'You called Jack your brother-in-law. Have you and William married?'

She is still annoyingly observant, Maggie thought.

'Oh, no, it's just simpler to say "brother-in-law" rather than "William's sister's husband".'

'Of course,' Briar said as she stirred her tea. 'Do you have any plans to marry?'

Maggie shook her head.

Why all the questions about marrying when she has not even asked why I brought her all the way to Durham? While she may have forgiven Briar Haines, Maggie was not yet sure that she trusted her.

'I was happy to receive your telegram,' Briar said, staring into the depths of her tea.

Maggie lowered her cup from her lips. 'I'm grateful you could tear yourself away from London. Is the private detective business keeping you busy?'

'There seems to be no shortage of thieving employees and philandering husbands in London, fortunately. Or unfortunately, depending on how you look at it.'

Maggie's mind immediately ran to her father. She attempted to focus on Briar.

'My business is blooming or booming or both,' Briar said with a grin.

Until Latey's unexpected arrival with George Eliot in tow, Maggie had not worked in a year. It had not been wholly by choice. After considering the chain of events her jealous streak had set in motion the previous year, Maggie feared the very notion of approaching the *Advertiser* for a position would set her green-eyed monster off once more. The last thing she had wanted was to imagine herself in competition with William again. It had nearly destroyed their relationship.

However, she had visited the *Newcastle Courant*, William's previous employer, with letters of recommendation from both William and Mister Latey. When she had effectively pestered the editor enough to arrange a meeting, he had stared at her as though she had two heads. Maggie realised then that despite the glowing references, Northern editors were never going to look favourably on employing a woman. While it was entirely expected for women not to work, especially in Durham, she felt the burden of it. As a result, she had felt her independence and confidence slowly evaporate, along with her spirit.

'I'm very glad to hear it.' Maggie brought her cup to her lips again and took a sip of fortifying tea. 'Now tell me, Briar. Do you still play chess?'

⊙⁂⊙

WINNING three games of chess against her old nemesis somewhat restored Maggie's self-esteem, and by the time William returned, the women had fallen into an easy camaraderie. However, she had told Briar nothing of the task she and William wished her to undertake, and her guest had not asked.

William had never met Briar. The fact seemed so strange to Maggie considering they had both played such fundamental roles in her transformation the previous year. When William walked into the sitting room of the family cottage, he shook Briar's hand and welcomed her to Durham. He was entirely pleasant, Maggie noted, but strangely aloof. It was an aspect of his character she had not witnessed before.

It was just the three of them. Grace was absent but had sent her apologies; she was spending the night at Beth's. Little Jack had croup and she had offered to help with the girls. This meant that during tea, Maggie could not fail to notice William eyeing their guest with suspicion.

When she and Briar parted by the Thames that awful day in 1879 – the day she had broken William's heart – Maggie knew Briar was as distressed as she to be ending their friendship. Although Maggie had seen her 'friend' attempt to keep her personal feelings in check, she could sense the pain threatening to escape from beneath her professional facade. Their friendship had blossomed despite Briar's occupation, not because of it. Maggie believed that Briar had developed the ability to separate her personal and professional life, even on occasions when they were one and the same.

It had taken Maggie a considerable amount of time and contemplation to understand this fully – after all, Briar was as complex as *The Iliad* and equally fascinating – and once she had, her attitude to Briar and her actions had softened. Maggie now wished to put the past behind her and focus on the future.

Over the course of the past year, Maggie had divulged everything to William regarding her experience with Briar. Liars had no place in William's world, and it was lying Briar engaged in for a living. Following her own revelation concerning Briar's behaviour, she hoped William would realise the detective could be their ally. Despite her occupation, Maggie had come to believe that Briar could be trusted in certain matters.

But as she observed William's manner, she quickly realised that it was proving difficult for him to understand her change of heart and the nuances of female friendship.

'Righty ho, then. Shall we get down to business?' Briar asked when they finished supper. She produced a notepad from her bag along with a pencil. She licked the lead.

Together, William and Maggie outlined what they saw as Briar's role. It had been on Maggie's return to London after the collapse of the Stanley Pit that she had met Briar, therefore Briar was aware of much of the detail.

'In a nutshell, you want me to find proof Drummond has ignored the union's recommendations,' Briar said when they had finished.

They nodded.

'The mine has been open for a week now,' William added. 'So far, Drummond has played for time when Fellowes has requested access for the union inspectors. It's just a feeling, but I don't think he has made any improvements. After their first shift, all the colliers were given a £10 bonus. Compensation, Drummond called it, for the loss of employment during the past year.' William gave a snort of indignation. 'With £10 burning in hole in their pockets, it's highly unlikely the pitmen are going to complain if all the improvements haven't been carried out.'

Maggie frowned momentarily, recalling Matthew's resolve to open the mine without fanfare. William viewed the £10 as a bribe but she speculated that Matthew's motives could be altruistic.

'Then the labourers from Yorkshire were a ploy, you think?'

William nodded. 'I saw their tents, but I saw no sight of them in town—'

'But Tommy Fellowes did,' Maggie put in quickly.

Since her visit, she had thought a great deal about the new colliery owner. If he was to be believed, all he yearned for was acceptance and friendship in the town, a desire Maggie knew intimately. She could not help fostering the hope that the man was honourable, for everyone's sake.

'Aye, in that you are correct. As did a few other colliers I spoke to. All of them to be trusted,' William grudgingly admitted.

Briar leant forward, her expression grave. 'What you both have to realise is that *no one* can be trusted.'

William nodded, then Briar looked directly at Maggie and raised an eyebrow.

'You, of all people, should know that.'

Maggie coloured, embarrassed anew that her mother and Briar had duped her so thoroughly. Could Matthew Drummond be deceiving her as well? She sincerely hoped that was not the case.

Having spent time with him and gaining a better understanding of the man, the meeting with Briar caused her to feel a mild nip of guilt. Maggie realised in employing her detective friend's services, she was betraying her newest friend in Durham. But she reasoned that she had to be certain that Matthew was honest. She refused to be fooled again and, most importantly, she refused to have William fooled.

'If we can find proof Drummond paid these Yorkshiremen,' William mused, 'we might discover just what he paid them to do.'

'That sounds like an excellent place to begin. Where would you suggest I might run into this fellow then?' Briar asked, closing her notepad.

'At the Old Inn on Sadler Street,' William said. 'It's where the pitmen spend their Friday evenings. I've heard that Drummond likes to join them.'

⁂

MAGGIE KISSED William before he climbed onto the cart. Then she walked round to Briar, who was already seated, and reached out her hand. 'Thank you for helping us.'

Briar clasped her hand lightly and gently stroked her fingers. 'As I said that afternoon by the Thames, if there was anything I could ever do for you ...'

The women smiled at each other before William flicked the reins and the horse moved on. The three of them had agreed he should take Briar into town immediately. It was imperative, Briar said, that she appear to be a stranger to everyone – especially to William and Maggie. William intended to have a word with Jack and Beth as well, seeing as Jack delivered Briar to the cottage. They – and Grace, of course – would be the only ones to know of their secret.

The new acquaintances were silent for a while as they journeyed through the dark. William wasn't certain what he was feeling. His grievance hadn't yet taken a distinct shape. During tea and the ensuing discussion, he had grown to like Briar. She was amusing and so much like Maggie in her manner and convictions that it was difficult not to feel like she was already a friend. What's more, it was heartening to see Maggie with like-minded company. The women had discussed the suffragette movement, the current state of politics and Maggie's plans for a school, which Briar showed particular enthusiasm for, even looking over Maggie's prospectus and suggesting several minor alterations. Yet William felt a knot in his chest that he couldn't undo. The woman made him uneasy and he wasn't sure why.

Briar held the lamp on the seat between them. It emitted an eerie glow in the light mist that was falling.

'Has Maggie ever told you how desperate she was after she returned to London?' Briar asked.

The sudden words startled William and the question even more so. Following the collapse of the Stanley Pit and the funeral of those who perished, including his father and two brothers, he had remained in Durham for a time. He and Maggie had agreed that it was important for her to return to the city and move forward with the Clairmont series. He hadn't pushed her away. Maggie had understood the reasons he needed to remain in Durham.

'Aye. I know she missed me. I missed her, too.'

'I said she was desperate,' Briar said more firmly. 'Why do you think she fell so easily into her mother's intrigue?'

William pulled on the reins, stopping the cart. He stared at his passenger for a moment. In the lamp's glow, her blue eyes were lit like a cat's.

'She was lonely as a ghost.' Briar said, meeting his gaze. 'Maggie had lost friends and her mother. And then ... you. I was the port in a storm for a deserted ship.'

'Maggie understood I was needed here. I didn't desert

her,' William said, horrified the woman he loved may have ever felt abandoned.

Briar shrugged. 'Seems that way to me.'

William flicked the reins and rode on, faster than before.

'You're just lucky, matey,' Briar informed him when they had reached her lodgings, 'that it wasn't a man you lost her to.'

CHAPTER 13

The Manchester Guardian
Wednesday, October 20, 1880

DEAR READER,

It is time now for me to move on to the part of my story for which, I know, you have been waiting. Englishmen and women relish scandal and while I have never sought it, scandal has always found a means of discovering me.

Our last instalment saw me determined to leave my past behind and transform into someone much different from the hysterical, bookish, judgemental young lady into which I had evolved. If the Brays had lit the fire of my change, then my beloved father's death acted as the tinder. I resolved that for me, provincial life would be but a distant memory. I was bound for the capital, ready and willing to be accepted by the free-thinking intellectual elite of London Town.

Hauling only one portmanteau, I arrived at Euston Station when I was thirty-two years old. I write 'hauling' because rather than clothes, jewellery and perfumes, I had packed my case with books. After all, why would I need to clothe myself elegantly? Londoners would accept me for my abounding intelligence and silvery wit … wouldn't they?

I had never been so mistaken.

MAGGIE ALMOND AND THE MASKED WOMAN

I stepped from the train and was instantly aware of my unworldliness. Compared to the hordes of cosmopolites scuttling back and forth along the platform, I was unkempt, unwashed, unemployed and astonishingly ill-prepared for London's life. Yet, I assured myself, my intellectual radiance would cast my defects into shadow.

Arrogant, you say? I heartily concur.

Through the Brays, I came to have some dealings with the publisher John Chapman. He was an exceptionally charming man with thick, dark curls and dimpled cheeks. He was also extremely well connected. Chapman rubbed shoulders with the likes of Charles Darwin and Thomas Huxley. He was, perhaps unsurprisingly, the most disgraceful name dropper I have ever met! But as I was often gloomy, the wit and warmth he shone on me during his visits were always welcome. If I ever were to follow through with my threats and leave Coventry, he informed me, he would kindly offer me lodgings at his home and workplace at 142 the Strand. If only I had known then how significant that address would become in my life.

From a backroom of their home, Chapman operated a publishing house with his wife Susanna. The residence was always in chaos, his daughters unruly and Susanna perennially ruffled. Despite his amiability and business acumen, John was a poor editor, a failing to which he readily admitted. He quickly discovered that my skills in this area were invaluable. Board and meals were the only payment I received for my labours but I did not mind in the slightest. Even though I had not a farthing to spend, I relished living as an independent woman in the capital.

Along with his wife and daughters, living with us at the Strand was his daughters' governess. She and Susanna were astonishingly beautiful women and, dear Reader, Chapman played husband to them both. Yet the peculiarities of the Chapman's home life did not strike me as unusual; after all, the Brays had initiated me into the notion of free love.

Soon, Chapman wished to expand his publishing empire by purchasing the liberal journal the *Westminster Review*. However, he did not know how to write a prospectus, so he handed this task to me while he met with investors. Once the journal was in his hands, he realised he did not possess the intellectual rigour to edit and amend the writings of the most brilliant minds in the country who were to be contributors: theorists, scientists and philosophers such as Herbert Spencer, Thomas Huxley, Charles Darwin, Harriet Martineau, George Henry Lewes and John Stuart Mill. Therefore, this task also fell to me.

Chapman's talents lay in other areas and our gifts complemented one another. The *Westminster Review* operated on a shoestring and, fittingly, our office was a shoebox at the back of his house. As I was the sole staff member, I worked day and night, but I relished every sleepless moment. I became the publication's anonymous editor. Officially, it was John Chapman who wore the crown. Although still unpaid and penniless, I told myself the privilege of working with the likes of the genii mentioned was payment enough for my efforts.

Working extremely closely for excessively long hours led Chapman and me to develop an attachment beyond the professional. Within the year, his 'wives' demanded I leave. Their free thinking clearly did not extend beyond a ménage à trois.

◈

'WOULD SUCH AN ARRANGEMENT HAVE SUITED YOU?' Maggie asked. The women were seated in Marian's sitting room. Mister Cross had agreed to accompany William on a walk. More a hike, really. They were travelling to Finchale Priory and it would take them the better part of the day.

'I arrived in London seeking something. I was hungry. Ravenous for books, essays and discussion, I gourmandised on intellectual debate. These things satisfied to a point, but John Chapman made me realise that it was love for which I was starved. As a child I was aware my parents and siblings loved me, but it was a distant kind of love with very little affection.'

'How did Chapman love you?'

'I don't believe he did truly love me. He never said those words. He spoke a great deal about beauty, about how men and women jointly present the beauties of nature. In retrospect, I realise that given my unattractiveness, he would never have dared to take our relationship into the light. It was only while I remained concealed in the dingy little back-room he called an office that he was free to love me.'

Maggie shook her head. *What a dreadful arrangement. Poor Marian ...*

'Do you consider him shallow?'

'I do indeed!' Maggie said. 'Chapman was a fool not to have recognised your intelligence as beauty.'

After all, it was Marian's incredible brain, she thought, *that his publication relied on.*

Marian shrugged, resigned. 'People can be astonishingly shallow, Maggie.'

Maggie supposed they could be. Her mother immediately came to mind, along with all the other millions of people who saw a woman's worth only in terms of beauty. *Surely not all men are so facile*, she mused.

'I believe you also formed a strong friendship with Herbert Spencer around that time.'

Marian smiled. 'Herbert and I came together because we were so alike. We were both from the Midlands, both from unlearned backgrounds, and he worked as assistant editor at the *Economist*, the offices of which were directly across the road from those of the *Westminster Review*. We really had no choice in developing an attachment – we were both incredibly lonely. It was that which drew us together like flotsam on the seashore.'

Maggie started in recognition. *Could it be a sense of shared isolation that led me to befriend Matthew?* She shooed the thought aside and tried to focus.

'I idolised him for a time. But he was an unusual man. He was always uncomfortable, always complaining of a headache or stomach pain. Herbert was peculiar, like George, but quiet. Quietly peculiar. I would never describe Herbert as ebullient. Yet for a brief time, we did everything together and I fell in love. I was feverish with love for that man.'

Feverish with love ... Maggie had experienced that disorder. Yet as she gazed at Marian now, so elegant and reserved, she could not imagine her in a fever of passion. Her behaviour towards Mister Cross was certainly no indication she was capable of such fire.

'And Spencer?' Maggie asked of the intellectual who had first developed the theory of social evolution.

'He pushed me away. I became impatient and so explained my feelings in a letter. It was an outpouring of my desire for him, actually. It was a deluge of love and Herbert was completely overwhelmed.'

Quickly reading what she had written, Maggie realised Marian approached love in the same manner she approached her studies, her evangelism and her work – with a devotion bordering on obsession.

But George Henry Lewes had been different.

Without the archives of the *Illustrated London News* close at hand, Maggie had spent a day at the university library researching the men in George Eliot's life. Prolific men of their era, Chapman, Spencer and Lewes had written much and had much written about them. It had not been difficult to sketch detailed portraits of each of them. All Maggie needed to do now was fill in the blanks with carefully crafted questions to Marian ... although she would need to write about them with discretion as both Chapman and Spencer were still living.

After reading their articles and biographies, Maggie reached the conclusion that the two men were brilliant. They simply weren't man enough to love Marian Evans. They were cowards, hiding behind outdated ideals and buried too deeply in words, concepts and ego to truly share themselves with another. Both could espouse views and promote revolutionary notions, but they could never love a woman like Marian.

George Henry Lewes, on the other hand, was a star. Lewes stood proudly in the light with nothing to conceal, not even the devastation of his own personal life.

'Tell me about George,' Maggie asked.

'My experience with the Brays and John Chapman gave me extensive insight into and tolerance for, the concept of an open marriage,' Marian explained. 'That George was raising his own sons, as well as his wife's three children to another man, failed to rattle me in the slightest.'

'But you and George could never marry?'

'Because he had fostered the free-thinking approach to marriage that he and his wife Agnes lived by, George had no legal grounds for divorcing Agnes. An end to their marriage was never in reach.' Marian shook her head. 'But it mattered not. Despite the absence of wedding bands, we both viewed our union as the true marriage.'

As Maggie wrote her notes, she glimpsed her own bare hands and wondered if she and William could ever be as enlightened and courageous as Marian and George Lewes.

WHEN MISTER DODD had arrived with Maggie, he had suggested a walk to John. It was more than a suggestion. He pressed, describing the delights of the Priory in such an entertaining and vigorous fashion, John would have been rude to refuse. Marian was certain Maggie was behind the plan, realising John's solicitous nature would prevent him from leaving the women alone for very long. *She is such an observant and assertive young woman,* Marian thought. *I wish I had been as confident when I was her age. Then I might have got on with my career, my life, so much sooner.*

Inching down in her chair, she laid her head against the leather headrest. How the interviews exhausted her. *When had the process of recollection become such an effort?* she wondered. But she had to admit it was less so in the comfort of her favourite armchair. When Maggie had agreed to write the articles and she and John had realised their stay in Durham would be lengthy, John had sent to London for it.

It had been a gift from Sara Hennell. Dear Sara; Marian

recalled the room they shared at Bridge Street following her eviction by Susanna Chapman. Each morning when they woke, they would look at one another and laugh about their hair, wild and unbrushed. Sharing a bed for so many months was when they had first begun to see each other as husband and wife.

Remembering how ruthlessly she had worked for Chapman, how tirelessly, Marian winced. She had not received a single penny for her efforts. But at least reward had come in the form as status and reputation, far more satisfying than monetary renumeration.

George had known that all along. His idea of a book which melded his scientific studies with her atmospheric descriptions of seaside creatures had been an odd one, but he always had thought of money not as a medium that needed to be earnt, but one that could be created. Marian laughed to herself as she pictured George explaining it to her. He was always so bad with money ... Nevertheless, while his theory was flawed, his hypothesis had led her to consider her own situation and attitudes. Once she accepted George's viewpoint, she had felt liberated. And then she had begun to write.

George had always supported her, always loved her. He had embraced her passion in every way. He never hid her. Instead, he brought her into the light ... unlike the men who had come before.

The Strand
London

AUGUST 28, 1852
  Dearest Herbert,

When we parted at the theatre on Wednesday evening, I sensed a discord. You took my hands in yours and stared at them for some time as though contemplating a dilemma. Did you wish to kiss them? If so, what prevented you from realising such a sensation? Why did you deny me the warmth of your lips pressed against my flesh?

You left me at the Strand with the heat from your palm branding an indelible mark upon my being. Your merest touch makes my heart burn with love for you. At night, when I am alone, I have envisioned my heart hammering beneath my breast, red and supple, forcing blood like a river throughout my body, raising my passions. I long to have your lips meet mine, and to embrace you in every way.

There I have said it! And I refuse to recant my words.

I realise no respectable English woman should write in this fashion, but I must. At thirty-two, I am well beyond a marriageable age; this I have accepted. It is not for a husband and children that I long. My entire world spins on my feelings for you, and I refuse to tamp down my passions or my yearning for you. You have my mind, you have my soul, but I long for you to have so much more.

Vulgar you may think me, but who does not have these feelings? They are as old as Adam and Eve. Your scientific mind would argue that humankind has evolved beyond such baseness, that we now possess the will to check our desires. Yet all at once (wouldn't you agree?) we have transformed into creatures of communication and expression, blessed with the ability to articulate our innermost thoughts and passions. I ask you, then, why should we hide our true selves under the veil of propriety?

Why should I not admit to my consuming desire for you, or the hunger I feel to have your body close to mine, heart against heart, flesh against flesh?

Now you have read my words, please do not forsake me. Even if you love another, please do not forsake me. For if I were to lose you, I would surely die.

Yours aflame,
Marian

❧

DISTRACTED BY HER THOUGHTS, it took a moment for Marian to notice the men's voices outside her window. Johnny and Mister Dodd had returned. Her musing had given her a sudden yearning, and she scanned the bookshelves in the parlour. The owner had lined them with Austen, Dickens and the published journals of Durham's archbishops. She could not help noting there were none of her own works. No matter, she would ask John to find her a copy of *Sea-side Studies* tomorrow. It had been too long since she had read the book she had written with her beloved.

❧

WILLIAM WAVED to Maggie when he spotted her waiting by Framwellgate Bridge. He farewelled Mister Cross and jogged to meet her, greeting her with a kiss and an embrace that lifted her from the pavement.

'What was that for?' she asked when he released her.

'I'll never stop relishing the sight of you, Maggie Almond.'

Maggie smiled and sensed herself blush, relishing her own good fortune in meeting such a gentle, loving and appreciative man as William Dodd. She thought of poor Marian and the disheartening run of men she'd had until finally falling in love with George Lewes. Marian had wasted so much time on lightweights, men who either were blind to her inner beauty or threatened by her passions.

'Did you enjoy the company of Mister Cross?' Maggie asked.

William nodded. 'Very much indeed. He has travelled widely, and knows something of the mining industry. In fact, his family once had interests in a Yorkshire colliery. And ...' He paused for a moment, thinking on his next words. 'He worships his wife. He related every topic that arose back to her.'

'There's nothing wrong with that,' Maggie said, smiling at the news.

William winked. 'A man after my own heart.'

Maggie looped her arm through William's and they began their walk towards the cottage. Before long, Maggie cast a sideways glance at him and grinned.

'What's taken your fancy?' he asked, noticing her good humour.

'Oh, it's nothing,' she said.

William looked at her, amused. 'It must be something.'

'I was just thinking about us,' she said casually. 'Marian and I were discussing inner beauty versus outer beauty.'

'Oh, aye.' He raised an eyebrow, puzzled.

They walked a short way in silence, then Maggie stopped and turned to face him. She smoothed her hands down her bodice and placed her hands on her hips.

William braced himself.

'Do you imagine you would have fallen in love with me had I not ...' Maggie tried to find the words.

Understanding dawned on him. 'Looked the way you do?' he finished for her, safeguarding her humility.

She nodded.

William did not answer immediately. Instead, they continued on their way. When they reached the gate of the cottage, instead of allowing her entrance, he halted her progress.

'It's a hard question to answer,' he said, rubbing his chin thoughtfully. 'In fact, a journalist such as myself might even call it "loaded". For a start, you are a beauty and to imagine otherwise is impossible. There's no denying you caught my eye the very instant I walked into the offices of the *Illustrated London News*. And I'd be lying if I told you I hadn't imagined how lovely it would be to bundle you in my arms and kiss you. Then, when I noticed that bonny sapphire on your betrothal finger, I tried to imagine the lucky lad who had won you. I was considerably disappointed, if not mildly crushed, that you were taken.'

'You imagined all that on your very first day at the *News*?' Maggie said, amazed.

'Aye, I did,' he said without embarrassment.

'However, it was when we spoke in the Archives Room that did it. Do you remember?'

She nodded.

'You were reading about the mines. It was not until then that I fell in love with you.'

He leant down and kissed her forehead.

'While you're a bonny-looking lass, Maggie, it was your head and your heart that won me over.'

CHAPTER 14

USUALLY, Briar would follow the subject of an investigation for days before she engaged. She had trailed Maggie for weeks before she sat next to her at the coffeehouse, although that was a longer than usual time for her to track someone. Most people followed a pattern, their routine defined them. But Maggie had been far more difficult to get to know. She was here and there, coming and going. Purpose imbued her every movement. The only constant seemed to be her visits to Claire Clairmont. When Briar had cornered Clairmont's girl one afternoon, offering her a shilling to air all she knew about Maggie Almond, the girl was as silent as the Trafalgar Square lions. Briar wasn't certain if she was being loyal to Maggie, protective of Clairmont or just slow-witted.

But now she didn't have the luxury of watching Matthew Drummond for weeks or even days, and nor did she want it. Such an exercise would be completely futile in Durham. Locals would spot her within the half hour. Briar didn't even have the option of conducting any research on the man. Maggie had informed her that his friends and family were all in Manchester, and archived editions of the *Manchester Guardian* held in the university library revealed little, nothing more than William had already told her. She had no choice but to engage immediately.

Briar dressed carefully for their encounter. She wanted to appear sophisticated but not aloof, convivial but not a toffer. It was an arduous task, especially when she didn't have her complete wardrobe at her fingertips. Eventually, she decided on a skirt the colour of goldenrod and a tartan bodice in shades of green. She finished her ensemble with a veiled bonnet. Colourful, but not lurid.

It was not the first time she had entered a public house alone. Briar took in the scene as she stood in the doorway. As expected, the inn was crowded and smoke-filled, but she saw a man – more attractive, more upright and less world-weary than the others – holding court by the fire. From the angle she was standing, the tongues of flame seemed to lick at his calves. Matthew Drummond, she assumed. Eventually, the landlord noticed her, taking her in from hat to toe. Briar lifted her veil as he formed his assessment of her. When done, he moved out from behind the bar and stopped before her.

'I'm sorry, Miss. You're not welcome here,' he said in a low voice. 'These here are family men.' He gestured to his patrons. 'There's a pub in Neville's Cross where you might find trade.'

She instantly realised her choice of outfit was far too flashy for Durham.

'You offend me, Sir,' Briar said, in her most plummy accent. She attracted the attention of the clientele. 'I am no doxy.' The word incited a low gasp from the clientele. 'I'm new here in Durham and I'd like to quench my thirst with a pot of ale, if your employment extends beyond aspersion and into hospitality.'

Her words took the publican aback. He was speechless and Briar's stare had frozen him to the spot.

In less than a moment, the attractive man she had noticed by the hearth was at her side.

'Miss, if I might be of service,' he said with a smile. 'Please, forgive Mister Farquhar. I doubt he has ever seen such a sumptuously dressed and imposing young woman.'

''Scuse me, Mister Drummond,' Farquhar muttered.

With her conjectures confirmed, Briar softened. She smiled gratefully at her 'saviour'. Maggie hadn't mentioned how handsome he was. Tall, raven-haired, elegantly slender. She wondered if the omission was for William's benefit. Was he the jealous type?

'I am much obliged, Mister ...?'

'Drummond. Matthew Drummond.'

WITH NOTHING more forceful than a raised eyebrow, Drummond cleared a table of its clientele. At his suggestion, the landlord offered Briar a pot of ale on the house. It appeared to Briar that in a matter of mere weeks, Drummond had gained an immense amount of sway with the men of the town.

For the next hour, they chatted about Durham, Manchester and London. He was charming (*one might say painfully so*, she thought) intelligent and amusing. Fortunately, Briar was immune to Drummond's allure. Although she didn't want to get into the habit of admitting it, she suspected William was right. His assessment of the man matched her own. He was not to be trusted; Briar could feel it in her bones, although she could not pinpoint why.

She was a milliner by trade, Briar informed him. 'But me shop fell on hard times. You see, I refuse to ornament my hats with real feathers, or genuine fur and animals. As a result, the elegant ladies of London left me for dead.'

'You're a woman of principle.'

'High principles, Mister Drummond. Me family originated in the North East. I decided it might be time to see the area and me birthright. Unfortunately, having wandered the High Street, I think the decision may have been too hasty. I can't imagine a posh millinery is needed or wanted in Durham.'

She noted a touch of sympathy in his piercing blue eyes.

'Perhaps it might be time for me to change occupation as well as digs,' she went on, the rim of the glass finding her lips. 'Although I'm uncertain I'd make a very successful pit brow lass.'

Drummond laughed. The sound was deep and resonate.

'As luck would have it, Miss Haines, I need an assistant.'

৩৵৩

BRIAR, Maggie and William had agreed to meet in public after Briar's evening at the pub, as though by accident. Maggie chose the cathedral's tower as the location for their rendezvous. If they arrived and departed separately, Maggie was certain Drummond would be none the wiser. And after all, he had visited the cathedral once already; surely a colliery owner wouldn't have need to climb the tower's 325 steps again so soon.

William had not mentioned his chat with Briar to Maggie. He had often thought of the evening he'd driven the detective into town. In his mind, he had judged her harsh censure as an attack, and an unwarranted one at that. It had been so unexpected, he was still unsure whether he hadn't imagined it.

He had never been a jealous man, yet he had sensed jealousy's persistent sting as he listened to Maggie and Briar converse on the evening of Briar's arrival in Durham. He realised then that there was no way he could ever understand Maggie's experience as a woman. Sympathy was easy; understanding was a completely different concept. It was clear to him that Briar understood Maggie's struggles.

Instead of sharing his conversation with Briar when he returned to the cottage that evening, he had woken Maggie quietly and they had made love. That was not unusual; his compulsion for Maggie never wearied. However, she had not been aware his passion had sprung from a different source that night. But William knew, and he was ashamed and disgusted with himself afterwards. While having no desire to own Maggie, that night he had marked his territory like a dog.

Now, as they walked hand in hand to the cathedral, Briar's attack came to his mind once again.

'Last year, after the funeral ... Did you ever feel as though I abandoned you?'

Maggie stopped and frowned. 'Why are you asking now?'

He shrugged. 'I was just thinking about it.'

'No, of course not. I understood you needed to stay and be with Grace. You were grieving. And I knew that following the disaster, it was imperative for you to finish the articles about the mine.'

They continued on their way. After a few moments, Maggie spoke again.

'I must confess, though, that at one point I was concerned you would decide not to return. Our relationship was still quite new and ...'

William sensed she was reluctant to voice her feelings. 'And what?'

'At the time, I was consumed by the many betrayals in

Miss Clairmont's life. She had noted in her journal that Shelley believed love, along with the words of love, would always be fleeting, ephemeral. And love had certainly played out that way for her, as I learnt over that summer. You had told me you loved me, but when you were away for so long and had not written ... Well, I grew to doubt your loyalty.'

William's heart sank. No person had ever doubted his loyalty before. Miss Clairmont's experiences may have caused her some concern, but he wondered what part Briar had played in fuelling Maggie's fears.

MAGGIE AND WILLIAM had already arrived when Briar made her way up the narrow, spiral staircase. The fresh air was welcome after the musty stairwell that reeked of mould. She breathed in deeply. The pair were leaning against a mossy wall, looking through a ragged embrasure at the view. Briar watched them for a moment. Side bodies touching, rock steady and so comfortable with one another. *They may be like that now*, thought Briar. *But it wasn't so long ago that Maggie had doubts ...*

Before she approached, Briar quickly scanned the area. They were alone. 'Day's dawning, you two,' she said merrily.

They turned, and Briar kissed Maggie's cheek. She nodded at William.

'What happened last night?' Maggie began eagerly. 'Did you meet Drummond?'

Briar could see that Maggie loved the game, the thrill of the chase.

'More than that. He offered me a job.'

'I've heard you were an expert in disguise,' William put in dryly, 'but I don't think you'd ever pass as a pitman.'

'As his assistant, as a matter of fact. I'm starting on Monday. It was as easy as shelling peas.'

'You'll have access to everything,' Maggie said, excited. 'We should know soon enough whether we can trust the man!'

Briar nodded, enjoying Maggie's enthusiasm. She observed her alert eyes and the bright colour in her cheeks from the excitement of their clandestine mission.

'What did you make of him?' William asked.

'I'm none too sure. For one thing, he's already got too much influence among the men who were gathered at the pub. They either admire him highly or they're terrified of him.'

She paused and took the couple in again, noticing the way their fingers brushed lightly. At the same time, Briar's information had made William's eyes narrow and Maggie frown. Before either could comment further on Drummond, Briar spoke.

'Nevertheless, he is an extremely attractive man. A person with that amount of charm wouldn't find it hard to attract admirers. Why didn't you tell me he was so handsome, Maggie?'

William looked at Maggie. Briar watched as Maggie's cheeks flushed even more. She hated placing Maggie in such an uncomfortable position, but Briar was thoroughly enjoying William's incredulity.

'Would you call him handsome?' Maggie replied, struggling to find her composure, the tone of her voice a touch higher than usual. 'I find his appearance rather common.'

An excruciating silence followed until Briar intervened. She clutched William's arm.

'Well, you've got too used to the cream of the crop, Maggie,' she said, winking at William. 'It's no wonder the charms of Matthew Drummond failed to bewitch you.'

THEY LEFT the tower separately so as not to be seen by anyone who might inform Drummond. Maggie and William made their way back to the cottage.

Maggie could see William was tense. During a stroll together, he would typically point out something of note, if only the colour of an unusual bird or flower, but he was silent as they walked.

'Briar was merely attempting to provoke you with her comment,' she began, looping her arm through his. 'I don't find him attractive at all.'

'Oh, I know, lass,' he said, patting her hand. 'I'm just contemplating what Briar said and wondering whether Drummond is on the up and up.'

Yet another expression she was not familiar with. Where did William come across them? But she guessed the meaning from the context. Maggie frowned. She had not yet told William about her visit to Drummond's house and their morning of chess. Perhaps this was the perfect time.

'I'm beginning to wonder myself, if I am completely honest. I cannot deny he is a peculiar character ...' Maggie paused, carefully curating the words she should use. 'You see, I visited Mister Drummond on the Saturday before last. It was the day of your union meeting in Ryton.'

He stopped suddenly, causing her arm to fall. 'Why?'

'I had bumped into him on the High Street a few days before and he asked my advice on making friends.'

'They've been other meetings?' William felt an unwelcome twinge of disappointment. He then had the uncomfortable thought that perhaps it was jealousy.

'Oh, no, not formal meetings,' Maggie hastened to assure him. 'It was an accidental meeting, but he expressed his loneliness and his intense desire to be accepted, a sentiment not dissimilar to what I'm experiencing, and I felt if I extended a courtesy and offered my friendship, perhaps I could learn more about him ...'

Even as she was explaining this to William, Maggie could not fully comprehend why she went to Drummond's that day. It took her a further moment to put her finger on it.

'In truth, William, I felt sorry for him,' she concluded. 'It's as simple as that.'

William stared down at her, thinking for a moment. Maggie's big heart would get her into trouble one day, he was sure of it. Yet it was not something he could tell her – any warning he may give her might just make her more determined to prove him wrong.

'I see,' he said eventually. 'Well, what did you make of him?'

'At first, he was charming, the perfect host.'

'At first?'

'We played chess, and he was an adequate player. But I continued to win. Before I departed, he insisted on a final match.'

'I see. And?'

'And he cheated.'

William's eyes widened in astonishment.

'He swiped my knight from the board when I wasn't looking.'

William opened his mouth to speak. Maggie held up her hand to silence him.

'But that's not the strangest thing. After I left, he ran after me and admitted his crime. He told me he didn't want me to think him unintelligent.'

William pushed his hands into his pockets and moved off the path to the water's edge. He stared towards the opposite bank, deep in thought.

'On the one hand, his behaviour suggests he is untrustworthy,' Maggie said. 'However, his admission ...'

William removed his cap and rubbed his forehead. He had suddenly grown weary.

'His admission suggests he is an extremely complicated man.'

CHAPTER 15

EARLY THE NEXT MORNING, William went to visit Tommy Fellowes. His godfather's home was a miner's cottage, one among a row of identical dwellings nestled in the village. Tommy was an early riser, as was any hewer who had ever worked at the coal face. Rising at four o'clock in the morn for forty years was an extremely difficult habit to break. William knocked on the door and Tommy promptly answered.

'Aareet,' William said in greeting, removing his cap.

Tommy nodded then let him into the cottage. Wordlessly, William followed him inside along a narrow hallway.

When Tommy's wife died, he was left with three young daughters. He soon proved himself to be the man everybody always knew he was: courageous, resourceful and caring. He pushed his grief aside and devoted himself to the care of his girls. Most importantly, he stopped gambling. There was a time when Tommy would bet on anything; horses, dogs, even fleas. Tommy Fellowes's hunger for a wager had known no bounds, but all that changed when his wife passed away.

Filled with admiration for the man, everyone in Durham pitched in to help in his sorrow. William recalled his own mother delivering meals to his front door and taking the girls to stay at the cottage before they were old enough to get themselves to school. The entire town wanted Tommy to succeed in his new life as a father alone. It seemed ungrateful to everyone when his girls married and moved away; unlike others in Durham, Tommy never had a harsh word for them. He never had a harsh word for anyone.

When they reached the kitchen, Tommy gestured for William to sit down and hastily produced a second cup of tea.

'What can I do fer yer, Willie?' Tommy asked, pulling out his chair to join his godson.

William glanced around at Tommy's neat kitchen as he took a sip of the hot tea. Colliers had a special way of brewing tea. It was three times as strong as the tea he ever drank in London and at least ten times as sweet. And it was never served with milk. Never. He'd go so far as admitting that in some instances, collier tea was better than whiskey ... although perhaps Maggie wouldn't agree.

'Have you had any luck getting the inspector into the Stanley Pit?' William asked after a time.

Tommy finished the dregs of his tea and placed his mug on the table. 'You'll be the first to know once I have, Willie.'

William detected an element of testiness in his tone. 'Aye, it's just that Matthew Drummond has hired an assistant.'

Tommy raised his thick eyebrows, interested.

'She is a friend of ours.'

'Aye, I see,' Tommy responded.

The men sat in silence as William sipped his brew. He and Maggie had agreed not to discuss Briar's true identity with anyone, apart from Jack, Beth and Grace. William wasn't certain why he was telling Tommy now. He simply felt he must. Tommy was his godfather; he'd been in his life since he was a bairn, a second father almost. He had always gone to Tommy with problems and grievances. The kind man's matter-of-fact way of perceiving the world would often shed light on a childhood complaint or adolescent concern.

He couldn't deceive him by keeping Briar a secret. And perhaps Tommy might keep an eye out for Briar if he knew of their connection. Even so, it took a moment for William to explain further. He eventually decided that for Tommy's sake, it was best he be kept in the dark as much as possible.

'She's new here, you see. Straight from London. I wouldn't want her to lose her position if the mine was closed. She needs the work.' Tommy nodded. 'But mum's the word, aareet? Drummond hasn't taken a shine to me, as you know. I don't want him to look badly on the lass because of that. And she doesn't want any favours from Maggie or me, either.'

Tommy nodded again. 'Aye. Mum's the word.'

'I'm sorry I can't offer you anything more sophisticated, Miss Haines,' Drummond said as he showed Briar into the office they would share.

The stone building had once been a miner's cottage, Briar guessed. One of the original dwellings, before similar residences were built in the town. It was one room with a hearth and nothing more. As Matthew Drummond's office, it housed two desks, two chairs and a set of filing cabinets. Overall, the room was cheerless and dull. William had informed her the previous owner had never lived in Durham and the manager had been a shiftless sort. Clearly, he was a tatty and untasteful sort as well, she concluded, examining the ragged curtains and worn upholstery on the chairs. She ran her finger along the window frame. It was thick with dust.

'We'll brighten this place up in no time,' Briar said, brushing her hands.

'I'm wholeheartedly in favour of any rejuvenation you can offer this tired old shack.'

'I won't be the only one rolling up me sleeves, Mister Drummond,' Briar said, raising an eyebrow.

He gazed at her, amused. 'It would be my pleasure to assist you in any way I am able.'

Drummond walked to his desk and produced two ledgers from a locked drawer. He placed them on what was to be Briar's workspace.

'These are the ledgers, Miss Haines. It will be your responsibility to note down all the incomings and outgoings, the tonnage of coal we transport from the colliery each week, where it goes and when payment is due.'

Briar nodded. She flicked the pages casually, searching the contents but without appearing to do so.

As Drummond outlined her duties, Briar scanned the room for anything out of the ordinary. Sadly, nothing seemed out of place in her dingy surrounds. Everything was equally dreary and soiled. However, when Drummond crossed the room to retrieve the invoice book from the filing cabinet, she noticed the rug that lay on the floor. She walked into the centre of it and examined the intricate design beneath her feet.

'Cor blimey!' she said, astonished at the sight of such a valuable carpet. 'This is an Axminster, isn't it?'

Drummond looked up. 'You have a keen eye, Miss Haines.'

'It's lovely,' she remarked, examining the delicate pattern of medallions and violoncellos. 'Does it belong to the old owner?'

Drummond laughed. 'Lord, no. The carpet is mine. I brought it with me from Manchester.'

Axminsters were worth over £300. Briar wondered why

Drummond would put it in the office of a colliery, where it might be ruined by sooty footprints.

'It belonged to my mother, you see. I have it here as a reminder of home. It's one of the few possessions I have that does.'

When she looked up at him to suggest it might be better suited to his lodgings, she was startled to find him staring at her with his blue eyes. She laughed to hide her surprise.

'You must be very fond of your family then, Mister Drummond. It does make a stunning centrepiece to the room,' she said merrily. 'I'll use it as the inspiration of our redecoration and then, with any luck, this place will feel even more like home to you.'

❧

'What do they mean when they say "aareet"?' Briar asked as she spread the picnic rug on the grass.

Maggie laughed. 'It's a greeting. The meaning really depends on the context. Someone could simply be saying "Hello" or asking "How are you?", or they might be concerned for your welfare.'

'Economical.'

'Very.'

Both women laughed.

Briar had been working at the pit for five days. So far, she hadn't found a single clue to what Drummond might be hiding. The women hadn't been in contact during that time, as they couldn't appear overly friendly, but at the end of their last meeting, Briar had suggested a picnic by the river so they could catch up on the week's events. William typically spent Saturday at the union which provided the women with an opportunity to talk alone.

'But you don't believe Drummond is entirely trustworthy?'

Briar shrugged. 'It's too early to tell. Plus, he's never out of the office for long enough to give the place a good going over.'

'Perhaps a distraction?' Maggie suggested.

'It would have to be a large one. He is never far away. He disappears at the change of shift each day, but not for very long. "Stretching his legs", he claims. The man does seem to have a curious amount of energy. I have, however, finally spotted some of those elusive Yorkshire men he hired. They've stayed on since the opening of the mine.'

'As pitmen?'

Briar shook her head. 'More like guards.'

'To keep the inspectors at bay ...'

'Exactly.'

Maggie realised that Drummond's refusal to allow the inspectors to do their job did not bode well. She sighed and closed her eyes.

'Let's end our discussion of Drummond today. The weather is too lovely to worry,' she said, turning her face towards the sky to feel the sun. 'The blue of a cloudless sky is my favourite colour. Before we know it, winter will be upon us. The river will be ice and this lovely green will be blanketed with snow.'

Briar looked up, too. 'What an evocative prediction ... Ah, but there is one cloud up there.' She pointed.

'Cumulous,' Maggie remarked.

'Who's a clever *gel*, then?' Briar smiled.

Maggie rolled her eyes and laughed.

'Do you remember our last picnic together?' asked Briar as she watched Maggie opening the basket and producing their fare for the day: sandwiches and cider. Briar was delighted to see a few of Grace's fruit-studded sly cakes make an appearance, too. Maggie had remembered her sweet tooth.

Before answering her question, Maggie looked at her with an expression of mock annoyance.

'Indeed,' she replied, pouring two cups of cider. 'By the time we departed the heath, you had me at sixes and sevens. I doubted myself, I doubted William ...'

Briar placed her hand over Maggie's and looked at her gravely.

'I'm sorry for that. Truly sorry.'

The women gazed at each other for a moment, both recalling that afternoon. It was one of the last days of summer. Over a game of chess, Briar had skilfully launched a series of queries at Maggie which had completely overwhelmed her, resulting in Maggie questioning the choices she had made and even her ability to play chess. In the end, she lost the game.

'I know,' Maggie uttered finally, patting Briar's hand 'All is forgiven.'

The women sipped their cider for a time, mesmerised by the ripples on the glassy surface of the river caused by daring dragonflies or colourful butterflies, or perhaps an undetectable trout.

'What is your opinion of country life, Briar?' Maggie asked. 'Do you prefer the trees, fresh air and space or the crowded lanes of the East End?'

Briar didn't answer. Instead, she rolled onto her back and stared into the canopy of an overhanging birch. She pulled Maggie down onto the rug beside her.

'Look at that,' she said, pointing.

It was a magpie, busy at feathering his nest for winter. The bird leapt jauntily from branch to branch and then to the ground, returning each time with a stick or leaf, even a piece of string. Occasionally, it would take him some minutes to choose the perfect twig or bud. His mate remained by the nest, adorning it to her liking while keeping a bright eye out for danger.

'I've always considered meself a part of the city. Tell truth, I've only visited the country a handful of times. I never much fancied the idea of rambles and riding,' Briar mused, still following the progress of the magpies. 'However, on this occasion, observing that busy little couple, I'm finding the countryside more to my liking.'

Maggie wasn't certain what Briar was attempting to communicate to her. Did she long for a home, a husband and children? Did she believe Maggie needed to begin the nesting phase of her life? She inhaled deeply and closed her eyes. She did not wish to press her friend to explain herself. Perhaps she was reading too much into the moment and Briar was merely marvelling at nature.

Eventually, Maggie sat up and the women ate their lunch, conversing all the while. Maggie learnt Briar had discovered her knack for subterfuge when a Scotland Yard detective had given her a shilling to follow a suspect.

'He told me to follow the gent for the afternoon, remembering all the places he stopped and the people he spoke to.' She smiled at the memory as she produced a sketchpad from her bag. 'I was small and could hide easily. The bloke never knew he was being followed.' Briar wet the tip of her pencil with her tongue. 'It felt wonderful to watch yet not be seen. The experience tickled me fancy, and I told the copper so. Anyway, it used to take me a week to earn a shilling as a milliner's girl. Following, watching, listening ... it was easy money by comparison.'

Maggie nodded, then remembered Briar had been raised by a milliner and his wife when her own mother could no longer afford to keep her.

'But millinery ... You possess such an extraordinary talent.'

Briar continued to sketch a scene of the river, with Prebends Bridge forming the background.

'My granny made hats. Not posh hats for Belgravia ladies, but straw hats for summer that anyone could buy. She sold them at the Petticoat Lane Market.'

Briar stopped her sketch for a moment and drew a hatpin from the creation she was wearing on her head. On this occasion, it was a white postillion with a burgundy velvet band. It looked to Maggie like a flowerpot with a narrow brim.

'Granny left me this.'

Maggie examined the object. 'Is it emerald?'

Briar nodded as Maggie turned the pin over in hands.

'Granny said a lady had fallen on hard times, so she exchanged the pin for one of Granny's hats.' Briar chuckled as she continued to draw, her hand sweeping across the page in large arcs. 'More likely, granny stole it.'

Maggie smiled and returned the hatpin to Briar. 'It must be precious to you.'

'It is.' Briar examined her sketch for a moment. She was pleased.

Maggie leaned in and examined the scene, too. 'It's lovely. You know, you really should be an artist.'

Briar offered Maggie the rough sketch.

'Thank you. I adore it, but why don't you complete the scene? I'd like to see what you're fully capable of.'

Briar shot her a playful glance.

'Artistically, I mean,' Maggie added with a laugh.

Briar took her hands. 'Our friendship is extremely precious to me as well, Maggie.' She brought Maggie's hands to her lips and kissed them.

The gesture warmed Maggie's heart. She had felt that their friendship had flowered since Briar's arrival. Maggie was pleased to have reached a renewed level of intimacy with her former best friend.

'I feel the same way,' Maggie replied, experiencing a sudden rush of sentiment.

Without Dorothea or another close female companion, Maggie had been concealing certain aspects of herself for more than a year. Perennially occupied in London or Gloucestershire, Dorothea had visited the North East only once in the past year, and Maggie's loneliness had grown even more profound after her mentor had departed. While she shared every thought and emotion with William, and Grace and Beth were always generous and welcoming, there were times she could not be entirely honest with them ... especially when the subject of living in Durham arose. She would have liked to discuss her confused feelings with an intimate acquaintance. Now in Briar's presence, the comfort of her warmth and amity offered Maggie a release of sorts.

Briar, sensing her friend's distress, placed a hand on hers.

'Since you arrived in Durham, I haven't felt as alone,' admitted Maggie. 'To have another woman who understands me ...'

Briar reached out and stroked Maggie's cheek softly.

'I love William and his family, but sometimes I feel as though I simply don't belong here. The more I attempt to be myself, the more I am ostracised. I am the definitive fish out of water, Briar. I know I would instantly be accepted if William and I were to marry, but I can't help thinking everyone is being entirely unfair. Why should I marry to be accepted? I am my own person, independent of William. Am I only to be validated if I am his wife?'

Tears spilled down Maggie's cheeks. Briar wiped them away, then drew Maggie close, embracing her.

'There, there. Cry as much as you like, my sweet,' she whispered. 'You can be yourself with me.'

CHAPTER 16

BRIAR SAT ON HER DESK, legs swinging beneath her, scanning the office. Matthew Drummond had given her a budget of £25 and she had purchased the items necessary to refurbish her shabby workplace. Taking inspiration from the carpet, dark green, maroon and cream made up the palette she had chosen; masculine colours that were both tasteful and commanding. She had found a second-hand gilt-framed mirror in Jack's ironmongery that she had polished to a shine, as well as a reproduction of Turner's *Norham Castle, Sunrise* that she'd caught her landlady throwing out. Briar thought the bursting lightness of the reproduction would complement the sombre colour of the wall.

Drummond insisted he supply the labour to paint the walls, although not his own, of course. One Friday after work, three thickset and unsmiling Yorkshiremen arrived at the office with brushes and paint, as well as cloths with which to cover the furniture. Briar wondered if these were the men who had 'improved' the pit. She had still not found any evidence in the ledgers or filed documents of the existence of the men, no record of payment for whatever it was they were doing at the pit now or had been doing in the preceding weeks. After at least a half hour of attempting to draw out information from them as she covered the desks and file cabinets, the men remained taciturn, as silent as saints ... although Briar would readily wager the three possessed not an ounce of virtue among them.

The fabric for the curtains and cushions was gold and burgundy damask. It had surprised Briar to find such a luxurious product in Wilson's, the town's haberdasher. Yet among the cambric and bombasine, she had discovered three yards of the most glorious damask. It was an offcut, Mister Wilson explained, from a special order. Dear old Mister Wilson sold it to her at cost. While she was in the store, Briar also purchased a yard of sky-blue silk and another of pearl-coloured tulle, remainders as well. Briar had in mind a hat. Stitching the curtains and covers by hand (it seemed not a soul in Durham owned a sewing machine) had afforded her some pleasure. She recalled why her mother had sent her to work at the milliner; her stitches were neat and uniform, barely visible.

Now, as she sat on the desk waiting for Drummond, she examined her surrounds. While they certainly weren't Buckingham Palace, she was pleased with her handiwork.

Drummond entered and stood next to her, looking around him for some time. He scrutinised the walls and the hangings Briar had chosen.

'Well done, Miss Haines.' He applauded, beaming at her. 'You have done such a remarkable job. Walter Crane himself could not have created such a pleasing aesthetic.'

'High praise indeed!' Briar said. While she was happy with the result of her efforts, she did not believe them worthy of such enthusiasm. But she had discovered that Drummond was unique in that way; it was often difficult for him to harness his emotions.

'Will you join me for supper tomorrow night, Miss Haines, as a celebration of your accomplishment?'

She eyed him squarely.

'It had occurred to me we are both alone here in Durham,' he continued. 'It only makes sense we keep each other company.'

Briar raised an eyebrow. 'What sort of company did you have in mind?'

Drummond grinned and took a seat next to her on the desk.

'Purely platonic, of course. A friendship is what I require. The pitmen are amusing, but they have their limitations. And men such as William Dodd, a man whom I suspect is of similar mind to me, seem intent on driving me out. That leaves you, Miss Haines – an intelligent and, might I say, extremely engaging young woman who, for whatever reason, tolerates my ill temper and vain attempts at humour.'

Briar had seen no evidence of an ill temper yet and, to be fair, she found his personality quite diverting and unpredictable. Striking up a friendship with the man, whatever that might mean, may well be the next logical step in her investigation, as it had been when she was following Maggie.

Briar accepted the invitation. If Drummond was not the scoundrel that William had him pegged as, it wouldn't hurt to have a powerful friend on her side should she decide to remain in the North a little longer.

❧

DRUMMOND DULY ARRANGED DINNER. At six o'clock the following evening, Jack arrived in the hansom at her lodgings.

'Drummond insisted,' Jack said when Briar complained a ride was unnecessary. She could walk perfectly well to South Bailey. 'Just go along with it, lass. I could well do with the extra few quid, to be honest.'

Briar wondered how much Drummond was paying for the four-minute drive to his house. Clearly, he wanted the evening to be memorable. Did he hope to show off his wealth by arranging a dinner at his home, rather than meeting at the pub for a pint and a pork pie? Instantly, she was glad she had borrowed a reception gown from Maggie.

And it was quite exquisite. Made from black and gold silk and velvet, the skirt was delicately embroidered with glimmering daisies. Featuring a square neckline that cut straight across the chest, the gown sat low over her bosom. The dress was more revealing than anything Briar had ever seen Maggie wearing. When she checked her appearance in the looking glass before leaving her lodgings, she concluded Maggie's shapely bust would do the gown far more justice.

When they arrived, Jack aided her descent from the cab. 'You look lovely, lass,' he commented. 'You'll certainly turn Drummond's head looking the way you do, if that's what you're intending.'

'Oh, I hope not,' Briar remarked. 'Matthew Drummond is not my type at all.'

Drummond's footman showed Briar into the parlour, where her host was already waiting. He had dressed formally, completing the ensemble with a dress coat lined with corded silk and a bow tie. He appeared even more handsome in a costume more fitting to his background. At the pit, he liked to get around in breeks and short coats in the style of the pitmen, but to Briar, they always appeared ill fitting and out of character. But now he wore his attire like a second skin.

While they discussed mundane topics, Andrew, Drummond's footman, mixed their gin slings at a small drinks table located at a discreet distance from them. Once he had departed, Briar sipped her aperitif and examined the room: the artworks and floor coverings, the host of ornaments that adorned every available space.

'Did you choose the furnishings, Mister Drummond?'

'Gracious, no. I purchased the house and all that was in it.'

'I thought they were far too tasteful for the likes of you,' she quipped, attempting not to reveal her surprise.

He laughed. 'You do amuse me, Miss Haines.'

'Tonight, however, you've dressed extremely tastefully,' she added, moving closer. 'What an elegant dress coat.' She rubbed the lapel between her thumb and index finger.

Their eyes locked for a moment.

'You must forgive me, Miss Haines, for not complimenting you on your appearance sooner. In truth, you have quite taken my breath away. It has been some time since I've been in the company of such an entrancing young lady. I suppose I'm a little rusty when it comes to the etiquette of romance.'

'Are you attempting to romance me, Mister Drummond?'

Before he could answer her, Andrew entered with their dinner of roasted game birds (partridge, Briar discovered later), turnips, brussels sprouts and cider gravy. The meal was delicious and Matthew Drummond the perfect host. They spoke of their backgrounds and families. Briar was honest (to a point) and Drummond entertained her with tales of his childhood in Manchester before mentioning his schooldays at Rugby.

'At times, it was extremely difficult.' His countenance darkened momentarily. 'My family was royalty in Manchester. The Rugbeians, however, treated me like a servant and beat me without redress.'

Briar sipped her wine and studied the man before her. She

considered herself an excellent judge of character (in her line of work she had to be) and she certainly wasn't a soft touch, but as she sat in Drummond's dining room enjoying his extremely fine claret, she sensed the unmistakable tweak of her heart strings being pulled. She began to understand a little of Maggie's desire to offer him friendship.

'Children can be cruel, merciless really.'

Drummond shrugged. 'I don't have the most pleasant memories of my school days, but the beatings and the hazing helped transform me into the man I am today.'

'And who exactly might that be, Mister Drummond?'

He thought for a moment, staring into the crimson depths of his glass. 'When I departed Manchester, I wasn't certain,' he said, meeting her gaze.

She noticed his eyes were awash with tears.

'But I believe I'm beginning to find myself again.'

Briar was touched by his earnestness. She reached for his hand across the table.

'Well, those days are long in the past. So, trouble yourself about them no more. What matters now is the future and making the Stanley Pit the most successful colliery in the North. Once that happens, you can finally give all those pigeon-livered bootlickers what for.'

Drummond smiled. 'You're good for my soul, Miss Haines.'

'Me mother used to say I was good for nothing.'

He laughed. 'I can't believe that.'

He rose from the table and drew her to her feet. He offered her a slight bow.

'Would you allow me the honour of this dance, Miss Haines?'

'But there isn't any music ...'

'We don't need music.'

Drummond took her in his arms. As they swayed to the

melody of the crackling fire and the flute-like strains of a nightingale nesting in a dense thicket beneath the window, Briar was confident Matthew Drummond was attempting to romance her. But to what end? Sex? There were many local girls who would offer themselves up on a platter to a man like him, and he wouldn't have to face them the following day at work. Was it possible he wanted something more? A lasting attachment, perhaps? Both options would certainly complicate matters, she mused as the dessert arrived.

৩১৩

JACK WAS WAITING in the hansom when she departed. Drummond did not press her to stay, although she sensed the offer hovering in the air between them like a bee around a flower. However, after assisting her into the cab, he kissed her lightly on the lips through the carriage window then said, 'Have a lovely weekend, Briar. You made the evening wonderful.'

'That was all?' Maggie exclaimed when Briar described the evening. She had arrived at the cottage late Saturday morning with her borrowed dress in tow.

Briar nodded.

'And you wore that dress?' Maggie pointed to the black and gold gown that was now flung over the back of a chair.

'I didn't intend to seduce the man, Maggie,' she said. 'Besides, while the kiss wasn't by any means passionate, I know I'm getting under his skin.'

Maggie cast her a glance. *It is the same strategy she used on me*, she thought. *Before long, I was sharing my most guarded secrets and divulging my greatest fears to her. Under his skin, indeed!*

'And you said he purchased the house and all the furnishings?' William asked.

Briar nodded. 'I asked around about that this morning. It

had belonged to Gordon Wenham, the previous owner of the colliery. However, Wenham never lived in Durham. But in order to purchase the colliery, one needs a permanent residence in the township. Drummond took the residence, lock, stock and barrel, off his hands.'

The trio were silent for a moment as they contemplated all that had occurred over a meal of partridge and brussels sprouts.

'The man is a mystery,' Briar said. 'I'll give him that. And I have to tell you that his sorry tale of growing up in the hallowed halls of Rugby broke my heart. Whether he's an angel or a devil, I'm yet to know. Either way, I'll go on investigating until we know for certain.'

'Do you think that is necessary?' Maggie asked. Without much evidence against Drummond, her pang of guilt at what they were doing was growing ever stronger.

'And if Drummond is as smart as he pretends,' added William, 'it might not be long until you're found out.' While William did not yet trust Briar, he did not want her to come to harm.

Briar looked at them then reached into her purse and drew out an envelope.

'I was going to wait to hear before I told you, but I've written to a gentleman friend of mine who works in the Manchester constabulary. Freddie's an honest copper. I've asked him to look into Drummond for me. Let's just wait and see if he turns something up.'

۞

BRIAR DEPARTED SHORTLY after their conversation, explaining she had a very important hat to see to. Maggie and William sat together over their unwashed teacups, attempting to understand Drummond. When their theories evaporated, William spotted the gown Briar had returned.

'I've never seen you in that,' he commented.

'As much as I love Durham, William, there's not a great deal of call for an elegant reception gown designed in the studio of Madame Tisseur of King's Road, London.'

'There's truth in that.' William touched the fabric gently, pensively. 'But I'd like to see you wear it.'

'Now?'

'Aye. Right now.'

'Why?'

'So I can watch you take it off.'

⁂

IT HAD TAKEN her almost an hour to dress. Maggie no longer wore a stiffly boned corset every day. It was not a requirement in Durham and William had told her he liked to 'feel her softness'. Donning all that was needed to fit into the Tisseur original took some time by herself. The last time she had worn the dress, Ada was by her side, at hand with a corset hook, then readying each layer of clothing in the correct order.

When Maggie gazed at her appearance in the mirror, she barely recognised herself.

She had sent to London for all her belongings shortly after arriving in Durham. Even though she knew there would be no need to have her complete wardrobe at hand, she had asked Ada to package all the garments – dresses, coats, hats, shoes and gloves included – and send them to her. Most of the garments remained unpacked and now, by London standards at least, they would all be considered outdated. Thinking on it as she looked at herself in the mirror, Maggie wondered what her motive had been. Homesickness? Vanity? A craving for what was absent? Or was ridding Chester Square of her presence a full stop of a kind? She still wasn't certain, but the dress she was wearing now was delightful and she enjoyed the way it made her feel: desirable and exciting.

She heard William's heavy tread on the stairs. He opened the door. The sight of her stopped him in the doorway. The neckline of the gown was cut low, and the skirt clung to her legs, emphasising her hollows and curves. He gazed at her at length then stepped into the room, closing the door behind him.

'When I see you, Maggie, I can't believe you're here with me. You could be on the arm of any man you choose.' He walked to her and breathed her in. He felt his heart quicken.

'I've chosen you.'

She kissed him softly, and his hands traversed her breasts and waist, finally coming to rest on her hips.

'Sit down,' she instructed, gently leading him to the bed.

William sat, and her fingers found the laces of her bodice. 'Is this what you want?'

He nodded.

Slowly and deliberately, she removed her clothing piece by piece. The garments that had been such an effort to put on seemed to slide off her body like water. Finally, clothed in only her corset and stockings, she walked to him and stood between his legs. He fingered the lace that sat flush against her bosom. Maggie shivered in anticipation.

'Pink,' he murmured, surprised at the colour.

'Flamingo,' Maggie corrected. 'It's exciting for a woman to know she is concealing something shocking beneath her gown.'

'Exciting?'

She nodded.

'I want you, Maggie,' he whispered. 'I want you now and forever.'

'I am yours,' she replied. 'Now and forever.'

Such was his hunger, William tore the corset from her. Hooks and eyes scattered on the ground. She looked at him, mildly stunned yet also aroused. He had never been rough before; Maggie found the change thrilling. Following his lead, she tugged at his shirt, lifting it over his head.

They clawed at one another, bit and thrust. Pinning her to the bed, he kissed her neck and breasts. His strength enraged her, and she scratched at his back. In that moment, William could do anything with her he wished and she wouldn't care. If he wanted to consume her, then let him. She couldn't have stopped him even if she wanted to.

When their bodies finally met, it was in an urgent and desperate way, as though it were the last time they would ever be with each other. They cried out together in pleasure, but there was a certain pain as well, resounding like thunder.

Are we attempting to claim one another, Maggie wondered, *or it this something more profound? Are we trying to hold on?*

Afterwards, they lay in bed holding hands, both unsure of what had just passed between them.

'I'm losing you,' William finally uttered.

Alarmed because only a moment ago it had been her feeling, too, Maggie rolled towards him and pressed her face against his chest. 'Never.'

'I overheard you talking to your father when he was here. And I can see how you're changed when you're with Briar.'

'Changed?'

'Aglow. You miss London and your life there.'

'I wouldn't be happy anywhere in the world if I wasn't with you,' Maggie said, sensing something else coming, a slow rumble in the distance like an approaching storm. She turned to face him. 'Do you want me here, William?'

He sat up and drew her close. 'Maggie, I want you so badly it hurts. There is no woman but you for me, and there never will be. Yet ...'

'Yet?' she echoed quietly.

'I'm losing you.'

CHAPTER 17

THE FOLLOWING DAY, their wonderful and strange lovemaking was never far from her mind, although they did not speak of it again. After William had admitted he sensed her slipping away from him, they had discussed his concerns for the better part of an hour. He worried their life in Durham would never satisfy her. She hoped he believed her reassurances. Despite her own confusion over her place in Durham, one thing she knew for certain was that she loved him. Maggie wished William could share in her conviction.

Now, as she attempted to work on her proposal for the girls' school, she wondered why he had doubted her commitment. What careless word had she uttered? What selfish thought had she voiced? It was not unusual for one pernicious, unsupported thought to take root and fester. She had almost pushed William away the year before in her stubborn and incessant pursuit of a principle. She hoped he wasn't now doing the same.

If he wants me that much, why hasn't he ever proposed? she wondered. Maggie knew he wanted to marry one day, but he had never asked her directly. She had never ruled marriage out, although she had been vocal about her feelings regarding the institution ...

Could that have put him off?

Thinking on the matter, she admitted to herself that she did have doubts about what marriage might mean for her independence. *But surely William would allow me the freedom I need to be myself ... wouldn't he?* She frowned, pondering. *Of course he would.* Besides, she reasoned, marriage to William would not be an institution or a transaction. She was certain it would be an ever-evolving relationship between equals. Perhaps she needed to state her position more clearly, although in that moment she wasn't quite sure what that position was.

By the time they travelled to the town hall together that evening, nothing had been resolved in Maggie's mind. The odd encounter between them had proved a distraction from her preparation for the meeting and had left her more nervous than she cared to admit.

Maggie, William and Grace took their seats in the hall. Following several muffled remarks by the mayor (none of them complimentary or heartening, Maggie noted), he called her to the lectern. Although no *boos* were audible, she heard a low rumble of disgruntled voices as she walked to the stage. She had never felt so nervous. Not the speeches she had delivered as a schoolgirl to the entire cohort at Cheltenham, nor her first day at the *Illustrated London News* had filled her with such terror. She realised that on those occasions, she had been in a world which was familiar. Even at the *News*, where she was aware every man in the office hoped she would fail, she had never experienced such extreme anxiety of the belly-twisting variety. But after a year, the Geordie attitude was still as foreign to her as a moment of calm in the finale of the *William Tell Overture*.

Maggie surveyed the audience when she reached the

podium. The townspeople appeared grizzled and haggard from a life either working below ground or a life spent above in worriment, waiting for the next collapse. A collier's life was harsh. To be the wife of a collier made life even harsher. All Maggie hoped to achieve with her notion for a girls' school was the choice of a more comfortable life for a collier's child.

As she gazed at the people seated before her, she concluded most present that evening were eager to condemn rather than support her. Why were they so opposed to the idea of education for girls? As she prepared to speak, she wondered what on earth she could say to alter their point of view. The sight of Regina Hartley seated in the front row did nothing to ease her discomfort.

She had purposely dressed in her most sober attire, yet it still seemed to Maggie that every woman in the audience stared at her with an expression of such horror that she might have been standing before them naked. She turned her gaze to William, then Grace, and finally to Briar. Her friend winked, a discreet gesture. She was sitting next to Matthew Drummond, who smiled at Maggie encouragingly.

In contrast, the mayor sat beside the dais with the expression of a gaoler.

'Thank you, Mayor Hardy, for permitting me to address the community this evening,' she began. 'I appreciate you all allowing me to explain my idea for a school for girls in Durham.' Maggie's mouth was dry and she attempted to swallow. There was no water on the dais. She was unsure if it was an oversight or intentional. She glanced at her notes. When she looked up, she noticed Marian and John Cross enter the room. The authoress was wearing a white mantilla. The couple slid into seats at the back of the auditorium, clearly wishing to be discreet. Marian offered a slight nod, but it was enough to buoy Maggie's spirit.

Maggie swallowed. How could she dare make a fool of herself in the presence of George Eliot?

'Ladies and gentlemen,' she continued with renewed purpose. 'I propose a school for girls in Durham. The daughters of colliers, farmers, shopkeepers, tradespeople, the mayor and the town aldermen would all be welcome. In short, the school would cater for all girls aged between six and fourteen. Neither status nor means will be prerequisites for enrolment.'

The audience instantly erupted into agitated chatter. Maggie wondered how she could have offended them all so quickly. Then she noticed Reverend Calder raise his hand.

'Reverend, you have a question?'

'The church school accepts both boys and girls. It has been good enough for the community for forty years, Miss Almond. Why do you think we should alter the education of our children now?'

Maggie attempted to smile with confidence. 'As you know, Reverend, it is now a government requirement for *all* children to attend school. Therefore, the curriculum must serve the needs of both sexes. While your school seems to accommodate the boys in Durham adequately, it does not suit the female students. That is why there is such a poor retention rate for girls. You must be aware that they remain a year in your school at best.'

She watched Calder take a long breath. He seemed to be gathering himself.

'Will you explain exactly *what* is so lacking in my curriculum?'

She had been determined not to offend anyone. Yet in only minutes she had raised the reverend's hackles. In the process, she sensed her own ire stirring, too.

'Well ... it is not balanced. The domestic sciences do not feature. Neither do art, or literature or philosophy.'

'Domestic sciences?' he asked, confused.

'Needlework, cooking, budgeting for a household—'

'The idea that a girl needs practical instruction in house-keeping as a part of her education is as absurd as would be the claim that boys need to be taught to plant barley or milk a cow,' the mayor put in.

Maggie was gobsmacked. *Does he actually believe the ability to cook, clean and sew is innately female?*

'I am a woman,' she responded, her voice rising. 'The skills of sewing and cooking are as elusive to me as milking a cow or sowing a field with barley as no teacher has instructed me. However, I would be a far more well-rounded individual if a teacher had. The curriculum at your school, Reverend, is weighted with arithmetic and religion. These are the subjects with which you are most comfortable.'

By this point in Maggie's presentation, Reverend Calder and much of the audience were red-faced with exasperation. However, their grimaces and expressions of annoyance did not deter Maggie.

'While there is a great deal children can learn from the Bible, there is also much that children would gain from reading Shakespeare and Socrates and Jane Austen. Likewise, learning about the works of Michelangelo and da Vinci would open their minds. For centuries, these writers and artists have taught humankind how to live in this world, how to recognise good and evil and beauty. They have instructed men and women in the art of compassion and humanity. What we need is a broader curriculum that considers both sexes. If you cannot provide one, then I am happy to!'

Reverend Calder and the mayor were outraged. Any other woman they would have dragged from the stage. But Maggie was an exotic species; after a year, they were still not sure whether she was a viper waiting to strike or a parakeet filled with colour and chatter.

Maggie looked at William. She read warning in his eyes.

In his carefully honed gaze, he was urging her to relent. Then her gaze fell on Briar. In her countenance, she read something completely different. Maggie took a deep breath and continued.

'I sincerely believe that if given the opportunity, women can do all things as well as or better than men. History shows us that women also make far superior leaders to men. Queen Elizabeth I and our current monarch Queen Victoria are but two examples of powerful, intelligent and enduring rulers this world has known.'

'They were anomalies,' Reverend Calder said loudly. 'They were born to rule!'

Maggie shook her head. 'That's ridiculous! They ruled because they were educated to be equal or better than their male counterparts.' Determined to be heard above the uproar, she raised her voice further. 'Shouldn't girls have the right to choose what future they desire? I'm not suggesting we prevent girls from becoming wives and mothers if that is what they want, but for a girl who longs for a career and a life outside of Durham—'

The hall erupted. Such a suggestion was too much for the audience's ears. For a moment, Maggie imagined she was about to be branded a witch and carried to the nearest stake.

'Good people of Durham, please quiet and take your seats,' the mayor cried above the din. 'Although it is a fruitless task, town legislature requires a vote.' Once the audience was still, he said, 'Raise your hands if you're in favour of funding a school for girls run by this woman.' He gestured towards Maggie, as one might point to a piece of particularly unpleasant refuse that had become adhered to the sole of a shoe.

William sprang to his feet. Maggie shook her head. The movement was almost indiscernible. The only act possible of making this moment more humiliating for her was William leaping to her rescue. Maggie had faced worse insults. She watched as William reluctantly resumed his seat.

A few hands eventually rose, and Maggie gazed at the pitiful array. Although defeated, she felt something blazing inside her. An inferno that needed release. She was Leonidas at Thermopylae and Lord Nelson at Trafalgar. Maggie was not about to surrender.

'Why are you all so afraid of change! If you weren't all so bloody narrow minded,' she shouted, 'you would be rewarded with a community of contented and flourishing equals!'

CHAPTER 18

'I MADE A FOOL OF MYSELF, a complete ass.' Maggie was close to tears but she refused to let anyone see her cry.

Maggie had noticed Marian, fearing, as always, that an admirer would recognise her, hasten towards the exit. However, she was deeply grateful that the authoress paused to give her a comforting embrace prior to leaving.

'Yours is a wonderful idea and I admire your courage.' Marian pressed her cheek against Maggie's briefly then clutched her arm and leant in. 'It is the mayor and reverend who are the asses.'

Maggie was drawn in by her gentle gaze.

'Girls' education will always be hard fought. I have some experience in the area. We should discuss the topic soon,' she said, patting Maggie's arm.

Maggie nodded, wondering what truths the writer might reveal to enlighten her own experience, and wishing she had discussed them with her before the evening's dismal performance.

Most of the crowd dispersed quickly, ashamed to be in Maggie's company. Even William was standing away from her, deep in discussion with his editor at the *Advertiser* Harry Armstrong as well as Tommy Fellowes. Grace, Beth, Jack and the girls were chatting to Reverend Calder, clearly attempting to assure him Maggie was not a heathen or a harlot or, possibly, both. Beth was rocking the baby furiously in her arms. He was grizzly, his small face red and contorted.

I know how you feel, Little Jack.

Had she ever felt so wretched? Her mother's betrayal had distressed her, but not in the same way. Public embarrassment could never be equalled as the catalyst for misery.

The only other people who remained in the auditorium were Briar and Matthew, who was conversing with the mayor. Briar stood obediently by her employer's side. Once the mayor departed, Matthew walked her way, Briar at his heels.

The women acted as though they were acquainted, but not friendly.

'Maggie, I was impressed by you tonight,' Matthew said.

'You'd be one of the few people who were.'

'It only seems logical to educate all young people adequately,' he said. 'Weavers do not differ from colliers. They demand their children be earning a wage as soon as possible. They need to be shown that with education, they might earn a better wage than they would trapped underground or chained to a power loom.'

Briar nodded in agreement. 'Your words, Miss Almond, certainly resonated with me,' she said. 'If I'd had formal schooling, my life would have panned out completely different. When me shop closed, I was at a loss. That's how I ended up here.'

Matthew looked at her and smiled warmly. 'And I'm very fortunate you did, Briar.'

Maggie flicked her friend a glance. *Briar now, is it?*

Then Matthew spoke again. 'Maggie, I want to offer you the funds you need to found your school.'

Maggie's heart stopped. She had never imagined the outcome of the most humiliating experience of her life to be this. Recalling Marian's comments on Charles Bray and the school he founded, she looked for William, excited at this new possibility, but he was nowhere in sight. Then her excitement was quickly tempered. *With the way he feels about Matthew,* she thought, *he will counsel against accepting.* Yet her strongest desire at that moment was to accept Matthew Drummond's offer and prove to the naysayers of Durham just what women could achieve given an appropriate education. She longed to say yes.

'If you're interested in my offer, I suggest you locate a suitable property, then determine a budget for your teachers' salaries, books, desks, chairs and other resources.'

'It would be highly unlikely that the school would run to a profit,' Maggie informed him, wondering why a businessman would wish to invest in a school. 'In fact, it will probably run at a loss. There are many families in Durham who can ill afford to pay. They would outweigh those that could three to one, at a guess.'

'I'm not interested in profit, Maggie. All industries should have philanthropic interests, don't you think?'

Maggie nodded cautiously, thinking once more of Charles Bray.

'If we act quickly, your school might be up and running by the new year.'

Maggie looked at Briar for any sign that she might trust Matthew on the matter. Briar widened her eyes, but gave nothing away. Maggie needed time to contemplate all the multifarious implications of the proposal.

Finally, she gave her answer. 'I so appreciate your offer, Matthew. However, I will need some time to think it over. My vision, you see, was of a community school, a co-operative, if you will.'

Matthew bowed slightly. 'Take all the time you need, Maggie.'

◈

THE FOLLOWING MORNING, Maggie's head ached as though she had drunk too much wine. She rose early with William and together they ventured to Causey Arch. They were meeting Briar there on her way to the pit.

'I want to take his money, but I know it could compromise the school.'

William gazed at her for a moment, attempting to read her expression. He knew what the school meant to Maggie, but he sensed something more was amiss.

'You still feel sorry for him, don't you?'

Maggie nodded.

'He is trying so tremendously hard to fit in and be a staunch friend ... Perhaps he is a good man. I want to believe he is and if I refuse his offer ...'

'You're worried he'll take it as a sign you don't value his friendship?' William finished. He walked away and leant against a sandstone pillar. She was about to go to him when Briar arrived.

'I've seen no one with a worse case of the morbs,' Briar said with a wink. 'What's the matter?'

'Oh nothing ... apart from just being handed my school on a platter and not being able to accept it, an act which will disappoint me and someone who I thought might be a friend.'

'Is that all?' Briar said with a laugh.

'No. I want to retaliate, too,' she fumed, suddenly angry. 'Allowing Matthew to fund my school would be the sweetest revenge on the mayor and that despotic and small-minded Calder.'

At this, William grinned. He loved to see Maggie fighting for what she believed in.

'Maggie, don't be disappointed. You really can't take his offer,' Briar said firmly. 'Believe me, Drummond is a businessman first and a friend second, if a friend at all. I'm sure he has an ulterior motive for funding your school.'

Maggie frowned. 'Why do you say that?'

'Your plan would allow him too much control,' Briar continued. 'Surely you see that he would own the school? He could pull rank on you at any time if he chose to.'

'That's true. He may try to influence your curriculum,' added William.

'And your plan could remove all female workers from the mine,' Briar continued. 'Why would he wish to encourage that? He needs those workers.'

'Really!' Maggie exclaimed, both disappointed by their suggestions and unconvinced. 'You are both allowing your imaginations to run wild. Profits aren't everything! The man said so himself. It's not completely unfathomable Matthew Drummond has a higher purpose in Durham,' Maggie said, holding her head high.

Briar gazed at her sympathetically. 'Your desire to think well of people is both your best and worst trait, Maggie.'

Maggie was affronted. She did not consider her willingness to trust people a character flaw.

'Perhaps this might make you think twice about Drummond,' Briar said, noticing Maggie's consternation. 'An inspector arrived yesterday, but Drummond told him he needed the agreed-upon notice before permitting entry. He sent him away. If he has nothing to hide, why did he do that?'

'What Briar says is true,' William added. 'Tommy told me as much last night. It's generally required by the union to give a fortnight's notice to the colliery before sending the inspector, but I didn't know Tommy had added that clause to the agreement.'

'Tommy didn't inform you?' Maggie asked, surprised.

'He's walking a very thin tightrope trying to keep the members both happy and safe,' William explained. 'He most likely knew I would disagree. Without giving notice, Drummond is well within his rights to sue the union and that is something Tommy can ill afford.'

Maggie nodded then returned her thoughts to Matthew's offer. Her school was within arm's reach, yet her dream had been for a community school funded by the town and its families. Briar and William were sure Matthew's involvement could mean the exact opposite of her vision.

After several minutes of internal debate, she came to a decision.

'Very well, then. I will not take Drummond's offer.' It nearly killed her to say it, but she had to admit that Matthew was likely a businessman first and a philanthropist second. Besides, there were still too many unanswered questions about his character for her to accept the offer in good faith.

Once the matter was settled, the women farewelled William, who was due at the *Advertiser*. They stayed by the river for a little longer to talk.

'You were magnificent last night, Maggie,' Briar said. 'I know the likes of the mayor and Calder have shredded your confidence, but you were wonderful.'

She certainly didn't feel wonderful. William had tried to comfort her after the meeting, but had advised patience, over and over again. Her school would come in time, he said. *Patience?* By the time they went to bed, Maggie had wondered if he knew her at all.

'Keep fighting,' Briar added. 'It's all we can do.' A mischievous expression suddenly formed on her face. 'Perhaps a rock through the mayor's window is needed?' She bent down and collected a handful of shiny pebbles from the bank and threw one of them into the water.

Plop.

Maggie laughed. 'I am tempted, but Durham is too small. Someone would spot us in an instant.'

Maggie found herself a handful of river stones and joined Briar in her meditative task. After a while, she realised it was not Calder or the mayor holding her back; it was money. Everyone believed it was coal that fuelled Britain, but it was money. Maggie considered asking her father for the funds, although she doubted her mother would look upon such an investment favourably. She had even considered approaching Raymond but was certain it would not thrill William. Or Raymond's wife, for that matter.

'Maggie, I know you want the school to happen and to happen soon. But Drummond is not the person to fund it. I have some money squirrelled away,' Briar said, as though she had read Maggie's mind. 'Quite a lot, actually. Will you take my money, Maggie? There is no one I'd like to invest in more.'

৩৶৩

WILLIAM FOUND it difficult to concentrate on his work. Thoughts involving Matthew Drummond, Briar Haines and Maggie darted through his mind like greyhounds. He couldn't catch any of them, no matter how hard he concentrated. He still believed Drummond was up to something, and the new stipulation of a fortnight's notice for inspection worried him. Or was it just that Drummond was a canny businessman? William had to admit that it would be daft of the man to allow the union to walk all over him with their demands.

Then there was Briar. Now there was a woman as complicated as a Greek puzzle. William was certain she wasn't to be trusted. He wondered if she could be working for Drummond as a double spy. Such news would crush Maggie.

And Maggie ... He rubbed his forehead, both marvelling at and confounded by her complexity. Her desire for immediate change was insatiable, and patience was a virtue she had never discovered. She filled his heart, yet he wondered if he would ever be enough for her. He pushed the thought from his mind and returned to considering Drummond.

Eventually, he rose from his desk with a path forward in mind and tapped lightly on his editor's open door. Harry Armstrong looked from the proof page he was examining with a magnifying glass. He gestured William inside.

'I was wondering,' William began, 'if an article isn't warranted about Matthew Drummond. He recently turned an inspector away from the pit.'

Armstrong placed the magnifying glass on the table, picked up his spectacles and put them on. He eyed William.

'As I heard it, the agreement stipulates a fortnight's notice. You can't think ill of the man for abiding by the agreement. Tommy told us as much last night.' He rose from behind his desk and placed his large hands on its surface. 'I lost people in the collapse, too, Will, but yer can't go after Drummond on a suspicion. Yer know as well as I that yer need evidence, man.'

William nodded and turned to leave. *Evidence.* He turned the word over in his mind. *A witness or physical proof that the seams remain dangerous.*

'Will, while I have yer here ... about the meeting last night,' Armstrong said, clearing his throat and moving out from behind his desk. William noticed his complexion redden. 'Your ...' He searched for the correct word.

'Maggie,' William offered.

'Aye, Miss Almond.' He nodded gratefully. 'Her presentation was ...' Once again, he searched.

'Thought provoking.'

'Inflammatory, I'd say.'

Harry Armstrong was in his forties. He and William shared similar backgrounds. They both came from colliery families and they had both attended the University of Durham. They had always had a strong relationship and their opinions and ideas had been in tune. However, now the men seemed to be playing different melodies entirely.

William nodded with a grin. 'I will not deny Maggie has a mind of her own.'

Armstrong sighed. 'I've already had complaints, you see. Several readers don't hold with the idea of you and she living ...' He waved his hand in the air.

'Being unwed, you mean?' William said.

'Aye. Now, if you and Miss Almond were married, and she were to call the entire township of Durham "bloody narrow minded", then perhaps people might not view her in the way they do, as a ...'

'Intelligent and forthright woman.'

William wondered where this conversation was heading, but it was a tribute to Maggie that she made men check their vocabulary so incessantly.

'Aye, tha's right,' Armstrong muttered uncomfortably. 'And her actions are reflecting poorly on you, Will, I'm afraid to say. I'd hate to see her views ...' He cleared his throat.

'Affect my performance at the *Advertiser*?'

'Tha's one way of putting it.'

William nodded and rose. He pushed his hands into his trouser pockets and considered Armstrong's words. He had been in a similar situation at the *News* when Latey received anonymous letters regarding his relationship with Maggie. Those letters – written by Briar, he now recalled, irritating him further – threatened both their careers and reputations. He and Maggie had ridden out the storm together. But he could not tell Maggie about his meeting with Armstrong today.

William did not fear dismissal or public opinion. Durham was in his blood, it was his home. People would come around eventually. And he knew his editor would support him.

'Why don't you just propose, lad?' Armstrong said after a moment.

William smiled half-heartedly, in a wane and woebegone way.

'I wish it were as simple as that, Harry.'

CHAPTER 19

The Manchester Guardian
Wednesday, October 27, 1880

DEAR READER,

Anything is more endurable than changing our established views about women. It seems that for many, nothing could be more abominable than looking up to the females in our society instead of down on them. For centuries, women have been idols or whores, mothers and wives, but never the equal of men. Never as people to be treated justly and with respect.

Throughout the years, I have often heard women complain their lives would be far more satisfactory had they been born male. There is no doubt that is true, however I have never in my life wished to be any other gender than that which I was born.

You may ask, then, why I wore the mask of a man for so long? The answer is quite simple: my novels would never have been published otherwise. Would the literati of London society ever have accepted Marian Evans, concubine of George Lewes?

I doubt it very much.

When Herbert Spencer rejected me, I was downcast. I could not imagine a man existed who might deign to love me. Then I met George. Complications crowded his life like Oxford

Street on Christmas Eve. He was married to a woman who had given him three strapping sons. She had also given Thornton Hunt, George's one-time business partner, three children. George kept the entire brood financially secure as best as he could. He, Agnes and the children all lived at his home on Bedford Place in Bloomsbury.

Some may be shocked by this arrangement. However, George, devastated by his own father's abandonment, refused to allow Hunt's three offspring to grow up fatherless. Despite no longer having feelings for Agnes, he courageously signed his name to each child's birth certificate, fully aware of the emotional and financial consequences of this act.

Then, trapped in a loveless marriage and penniless, he fell in love with me. How fortunate I was and how happy we made each other! When the living arrangements at Bedford Place became too fraught, George moved out. Following his lead, I resigned from my position at the *Westminster Review* and we embarked on a life together as 'Mister and Missus Lewes'.

We boarded the *Ravensbourne* and headed across the English Channel. Our ultimate destination was Weimar, the centre of German Enlightenment, and home to Goethe – George's obsession at the time. When we 'married', he was working on his book, *The Life and Works of Goethe*.

The liberal-minded and sophisticated Germans accepted our arrangement without question. We dined with Franz Liszt at his summer residence, located on the edge of the magnificent *Park an der Ilm*. He was such a handsome, charismatic and brooding fellow … It was no wonder his life was a series of adulterous affairs and liaisons. We played the piano together and I shall never forget the feeling of being in the presence of such mastery.

Our eight months abroad forged George and me as a couple, two units melded into one. Unfortunately, when we returned to England my dearest friends found it difficult to accept us. Confounded that I should call myself 'Missus Marian Lewes', they soon shunned me.

Since birth I had changed my name twice. Why not a third? And, indeed, why not a fourth? For when my first novel, *Scenes of Clerical Life*, was published in 1858, I chose to use the pen name 'George Eliot'.

The reason I took the Christian name 'George' as my pseudonym is obvious. As for Eliot … It was simply a strong, mouth-filling, easy-to-spell surname. In retrospect, I believe my unconscious was at play and my choice was not so straightforward. 'George' could well have reminded me of George Sand, a writer I admired greatly. As for 'Eliot'? George and I were reading *Persuasion* to each other that spring. Anne Elliot's journey to romantic maturity and happiness resonated with me greatly.

Juliet asked, 'What's in a name?' Everything, I say.

When *Scenes* was published, there was considerable speculation about the identity of the author. After *Sea-side Studies*, George encouraged my fiction writing relentlessly. He was also the one to suggest I use a pseudonym. George had faith in two things – my talent and the conventional views of my audience.

There have never been rules for the writing of men. If I was going to write fiction, as my dear husband urged, it needed to be free and unconstrained by the limitations imposed upon female writers. My style of fiction would be realistic, passionate, observational and sympathetic.

My fiction would never be a 'silly ladies' novel' by a 'lady novelist'.

My male disguise was so expertly painted that even my publisher, John Blackwood, did not recognise the author of *Scenes* as a woman. Only Dickens took a lucky guess at my gender in a letter he wrote addressed to the author of the book. He sent it via Blackwood. He addressed it 'Dear Sir' but made a point of complimenting my novel's 'womanly touches'.

When George read the first part of *Scenes* to a party he attended in London, all assembled believed the writer to be a clergyman – a Cambridge man, no less! The success of my mask delighted me. Fortunately, I had George to act as my agent and go-between. Whenever he returned from a meeting with Blackwood, he would laugh heartily; the old Scot's determination to wrench from his lips the identity of his anonymous new author delighted him so.

Writing fiction transformed me, physically and spiritually, and *Scenes* was just the beginning. I had been ostracised, but writing gave me a voice, a means of expressing my views. The energy I possessed was boundless, and all I perceived shone as bright as daydreams. Whenever George and I took a ramble along the river, the trees, the sun, the water seemed to expand before me. It is true that my relationship with George had sent me into hiding. Why, even through my fiction, I was concealing my identity! I was a recluse … but I had never been happier.

Despite my joy, the idea of deceiving those I loved was an anathema to me. So, I wrote to my brother Isaac and sister Chrissy. Although I could not be completely open, I informed them of my marriage to George. I divulged everything about my life in Richmond, the place we chose to call home, and that I was happy writing. Then I walked to the end of my street and kissed each letter reverently as I placed them in the postal box.

THE WOMEN SAT in the sunny conservatory of Marian's home by the river. The glass seemed to intensify the sun and Maggie felt herself growing warm. She loosened her collar and was reminded of Clairmont's over-heated attic room in Islington. It was always so stuffy. But this heat was different. Neither stuffy nor claustrophobic, it was the type of warmth one welcomed ... the kind of heat that made a person wish they could curl up cat-like and purr.

Maggie shifted her seat a little. The sun was glinting off the glass and into her eyes. The women had planned to meet at the university library on this occasion, as Maggie liked the quiet and the dark mahogany tables and bookshelves. She had reserved the Wolsey Room for them. However, Mister Cross had sent a message early in the morning, explaining his wife's preference to remain at home.

Since the interview had begun less than fifteen minutes before, Mister Cross had entered the conservatory twice to see to the wellbeing of his wife. When he materialised a third time, Marian had tactfully sent him away, implying the proceedings would move more quickly if they were not constantly being halted by his interruptions. Cross seemed to take the criticism well. Maggie suspected he was used to such censure.

'Very well. I am leaving until this afternoon,' he said. 'I have several errands I must attend to. If you need anything, Julia—'

'Is here. I know.'

Mister Cross kissed his wife on the forehead and bid Maggie farewell, then left the room.

'Are you feeling poorly, Marian?' Maggie asked. 'We can continue the interview another time if you wish?'

'No. It does me good to have you here. It's my kidneys, you see. They cause me trouble.'

'Bright's disease?' Maggie asked, concerned.

The authoress nodded. 'It is uncomfortable, but not life threatening, I am told. However, the warmth helps the pain.' She smiled and adjusted the cushion at her lower back. 'Shall we continue?'

Maggie nodded. 'Did you receive replies to your letters to your brother and sister?'

'One reply only, and that from my brother's solicitor, Mister Holbeche. He had been the family's solicitor even when my father was still living.'

Maggie looked up from her notes.

'My siblings wished to know the details of the marriage, as well as the occupation of my husband. Holbeche informed me my brother and sister were most alarmed at me having married without their knowledge. It seems that Isaac was a traditionalist and had expected George to ask for my hand.' She smiled at the absurdity of the notion. 'Isaac had planned to arrange a dowry. The very idea ... while I appreciated my brother's generosity, even if George and I were free to marry, such ridiculous notions would never have crossed our minds.'

Maggie nodded. They were indeed outdated notions based on a belief that females could be owned and sold like chattel. She had said the same to William many times. In the light of their recent conversations, she wished she had kept her mouth shut.

'Were you honest in your reply?' Maggie asked.

'I replied, honestly and nobly. I explained George was a renowned writer and a very learned scientist, and that I regarded our marriage as sacred, although it was not legal in the eyes of the church or government.'

Maggie's chest tightened. In the same predicament as the authoress, she had been nothing but entirely truthful regarding her relationship with William. Her honesty had won her no friends or allies. After the Town Hall meeting, she wished she had been less so.

'My siblings ceased all communication with me. My brother did not contact me until I married John in May this year.'

'What?' Maggie exclaimed, astonished. 'For more than two decades, you were estranged from your brother?'

Marian nodded. 'Ludicrous, isn't it? I recall the day that Holbeche's second letter arrived. When George entered the sitting room, he noted my ashen complexion and snatched the correspondence from me immediately. On reading it, he was furious. He called my brother and sister ignorant and shouted about their narrow minds.' Marian flicked her gaze to Maggie.

Only two days ago, she had shouted the same.

'"How dare they!" George cried. You see, I had supported Chrissy and her children for many years after she was widowed. George and I often went without so that Chrissy's children might not. He was so upset, his diatribe lasted for hours. All the while, I sat in my armchair and thought of Isaac and me fishing together when we were children, and how he had taught me to ride and tie knots. Finally, George threw the letter into the hearth and departed, still raging.'

'Did you have any female friends to support you through this time?' Maggie asked. Marian's experience reminded her of her own, and how much she had come to appreciate Briar's friendship and support.

'No. Many of my friends deserted me. Chapman, despite our history, was concerned for me, as was Cara Bray. George had a reputation as a rake, and they refused to believe it was merely a character trait he had invented and nurtured to justify his muddled private life. Sara ...' She winced as though the memory was a painful one.

'Sara Hennell?'

Marian nodded. 'Despite the unorthodox living arrangements at Rosehill and her initial acceptance of our relationship, Sara became furious about my decision to be with George. We had been so close that I had considered her my wife for some years.'

At a questioning look from Maggie, Marian stared seriously at her for an instant. Her lovely blue-grey eyes were eloquent, expressive.

'I believe when she realised George and I were not a passing fancy, she became jealous.'

Maggie leant forward and offered Marian more tea, sensing the break from Sara Hennell all those years ago still stung.

'Only a few, such as Barbara Leigh Smith, were loyal. I recall writing to her about George and our relationship. She replied, "George and you living together is a manifestation of your strong and noble nature." I cried with happiness when I read those words.'

'Tell me more about Barbara,' Maggie asked. She knew the woman as 'Barbara Bodichon', artist and a women's rights advocate, but Maggie wasn't aware of her connection to Marian.

'We met through the *Westminster Review*. We were little more than acquaintances for many years. But following her letter of support, our friendship matured. I invited her to visit us at Tenby and Ilfracombe. George and I were living between those two places throughout the summer while he continued to research *Sea-side Studies*. I'm not certain why, but I felt compelled to ask her advice on our impossible situation. How long could I hide from society? Yet I could never give up George … She had always seemed wise, so I trusted her opinion. I was glad I did. Barbara was immensely sensible, and she held similar views to my own.'

'And what did she advise?' Maggie asked, eager to know both for her article and for her own benefit.

'"Your own heart must decide", she told me.'

❧

BY THE TIME Maggie farewelled the Crosses, the conservatory had grown cold. She thought on their parting. Mister Cross had arrived home in the mid-afternoon, just as the sun was setting. He'd entered the conservatory and, less tactful than his wife, suggested the interview be drawn to a close.

Now Maggie waited for William by Prebend's Bridge. A creature of comfort and habit, he always walked the same way home. Marian had offered her a shawl for her journey. When she had set out earlier in the day, she believed she wouldn't need anything warmer than what she was wearing. But Missus Cross insisted she take the shawl. The Crosses were so wary of the weather; perhaps that's what happened when one aged, although it was true that the days were growing colder.

Maggie drew the shawl tight around her shoulders, thankful for its warmth, and sat by the bank. The over-hanging amber and russet leaves blended with the dwindling flames of the sunset and the air smelt as only it can smell in autumn – crisp and grassy, like a pippin apple eaten straight from the tree. After a moment, she opened her notebook and began reviewing her notes. Maggie read the last words on the page and her thoughts flew to William. Could her heart decide her fate, like Marian's had done for her? If only it were that easy.

❧

'I FOUND you a copy of *Sea-side Studies*,' John said as he followed his wife up the stairs to her bedroom. 'I've left it on your nightstand.'

It must be strange for him to be married to me now, she thought. John had witnessed her love for George, and had played a significant role in both their lives. Perhaps that was why he scoured the bookstores of the North East, tracking down a volume of the book she and George had written together. *God knows where he came upon it ... Perhaps I should not resent John for his attentiveness. Rather, I should love him for his forbearance and consideration ...*

Once she was settled under the counterpane and John had departed, she reached for the book. Holding the pages to her nose, she breathed in deeply, as if hoping to ingest George Henry Lewes through the words he had written so many years ago. She opened on a page and read. It was George's description of an annelid, 'the millipede of the sea,' he called it. His words were accompanied by a sketch Barbara had drawn when he had found it, a beautiful pencil sketch. When her friend had come to visit them in Tenby, she had brought with her an easel, brushes and paints. Yet she chose pencil for this particular creature. The perfect choice.

8 Park Shot
Richmond

DECEMBER 2, 1858

Dear Barbara,

I am happy to report that the Royal Society gave George permission to name the beastie you sketched. It is now known as the 'Tenby Bristle Worm'. It is the very first of its kind to be discovered. Do you recall that you highlighted its similarity to a bristle brush? It was an offhand comment, probably one only George remembers. He was so pleased with the likeness you made for Sea-Side Studies. 'Barbara has made a Thomas Huxley of me!' he cried when he received the correspondence in the post this morning.

The episode led me to recall our time by the seashore in Wales.

Although I never spoke of it, your visit and friendship meant every-thing to me then. Apart from you, all my female friends had deserted me. Even Cara and Sara were slighted I had not sought their counsel when George and I became one. For a reason I cannot identify, their neglect of me made me ashamed of myself and our love.

Usually, my secluded, solitary life within my ivy-clad confines does not bother me. George ventures into London weekly to peddle my wares. He presents the news of his adventures when he returns in such an animated and amusing way (you know what a showman George can be) it's as though I am transported with him. However, on Monday I had the urge to go up to London myself. A strange irrita-tion nagged at me. Bored and restless, I snapped at my poor husband like a mad dog.

My purpose was to nab a copy of Vindication. I had the notion that if anyone could light my murky way, it would be Wollstonecraft. Copies of it are so scarce these days. People view her in the same light as they view me; it is a tragedy that she is so shunned. I expect if we had met, we would have been kindred spirits.

I set off on the eight o'clock train to Euston alone, with the deter-mination of Marco Polo and the fearlessness of James Cook. After many hours of indignant searching, I finally found the book in a nameless bookstore in Cecil Court for 3s 6d. Once I had the precious tome in my hands, I realised why I had treated George with such ferocity: I have been missing my friends. While he visits London each week and meets with his old chums, I am not able. That morning, I resented his freedom. Envy, pure and simple, ran like hellhounds through my veins. Once I realised this, I placed the book in my bag and returned to Kew on the next train.

Although I miss society and my friends, whenever I am away from him, I miss George far more.

You were correct, dear Barbara, in your advice; my heart leads and I follow.

Yours in accordance,
Marian

CHAPTER 20

WHEN MAGGIE and William arrived at the cottage, a young woman and three children were waiting in the kitchen. It was Lucy Owen. Maggie remembered her from the September meeting of the Society. How could she forget the face of the only woman to support (albeit meekly) her idea of a girls' school in Durham?

The woman's angled face was more familiar now. She had seen her on the High Street occasionally. At those times, she had been sheepish and reluctant to meet Maggie's eye, but had said hello nonetheless. Her reticence was not surprising. Maggie's reputation preceded her everywhere she went, even on Durham High Street.

Maggie had also noticed Lucy at the Town Hall meeting. She was seated next to a large, burly man. From his attire and overall darkened patina, Maggie assumed him to be a pitman.

Grace had poured the woman a cup of tea and the children sat beside them eating stottie cakes. William liked to boast that Grace's stotties were the best in Durham.

'Here they are,' Grace said as the couple walked through

the door. 'Do you remember Lucy Claymore, Willie? Gerald's wee sister?'

William nodded in recognition. 'How is Gerry? I haven't seen him in an age.'

'He moved to Bristol about five years ago,' she said in a delicate, refined voice. 'He's a bookkeeper.'

Golden curls framed her fine features and her wide grey eyes shone with intelligence. They roamed the room cautiously. She reminded Maggie of the mother magpie she and Briar had observed during their picnic. Lucy was taking in her surrounds, wary of danger. *She is very attractive*, Maggie concluded. *Perhaps that pitman wasn't her husband, after all. They would be an ill-matched pair if he was.*

'Gerry always had a knack for numbers,' William commented as he took a seat.

Grace cleared her throat and glanced at her son. 'Were you aware that Lucy married Reggie Owen?'

Maggie noticed William's frown. The information didn't sit well with him.

'Did you, now? Well, it's lovely to see you again, Lucy.'

Maggie joined the party at the table and Grace introduced the children – Max, Ronald and Geraldine – before producing two more cups of tea.

'Lucy attended our last suffrage meeting,' Maggie informed William. 'And she is open to the idea of improving girls' education in Durham.'

'Well, it is no wonder. I seem to recall you being sent off to fine boarding school when you were still a bairn.'

Lucy laughed. She had a charming laugh, effervescent. Yet judging by her manner, Maggie suspected it was rarely heard.

'Well remembered. I was six.'

'What school was it?' Maggie asked.

'Miss Beecher's School at Hartlepool. I was hoping I

might enrol Geraldine as well, but ...' Lucy's face darkened for a moment. When she looked at Maggie again, it was with a downcast expression.

'Lucy is actually here to speak to Maggie,' Grace said.

'Really?' Maggie said eagerly, excited at the prospect of a woman needing her advice. 'We could go into the sitting room if you'd prefer to chat there?'

Lucy nodded and rose from the table. Maggie led her out of the kitchen.

Once the women were inside, Maggie gently prodded the fire back into life. She gestured to the seats around the hearth.

'What would you like to talk to me about, Lucy?'

The young woman took a deep breath before a merry shriek coming from the kitchen startled her. She went to rise.

'Don't be alarmed,' Maggie said, touching her hand softly to settle her. 'It's probably just William entertaining them, that's all. He has a quite a knack with children ...'

Her words petered away, distracted by a sudden image of herself and William with children. She had still not quite decided what she wanted in that regard.

Lucy nodded. 'He was always a kind and gentle boy, always looking out for his younger brothers and such.'

Lucy's words drew Maggie back to the situation at hand. She enjoyed hearing William praised and complimented, but she was concerned Lucy would happily talk about any subject other than the one she had come to discuss. Rising, Maggie walked to the window and drew the curtains together, waiting for Lucy to gain courage enough to speak honestly.

When she sat again, Lucy said, 'It's my husband, Miss Almond.'

'Yes?'

It took some time before Lucy was ready to tell her more.

As Maggie waited, she wondered what the young woman was preparing to utter. She watched as Lucy's eyes filled with tears. The words that finally came were barely a whisper.

'He hits me.'

Lucy's admission, stated in three simple words, hit Maggie, too. Hard. A woman had never confessed such a thing to her before. Maggie sensed her temper flare, but she knew she could not express her outrage to the woman in front of her. She needed to be calm, for Lucy's sake. Apart from the law which gave husbands the right to own their wives, to even beat their wives, Maggie could not fathom what gave men the moral justification to do so. She quickly scanned the woman's face, but she saw no signs of injury or bruises. She waited for Lucy to continue, realising why Regina Hartley had mentioned the suffragette meetings to the poor woman. Perhaps the butcher's wife was more in favour of female emancipation than Maggie had credited her for.

'Last week, he took to me with a strap, worse than ever,' Lucy said rising and slowly lifting her skirts, then turning.

Maggie reached out and gently inched up Lucy's drawers. The backs of her thighs had been savaged. Red raised welts criss-crossed her legs.

'He's never touched my face, though. He says it's the only tolerable thing about me.'

Maggie felt her anger rise. She walked to the mantel, considering a course of action. She gripped the edge of the oak beam. If she were physically strong enough, she would have enjoyed ripping the timber from the wall, finding Reggie Owen and beating him across the head with it. How she would relish hurting him the way he had hurt and humiliated Lucy.

Slowly, as she calmed, she wondered why Lucy had confessed to her. After all, they were barely acquaintances.

She remembered a friend of her mother's, Rose Wickham. When she arrived at Chester Square early one morning with a bloody lip, a single carpet bag and her two children, Lydia had taken charge. Without rousing the maids, she had prepared a bedroom for Rose and another for the children. She had directed Maggie to make them all cocoa. Once they were all settled in bed, Lydia had entered Maggie's room and lay down with her, her head resting on the same pillow. Her breath, still sweet from the cocoa, tickled her face like a zephyr. 'I shall talk to your father in the morning. He will know who will help. I will send Rose and the children to Hampshire for the time being. They can stay at our house in the country until everything is arranged.' Then she stroked her daughter's hair until she fell asleep.

At just ten years old, Maggie did not know that 'arranged' meant divorced. Until now, she had forgotten her mother's compassion and mastery during that early morning in Chester Square.

'You and the children need to stay here for the time being,' Maggie said, attempting to muster the same command as her mother had all those years ago. She didn't have the political connections or the finances of Henry and Lydia Almond, but she knew she couldn't send Lucy and her children back to Reggie Owen.

'You must stay until we can ensure you will be safe,' Maggie rephrased, hoping Lucy would understand the perilous nature of her predicament.

'It will only make him angry,' Lucy said, becoming agitated. The consequences of leaving seem to have overcome her. 'He's never touched the children, and he is their father ...'

Maggie felt the tight knot of anger blaze in her chest again.

'I cannot do anything to help you if you go back to him, Lucy. If he is violent, he has no right to be their father.'

Lucy nodded unsteadily, then turned her gaze to the hearth. The flames flickered in her grey eyes. Maggie remained silent, watching the woman consider her future. To push Lucy now might mean pushing her back to Reggie. Women were raised to consider their husband first, even over their own wellbeing. It was a terrifying prospect to make a stand against a brute, and heart-wrenching to tear apart one's own family.

'Lucy, why did you come to see me?' asked Maggie gently.

'We went to your meeting the other night,' Lucy said eventually. 'What you said about choice. If I'd only had a choice ...' Tears formed in her eyes. 'Reg was handsome once and quite dashing. He had a modest charm in those days. One afternoon when he took me walking by the river, one thing led to another and ...'

'You became pregnant.'

Lucy nodded. 'I was carrying Max when we wed. Even though I didn't love Reg, my parents forced the marriage. When I heard you speak at the meeting, something in me snapped. I realised I needed to do something, and I knew that you'd understand my situation.'

Maggie went to her and took her hands. Tears cascaded down Lucy's cheeks.

'Lucy, your parents didn't know you had a choice either.'

The women looked at one another for a moment. Maggie could almost feel Lucy's anguish. She could see Lucy didn't believe she could have taken a different path all those years ago. And now? It depended on Maggie to show her it was possible. She wrapped her arms around Lucy's shoulders and embraced her, hoping to assure the young woman all would be well.

LUCY INSISTED she sleep with her children in the same room. Maggie guessed that Max, Ronald and Geraldine fell asleep quickly, but she could hear Lucy's tears through the wall for a long time after they had retired. She hoped they were tears of relief.

Once Lucy uttered her initial confession, she divulged every thrashing, berating and humiliation she had received from Reggie Owen. The poor woman had told no one. She had endured the abuse for years, since Max was a baby. Maggie hoped that by Lucy laying her burden onto another's shoulders, it might ease a little of her torment.

There was no possibility of Maggie falling asleep soon. Rage, like a demon, possessed her. Her skin tingled with it. She had helped Lucy undress and saw the bruises and scars on her body. The man was a beast. Maggie inhaled deeply and attempted to still her mind.

She took William's hand in the dark, grateful for her good fortune. He was a lamb. Had he ever even raised his voice in her direction? She sifted through her mind. If so, it was rare.

As she struggled to find sleep, Maggie considered the next steps for Lucy and her children. They must leave Durham, she decided. A man such as Reggie would not let them go easily. Maggie thought there was the strong possibility he would demand ownership of the children. And he could – ownership was his by law. Lucy would need to escape, to go into hiding. Maggie resolved to write to Lucy's brother, Gerald, in Bristol. William had described him as a sensible and upright character. Surely, he would be willing to care for his sister, nephews and niece ...

Another woman forced into a life of concealment by her circumstances, Maggie thought ruefully. She was only grateful there had been no violence in Marian's life, or her own.

'Reggie was always a lout,' William murmured into the

dark, as though attempting to reason why a man could be so beastly.

'How so?'

'He was always eager to start a fight, just as keen to finish it. My little brother Johnny ...' William paused before continuing. His brother's death in the pit disaster was still so raw. 'He was a wee lad, but he had a mouth on him. Also, he was ten times as clever as an oaf like Reggie Owen, even when Johnny was but a lad in knee socks. One day, Reg beat him to a pulp over something Johnny had said. By the time I got to him, his nose was bleeding and his eyes were black. Poor wee blighter ... Reg is a thug, always has been, but I never thought he would be capable of abusing a woman.'

'Did you turn the other cheek?' Maggie asked, rolling against his side, 'Or was it just deserts for Reggie Owen?'

'I pushed him off Johnny, but once I saw the state of my brother, huddled like a beaten cur in the dirt, all I could think of was getting him home. Reggie went unpunished, by me anyway.'

'You're one of the good ones.' She kissed his cheek.

'Are you suggesting I'm a dying breed?'

Maggie sat up and turned on the lamp. She spoke softly, but seriously.

'Wife sales still occur, did you know? Men are permitted to beat their wives, and a married woman has no separate legal identity to her husband's. These atrocities are legal, William. So yes, I believe you are a dying breed and I count my blessings you aren't dragging me to the nearest auction where I might fetch the best price.'

'But you're not my wife.'

'Exactly,' she said and turned out the light.

THE FOLLOWING MORNING, the shouts of men and the cries of children woke Maggie. For a moment, she believed herself to be in the strange point between sleep and waking, where it was possible for one's dream to guide the sleeper into coherence before it scurried back into the realms of the subconscious to be lost forever. She touched William's side of the bed. It was empty and cold.

When she realised the clamour was occurring downstairs, she sprang from the bed and hurried from the bedroom. Checking in the room Lucy and her children had been given, Maggie found them crowded together on one bed. Lucy clutched her three children tight, attempting to soothe them. Grace was with them, standing near.

'Stay here, Maggie,' Grace cautioned. 'It's Reggie. He's as angry as a hot horse.'

Maggie ignored the warning and left the room. She had no intention of allowing William to come to harm.

From the top of the stairs, she could see him at the door, holding back an enraged Reggie Owen. William was at least a head taller, but Reggie was wide and muscled. He looked as fearsome as a wounded bull. William was attempting to calm him; his tone was even and his words reasonable. Maggie took a few steps closer and Reggie spotted her.

'Tha she is,' Reggie shouted, pointing towards the stairs. 'Tha's the miscreant bitch who started all this.'

In an instant, William had raised his arm and swung. Reggie fell against the doorframe and then to the ground.

'I'd have it you were the one that started it all, yer great doylem,' William shouted, standing over the prostate form of Reggie Owen. After a moment, William seemed to calm, and he helped Reggie to his feet. 'And I'll thank you for not using that sort of language regarding Maggie ever again, in her presence or no, or you'll be gettin' far worse.'

Reggie rubbed his jaw and stumbled away through the gate.

Maggie ran down the remaining stairs and into William's arms. He was shaking. She closed the door and led him into the kitchen. Tea was what one required in these situations. She placed the kettle on the stovetop.

'Thank you,' she said once he had calmed further. 'You're the first person ever to defend my honour with their fists.'

He looked at her gravely. 'Wedding band or no, Maggie, you are my wife here.' He placed his hand on his heart. 'We are one and I'll defend you 'til my dying day.'

❧

FOLLOWING BREAKFAST, William was still feeling agitated by his encounter with Reggie Owen. He felt as though he could run for miles across the dales given the chance. Instead, he set to work in his mother's garden. For weeks, she had been asking for repairs to the fence surrounding it; Arlo the goat would not listen to reason when it came to resisting the urge to devour the season's cabbages. William was not a remarkable carpenter, but he knew enough to repair a fence.

By mid-morning, the sun had grown warm. He removed his waistcoat and rolled up his sleeves. As he did so, Grace approached with a mug of water straight from the well. When he put the cup to his lips, it was like ice. There was nothing quite as good as the taste of water, crisp and biting, cooled by the earth. Grace admired his handiwork then she sat beside her son on the grass. He offered her a sip of his water.

She shook her head. 'You're the one who's sweating like a groom at the altar.'

William flashed her a look then immediately regretted it. *When did I grow so sensitive?* he wondered.

'It's just an expression,' she said, patting his knee.

'Aye, I know.'

They were quiet as William sipped his water. Gazing towards the dales, he realised he loved his life in Durham. There would always be thugs like Reggie Owen; those he would handle. What he couldn't manage was Maggie and he hated himself for feeling the need to do so.

Grace produced a small velvet box from the pocket of her apron and handed it to her son. He held it in his hand for a moment. Sighing, he returned it to Grace without even opening it. Instead, she opened the box and gazed at the ring cushioned in the silk hollow.

'Your father gave this to me on the day he proposed. It was his nineteenth birthday, and he suggested a walk to Elvet Bridge. It was a beautiful spring afternoon. We'd been courting for a month or two and that day, Archie told me I was the most beautiful girl he'd ever seen. If he couldn't have me, his heart would break, he claimed, never to be mended.' She smiled at the memory. 'Then he gave me this box.'

William took the box from her again and examined the ring. Grace had stopped wearing her betrothal band when the children were bairns. She worried the setting would scratch their soft baby skin. To William, the ring looked brand new. He could remember his mother wearing it on only a few occasions.

'It's sweet, isn't it?' Grace said. 'A rose-cut diamond. It would have cost Archie a fortune. He never told me how much he paid for the thing. But you know your da, he enjoyed romancing me.'

William nodded, recalling how he would often catch his parents locked in an embrace when they thought the children weren't about.

'Why are you showing it to me?'

'I'm giving it to yer, lad.'

William frowned, confused.

'Ask Maggie to marry yer. She loves yer, Willie. I can see it in her eyes every time she looks your way.'

William did not doubt that Maggie loved him, but for Maggie, there was more involved in marriage than love. If she said no, things would never be the same between them. He didn't believe he could go on with her in the same way if she refused him.

CHAPTER 21

THAT AFTERNOON, Maggie walked into town along the river. William's words had made her contemplate her choices. William *was* one of the good ones. He would never treat her like property, beat or abuse her. Of that, she was certain. She hoped that her words did not imply she thought otherwise.

She frowned. She knew William was not like other men. Then why couldn't she commit to him in the only way that mattered? To him, at least. She loved William solely, passionately, intensely. She would lay down her life for the man. So why wasn't she able to allow her feelings to soften her principles? It was fear, she reasoned by the time she had reached her destination.

The fear Maggie Almond would cease to exist.

Maggie was heading to the post office to send a telegram to Lucy's brother Gerald. Before she had departed the cottage, Grace had warned her again about the dangers of a confrontation with Reggie Owen, but Lucy had intervened.

'Don't concern yourself,' she had said. 'Reggie will be at the pit. He hasn't missed a day's pay in his life. The new owner seems to have taken a shine to him.'

'Oh, how so?' Maggie queried, interested.

Lucy shrugged. 'Mister Drummond has invited him twice to the pub. I get the impression the man likes him.'

William had described Reggie Owen as oafish, and she had witnessed it with her own eyes early that morning. What would Matthew see in the likes of him?

As though she had summoned him with her thoughts, Matthew Drummond appeared on the opposite side of the street, strolling along in that carefree way of his. She called to him then ran across to speak to him. They continued their journeys together.

'Have you given any thought to my offer, Maggie?' he asked.

'I have and I am so sorry to say I must decline it.'

He stopped and turned to her. Disappointment swept like a gale across his face, blighting the landscape of his handsome features for an instant.

'I assure you that your kind offer means so much to me, but I do not believe it is wise for a business so wholly involved with the workings of a town to fund a school. Schools should be independent, free to evolve as they would naturally, free from pressure.'

'There'd be no pressure from me, Maggie, I can assure you. Besides, we're friends.'

'That places me in an even more compromising position,' she said earnestly. 'A disagreement over my handling of your finances might lead to a rift between us. And I would not wish to lose your friendship.'

Her words seemed to brighten him no end.

'You are correct, of course. My father always said never go into business with friends.'

'As did mine!' Maggie smiled.

She had imagined it would be a far more difficult conversation. With that matter resolved, she looped her arm through his and leant closer towards him.

'Matthew, as your friend,' she whispered, glancing around her to be sure she wasn't overheard, 'I'd like to inform you of the character of one of your employees.'

He looked at her gravely.

'Reggie Owen is a violent and heartless man. I can say no more now, but be wary of him.'

Matthew nodded, considering all she had told him. 'Thank you for confiding in me, Maggie. I appreciate your concern. I shall keep an eye on Mister Owen from now on.'

When they reached the saddler, both agreed another morning of chess was warranted, then they parted ways. Maggie watched him drift along the street as though on a cloud. *Surely Matthew Drummond is an honourable man?* She hoped it was so. In truth, it buoyed her confidence to have made a friend in Durham other than William or members of his family. She hoped that one day, William would grow to trust Matthew, too.

Distracted by her thoughts, she bumped into Beth, hustling her children towards home. Little Jack sat on her hip, looking back and forth with an interested expression on his round face.

'I've heard Lucy Owen and her bairns are staying at the cottage.'

Maggie nodded and wondered who else the ripples of gossip had reached.

'She needs some time away from her husband.' Maggie did not want to reveal the depths of Lucy's humiliation at the hands of Reggie, even to Beth.

'Be careful there,' Beth advised quietly.

Jack gripped Maggie's finger, fiercely intent upon drawing it into his mouth.

'Why do you say so?'

'Breaking a family asunder will not win yer any friends in this town,' she said. 'I'm no' suggesting you're in the wrong,' Beth added pointedly, 'just make sure you know what you are doing.'

As Beth hurried her brood along the High Street, Maggie looked after her. What else could she do but assist Lucy? There was no way she could suggest the woman go back to her thug of a husband. Maggie was sure she was in the right. The matter resolved in her mind, she opened the door to the post office and walked towards the telegraphist's desk.

❦

EARLY THE FOLLOWING MORNING, Briar arrived at the cottage with a large hatbox and was glad to find Maggie and William alone. Maggie explained to her that Lucy had taken her children for a walk by the river and Grace had only recently departed for the university library.

'A man arrived at the pit yesterday, late,' she began, placing the box in the centre of the table.

'An inspector?' William asked eagerly.

'I don't know for certain, but I assume so. The required time of the notice has passed,' Briar answered. 'Although, Drummond ushered the man so quickly from the office, I barely had time to get a good look at him.'

She removed her gloves, then added, almost as an afterthought, 'Oh, and Drummond informed me yesterday afternoon that Reggie Owen was moving into a hurrier's role.'

Maggie and William glanced at each another in surprise.

'The salary he is to receive is a pound more a fortnight than the other hurriers earn,' added Briar. 'When I questioned Drummond, assuming it was an error, he informed me Mister Owen was doing a second job for him privately, and I was to leave the extra off the books.'

The three of them glanced at each other, all musing silently about this unexpected turn of events and what Drummond's 'private job' might be.

Sinking back in her seat, Maggie crossed her arms at her breast. A strange sense of hollowness formed in her chest. Matthew had promoted Owen only hours after she had described his beastly nature.

'It could be something entirely above board,' Briar continued. 'Owen might be trimming Drummond's hedges, for all we know ... although I doubt it, because Drummond asked Reggie Owen to escort the inspector back into town. The poor blighter didn't look overly pleased by Drummond's hospitality.'

William raised an eyebrow.

'I'll keep my eye on both of them. It's no use worrying until we know more, is it? And to that end ...' Briar lifted the lid from the hatbox.

Maggie cleared the table, and her friend tipped the contents of the decorative hatbox onto it. The box was large enough to fit a top hat, so a huge amount of rubbish spilled out of it across the table's surface – mostly scrunched up documents and papers. *How ingenious she is*, Maggie thought. After only a few weeks, Briar had become renowned in Durham as 'the lass with the hats'; nothing would seem amiss if someone were to notice Briar walking down the High Street carrying a hatbox. *No one would suspect she had stolen the contents of the colliery's wastepaper bins ...*

William took a seat at the table. Systematically, the three began flattening each piece of paper and scouring it for a clue, a hint that might expose Drummond as the liar they suspected him to be. If she hadn't learnt about Reggie's sudden promotion, Maggie would have felt extremely guilty fossicking through Matthew's rubbish. Now she realised her view of the man had been perhaps a shade rosier than warranted. Her doubts about him were swelling by the minute.

'Scrutinising a person's rubbish is the surest means of discovering as much as possible about them,' Briar said as she examined a train ticket particularly closely. 'I couldn't tell you the amount of dross I've had to stick my nose in over the years.'

Maggie envisaged her parent's maid Beatrice setting the bins in the back lane of Chester Square, as she did every Monday evening. What had Briar found in the refuse of number 12? Had Briar crept from the shadows, cloaked in black, to comb through the household's detritus? Maggie's mouth curled into a smile. Then she glanced at Briar. Briar winked as though she could read the thoughts flitting like sparks around Maggie's mind.

After an hour of painstakingly sifting through Drummond's wastepaper, William sat back, disappointed.

'There's nowt. There's nothing here to indicate that Drummond is anything but aboveboard. Am I looking for something I'm never going to find? Am I so desperate to lay blame for the collapse last year that I'm willing to harass and persecute an innocent man?'

Maggie placed her hand on William's thigh. She wondered if she should tell him about Matthew promoting Reggie contrary to her counsel. *It would reassure him his suspicions are not entirely skewed* ... However, before she could say anything, Briar answered William's question.

'Oh, Drummond isn't innocent. I'd stake my favourite Gainsborough on that,' she said, making Maggie chuckle. 'Besides, he wouldn't be the first person to cover his tracks well, especially if he's in the habit of doing so.' She drummed her fingers on the table, thinking. 'There are clues everywhere, I am sure of it. We just need to find them.'

They sat in silence for a few moments, considering the

location of the elusive clues Briar referred to. Then she spoke again.

'His rubbish is clean. His ledgers are clean as well. They're so spotless they make me suspicious.'

'How so?' Maggie asked.

'A company's ledgers are always peppered with errors of the unintentional kind. Minor mistakes in the addition or subtraction of figures are usual. I have scoured Drummond's books a hundred times and I haven't noted a single error.'

'Do you think he might keep a second set of ledgers?' William asked, eyes lit by Briar's suspicions. 'Dirty ones?'

Briar nodded as she gravely scanned the piles of paper.

'I'd bet my eating money on it. All clever businessmen, even the crooked ones, must keep an eye on their finances. Drummond could be skimming off the top to line his own pockets. He could be paying his workers less than the union agreement, so keen they all were to get back to work.' She paused for a moment, contemplating the possibilities. 'Why, Lloyds hired me once to investigate a broker of theirs. The cheeky blighter had raised all his client's premiums by at least fifty quid. Needless to say, Lloyds saw nothing of the extra profits and the broker's ledgers were spotless. It took me months to discover the evidence.'

'And how did you?'

'The dirty ledgers were concealed in a safe box attached to the underside of his desk.' Briar sighed and leant back in her chair. 'The only problem is, I have no idea where Drummond might be hiding his.'

'Just like a man,' Briar commented pointedly when William departed for work. The rubbish was still strewn all over the table.

Maggie raised an eyebrow. 'He has a job to go to.'

'As do I,' Briar said. 'And, if I'm not mistaken, aren't you working at the moment, too? Aren't you writing an extremely important series for the *Manchester Guardian?*'

Maggie smiled at the compliment but was perturbed by Briar's words. William was a considerate partner and Maggie had never heard him utter a single disparaging word about the opposite sex. But it was the way of men, especially Northern men, to leave domestic chores to women, although she had to admit William was an excellent cook when Grace allowed him into the kitchen. Grace was wonderful, but she pandered to William's every whim. After all, it was her household. It would be rude and ungrateful of Maggie to criticise how Grace ran it.

Still, Maggie reassured herself that once she and William lived in their own home, the situation would change. Briar had also reminded her of her own work. She had an article to finish and if she didn't get the current instalment finished by five o'clock, Latey wouldn't receive it by the deadline. The *Guardian* had published the first three of her articles and Latey had posted each one to her, hot off the press. There was no other way she could have seen them; the only newspapers available in Durham were local.

'You go on,' Maggie said. 'I'll clean this up and then get on with my article.'

'Don't be silly. It won't take a tick with the two of us,' Briar said. 'Put on the kettle. We'll have a cup of tea to look forward to once we're done.'

Maggie did so, and then the women began their task, stacking and arranging. Briar suggested they keep the documents in case they might need them in the future.

'Something we've seen among it all might strike a chord one day.'

Once they had finished and they had secured the papers in the hat box again, the pair sat back, admiring their work.

Maggie poured the tea. For the next little while, the women conversed freely on various topics, including their hopes for the future. Briar dreamed of her own millinery – it was the truth, she assured her friend – while Maggie talked of her dashed hopes regarding the girls' school.

'Then accept my offer, Maggie,' Briar pleaded.

'I cannot. You'll need your savings to make your own dreams come true. Besides, it's as I told Matthew ... one should never go into business with friends.'

'It wouldn't be a business transaction. I see it as an investment in the future of womankind,' Briar said. 'Just think on it a little longer, is all I ask.'

Maggie nodded her agreement as they sipped their tea.

'It's Halloween on Sunday,' Briar said finally, as though wishing to draw out the moment.

'So it is,' Maggie replied.

'Are there any Durham traditions?'

'Not really. The odd jack-o'-lantern about the town ...' Maggie thought a moment longer. 'That's about all.'

'Well, I'll show you a Halloween tradition me granny showed me.'

Briar carefully suspended her teaspoon across the rim of her teacup. Then, taking Maggie's spoon and cup, she dripped tea slowly into the balanced spoon. Listening to Briar as she counted each drop as it fell into the recess – 'One ... two ... three' – became somewhat mesmerising for Maggie.

On the count of twelve, the spoon overbalanced and fell into the cup with a polite splash. Startled, Maggie looked at Briar.

'What does it mean?'

'Twelve years until you're wed.'

Maggie frowned, instantly disturbed.

Noticing her unease, Briar attempted to reassure her. 'It's just a silly parlour game of me granny's. She could read tea leaves as well. At least, that's what she claimed.'

Maggie, speechless, nodded.

'I hadn't meant to upset you,' Briar went on, startled by Maggie's unexpected reaction. She rose and walked to her friend, sat down and took her hands. 'It was just a bit of fun, that's all.'

'Yes. Yes, of course ... In all honesty, I don't know why I'm so distressed.'

They looked at one another. The blue of Briar's eyes received Maggie's brown and before the latter could object, Briar leant in and kissed her.

Initially, Maggie was stunned. Too stunned to act. But soon she closed her eyes and found herself unable to resist Briar's advances. The silken softness of Briar's lips and the sweet scent of her breath were enchanting. Their bodies edged closer and Maggie, responding to Briar's passion, surrendered completely to the sensation, her hands finding Briar's slim waist. But when Briar's hand skirted Maggie's breast, she drew back, shocked from her rapture.

Breathing hard, Maggie was instantly ashamed. Not at that fact she had kissed Briar, but because she had betrayed William. She blushed, sensing the warmth spread from her chest to her cheeks. She could not understand what had led her to respond to Briar's advances.

'Don't be embarrassed, Maggie,' Briar said, taking her hand. 'It's entirely natural.'

'It's not that.' She disentangled herself from Briar, and walked to the window, flustered and confused. She fixed her hair as she tried to find the right words to say. 'You're my friend, Briar, and I have so valued spending time with you. But my feelings for you are ...'

Before she could fully articulate the scramble of her

emotions, Briar rose and walked to her. She flattened the lace at Maggie's collar, her hands coming to rest lightly on her shoulders.

'I have a lovely town house on Calvert Avenue in Shoreditch. There's a room at the back overlooking the garden. It would make the perfect salon for you. Sunlit and warm, I have imagined you writing there many times, ink smudges on your cheek and your hair worked loose from your exertions.' She gently twisted a tendril of Maggie's hair that had escaped a pin.

Maggie was stunned. *She sees me as a kept woman?*

'But you wouldn't need to write for a newspaper. You could write fiction. You are perfect for that kind of work. I can see it now: a novel about female emancipation would be right up your alley.' She paused and smiled.

How have I been so oblivious? Maggie wondered, her heart sinking.

'I have a maid, you know, just one, but Clara is all that I need. You could live in the manner to which you've grown accustomed ... Hot running water, indoor plumbing, a footman. You aren't the kind of woman to live in a small way ...'

As Briar continued to wax lyrical about their future together, it all became clear. The picnic, Briar's pointed comments about William, the inadvertent caresses and her offer to invest in the school. If Briar had been a man, Maggie would have stoppered the overtures weeks ago.

'... once we find evidence Drummond is the tyrant we suspect he is, we can travel to London together and—'

'Please, stop, Briar,' Maggie interrupted, breaking away. 'To live with you in London ... It's impossible. I love William. I do. My home is here now.'

Maggie needed Briar to believe her.

'Briar, my life is with William wherever he is, be it big or small.'

Briar turned pale, but her eyes flashed. She was angry and rightly so. Maggie knew that kiss should never have happened.

'Why did you kiss me then?'

Maggie wasn't certain. William satisfied her in every way; he was a dedicated partner and a devoted lover. They were friends as well. They shared every thought and feeling. But then there were their fears about the future ... they never shared their fears. Skirted, touched upon and hinted at, but never shared.

'I am so sorry,' Maggie said. 'If I have led you to believe ...'

Briar sat, almost collapsed into, a chair and buried her head in her hands.

As a friend, Maggie wanted to comfort her, stroke her strawberry hair and offer her solace. Instead, she kept her distance and watched the woman who had become her dearest friend in recent weeks suffer her heartbreak alone.

After a few minutes of excruciating silence, Briar raised her face to Maggie's. She smiled wanly.

'No, you haven't led me to believe anything, Maggie. I see that now. Your words have made me realise that I've constructed this fantasy because I wanted it to be so. I've wanted it to be so since I first met you in that coffeehouse near St Pancras.'

Maggie hadn't realised Briar's feelings for her had ignited so long ago. She sat also, astonished that she had been so blind to her friend's desires.

Briar shook her head in disbelief. Or perhaps in an attempt to dislodge the idea of a life with Maggie from her mind. Her complexion reddened.

'I pride meself on rooting out the truth during an investigation. However, I can never see me own personal life clearly. It's a failing of mine.'

'Your affections began at our meeting at the coffeehouse?'

Maggie asked gently. All that Briar had done in the past had been undertaken while she'd had feelings for her. Last year, Maggie had considered Briar's actions unscrupulous. Now, they just seemed pitiable.

'Before that, even. I followed you for weeks before I contrived the meeting in the coffeehouse.'

Maggie sighed. Her thoughts wandered to more recent events. 'Was it your feelings for me that led you to offer the funds for my school?'

'Partly,' Briar said. 'But I truly do admire you a great deal and I want to see you succeed.'

Maggie straightened. 'Then I must refuse your generosity.' She loathed to utter the words. Without Briar's finances, she could never open a school.

'Oh, don't be such a ninny, Maggie. My offer still stands. My belief in your venture hasn't changed.'

Briar's demeanour had returned to usual: bright and cheery with a hint of scorn. Although Maggie was certain it was for show, she was pleased her friend was attempting to restore her equilibrium.

'Besides, I've been knocked back before. Although, I must admit, none of the others have stung half as much as this.'

'Friends?' Maggie said, holding out her hand.

'Always.'

CHAPTER 22

MAGGIE KNEW she had to tell William about what had transpired between her and Briar, although the reason it had happened remained elusive. She spent the entire day at war with herself, slicing through the tangle of feelings. She was a conquistador navigating the Amazon.

Finishing the article provided a healthy distraction and Marian's life offered Maggie insight into her own. Although devoted to George Lewes, Marian had experienced complex relationships with a number of women. There was Barbara Leigh Smith, a woman to whom Marian was still exceedingly close. They had shared intimacies ... If not physical, then certainly emotional. And then there was Sara Hennell, sister of Cara Bray. Marian was 'husband' and Sara was 'wife' ... Maggie believed the endearments suggested a relationship that went beyond the bounds of mere friendship. She guessed that with Sara, those emotional connections had spilled over into something more tangible.

How can I ever make William understand the intricacies of female friendship? she thought in frustration.

'We had news from Bristol today,' Maggie said to those

present at the table that night. 'Jack drove this out. It's from Gerald.'

She produced the telegram from her pocket and handed it to Lucy. As she read, a smiled formed on her lips.

'He was always a good brother,' Lucy remarked, folding the telegram.

'William and I will accompany you to the station tomorrow. The Bristol train leaves at half ten.'

'I can't thank you enough for your kindness,' Lucy seemed to address the entire party. 'But especially you, Maggie. Without your presence in Durham, I would never have mustered the courage to leave Reggie. I would never even have considered it a possibility.'

Such an admission was heartening for Maggie to hear. Until that point, it appeared every choice she had made in life had been wrong. Most of Durham had certainly made her believe that was the case.

'You showed me there was a different way,' Lucy finished, squeezing Maggie's hand. The women embraced. Then Lucy promptly ushered her children upstairs. They would need to prepare for their journey tomorrow. Grace soon followed behind them. She had promised to find some clothes for Lucy and the children; they had departed their home with nothing.

A different way, Maggie thought. Perhaps Lucy's words had provided the starting point for a conversation she had been waiting to have with William since his return to the cottage that afternoon.

The two of them sat at the table relishing the peace and time alone in one another's company. Their investigation of Drummond, William's union work and Maggie's writing, not to mention the presence of Lucy and her children in the cottage, had seemed to keep them apart. Maggie inhaled deeply and recalled the early stages of their relationship in

London the year before. They had been in one another's company constantly, their desire all consuming.

'What is it, Maggie?' William asked. 'I can see there's something you want to tell me.'

She smiled. He knew her so well. 'How can you tell?'

'Your poker face is terrible.'

She nodded then took a bolstering breath before speaking.

'Briar kissed me today.'

William didn't react. He was inert, waiting.

'And I kissed her back,' she added, seriously.

He stared at her, confused.

'Passionately.'

William, finally comprehending what she was trying to tell him, rose from the table. Maggie could not discern whether he was angry or upset, disappointed or frustrated. Unlike her own, William's poker face was excellent.

When he finally spoke, his tone was heavy with sadness. 'Do you love her?'

Maggie rose and hurried across the room to him. 'Goodness, no. I love you and I told Briar so.'

'Then why did you kiss her?'

She shrugged. 'I've been struggling with a reason since she departed this morning.'

The couple sat again and Maggie talked through what she suspected were her motivations.

'I am no stranger to ...' she paused until she latched onto the appropriate term. 'The affectionate nature of female friendship.'

William looked at her, astonished.

'You forget, William, that I attended a girls' boarding school. Our need to be close was born from loneliness. We saw our families so little. Many of the girls at the school had come from homes where affection was rarely exhibited and ... Well, no one frowned on this type of intimacy.'

'Are yer saying you're lonely, Maggie?' William asked quietly.

'Briar's visit has shown me that I have been. My life is here with you now, but I must confess to missing London and the company of women such as Briar more than I could ever realise. I am not a homemaker, William. I cannot chat with local women about the quality of Craster's kippers or the most effective cure for croup.'

He smiled.

'And even if I wanted to, they wouldn't let me. Not a soul responded to my notice about a sewing circle. And the incident at the town hall has made me completely untouchable.'

She paused for a moment, readying herself for what she was about to say.

'What makes it even worse is that you are tied to me. My reputation is sullying your own, and I worry ...' She stared at him gravely. 'I worry that I don't suit you. Until Marian arrived and then Briar, I wasn't even aware I was wanting. But since then, I have wondered if perhaps a pretty Durham lass who is more amenable than I might be better for you.'

Her obvious anxiety softened him into understanding. He gripped her arms.

'I don't want a woman who's biddable. I fell in love with you partly because I knew I'd never be able to tame you, and I'd never seek to. I want only you, Maggie.'

Relieved, she melted into his arms. She hadn't realised she had been so tense.

'While your stubbornness and principles can madden me occasionally, I'd have you no other way. Anyhow, after your performance with Briar, I'd say it would more likely be you finding the pretty Durham lass.'

Maggie gazed into his laughing eyes, then she rested her

face against his chest. William could always cheer her. He had a unique perspective of the world.

'What are we to do, then? I don't want yer bussin' every lass you hit it off with.'

'Bussing?' Maggie asked, frowning.

'It just means kissing, nothing fruitier.'

They laughed, and Maggie was flooded with relief.

'But seriously, what are we to do?' William asked. 'I want you to be happy, Maggie.'

Maggie sighed. The problem was that she was no longer certain what would make her truly content.

❧

MAGGIE WAS STILL CONTEMPLATING the question when she went to town two days later on an errand. William had suggested a dinner between the three of them – him, Maggie and Briar. He had his heart set on cooking a topside roast, hang the expense.

He took her by surprise as she was exiting the Hartleys' store.

'Well, well, what do we have 'ere?' Reggie Owen smirked, blocking her path. 'It's the trollop responsible for breaking up me family.'

Maggie's heart pulsed frantically in her throat. She gripped the package from the butcher shop against her chest.

'I believe you managed that all on your own, Mister Owen,' Maggie said. 'Please, step aside.'

'Not until yer hear me out.' He took a step closer.

Maggie did not budge despite her terror, despite her heart beating like a cornered rabbit's. She just hoped Reggie possessed the foresight not to throttle her on the High Street. She certainly had no intention of listening to any excuses for his abuse.

'I've heard about as much from you as I can stomach. Lucy did well to come to me for help.'

The Hartleys walked out onto the street to witness the scene.

'She showed me her injuries, the wounds on her legs. She doubted I would have believed her otherwise. I did the only thing a woman could do in my position.'

Now there were witnesses, and she was confident Reggie would not physically harm her, Maggie let loose in the only way she was able.

'I placed Lucy and her children out of your reach. Even though the law doesn't support her, I will be Lucy's advocate. And if I have my way, Mister Owen, you will never see Lucy or the children again!'

Reggie seemed pained by Maggie's words. 'They're my children, too!'

Passers-by had stopped to witness the confrontation. Proprietors walked out of their stores. Maggie's terror had eased, and she felt a flush of valour and pride, even victory, as she stood toe to toe with Reggie Owen.

Reggie's face showed a mass of different emotions. Anger, confusion, torment and heartbreak. Maggie wondered if Reggie believed his actions were justified. But remembering all that abuse Lucy had recounted to her, she would not relent.

'You relinquished that right the first time you lay your hands on your wife, you brute.' She could see that Reggie was confused. 'No man should treat a woman that way. It is unfortunate that Lucy had a moment of weakness when she was just a girl.' Maggie looked at the man with contempt. 'She has regretted that lapse ever since, I assure you.'

Reggie's fists clenched by his side. His knuckles were white.

'You're a beast, Reggie Owen,' Maggie continued, unable

to cease. 'Plain and simple. And I ask you to steer well clear of me in future.'

She was about to walk away when he gripped her arms. His powerful fingers thrust deep into her flesh. She was instantly enraged.

'Go on, Reggie, strike me,' she hissed. 'It's not a crime to beat your wife, but if you harm a hair on my head, you'll find yourself in Newcastle Gaol.'

Reggie released her, pushing her back. Maggie stumbled but remained standing.

'You'll get what's coming to yer,' he spat. 'You and the likes of the doxy who works for Drummond.'

With that, Maggie and the crowd that had gathered watched as the loathsome man disappeared along the High Street.

Shaken, jubilant and dismayed ... conflicting emotions coursed through Maggie's body like wildfire, but only one question filled her mind.

What on earth does Reggie Owen have against Briar Haines?

CHAPTER 23

THE DINNER WAS SUCCESSFUL, although her encounter in front of the butcher shop was never far from Maggie's thoughts. Briar arrived on time with a gift for each of them, a cravat for William she had made herself and some writing paper for Maggie. In their nervousness, the women made a show of tying the cravat around William's neck. It was forest-green velvet; the fabric brought out the colour of William's eyes, Briar remarked when it was successfully tied in a fashionable Windsor knot. Maggie believed all three of them were slightly anxious.

However, by the end of the evening, William and Briar seemed more content in each other's presence. A profound truth had been revealed that affected them all. Now they had to adapt to each other and build a different sort of relationship. Maggie was relieved she had divulged to William what had occurred between herself and Briar.

When she arrived home from the university, Grace relieved the younger people of the burden of washing and drying the dishes. After a tutorial, her mind would always be buzzing; she assured them that sleep would evade her for some time.

Since Henry's departure, Grace had become devoted to her studies, spending hours at the university. To Maggie it seemed as though Grace was in want of a distraction, a conduit for her energy. She had tried to ascertain if it was heartbreak or hope that was driving Grace, but had not yet come to a conclusion.

As Grace busied herself in the kitchen, Maggie, Briar and William took a stroll, just to the point in the river from where Briar would take the path into town. It was William's suggestion. He wanted Briar to arrive safely to the boarding house but it would be unwise for him to drive her all the way to the High Street, where people might see them and question their acquaintance.

The women complimented William on the dinner again and then the group fell silent for a while. Maggie drew her shawl tighter around her shoulders, and as they walked in a line across the path, the fog of their breath merged, creating an eerie and baleful mist. Several ducks took flight from the bushes and skimmed along the water's surface when they approached. Startled, the threesome stopped and looked around to ensure no one else could see them. While they were now perfectly comfortable in each other's company, they didn't want Matthew Drummond to discover just how friendly they were.

They paused for a while by the river.

'I saw Mister and Missus Cross yesterday,' commented Briar. 'In Wilson's, when I was buying the fabric for William's tie. He was fussin' about his wife like an old mother hen.'

'They are an interesting couple, are they not?' Maggie asked. She gazed at the moon glowing bright in the sky, bright enough for them to see by.

'Interesting,' Briar said. 'That's one way of putting it.'

'He does seem to fawn over her,' William added. 'While I'm in favour of a man worshipping his woman as though she were a goddess,' he doffed his cap in Maggie's direction, 'his behaviour is a wee bit ...'

'Obsequious?' Briar put in.

William nodded.

They walked on for a time. Maggie wasn't certain what to make of the Crosses. There was the age difference, and a certain inequality in their intellect ... but there was something else, as well. While they were comfortable with each other, they did not seem to connect as a husband and wife should.

'It can't be easy being married to a man like that,' Briar continued. 'Although it can't be easy being married to a genius like George Eliot, either.'

The trio were silent for a while as they each contemplated the Cross's relationship. When they reached the bridge, they stopped again.

'I had a run-in with Reggie Owen this morning,' Maggie said. She had been torn whether to confide in William and Briar, fearing both would overreact. However, as Reggie had mentioned Briar by name, Maggie believed that in this case, honesty was the best policy.

Alarmed, her companions immediately drew closer to her.

'What happened?' William asked. 'Did he hurt you?'

She related the events on the High Street.

'With so many witnesses, he couldn't have harmed me, but ...'

'But what?' they asked in unison.

'He seemed peeved by you, Briar.'

Briar raised her eyebrows. 'My offence?'

'Nothing specific.'

Briar waved away the threat like it was a pesky fly. 'Because his wife has left him, he blames all females when he should be sick with remorse. That poor woman ...' She shook her head in disgust.

'Briar,' William said, approaching her with a new serious-ness in his eyes. 'Reggie Owen could snap you in two. Please be careful.'

Briar nodded solemnly, taking in William's warning. They were about to part when Briar remembered something.

'I believe I have an idea where Drummond has hidden the second set of books.'

William and Maggie looked at her expectantly.

'But the less you two know, the better,' she said with a wink. 'Let's just say I knew something was amiss the minute I walked into his office.'

'I'm aware you have forged a connection with Matthew, but do nothing foolish,' Maggie counselled, taking Briar's hand. 'We're yet to determine of what he is capable.'

William placed his hand on the small of Maggie's back. 'If he's not averse to putting the lives of 300 men at risk, I don't think he'd balk at causing a woman harm.'

Maggie nodded sadly. She knew now that William's opinion of the man was more than likely right.

Briar smiled and kissed the cheeks of her protectors, first William and then Maggie.

'You two fret like my old Aunt Mary. I've been in stickier situations than this.'

The three embraced together. They had reached a new understanding. With a last wave, Briar headed off towards her lodgings.

CHAPTER 24

The Manchester Guardian
Wednesday, November 3, 1880

D<small>EAR</small> R<small>EADER</small>,

You will recall in our last correspondence I was telling you of the years I hid away from the world in Richmond. During that time, finally content in love, my blessed union with George blossomed daily. Each hour there would be a new bud opening, another discovery. Of course, we squabbled and grew moody with each other occasionally; George, in his constant state of exuberance, and I, who could succumb so easily to fits of melancholy, were not a textbook match by any means. Yet we complemented each other so perfectly. At Griff House, when I was a girl, we had a scruffy old sheep dog called Rusty and an ill-tempered cat we named Tabby. The pair would often curl up by the hearth together in the evening, content and completely comforted by the other's presence. That was George and me. Our life was a blissful succession of walks and writing, playing music and reading.

However, while I was ecstatic to have George by my side, I would often grow frustrated by the limitations of my small world in Richmond Park and Kew Gardens.

Even though *Scenes of Clerical Life* had not been a resounding success with readers, George was determined I continue to write fiction. His encouragement, combined with the pressure of our dire financial predicament and my siblings' ostracism, led me to hit upon an idea for a novel. *Scenes of Clerical Life*, while a full-length work of fiction, was merely three novellas joined, as George enjoyed pointing out. He called me a coward for not committing to a meaty tome, a fleshy novel of substance and ideas. He would constantly remind me that readers longed to immerse themselves in a sustained world which a writer such as myself could bring to life.

George was correct, as always.

I had been holding back with *Scenes*. It was an experiment for me; I wanted to see if I could write fiction in my style. That is, I wanted to paint a realistic portrait of women's lives. Even though I concealed my gender to the world, I wanted to prove a female novelist could combine the feminine virtues of sympathy and tolerance with the gifts of my favourite male authors: humour, observation and passion.

Yet before I touched pen to paper on my second novel, my new story haunted me a great deal. I knew it would be a country story; the low moan of cattle and the scent of hay followed me wherever I went. Besides, it was the world with which I was most familiar. As you know, dear Reader, I spent countless hours as a child with my father in his cart, travelling the estate that surrounded us. Those experiences blazed images of country life into my memory. Once I took my time shaping the story in my mind, I set about writing it without delay.

By that stage, I had learnt that my imagination was my best friend and I was able to give it its head at last. Rather than fearing the world of my imagination, I allowed it to besiege me. I finally destroyed the fortress I had erected when I was a girl. I began *Adam Bede* in October 1857 with a scene of a young woman preaching outside to country folk. Perhaps you recall which of my relatives inspired this beginning?

At the time I was writing my new work, the identity of the author of *Scenes* was still a source of great debate. Critics who reviewed the novel favourably persisted in trying to discover the 'real' George Eliot. People from all over the United Kingdom claimed to be me – can you imagine? While I longed to tell those who were closest to me (my dear friend Barbara Leigh Smith, for one) George advised the contrary. He hoped to secure a lucrative deal from Blackwood's for my new novel. He was sure that if John Blackwood was aware a woman was the author, he would strike *Adam Bede* from his list immediately. The conventional old Scot was always wary of bold tales, but one written by a woman ... and if that woman was the scandalous Marian Evans! Who knew what misfortune he may be inviting?

'JUST BEFORE CHRISTMAS, George sent Blackwood what I had written. It was only a few chapters, but they were powerful,' Marian said. 'In fact, Blackwood thought them too powerful to be serialised in his magazine. I can still recall the words he used in his response to George. He wrote that "the nature of the tragedy was too sexual to be serialised".' Marian laughed quietly. 'Writing those words would have been tortuous for him. John was a Puritan at heart.'

Maggie smiled. They were sitting in the Cross's sitting room as Marian had preferred to stay in for the interview. It was an overcast day and Julia had lit a fire, yet the room kept a chill. Durham Castle cast an imposing gloom over the scene. This time, Maggie had worn a frock coat to the interview; Mister and Missus Cross were always so concerned with her comfort. She knew if she arrived in her usual outing jacket, the couple would fuss and worry until she was cocooned in layers of Marian's wraps and shawls.

Maggie recalled her own reading of *Adam Bede*. The author's description of Dinah's sexual awakening still stirred her whenever she recalled the lines, but for a fourteen-year-old at Cheltenham Ladies College, they were positively inflaming. As for the infanticide which occurs in the novel, Maggie could imagine any publisher being shocked by it, let alone someone like Blackwood. Such a plotline coming from the pen of a man would have been challenging, let alone from a woman's. She flicked back through her notes.

'You based the character of Dinah on your Aunt Elizabeth, is that correct?' Maggie asked.

'Yes and no,' Marian answered. 'Aunt Elizabeth, in her role as lay preacher, had occasionally offered console to the inmates of a women's gaol near Nuneaton. She once told me a story about a young girl who was imprisoned for murdering her baby.'

'Like Hetty Sorrel,' Maggie said, referring to another character from the novel.

Marian nodded. 'Aunt Elizabeth told me the poor girl abandoned the infant in the woods. It was born out of wedlock, you see. An hour later, filled with sorrow, guilt and remorse, she had returned to take her baby home. But it was too late. The child was already dead.'

Maggie had not known the writer had drawn the storyline from a real woman's experience. *But then*, she thought, *realism has always been Marian's goal with her fiction.*

'I suppose it was a combination of Aunt Elizabeth and her experiences which inspired much of the novel,' continued Marian. 'And although it was not intentional, I can now recognise my father so clearly in Adam. Like my father had been, Adam is a carpenter, strong and industrious. He believes hard work is a means of carrying out God's work. While he is not educated, he is not ignorant either.'

Maggie nodded. While Marian had fled country life, a life which had not offered her enough scope for her passions, it was the world to which she returned in her fiction.

'You began writing *Adam Bede* in October 1857 and Blackwood did not publish it until February 1859. Forgive my ignorance, but that seems such a long time, considering ...' She looked at her notes, '"The low moan of cows and the scent of hay" followed you everywhere.'

'It was! It was an extremely long time considering how enraptured I was by my premise. First, I didn't have the impetus of a monthly deadline. *Scenes* was written in serial form and while it had been a foray into my imagination, I remained guarded.'

Maggie lifted her eyes from her notes.

'You see, writing in short bursts was akin to ... dipping my toes into the waters of my imagination, so to speak.'

Maggie nodded, understanding.

'However, Blackwood planned to publish *Adam Bede* as a novel. It was imperative that I allow my imagination free rein. While I had Adam, Hetty and especially Dinah sketched in my mind, and the plot in place, the words were very slow in coming.'

Marian paused. She looked for a moment beyond Maggie to the stone walls of the castle.

'I believe I knew the impact *Adam Bede* would have. Hetty's sexual undoing, the murder of her child and Adam's tirades about sexual double standards could have been my undoing as an author.'

'What eventually spurred you into completing the novel?' Maggie asked.

'We travelled to Switzerland, then on to Germany. George's sons were in school at Hofwyl, in Berne. Although we could ill afford to have them there, George insisted on removing them from the chaos of Bedford Place. It was my first meeting with them and I proved to be a terrible step-mother. I had no clue how to act around children, especially boys. And they were such dear lads. But I was awkward and, well ... Children have a knack of throwing into stark relief one's own shortcomings.

'George was a natural with children – all children, not just his own. He seemed to be able to speak to them on their level ...' Marian sighed. 'Yet, I avoided them as much as possible. While George and the boys went hiking or camping, when they visited museums, I remained in our room and wrote.'

'Did his sons object to you?'

'Not in the slightest. Although I was the cause of their father leaving the family home, they accepted me wholeheart-edly, lovingly. They even called me "Mutter". You must remember, they had been raised in an entirely unconventional household, so took no issue with me and George being together. But I was dreadfully self-conscious around them, and I could never figure out why. They were George's sons, after all, and I could recognise a different aspect of his personality or appearance in each of them. Those boys were part of him and my heart burst with love for them, but I was too terrified to show it. Eventually, when the boys became adults, I was able to forge a deeper relationship with them.'

Maggie nodded, interested that such a passionate woman was incapable of showing any motherly affection to her step-sons. Although Maggie had not spent a great deal of time around children, she was certainly not averse to them. She had enjoyed being in the company of Lucy's three. Her boys were so full of energy and excitement, Maggie could amuse them with the simplest rhyme or game. And she had to admit that braiding little Geraldine's golden hair with emerald ribbons had been an extremely agreeable chore.

'Was it merely that you found yourself at a loose end that *Adam Bede* progressed?'

'Oh, my dear, no!' Marian gasped. 'Being in Switzerland and Germany inspired me. For one thing, George was working on a book which was later published as "*The Physiology of Common Life*". His findings and our subsequent discussions of the human body – of its veins and muscles, tissue and organs were so incredibly satisfying. Discovering vocabulary such as "thoracic", "cerebellum" and "pectoralis" was wonderful. I longed to employ words of similar force in my manuscript. Besides, I witnessed how much joy writing offered George; he wrote with such effervescence, always allowing his imagination and his creativity to possess him entirely. I wanted to taste that as well.

'After Switzerland, we travelled to Munich and then Dresden. These were places we were accepted. George and I could appear in public as a couple without a hint of scandal. It was invigorating to attend soirees and museums on the arm of my husband. It was such an intensely joyous sensation to be myself.'

'It wasn't only your imagination then,' Maggie put in. 'You dropped other defences as well among people who were more open-minded than the English.'

'Indeed. I was also inspired by the galleries I visited daily, paying particular attention to the works of the Dutch realist painters. I hoped I had imbedded *Scenes* with a similar type of realism to what I saw in those magnificent paintings. But I aimed to go so much further with *Adam Bede*.'

'Did you hope to eradicate the idealistic view of women in your novels?'

She shook her head. 'There was room for the Madonna among my pages, but I longed to balance *Adam Bede* with a more practical view of womanhood – an old woman peeling carrots, or a young woman forced into an impossible situation by an unwanted pregnancy. Male writers cannot capture with honesty the mundanities and the hardships of a woman's existence.'

Maggie nodded. 'It was exactly that which I hoped to reveal in the Clairmont series. Those poor sisters struggled so in the face of insensitive and selfish males. People read Mary Shelley's works and all they see is the renowned writer. They never see the woman. And as for Claire and Fanny—'

'Until your articles, they had been completely forgotten by society,' Marian said. 'It is why I chose you, Maggie. I read in your articles what I hoped to imbue in my own novels.'

Maggie felt her cheeks flush. While she was aware the Clairmont series was good work, whenever she had reflected upon it, she most often viewed the articles as a source of her greatest downfall. Hearing Marian's praise now, her perspective shifted, like a scene in a diorama. Maggie was instantly proud of the series, immensely so. She could barely concentrate on her next question. She glanced down at her notes.

'How was your identity discovered?' she asked eventually.

Marian pursed her lips and snorted. 'Herbert Spencer revealed my secret.'

Maggie raised her eyebrows. 'Why? Out of malice?'

Marian shrugged. 'Malice, jealousy and ignorance. He could never fathom my experience as a female writer.'

Mister Cross entered before Maggie could ask her next question. She smiled and closed her notebook. She observed him as he plumped the cushions behind his wife's back and examined the fire. He stood there for some time, silently debating whether he should add another piece of wood.

'I can keep the fire ablaze, Mister Cross,' Maggie said when she understood his dilemma. 'In fact, I am rather handy at maintaining a healthy blaze. Northerners never seem to feel the cold, and I have taken to lighting my own fire to keep frostbite at bay.'

Maggie's assertion failed to amuse Mister Cross. Moreover, he did not seem convinced of Maggie's talents. He went about positioning the wood, then poking among the ashes. The gentleman had been well behaved until that point. She wondered what words had passed between husband and wife before Maggie had arrived.

At a look from Marian, John nodded to Maggie and left the room.

'Please excuse him, Maggie. John dotes on me so. He does his best to look after me.' Marian frowned. 'He doted on his mother, too.'

'When did Mister Cross's mother die?'

'Anna passed only ten days after George. It nearly destroyed Johnny.'

Her subject's mood altered. Maggie sensed the new, sombre atmosphere create a vacuum in the space between them. She watched Marian stare into the hearth mournfully. To Maggie's dismay, the interview ended there.

AFTER MAGGIE'S DEPARTURE, a hole remained in the sitting room; Marian always found Maggie's spirit so uplifting. John had shown her to the door, and she had discerned echoes of their casual chat before Maggie bid a cheerful adieu.

Marian's back ached so profusely she did not believe she could stand. When her husband entered the room, he came to her and knelt beside the armchair, placing his hand gently on her arm.

'Can I do anything for you, *mia Madonna*?'

'Please bring my slope, John. There is a correspondence I must see to.' It was a lie. In her agony, she could not generate another plausible excuse for remaining in her chair.

Her husband scurried hastily up the stairs and to the bedroom. Within a minute, he had reappeared with her writing slope. He placed it on her lap. The weight of it against her thighs sent ripples of pain into her kidneys.

'Thank you, dear.'

He hovered for a moment, then moved to depart.

'Close the door, please,' she said.

A moment later, she heard the latch click.

The pain traversed the backs of her thighs, then reached all the way into her heels. With the writing slope on her lap, she closed her eyes, waiting for the sensation to subside.

Holly Lodge
Wandsworth

April 22, 1859

Dear Sir,

Although it has been some years since I called you 'Herbert' and you called me 'Marian', I wish to call on our past intimacies now as I write this letter, hoping to melt your glacial heart. I know this is possible because I read your criticism in February of Adam Bede for the Review. You declared yourself 'unusually affected' by the prose. High praise coming from the Ice King.

Did you read William Hepworth Dixon's rebuke of me in the Athenaeum? He declared Adam Bede a tale 'such as a clever woman with an unschooled moral nature might have written, a rather strong-minded lady, blessed with an abundance of showy sentiment and a profusion of pious words'. It was as though he had guessed at my identity before anyone else. He might well have written 'Marian Evans is the author of Adam Bede'.

George and I can only conclude it was you who revealed my secret to John Chapman and others. John Chapman can be a persuasive man, as I well know, and he is a shameless gossip. Dixon and he are such chums. It was Chapman who visited us and divulged that he knew the truth.

I expected you to keep my secret for longer than the six nights that had passed since you dined with us at Holly Lodge. Now I realise why you wondered aloud how George and I could afford such a charming residence in Wandsworth. It was your relentless probing, so direct, that caused us to admit the truth.

You vowed to me, with hand on heart, that you would never share the knowledge ... yet you broke that vow within days of making it.

How I wish we had not revealed to you my identity as George Eliot!

Fortunately, your ethical failure has come too late. The success of the novel and the funds George secured for its sale to Blackwood's has set us up quite nicely. Readers and reviewers seem willing to overlook my moral failings and gender when great writing is at stake. Why, even the Queen has praised my words! And I believe the term 'genius' has been mentioned more than once in regard to my talent.

Therefore, I take great pleasure in telling you that your betrayal has failed to wound my status and reputation. My skills as an artist, the novel's moral voice and the emotions it has generated among readers means Adam Bede has lifted me above the status of outcast.

Indeed, I am now untouchable.

Given this, I will not allow myself to ponder the motivations for your maleficence. Jealousy, mean spiritedness or sheer bloody-mindedness – I will never know, and I refuse to allow myself the distraction of caring. We were once the closest of companions, but your actions have formed a chasm between us that will never be bridged.

My writing desk awaits. A new novel awaits. Shall I await an apology?

Yours expectantly,
Marian Lewes

CHAPTER 25

W‍HEN M‍AGGIE DEPARTED Marian's house, she headed towards the High Street. She had not told William what she intended to do because he would most certainly have attempted to stop her.

'It's only been three days, lass,' William had counselled that morning. 'Briar is biding her time. She'll contact us when the coast is clear, when Drummond isn't likely to be alerted to our connection.'

Maggie had brooded over her tea. It wasn't Matthew she was concerned about. Reggie Owen's words in the High Street tormented her and Briar's comment about Reggie despising all women ... The thought he might take out his frustrations on Briar was maddening her. Yet Maggie could not fathom why he would target her friend.

'But she has never been out of touch for this long,' Maggie said, lifting her face to William. 'The last time we saw her, she was planning something. What if she ...' Maggie stopped, unable to complete the sentence.

William kissed her forehead. 'I'll ask around on my way home this evening. Aareet?'

Maggie nodded, but she wasn't satisfied. If William waited until the evening it was another day – an entire day – that Briar would be missing.

Missing.

Realising she was allowing her imagination to run away from her, Maggie attempted to rein in her thoughts and fill her mind with more reasonable possibilities.

Briar was called back to London urgently.

She's come down with a terrible case of the flu.

She's too busy keeping an eye on Drummond.

Yet none of them seemed reasonable. Even if Briar hadn't wanted to make contact in person, she would have found a means of relaying a message. She would have slipped a note to Jack or Beth. Briar was the most resourceful person she knew. Maggie bit her lip.

When she reached town, Maggie went straight to the blacksmith's yard. She discovered Jack standing at the forge staring into the flames pensively. He was holding a piece of iron in the heat. His large, spindly hand gripped a pair of heavy tongs. He didn't turn as she approached, and Maggie wondered what had captured his thoughts. When he noticed her, he paused his work and smiled.

'Mags! What brings you here?' he said merrily. 'I don't see many lasses as pretty as you venturing into a smithy's yard. Except for Beth, of course.'

Maggie was in no mood for chitchat. 'I'm looking for Briar. Have you seen her?'

Jack drew the tongs from the flames and examined the piece of iron. It was glowing red. He nodded, satisfied.

'Not since ... let me think ...' Jack stared into the sky for a moment, then closed his eyes tight. 'She was on her way to the pit. It was the morning after you three had dinner together.'

Jack had known about the dinner as Maggie had stopped

by to borrow a large boiling pot. Married to an ironmonger meant Beth had saucepans for every occasion.

'I was walking out of the store and she waved to me from the across the road.'

'How did she seem?'

'Cheeky, as usual. "Little Jack Horner", she called.' Jack smiled. 'She's a brass-necked wee lass, isn't she?'

'Yes, she is,' Maggie murmured, thinking. 'But you didn't notice her in the evening coming home from the pit?'

Jack shook his head. 'But I had nowt collections that day, from memory. I spent the entire day here, at the forge.' Jack cocked his head, noticing her concern. 'You seem fashed.'

Maggie was fashed. And growing more so by the instant.

After making a few more enquiries around town that revealed nothing, Maggie arrived at Briar's boarding house. The owner, Missus Chandler, was standing at the reception desk, as though she were expecting someone. Maggie supposed the landlady of a boarding house was always in a state of anticipation. After several irritating pleasantries, Maggie got to the point.

'I was wondering if Briar Haines is in her room. I have a letter for her.' Maggie rummaged in her bag to convince the landlady of her sincerity. 'Mister Darlington asked me to drop it off.'

'I'm afraid you can't, Miss Almond. Miss Haines moved out on Tuesday,' she checked the ledger that lay open before her on the counter. 'Yes, Tuesday evening. She came in from work at about half five, went straight to her room and had departed before six with all of her belongings.'

Maggie was stunned. She gathered herself as best as she could. 'Do you know what hastened such an unexpected departure?'

Missus Chandler shook her head. 'She didn't say, but a cart was waiting for her outside.'

'Did you see who was waiting for her?'

'Na. I didn't see who was at the reins. It was dark, yer know.'

Maggie felt her anxiety mounting. 'Would you mind if I saw her room? If it's unoccupied, of course.'

Missus Chandler removed a key from a set of hooks behind her and led the way up a wide staircase. She had inherited the premises and the business from her husband. It was a grand residence. Students from London who found the college residences not sophisticated enough for their tastes were who typically rented the rooms. The worn tread on the stairs indicated the establishment's popularity with heavy-footed youths.

When they had reached the top of the second storey, the women heard the shopkeeper's bell ring.

'Would you mind, lass?' Missus Chandler offered Maggie the key. 'Hers was the room at the end. Number seven. I haven't had time to touch it yet, so excuse any mess that might be left.'

Maggie took the key and walked to the room. She was certain Briar had departed just as Missus Chandler had described, yet she was anxious about what she might find when she opened door.

❧

Missus Chandler was at the counter with a guest when Maggie returned to the lobby. She placed the key on the dark timber. Maggie thanked the woman for her time as she hurried from the premises. Once outside, she ventured to the back of the boarding house where a hat box lay on the ground waiting for her. She had dropped it from the window moments before.

Now that she was alone, she drew Briar's portfolio from

beneath her frock coat. Maggie had found it, along with the hatbox, beneath the bed in Briar's otherwise empty room. She was sure Briar had meant her to find the items.

'Lass!' William called from across the street when Maggie emerged from the laneway. 'What are you up to there?'

Maggie clutched at the box and the portfolio, breathless and perturbed. She didn't know what Briar meant by leaving those particular possessions behind, but she was positive it wasn't good.

'Yer as white as a bean.'

'Briar has gone.'

William frowned, gazing up and down the High Street, concerned.

Maggie related all she had discovered during the afternoon. 'I know Briar left these for a reason,' Maggie said, holding aloft the hat box and portfolio, 'but I don't want to examine them here, for all of Durham to see. Let's go back to the cottage.'

<hr />

WILLIAM AND MAGGIE scoured the items as soon as they arrived home. William took the portfolio and began sifting through Briar's collection of sketches and watercolours. He stopped when he came to a striking watercolour. It was of a country idyll; the Wear and Prebends Bridge made up the background. At the centre of the painting was Maggie, lying on her side on the grass, gazing at a pair of magpies beside her. She was wearing a serene expression on her face, almost drowsy, as her chestnut hair fell in waves over her shoulder, reaching for the grass beneath. The skin of her bare arms was creamy and her blouse sat open at the collar, revealing the soft curve of her bosom.

William stared at it for some time. 'She's in love with you.'

Maggie walked to his side of the table and stared at the image. Briar had finished the pencil sketch she had drawn by the river on the day of their picnic, but she had done so in a seraphic, almost erotic, style.

Is that the way she sees me? Maggie wondered, sadly. *As a nymph?*

'It's bonny,' William murmured, swallowing. 'Beautiful.'

'Indeed.' Maggie said, feeling a huge hole form in her belly. If Briar departed willingly, she would never have left the painting behind.

Maggie trembled as she lifted the lid from the hatbox. In it, she found a small sky-blue side toque. It had a narrow brim and a butter-coloured ribbon wrapped around the crown that was secured with a cameo. Maggie looked closer at the piece. It was of a mythological figure, a woman with a laurel wreath encircling her head. Maggie could not determine the goddess the object depicted.

She put the hat down and examined the hatbox. Briar had scrawled something on the inside of the lid.

'Sent packing. 10 pm train from N.,' she read to William.

Maggie swallowed. Briar had clearly been in a rush, or she had been rushed by someone. Briar's words returned to her.

There are clues everywhere. We just need to find them.

Looking more closely at the hatbox, she felt around the interior, running her fingertips over the base. Securing her fingernails beneath the edge, she lifted it, discovering the six piles of bank notes it covered. Maggie knew in an instant it was the money for the girls' school. Even when facing danger, Briar had not forgotten her promise.

Maggie's heart sank like a stone.

LATER THAT EVENING, Grace mused over the objects Maggie had found in Briar's deserted room as keenly as Maggie and William had done. She stared at the cameo for an age, then at the sketches in Briar's portfolio, although Maggie had thought it prudent to remove the painting of Maggie-upon-Wear.

'It could mean she intends to return,' Grace conjectured. 'Or ...'

'She suspected she was about to come to harm,' Maggie put in quickly. 'And left these as messages.'

'If that's the case,' William said. 'What do they mean?'

Maggie shook her head. 'I don't know. Apart from what she wrote in the hatbox, I can't connect them to anyone. Not Matthew, at least. Or Reggie, for that matter.'

Grace rose and flattened her skirt. 'Perhaps they express a message of a more personal kind.' She cleared her throat, then went up to bed.

WILLIAM WOKE and glanced at the clock on the bedside table. Two o'clock. A lamp burned softly in the room. He sat up in the bed, groggy with sleep. Maggie was standing in front of the mirror in her nightdress. She was wearing the hat Briar had left behind. It suited her perfectly. The jauntiness of the style matched her personality. Even dressed in her nightclothes, Maggie looked bonny wearing that hat.

'Sky blue is my favourite colour,' Maggie said quietly. 'I told Briar on the day we picnicked by the river. It was the same day she began that picture.' She looked to her right. The artwork lay over the back of a chair.

'What could have happened to her, William?'

William sighed and caught her eye in the mirror. 'I don't know, lass. But we'll do everything we can to find out.'

Maggie stared at herself in the half light. Were the items a goodbye of sorts? If so, then Briar's fate grew even more bleak. Attempting to close off the place in her mind that housed her darkest fears, Maggie shivered and removed the hat. Closing the lamp, she crawled back into bed and pressed herself tight against William's side, not allowing her thoughts to travel to the dark places of her imagination.

MAGGIE ROSE EARLY the following morning, slipping from the bed like a drop of quicksilver. She wanted answers to the questions that had swarmed in her mind like bees for most of the night. She felt certain the only way she could find them was to talk to Matthew Drummond.

When she arrived in South Bailey, he was just leaving for the colliery. On seeing her, he removed his bowler hat.

'The sun has barely risen, Maggie!' he cried merrily. 'I hope you're not hoping for a rematch now. I'm late for the pit.'

'No, it is far too early for chess,' Maggie responded. 'I was wondering about your assistant, Miss Haines. I can't seem to locate her.'

Matthew frowned. 'I didn't realise you were friends.'

'Not quite. She was interested in the girls' school and had asked me to call on her yesterday at her boarding house for tea to discuss it. Yet Missus Chandler informed me when I arrived that Miss Haines had departed Durham on Tuesday evening. It seems odd that she made a date with me, then hastened from the county ... You know how challenging it is for newcomers to make friends, I had hoped Miss Haines and I—'

'Miss Haines would not be worthy of your friendship,

Maggie,' Matthew said, an uncharacteristic hint of bitterness in his tone.

'How so?'

'I caught her attempting to ... Well, I'm not really sure what she was doing. Stealing or prying? I'm uncertain. People have attempted to blackmail my family before, you see. She was rummaging through the office, searching for something. She refused to say what. I had no choice but to dismiss her. I am certain that is why she chose to leave. Her failure to confide in you regarding her hasty departure is proof enough of her character.'

Maggie's heart fell into a series of palpitating rhythms and her mouth grew dry. She stared into his pale blue eyes. It wasn't unthinkable that he had caught Briar searching for the ledgers ...

But then why would Briar have left without telling me?

'I am doubly disappointed, Maggie,' he said eventually.

She held her breath.

'Our relationship had blossomed into something greater than employer and employee. I believed her feelings were genuine ... It was early days, but I had hope of our affection growing.'

Maggie looked at his expression. It revealed nothing but sorrow and bewilderment. She touched his arm.

'I am sorry,' she said. 'Those first moments when an affection is newly formed are quite wonderful. But perhaps it is fortunate you had not yet formed a more lasting attachment.'

Matthew nodded, and the pair stood in silence for a moment. Despite her concern for Briar, something in his countenance – the disappointment of a lost opportunity, perhaps – gave Maggie a strong compulsion to comfort the man.

'Well, Matthew, I will allow you leave to get on with your

busy day. I suppose it remains just you and I as the founding members of the Durham Lost Souls Society.'

Matthew smiled warmly. 'Given recent circumstances, I would have it no other way, Maggie,' he said, before donning his hat and bidding her farewell.

CHAPTER 26

WILLIAM HAD a late start that morning. Maggie was upset, still concerned at Briar's whereabouts. They spent longer than they should over breakfast developing a series of realistic theories regarding where she might be. However, the more they talked, the more they kept returning to the worrying idea that Briar had run foul of Reggie Owen.

'If that's the case,' Maggie said, 'then I'm entirely at fault.'

The piteous expression in her brown eyes stabbed at William's heart.

They eventually resolved to send a telegram to Raymond Turner in London asking him to call at Briar's home on Calvert Avenue in Shoreditch. There was a chance she had returned to London, and they were both worrying needlessly. Although Briar had not revealed the street number of her dwelling, Maggie was certain Raymond was resourceful enough to find her residence.

They would also send a telegram to Mister Latey asking whether he could use the resources of the *Manchester Guardian* to unearth any further information about Matthew Drummond. William sensed Maggie still wanted to believe the man was aboveboard, but her journalistic instinct, combined with his own doubts, were forcing her to continue Briar's search. Even if Drummond had nothing to do with Briar's disappearance, it was possible the man was hiding something.

The couple walked into town together. When they farewelled, Maggie turned towards the post office. William walked to the office of the Durham Miners' Union. He had decided to speak to Tommy to see if he knew anything about Briar, anything that might ease Maggie's mind.

The union office hadn't changed at all since William had first worked there a decade ago. Playing host to colliers all day and into the evening, dust shadowed the office's floor, windows and curtains. Coal dust. It was a smell very familiar to William; it reminded him of his father.

'Aareet, Tommy?'

William's godfather, poring over a pile of papers, nodded a distracted hello.

'Do you have any idea what happened to Drummond's secretary?' William asked.

Tommy looked up then settled further into the seat behind his desk.

'The lass you mentioned a while back?'

William nodded.

'Na. I've no clue. Why do you ask?'

'She left town a few days ago.'

Tommy shook his head. He seemed dismayed. 'If I know Drummond, he most likely tried it on.'

William raised his eyebrows. 'He's a ladies' man then, is he?'

He recalled Briar's description of their dinner. Despite the kiss, her preferences ruled Drummond out as a potential suitor. He wondered if this could be a case of unrequited love. After all, it had been at the source of some of the greatest tragedies in literature. William shook off the thought. What-ever was happening was stuff of the real world, and he was certain something more nefarious was at play. Besides, Briar was a canny lass. She would realise if Drummond held any genuine affection for her.

'Aye, or so I've heard,' Tommy answered.

'From who?' William asked, observing his godfather's demeanour. He looked tired, fed up, annoyed William was asking questions. It appeared that union business was wearing Tommy down.

He shrugged. 'I canna remember.' He shifted in his seat and moved a document lying on the right side of his desk to the left. 'I'm speakin' to colliers from all over. One of them most likely let something slip.'

William nodded, thinking. 'You know Briar was a friend of Maggie's. It seems a wee bit odd she'd up and leave Durham without even a word to her.'

Tommy shrugged once more. 'Sorry, Willie, but I canna help yer. An old hewer like meself has little to nowt insight into the mind of a young woman such as Briar Haines.' He rose to show his godson the door, hitching his pants and straightening his waistcoat.

'I heard Maggie had a set-to with Reggie Owen on the High Street a few days back.'

William had interviewed enough people in his career to know when a person was changing the subject.

He had heard news of the argument from at least a dozen people. Even Harry had mentioned Maggie's 'bold spirit'. Most people he'd spoken to about it, women and men alike, applauded her actions. William hadn't realised that quite a few people knew about Reggie's treatment of Lucy; yet Maggie was the only person in Durham to defend her and take a stand. William's heart swelled with love and pride for Maggie. It also filled with something else.

Concern.

'She gave as good as she got, though.' Tommy continued. 'In fact, she had Reggie on the back foot.' He paused for a moment before adding gravely. 'She's a brazen, wee lass, Willie. You should watch out for her.'

William left the office with his concerns no less allayed. They nipped at him from all directions like midges. He looked around him, wondering if Maggie was still about. With Tommy's parting words, a feeling of dread took root in his chest. He could not shake the sense Maggie might be in danger. Without proof of foul play and armed only with his instinct, William turned towards the Chief Constable's office to report Briar Haines missing.

❧

MAGGIE WAS WAITING at Prebends Bridge. William saw her when he rounded the bend in the river. He continued to the bridge at a run. Although he hadn't realised it throughout the day, since his meeting with Tommy, he had been concerned for her safety. His godfather's warning words and the hour he'd spent with the police had made him anxious. The constable was a friend, a local lad William knew from school. Andy Stackhouse had completed his training in London. He made no bones about his plans to return to the capital one day as a Scotland Yard detective, but he recognised the need to tally up a few more years of experience before he might realise his dream. Content to do this in Durham, Andy was one of five constables who protected the county.

When she heard his footsteps on the stone, she turned and smiled. They came together. Feeling the need to keep her with him always, he held her tight. When they broke apart, she looked at him strangely, sensing something different in his embrace.

'Has something happened?'

A flock of geese cried as they traversed the river. Their strident sounds echoed across the water.

'Na,' he replied. 'I love you, that's all.'

'I love you, too. Now tell me what's troubling you.'

'You can read me like a book, Maggie Almond,' he said, smiling, then leant his arms on the stone wall and gazed down at the still water below. She waited for him to begin and when he did, he revealed his distressing discussion with Andy Stackhouse at the Chief Constable's Office.

'I told Andy about Briar's hasty exit from Durham and her message written in the hatbox. I also mentioned Briar's friend in the Manchester constabulary. Andy promised to make further inquiries.' He took a deep breath before continuing, unsure what Maggie's reaction would be to his next words.

'Andy thinks that Briar realised she might come to harm. He said her actions on Tuesday suggest she was getting all her ducks in a row ... so to speak.'

Maggie observed the river's course over and around rocks. 'It would explain the money ...'

William watched her face turn pale.

'I dropped into the bank after sending Raymond the telegram. Briar had visited on the morning of our dinner. The teller informed me it wasn't on colliery business.' She gripped the stone wall. 'I think she left those things behind for me. She knew I would find them. It was her way of telling me she loved me ... to say goodbye.' Maggie's eyes filled with tears. 'Heavens! What has become of her, William?'

He took her in his arms but remained silent, unable to voice the unthinkable.

LATER THAT EVENING, as the three residents of the Dodd's cottage went about their various pursuits in the sitting room – William checking the wording of a petition the union wished to send to parliament, Grace busy at her cross-stitch (her mind was too distracted, she said, to attend to her studies) and Maggie completing her latest article for the *Guardian* – there was a knock at the door. Startled, the trio stood at attention. Neither William nor Grace nor Maggie were resting easily following tea, a meal which the three had only nibbled. Maggie could not recall William ever leaving food on his plate. She sensed he was as disturbed as she regarding Briar's whereabouts.

The women followed William through the cottage to the front door. Andy Stackhouse was standing on the other side. Although it was almost ten o'clock, he still wore his uniform. He secured his hat under his arm.

'Aareet,' he said to William, pushing his sandy hair from his forehead. 'Missus Dodd. Miss Almond.'

'Come in now, Andy,' Grace said. 'Can I get you a cup of tea?'

The constable shook his head. 'Na, but thank you, Missus Dodd. I was hoping Willie and Miss Almond might recognise this.' Stackhouse placed a drawstring purse on the table. 'We found it near Swin Bridge.'

Maggie's heart leapt into her throat.

The reticule of violet velvet belonged to Briar.

CHAPTER 27

The Manchester Guardian
Wednesday, November 10, 1880

DEAR READER,

Whether or not I liked it, Herbert Spencer had revealed my identity. He had revealed my secret to the world, and I became renowned and wealthy a woman as any living in England. I had never dreamt of such notoriety. After so many years of scraping by on a pittance, George and I wanted for nothing. But so much better than the financial rewards I received were the critical praises *Adam Bede* garnered.

Shortly after the novel was published in February 1859, John Blackwood revealed he had received correspondence from a carpenter who approved of the realism of the workshop scenes. To me, the commendation of a carpenter was far better than a rapturous review in the *Leader*. Blackwood was never an ebullient gent, but he agreed that the realism with which I imbued *Adam Bede* had surpassed even that of the great Charles Dickens in his works.

Such comparisons thrilled me. Although I truly believed, dear Reader (and still do) that although Dickens was a master of realism, many of his characters drifted into the realm of caricature. My strenuous endeavours to make the novel as true to life as possible had paid off, not only with reviewers, but with the public as well. I achieved everything I had hoped to in writing my first complete novel.

Sales of the book soared! Yet I remained reticent to leave my refuge after such a prolonged period of such public shaming. I was, however, desperate to hear not only further praise of my work but also whether opinion had truly altered regarding my status as persona non grata. I sent George to London weekly to retrieve news. He visited friends and frequented alehouses and coffeehouses, always with an ear to the ground. He assured me reviews were positive and public opinion fell in my favour.

At my request, George had Holly Lodge refurnished and redecorated. New sofas and chairs, as well as wall and floor coverings, were chosen and ordered. He even purchased a grand piano that was to be my very own. Yet our Wandsworth home did not completely content me. I often ask myself why this was so, and I believe the answer has something to do with pride. Holly Lodge was a hiding place and regardless of what improvements George made to the house, it would remain so in my mind.

After five years of concealment, I longed to be out in the world once more; it had been an age since I received visitors and I wanted to learn to do so again. However, my lingering feelings of humiliation and embarrassment prevented me from doing that at Holly Lodge.

Despite my discontent with my immediate surrounds, I began on a third book. Between ourselves, George and I called it 'the mill book'. The idea came to me when, for whatever reason, we were reading about cases of inundation in the Annual Register. Dear Reader, as you might have well guessed, Blackwood's eventually published this book as *The Mill on the Floss*.

As I was picking up steam on 'the mill book', I received a letter from my sister Chrissy. When the postmaster handed me the envelope, I recognised her hand immediately. I stood at the post office counter for an eternity, pondering what it contained. Would it be another rebuke? Had I scandalised my family a second time when it became known that I was George Eliot? After such a lengthy silence, I feared my sense of success and achievement would surely wither under any further criticism from my family, flattened to unimportance.

When I arrived home, George was waiting for me in the drawing room. He saw my waxy complexion and realised immediately something was amiss. We read the note together. Once the contents of her message became clear, a wave of remorse upended me. My immediate fears of further censure from my siblings could not have been more wrong.

'THE CONTENTS of that letter were a shock to me. Chrissy praised my writing and my courage,' Marian said.

Maggie sat opposite the authoress in the Wolsey Room. She had received a message from Marian saying she was in need of an outing, so she had reserved the room a second time. Now, they were comfortably nestled among the mahogany and the books and the portraits of past Bishops of Durham. Observing her in the scholarly environment, Maggie felt that Marian Cross was exactly where she belonged.

Maggie did not know if she had ever met such a learned woman. Of course, she would never mention this to Dorothea. Marian was clearly persuasive as well. Mister Cross would normally not allow his wife out of his sight willingly. Maggie imagined that to allow her to sit for most of the day on a cold wooden chair was completely unacceptable to him. Yet it appeared that under the force of Marian's will, he had relented ... but insisted Marian take with her a cushion to sit on and a rug for her lap.

'Chrissy wrote she had bowed under pressure from Isaac to exile me,' Marian continued. 'She said she would never have acted as she did otherwise. My heart swelled with love for her, for divulging the truth. Recalling our closeness as youngsters, it amazed me that such a sweet and caring boy such as Isaac could have grown into a such a tyrannical man. I remember Chrissy wrote, "You were always a different child and because you live differently now should be no cause for alarm. When you are in Warwickshire again, it would honour me to meet Mister Lewes." What those words meant to me!'

Maggie smiled and looked up from her notepad, wishing she might receive a similar letter from her mother Lydia.

'Why do you believe she contacted you after such a long time?' she asked. 'Was it your sudden fame?'

Looking down at her long, elegant fingers spread wide on the table, Marian answered quietly.

'She was dying. Chrissy had been widowed some years before. Her husband was a doctor; when they had married, he desperately wanted to do good in the world. The truth of it is, Maggie, doing good often goes unrewarded. He left her and their five children impoverished.

'George and I visited her in Warwickshire. My beautiful sister with the golden curls and exquisite features was but a shell, a dried husk. I barely recognised her. I could tell immediately that she did not have long to live, so we made the decision to stay with her. And besides, we were finally reunited; I was desperate to spend time with my sister.

'I'm grateful we chose to stay; she succumbed to consumption not ten days after our arrival.' Marian shook her head sadly. 'I believe she wanted to apologise for her behaviour before she died, to explain her actions to me. And she did.'

Maggie sighed inwardly and lowered her head. She thought of those she had in her life. William and his family, her father, Dorothea, Mister Latey and ... Briar. She felt her chest tighten. Would her own anguish be lessened if she had been able to say farewell to Briar? Or if she knew what was to come? She closed her eyes for a moment, staving off her tears.

'What happened to Chrissy's children?' Maggie said urgently, hoping they lived happily ever after.

Marian shifted slightly in her seat and cleared her throat quickly with a sharp, curt *ahem*.

'I sent them to boarding school and paid their fees until each of them graduated.' Noticing the narrowing of Maggie's eyes, she went on. 'They did not know me. To uproot them and bring them to live with us in London would have been impossible, not to mention grossly unfair.'

'Of course,' Maggie said gently, recalling the previous

interview when Marian had spoken of her discomfort in the presence of George's sons. She sensed she should continue down a different path.

'You mentioned George purchased a grand piano. Do you still play? I haven't noticed an instrument in the home you've taken here.'

Marian smiled. 'Unfortunately, a home with a piano was not available for rent in Durham. But when I'm at home in London or in Surrey, I play every day. It relaxes me.'

It seemed to Maggie if she were with Claire Clairmont now, the old lady would enquire after her ability to play. And enquire about everything else in Maggie's life ... She could imagine discussing Briar at length with her. *Briar* ... Maggie tried to clear her mind once again.

Marian was so used to being adored. Maggie had noticed that she rarely took an interest in others, although it wasn't rudeness exactly, more a learnt aloofness. It reminded Maggie of Dorothea's story about attending the salon and the girl seeking permission to kiss her feet.

'I don't play an instrument myself,' Maggie commented, eager to observe Marian's reaction. 'It's chess that relaxes me.'

Marian nodded slowly, a little stunned Maggie had offered the information uninvited. A moment's silence followed before Marian continued more easily.

'I am an excellent pianist, you see,' she ventured, leaning across the table conspiratorially. 'And to be honest, I have always enjoyed the notoriety playing brings me.'

Maggie nodded and leant closer herself, lowering her voice. 'For me, it's the battle at play on the board and the exhilaration following a win.'

'And if you don't win?'

A smile formed on Maggie's lips, and she lowered her eyes to her notes.

'It must have been difficult for you,' Maggie said, deciding to return her focus on the interview. 'You had lost your sister, and you were estranged from your brother. You had not yet ventured back into society and still considered yourself outcast. It strikes me that George was the only person you had in your life. I mean, the only person who you could rely on completely.'

'There was one other person,' Marian replied.

'Oh?' Maggie looked up from her notes, surprised.

'A young lady I knew in my childhood, Maria Congreve. During my time at Holly Lodge, we became extremely close. She and her husband were our neighbours, you see. Our friendship was such a contradiction.'

'How so?'

'Maria differed vastly from all my other female friends. Reserved and unassuming, she led an entirely conventional life and held no opinion about female equality whatsoever! Yet she was remarkably intelligent ... emotionally intelligent. Never an ill-timed phrase or harsh word escaped her mouth. Maria reminded me of a mute swan: graceful, elegant. Quite the opposite of me. Yet we got on famously.'

❦

MAGGIE ACCOMPANIED Marian back to her town house and the women shook hands at the gate. It was then Marian noticed the cameo Maggie was wearing on her jacket lapel.

'That's a lovely piece.' Marian looked more closely. 'Atalanta, I believe.'

'Really?' Maggie said, interested. She had been unable to identify the figure. 'And she was the goddess of ...?'

'Not a goddess at all. Atalanta was a swift-footed huntress, famous, in fact, for killing two centaurs who attempted to rape her. She refused to marry, but on one occasion she proclaimed to all men in the surrounding areas that she would wed anyone who could outrun her. Do you know what she did?'

Maggie shook her head. The myth was familiar, but she couldn't recall the details.

'She speared any man who came even close to overtaking her.'

Their laughter must have alerted Mister Cross. He opened the front door and stood there warily before walking to the women and examining the cameo himself, gripping it gently between his thumb and index finger.

'This is Atalanta. Her name means "equal in weight",' Marian explained.

Mister Cross released the cameo as though it were on fire and shot his wife an expression of ... anxiety? Concern? Maggie was uncertain which. Perhaps it was both.

'There are hundreds of tales of Atalanta besting her male rivals,' Marian finished, oblivious to her husband's unease.

The younger woman nodded gravely. Unbeknown to Marian, the information she had offered Maggie revealed a more profound meaning to her.

She bid a last farewell to the couple and walked away.

છાજી

MISTER CROSS TOOK his wife's arm and led her inside.

Marian pulled her arm from his grasp.

'I am well, John. I am not an invalid yet.'

She walked towards the conservatory, asking Julia for a pot of tea as she passed the kitchen.

Marian was relieved when John did not follow. She needed time to sift through the contents of the interview, alone. Her young interviewer had an uncanny knack of disarming her. While she was wholly prepared to reveal herself to the world, she found that her old reclusive habits died hard.

೧ஜ๑

Holly Lodge
Wandsworth

MARCH 7, 1860

Dearest and most darling Maria,

How lovely it was to see you today after so many years. Coventry and Bird Grove House, while so vivid in my memory, seem like a century ago.

When George announced our Wandsworth neighbours, the Congreves, were joining us for lunch, he only mentioned your husband, Richard – the Oxford scholar, the great and renowned Comtist! If only he had mentioned his wife, for she is far greater in my eyes.

I must confess, I did not recognise you at first, although there was something in your appearance that sparked a recollection in my mind. I believe it was your shy smile and the discreet way you have of looking at me. Then you spied my piano and mentioned Beethoven. Your expression! Any doubts I'd had as to your identity vanished in that moment. Once I realised it was young Maria Bury standing in my drawing room, I found it difficult to contain my joy.

I apologise for not confessing that I recognised you before now, but I feared I might shed tears over our unexpected reunion should I voice my happiness. What would your husband think of me then? The two of you were the first guests we have received in England as a couple, despite the many years George and I have been together. You have likely discerned this to be so already. George is not usually so blustering, and I am not typically so clumsy.

I am a little embarrassed when I recall our first meeting all those years ago. Your father, the good doctor, had arrived to attend to my father, who was ill. He asked you to wait with me in the sitting room, where I was practicing the piano. You were such a circumspect child and I so unabashed, I continued the piece I was playing. For you to remember it was Beethoven proved to me our meeting had affected you.

I remember playing with an abandon that was spurred on by your gaze on my fingers moving over the keys, as though the digits were enchanted. Then, when I stopped (I must admit, the passion with which I played for you made my fingers ache), you asked quietly if you might look at the books on the shelf behind me. While intensely shy, you were still brave enough to make that request. That was when we discovered we were like-minded souls. Neither of us lived in bookish homes, yet our adoration of books was incurable.

From that day to this ... It heartens me no end to believe that despite knowing of my arrangement with George, you pay no heed to rumour and gossip. To know I have you in the neighbourhood steadies me and, like a spell lifted, I no longer view Holly Lodge as oppressive in the way I have done for so long.

I look forward to discussing everything with you when we next meet, as arranged, on the Common. The past, present and future is ours to explore.

I am forever in your debt for your renewed friendship,

Yours beholden,

Marian Lewes

CHAPTER 28

MAGGIE EXAMINED the cameo as she waited for William on the bridge. While the hat Briar had made was gorgeous, Maggie could never wear it in Durham. It was a Royal Ascot style of hat; such lurid headgear would surely invite even more scandal. However, she had decided to wear the cameo on her lapel for her meeting with Marian.

Atalanta ...

When Marian had related the tales of the Greek warrior woman that afternoon, Maggie had searched her mind for a hidden message in the myth. Now she realised the message wasn't cryptic at all. It was Briar and Maggie who were the warriors now.

But where is Briar?

Maggie needed to take action to find her friend. She wanted to be as valiant as Atalanta, but she wasn't certain how she could act.

'I promise you, Briar, I will get to the truth,' Maggie whispered into the water below, hoping her pledge to action would somehow magically reveal the way forward.

She pinned the cameo back on her coat, then looked up at

the sky. The sun was dying and the willows queued along the bank had been stripped bare of their leaves by the season. Their skeletons reflected harshly in the water. It struck Maggie as a ghoulish image. She was reminded of Mary Shelley's nightmares and the losses that had so relentlessly haunted the authoress.

Maggie turned away, wishing to dispel the image, then checked her wristwatch. It was half five. William was usually at the bridge by now. She waited a moment longer then reasoned he most likely finished early and was waiting at home for her with a chicken roasting in the oven.

⚜

WHEN SHE ARRIVED at the cottage, she found it empty. It was Wednesday and Grace would be at school until eight. William would never be late on a Wednesday. It was the only evening when they had the cottage to themselves. She stared at her wristwatch. With each minute that ticked by, the sun sank lower and her anxiety mounted. Briar had so suddenly disappeared from her life. What if William ... She heard the gate swing shut, and she hurried to the door. It was William, making his way to the washroom at the back of the house.

'Where have you been?' she cried.

He stopped and turned, then looked her way somewhat guiltily, she noticed.

His trousers and shirt were black with coal dust. Grime coated his face, reminding her of the evening when she had arrived at the Stanley Pit following the collapse. William had laboured all day and into the following morning to free his trapped father and brothers, without success.

'You've been down the pits, haven't you?' she asked, alarmed.

William removed his flat cap.

'I had to know, Maggie,' he said imploringly. 'I had to see for my own eyes whether Drummond had made any of the improvements. He's never going to let the inspectors in, despite Tommy's optimism that he will.'

Maggie was still and silent, overcome by such a strange and powerful combination of emotions. Relief, love, anger and pride were all present in her heart, battling for dominance.

'Maggie?' William whispered.

Clenching her fists, she screamed. Loud. Angry. Primal.

Maggie had never behaved that way before and her actions momentarily surprised her. William, too. Instinctively, he took a step back.

Maggie swallowed. The release hadn't offered the alleviation of her strained spirit that she had hoped. The pair stared at one another for a moment, then drew together and kissed. Greedily, ravenously, they took each other in.

❧

Once they were both clean, the couple sat contritely sipping the whiskey Maggie had poured. They had not spoken since her outburst. William had taken her in the garden against the cold stone wall of the cottage, then they had washed and silently entered the cottage, feeling comforted and somewhat ashamed all at once.

Finally, when the whiskey had restored her temperament, Maggie laid her hand on his.

'I'm sorry,' she said. 'I was angry. Everything happening is out of my control and I feel helpless, utterly useless.' She sensed her eyes filling with tears. 'If anything ever happened to you, I ... I couldn't bear it.' She placed her hand on her throat. 'I would suffocate. You're the air I breathe, the person

in the world whom I love the most, and without you, my life
... It doesn't bear thinking about.'

'Oh, lass,' he replied. 'Don't apologise. Your words and
actions mean everything to me. I know they were not from
anger, but from love. I'd hoped to be home and washed
before you returned.' He clutched her hand and drew her
onto his lap. 'I love you, lass, more than I can express in mere
words. You are the sun that warms my heart on a wintry day.
Being with you is my nourishment. You make me strong.'

Fear prevented him from saying more. Maggie pressed her
face into his neck, and they sat silently together until the sun
set completely, each longing to utter what was actually in
their hearts.

But how could she give herself over to William completely
without losing a part of herself?

உஆ

'I WAITED for the end of the shift, then I was in and out
before the beginning of the following one,' William said as
they ate the Welsh rarebit he prepared. 'I grew up at the
colliery, Maggie. I know those seams like the back of my
hand. So I entered a disused shaft away from the main pit and
followed it until I reached a more recent seam.'

'And?'

'There's still inadequate shoring and ventilation shafts,
nothing like the amount the union stipulated in their
demands. Drummond has been lying this entire time and
Tommy has believed him.'

They ate silently for a few moments as they processed the
information. Maggie wiped her mouth, unable to finish her
supper. She shared in William's sorrow, but there was another
distinct sadness she was experiencing, too. Matthew was not

the type of man who could be a friend. And she realised, not without sorrow, that he was not a man she could ever trust.

❧

IN THE MORNING, William resolved to speak to Tommy Fellowes about the mine. Maggie suggested she come along as well.

'I worry your close feeling towards Tommy might colour your judgment. It will be easier for me to ask the more troublesome questions.'

William nodded. 'You're probably right, lass. But I'd lay my life on the fact Tommy is as clean as a new pin.'

The pair set off together. Although much had been aired between them, still something remained dowelled in the tight joins of their relationship. Maggie knew it was the subject of marriage. The words they had spoken the evening before were vows of a sort. But she came to the realisation that William was hesitant to propose, fearing she would say no. In truth, he was right to be cautious. While the words she had uttered were true, while she wanted no one but him, the fear that people would instantly view her as William's Dodd's wife and nothing more was still holding her back.

When they reached the offices of the miners' union, William explained to his godfather what had occurred. He admitted to descending the shaft. Maggie watched Tommy Fellowes closely as he spoke. He seemed uncomfortable, incapable of meeting William's eye.

'Are yee daft? There's nothing I can do now. Drummond can never know you were in the seams, or he could have yer arrested for trespassing.'

'Aye, but now yer know he's lying. You should press to get the inspectors down there. Andy Stackhouse will help you.

He's a good man and I'm certain he'll overlook the trespassing.'

Tommy sighed, shaking his head.

'Mister Fellowes,' Maggie said. 'Briar Haines has disappeared. Matthew Drummond told me he caught her prying. What if she found something?'

Tommy's eyes lit up. 'Like what?'

William nudged Maggie's foot with his boot.

Maggie shrugged. 'I'm none too sure,' she said casually. 'It could be anything, perhaps something to do with the mine, or a connection to his personal life ...

Tommy rubbed his brow. 'What are yer suggesting, lass?'

'I'm not suggesting anything. It simply seems like too much of a coincidence that Drummond found Briar snooping and then she disappeared.'

'Yer reading too much into this, the pair of you.' He rose and laid his hands flat on his desk, leaning towards them. 'Aareet, so we know Drummond has been delaying the inspectors because some demands have yet to be met. But yer need to understand that the pitmen, the hurriers ... Everyone that the union represents don't want the mine to close. I would have a riot on my hands if I forced a closure.'

'Tommy, you can't be serious!' William cried, rising.

'Leave be, lad. I know you're still hurting from the collapse last year but, whether you think it's justice or no', my hands are tied.'

When they departed, Maggie walked William to the *Advertiser*.

'He's feeling the pressure,' William said when they reached the door to his office. 'He's stuck between the members, Drummond, the union's ethos to uphold safety and fair pay, then there's me in his ear ...'

Maggie squeezed his hand. She felt for William, but she

couldn't help feeling that Tommy knew more than he was saying ... and William was too blinded by his respect for his godfather to see it.

CHAPTER 29

MAGGIE WORKED on her article in the cottage's quiet. William was at the *Advertiser* and Grace had only recently departed for the university. She was attending a lecture on Dalton's atomic theory. She was the only female enrolled in the College of Science and she endeavoured to research every lecture before attending. Grace suffered a similar experience at university as Maggie had at the *Illustrated London News*. Her male peers were always eager to see her fail or stumble over questions the professors might ask. Maggie knew all too well that women had to work ten times as hard as their male colleagues to receive just an ounce of recognition.

'Can you believe, Maggie,' Grace said as she was readying to leave, 'that one day long ago someone actually asked: how big is small? Why, that's what atomism all comes down to in the end.' It always thrilled Grace when she had discovered a means of making sense of a concept.

Maggie smiled at her enthusiasm and her dedication. 'Indeed it does. Well done!' she said, then kissed Grace's cheek in farewell.

Now, left to her own devices, Maggie struggled to concentrate on her writing. Her mind was awash with thoughts of Briar, Matthew and Tommy Fellowes. She needed to act, but she wasn't certain how. At that moment, as though she willed it, there was a knock at the door. It was the postmaster's girl, Mister Darlington's daughter. Maggie searched her mind for a name ... Isla, she believed.

The girl handed her the envelope she was holding, then waited a moment, craning her neck to see the inside of the cottage as though the occupant might be hiding something valuable.

'Would you like to come in, Isla?' Maggie asked.

'Thank yer, Miss,' Isla said, propping her bicycle against the wall and stepping over the threshold.

'If you don't mind, Isla, I'd like to read the telegram you've brought immediately. It may contain some very important news.'

Isla, Maggie guessed, was about eleven, the same age as Maggie when she started at Cheltenham. She gestured for the girl to sit, then she tore open the envelope. Holding her breath, she read the contents. Raymond had paid a visit to Briar's house on Calvert Avenue and spoken to her maid Clara. She'd had no word of Miss Haines since her departure from London some weeks before. Usually, the telegram went on, Miss Haines was excellent at keeping Clara informed of her movements. Maggie exhaled a long voluminous sigh, then sank into a chair.

'It's not good news, Miss?'

Maggie shook her head. 'I'm afraid not, Isla.' Maggie folded the document and slid it back inside the envelope. 'Now, what can I do for you?'

It took the girl some time to speak. Maggie could almost see her ordering the words in her mind.

'Mam and I saw you t'other day on the High Street,' she said. 'The day you gave Reggie Owen what for.'

'Oh, yes.' Maggie wasn't sure where Isla was heading. Half certain she was going to be rebuked by the child, she added. 'It wasn't my finest moment, I suppose, but ...'

'Oh na, Miss,' the girl put in beseechingly. 'You were canny.'

Maggie looked into Isla's earnest grey eyes. They were misted with tears. She took the girl's hand.

'Mam and me, we thought you did fine. Mam said you showed her what a woman could do. And she wants you to know that when your school opens, she'll be enrolling me and me brother, too ... if he were a girl, I mean.'

'Why, thank you, Isla,' Maggie said, amazed. 'And please pass on my good wishes to your mother.'

Her behaviour on the High Street with Reggie Owen had been spontaneous, fuelled by her rage. When she reflected on the moment later, she was certain the incident would have won her no friends. Never in her wildest dreams would she have expected her words to inspire the onlookers.

'Isla, I will contact you when my school opens. It would be my pleasure to have you as the first enrolment.'

As she watched the girl peddle along the road towards town, her spindly legs revolving at a rate of knots, Maggie's heart welled and she finally understood how Dorothea must feel inspiring young women. Then the girl disappeared among the hedgerows, and Maggie turned her mind back to Raymond's telegram.

❧

WILLIAM READ the message when he returned that evening.

'Your Raymond is very thorough, isn't he?'

Maggie raised an eyebrow. 'For a start, he's not my Raymond anymore. And second, of course he's thorough. He's a Harley Street paediatrician. He is trained to be so.'

William smiled, seemingly happy he could still rile her about her former fiancé.

'But it doesn't help us any.'

'I think it does. This is confirmation Briar has run foul of ...' Maggie couldn't bring herself to say what she was thinking. 'William, if she had travelled to London directly, she would have been home days ago!'

'What if she stopped along the way?' William suggested. 'It would not be out of the question for an independently minded woman such as Briar to stop en route and visit a friend, or—'

Maggie thrust her finger towards the telegram. 'But her maid told Raymond that Briar always kept her abreast of her comings and goings. If her return to London was planned, she would have telegraphed ahead. Likewise, if Briar had made a detour on the spur of the moment, she would have advised Clara, I am certain of it. Briar is meticulous in all her actions. And what about the purse? She would never be so careless as to lose such a thing!'

William nodded gravely. 'Very well. We'll go see Andy tomorrow. There's naught we can do now.'

❧

THE FOLLOWING morning as they made their way into town, they spotted a horse coming towards them along the road.

'It's Andy.' William stopped, waiting for the rider to get closer.

When the young officer reached them, he dismounted and removed his hat, wedging it snugly under his arm.

'Good morning,' he said. 'I was just riding out to see you, Miss Almond.'

'And we were just coming to see you, Constable,' Maggie

said, reaching into her purse for Raymond's telegram. 'We received—'

'Miss Almond, it's my unhappy duty to inform you we found yer friend early this morning.'

Maggie could discern from his tone and the sudden sallowness of his complexion that the words he would speak next were going to be grim.

'Drowned.'

Maggie released a choked cry, and she sensed William's arm slide around her waist. The strength of his body against hers acted as a support. Without it, she would have collapsed.

Andy cleared his throat. 'There's more.'

Their anguished faces turned to him.

'I found Reggie Owen nearby with his skull staved in.'

❦

ANDY STACKHOUSE ACCOMPANIED William and Maggie back to the cottage, where Grace was waiting. Within an instant of hearing the devastating news, she had the kettle on the stove and the teapot heaped with Tetley's. William had placed his coat around Maggie on the short walk home. She'd started to shiver uncontrollably and the colour washed from her face, as though she'd been instantly stricken with fever. Silent on the journey, she was in a state William had never witnessed before. Now they were home, he bounded up the stairs and pulled the eiderdown from their bed. Rushing back to her, he wrapped it around her shoulders.

'Shock,' Andy Stackhouse murmured sombrely to William. 'Perhaps I should come back when you're feeling more yerself, Miss.'

'No,' Maggie said immediately. 'I need to know what happened.'

'Lass, please,' William said. 'Andy's right. You're not your-self. Just give it an hour or two.'

Maggie shook her head. Large pools of tears formed in her eyes. William wrapped his arms around her body. He wanted to take her pain away, squeeze it out of her, but he knew that wasn't possible. All he could do was to be by her side while she heard the unendurable. It had been what she had done for him following the collapse of the Stanley Pit.

'A fisherman and his son,' Andy said. 'They were down river near Maiden Castle when they made the discovery early this morning.'

Maggie needed to focus. She wanted to ask the right ques-tions, but her mind was full of Briar as she had been – mischievous, autonomous, intelligent ... alive.

'If, as you believe, she was being forced to leave Durham,' said Andy, 'it appeared that Reggie was the one to escort her.'

'Drummond must have sent him,' William said gravely.

Maggie felt even sicker. It had been only a few days since she had spoken to Matthew about Briar and he had made no mention of Reggie.

Andy continued. 'It's possible she got the better of Reggie on the way and thrashed him.'

'How could a wee lass like Briar Haines get the better of Reggie Owen?' William asked. 'He was over three times her size.'

Andy shook his head, puzzled.

'And how could he have drowned her after she'd smashed in his head?'

'Unless he died afterwards of his injuries,' suggested Andy.

'It makes no sense,' Maggie put in after a time. She was feeling more like herself after the fortifying tea. She let the eiderdown fall from her shoulders. 'Briar wasn't violent. She would never have attacked Reggie unless she felt he was threatening her life.' She paused, trying to imagine the awful scene. 'You said the fisherman found her down river. The note Briar left explained she was leaving from Newcastle Station on the ten o'clock train. If that was the case, Reggie was taking her the wrong way.'

'Unless he never intended to take her to the station,' William added, his face grim.

'And if Briar felt in danger, it could explain Reggie's injuries,' Grace said.

William frowned. 'Even so ...'

'Even so,' Maggie continued. 'It's as you said, William, a woman of Briar's size would not have the strength to stave in Reggie Owen's head ... it just doesn't make sense.'

Andy nodded. 'His injury was severe. Doctor Carmichael is yet to examine him, but I cannot imagine after a blow like that, he would have had the will or the strength to drown a woman.'

Maggie moved the pieces of the macabre puzzle around in her mind, determined to understand. Then she had it.

'There must have been a third person. It's the only way to explain it.'

※

WHEN ANDY LEFT, Maggie told William and Grace they should get on with their day. At first, neither of them wanted to leave her alone, but she had insisted. Finally, they both relented and departed. William and his mother accepted death so courageously, as though holding their grief an unwilling captive; they wrestled with it until eventually it was conquered.

But someone had murdered Briar. Maggie could not accept such a death for her friend, and neither did she want to. The knowledge she would never see her again, never hear her merry laughter or feel the warmth of her friendship, made her body ache. Maggie wanted to tear her mind to shreds at the thought of what Briar had suffered. The injustice of losing her!

Once she heard the gate close, she sat down and allowed her tears their release. Alone in the kitchen, the weak sun filtering its soft light across the table, Maggie sobbed with such immense sorrow, she believed she might never find joy again.

CHAPTER 30

The Manchester Guardian
Wednesday, November 17, 1880

DEAR READER,

It may surprise you to know that George Henry Lewes and I began our relationship on a far from passionate footing. Given this, I am so grateful those elegant almond-shaped eyes of his could see through my haughtiness and pride, and forever thankful he continued his pursuit of me. He was a terrier, a Jack Russell – energetic, tenacious, loving and oh, so loyal. These were the qualities that captured my heart and what eventually evolved between us was a passionate and wonderful love.

The first time I met George Lewes was when he visited the *Westminster Review*. He was a contributor to our various sections. He was a jack-of-all-trades and master of none, or so I thought. Literature and theatre reviews, science writing and philosophical debate were all in his wheelhouse.

I met him when I first began at the publication. He came to the office to look over the edits I had made to a piece of his on positivism. The stubborn man disagreed with every one of my suggestions! He even had the gall to suggest that I knew nothing about the philosopher Auguste Comte and was in need of an education. How dare he! When he departed, he left me feeling wretched, my confidence shattered. Oh, how I despised the man!

The second time I met George Lewes was at an opening of a Constable exhibition at the National Gallery. He was holding court by the artist's rendering of *Flatford Mill*, telling those who had assembled around him (as though he were Constable himself) of his visits to Suffolk and how Constable's romantic depiction of the place captured the atmosphere perfectly. The fact he'd once been an actor was obvious. He enjoyed the limelight like no person I had ever known.

As he sermonised, he caught my eye over the heads of his audience. He nodded. There was a glint in his eyes – mischievous, arrogant, interested? I could not quite determine. My hackles rose. I ignored him and walked to the exit. By this stage in our relationship (if you could call it that), I could not stand being in the same room as the man!

The third time I met George Lewes was in a bookshop on the Strand. I was on the arm of Herbert Spencer and we were glancing through a copy of Hegel's *The Philosophy of Religion*. George saw our interest in the publication and began, at length, to inform Herbert and me of its publication history. This led to a discussion of Karl Marx, who had critiqued the work, and the German's recent move to London.

'He has lived in exile for most of his life,' George informed us. 'In part, his exile had to do with his devotion to Hegel, and his atheism, of course. You probably know he is living now in Soho, on Dean Street. His home is also the headquarters of the Communist League. They followed Marx to London ...'

And so, he went on. But this time, in my eyes, at least, he was not holding court or being grandiloquent. He was simply a man with an endless amount of knowledge. I wondered if his head might burst at the seams if he did not give his wisdom release.

Herbert, who liked George Lewes even less than I, made a rather scathing remark about Marx and strolled to another section of the store. He left me alone with Mister Lewes. George seemed to alter then; he relaxed in my presence. We flicked through several other philosophical tomes together, remarking on the various theories, or our understanding of them. We even discovered an edition of his most recent book on the infamous Robespierre. I had written about it in the *Review* and, I must confess, I hadn't been kind. George acknowledged my 'strident critique' and we laughed. Shrugging, he said, 'I will not be so cruel when you publish your first book, Miss Evans.'

Somehow, he saw in me what I could not, even then.

As we stood in the bookstore, gradually getting to know one another, his alert blue eyes darted around my face without ever landing on it. Acutely aware of my appearance as always, I thought perhaps I was too hideous for even George Lewes to gaze upon. Most women found George unattractive. Simian, if I am to be frank. Yet he had a sturdy, muscled look about him which I found very appealing. Finally, after some minutes, his lovely eyes lit upon mine like feathers. They contained such earnestness and admiration that I couldn't help but take his next words seriously.

'Miss Evans,' he began. 'I was hoping you might do me the immense honour of joining me for tea at a time acceptable to you. I have very much enjoyed our conversation.'

I knew of his family situation. Everyone in our industry did. Yet no man had ever looked at me the way George Lewes did at that moment – with such respect and longing.

It was then Herbert emerged from the stacks and suggested we go. My response to him was hasty.

'You go on, Herbert. I am joining Mister Lewes for tea … today.'

❧

'I AM SO VERY sorry to hear about your friend, Miss Almond,' John Cross said when he opened the door.

He really is a considerate man, Maggie thought. She did not fail to notice that it was he who had been waiting for her rather than Julia.

'It is a hideous thing to lose someone to whom we are close. We ran into Miss Haines at Wilson's on several occasions. She sung your praises endlessly. She clearly admired you greatly. I've no doubt you felt the same.'

Maggie nodded her thanks. She feared if she were to voice her feelings about Briar's death, she would cry again and be unable to stopper her tears. William had wanted to send her apologies to Marian that morning, but Maggie had prevented him. Blindly groping for answers in the dark, she needed a focus for her pent-up energy at a time when everything around her seemed misted. She needed the distraction of conversation. Concentrating on another life for a few hours would give her room to breathe. At least, she hoped so.

Maggie took her seat opposite Marian in the drawing room. She glanced through the window. The cold stone castle appeared more ominous than usual. Marian leant forward and gripped her hand. Immediately, tears stung at Maggie's eyes.

'When George died,' Marian said. 'I was at a loss for so, so long. It was months before I'd allow anyone to see me. I refused to venture into the world.' She smiled wistfully. 'You would appreciate my mourning, Maggie. I wore a most unappealing black crepe dress and insisted on donning a widow's cap.'

Maggie looked at her gratefully. 'A la Dorothea Casaubon,' she said, remembering that George's Eliot's *Middlemarch* heroine admits to using her widow's cap as 'a kind of shell'.

'Exactly.'

George Lewes had been in Marian's life for twenty-four years. Briar had been in hers briefly by comparison, yet Maggie felt the loss profoundly. Somewhat put right by Marian's words, Maggie opened her notebook.

Focus, she thought. *Focus on anything but Briar*.

'Was George ill for a very long time before he passed?'

'Died,' Marian corrected her. 'George didn't pass, he died. Passing seems so transient. Death is forever.'

Maggie nodded, noting the difference. 'Was he ill?'

'He was extremely ill, but only for a brief time, thankfully,' she recalled, closing her eyes for a moment. 'We first realised the seriousness of his illness in September of 1878. We had just bought our new home, The Heights, in Witley. Nine acres, George enjoyed boasting. Witley is a beautiful village, and our house was perfect. The property had gardens and fields, even a wood. Johnny found it for us. He is a very shrewd negotiator.'

Maggie knew Witley; her father had ties in the area. In fact, his ancestral lands lay very near the Saxon village.

Godwin, one of the first earls of Wessex, lived there nearly 700 years ago.

'George lost a vast amount of weight extremely quickly and suffered the most intense stomach cramps. He described them once to me. He said it was as though a rope ran from his neck to his lower abdomen and someone was intent on tying it into a constrictor knot.' She smiled sadly. 'Even when he was suffering, he could amuse me.'

'And himself,' Maggie added.

'Indeed. It was his way. The cramps came worst in the early morning. At dawn he would waken me and we would go for long walks around our nine acres, sometimes going further into the Common. Walking eased the pain. So frail, he was. His arm looped through mine was unrecognisable. He'd always been the person supporting me.'

'What did you talk about during these walks?'

Marian sighed and closed her eyes again. 'The future. We both knew the end for George was coming. Without my knowing, he had arranged all our affairs with Johnny. So when we were alone, we'd discuss the future. Silly, I know.'

'Not at all,' Maggie said. 'You were enjoying each other until the last moment.'

'I suppose we were.' A cloud of grief seemed to descend upon her.

Maggie realised that George's death was still so recent; not yet two years had gone by.

'By November 30th, he was dead,' Marian continued. 'He died at fifteen minutes to six o'clock in the morning.' Tears welled in her eyes. 'I stayed in our chamber for seven days. I even refused to attend his funeral, a decision which I regret immensely. I cried and wailed, alarming our household servants Brett and Missus Dowling, who knew not what to do with me. Johnny called, as did Barbara, Cara and lovely Maria Congreve. Even Herbert came to pay his respects – we had resolved our differences by then. John Blackwood, chronically ill himself, sent notes and flowers. I ignored them all and refused to see them when they drove out from London. There was a hole where George had been and all I could manage, all I wanted to do, was fill it with grief.'

'How long was it before you could face the world again?' Maggie asked, hoping she could see an end to her own agony.

'I did not venture outside the walls of The Heights until the following year. It was not until March 1879 that I finally received visitors, but only because I was forced to.'

'How so?'

Marian rubbed her brow. 'Our properties, bank accounts, our shares and investments were all in George's name. He had managed my money and career for over twenty years. If I wanted to have the means to live, I had to venture forth and plan. But it wasn't a simple matter. I had to change my name by deed poll to Mary Anne Evans Lewes in order to be granted access to deeds, investments and the like. For twenty-four years I had been Marian Lewes, yet no one would believe me.'

Maggie's thoughts turned from Briar to William. She recalled the panic she had felt when she learnt he had descended into the disused pit. She wondered how close he had come to death. What if he had died? How would she react to such a loss?

Julia brought in tea and the women paused their interview. The topic of the day was such a mournful one that somehow Maggie's grief for Briar and her fear of losing William had merged with Marian's own loss. Usually, Maggie would take this hiatus in the interview to converse with Marian on a different topic, one unrelated to their discourse. It was a means of gaining background and colour for her articles. However, today she remained silent, pensively sipping her tea. With some magical intuition, Marian refrained from speaking, too, judging silence was best. Maggie was grateful for her consideration.

MISTER CROSS SHOWED Maggie to the door and once again expressed his condolences.

'Would you mind if I walk you to the bridge, Miss Almond?' he asked.

'Of course not, Mister Cross.' As they strolled along, Maggie wondered what prompted his unexpected courtesy.

'You were discussing George today,' he remarked.

Maggie nodded. 'It was not my intention. However, Missus Cross is such a remarkable observer. I believe she read my mood and hoped sharing her life with Mister Lewes might somehow ease my own grief.'

'Yes, she is quite remarkable in that way,' he said, nodding, seemingly satisfied with Maggie's answer.

She looked sideways at him. 'Mister Lewes seemed like an extraordinary man. Was this your experience of him?'

Mister Cross looked thoughtful for a few minutes and Maggie feared she had spoken out of turn.

'I had heard stories of George Lewes before mother and I met him in Rome,' he said eventually. 'In his youth, he had been a follower of Shelley and enjoyed the company of other hedonists such as Leigh Hunt, who, as you well know, Miss Almond, embraced the principles of free love.'

Maggie nodded. *Did you ever embrace those principles, Mister Cross?* she wondered.

'I'd heard George Lewes shared his wife with his business partner, Thornton, the son of Leigh Hunt,' he continued. 'It was a scandalous arrangement, and I imagined George quite the *débauché* ...'

Perhaps not.

'But my experience with George was quite the opposite. In the years I knew him, his one and only concern was for Marian. His duty in life was to love and protect her – indeed, to cherish her. While he was a talented writer, he was never a great success in terms of financial rewards. But he was highly successful at loving Marian. When he died, I vowed to care for Marian in the same way as he had done.' Mister Cross stopped and looked around him for a moment. 'Well, here we are.'

They had reached the bridge.

He took Maggie's hand in both his and gripped it warmly. His sudden compassion touched her. She wondered if it was this compassion that had led him to care for Marian, or if it was their shared grief that had drawn them together.

🙘🙚

'Poor girl,' John remarked to Marian when he returned to the drawing room. 'I wonder what occurred. It seems Miss Haines's death was not as simple as a drowning. Julia heard talk in town, you know. There was a man involved … a brute of a fellow who Miss Almond publicly rebuked for the treatment of his wife.'

'Oh, how you like to gossip, Johnny,' Marian smiled. 'But I cannot say it would surprise me to learn Maggie Almond publicly humiliated a man who was in need of some humility.'

'Well, it is quite intriguing, don't you agree? Never, in my wildest dreams, would I have imagined Durham to be a hotbed of crime and scandal. I had thought our time here might be a period in which you could relax and renew your strength.' He leant back into the chair and crossed his legs. 'I wonder if Matthew Drummond plans to make a public statement. He was Miss Haines's employer, after all.'

As John Cross conjectured and hypothesised about the

death of Briar Haines, Marian's thoughts returned to the aftermath of her own loss, still so fresh in her mind.

The Heights
Witley, Surrey

FEBRUARY 13, 1879

Dearest Barbara,

Bless you for all your goodness to me, but I am a battered creature and draw away from even the tenderest touch. As soon as I feel able to see anybody, I will see you.

Bless you, too, for your loving thoughts. But for all reasons, physical and spiritual, I cannot move. I am entirely occupied with George's manuscript and must be on the spot among his books. Even if I were able, I could not bear to go out of sight of the things he used and looked on.

Bless you once more. If I could go away with anyone, I would go away with you.

I walked past his study last night and glimpsed his fountain pen and the funny little porcelain dachshund which sits on his desk, a memento from our time in Weimar. I sobbed inconsolably. That silly little figurine pulls at my heart so.

For me, being in his study, carrying on his work, keeps an idea lit in my mind that he is still alive. If he were to walk through the front door this instance, it would not surprise me at all.

'What a jape!' he would cry, laughing. 'You've always been so lovingly dupable, Polly.'

Johnny Cross came to visit this morning. He has been writing incessantly, dreadfully concerned for my wellbeing. I finally permitted a visit. My grief has eclipsed my compassion, Barbara; I had forgotten that he had lost his mother only days after George died. Poor man, he is grieving, as am I. He was devoted to his mother, and he was a friend of George as well.

I had hoped to find peace in his company again. I felt sure our sorrow could marry and, in the process, be diluted.

However, as he sat opposite me in the library, everything about the man caused irritation. All he spoke, every action, seemed to have an association with George. Brett had propped our tennis rackets in the corner, and Johnny reminded me of a match we played together in the summer. The suit he was wearing was from Hamilton's, a clothing store which George had recommended to him. He sat with what seemed to me lordly airs in George's armchair in such an overbearing manner that I had to bite my tongue to prevent myself from throwing him from the house. Eventually, I dismissed him, citing a sick headache. I could bear his presence no longer. As you can see, my sorrow makes me fiendish. Can you believe that once he departed, I began to miss him?

Oh, Barbara, will I ever feel whole again?

George was so intent on finishing his manuscript. He had promised it to Blackwood's. I am endeavouring to complete it for him. It is the least I can do for my husband in my melancholy.

Your loving, but expiring,

Marian

CHAPTER 31

THE MOOD in the cottage remained sombre and William and Maggie prepared tea wordlessly. Following her interview with Marian and the ensuing conversation with John Cross, Maggie's thoughts were a jumble, an ugly, tangled mess. Although Constable Stackhouse had assured Maggie he would get to the bottom of Briar's death, it concerned her that the trail would go cold if he didn't act with more haste.

It was just the two of them tonight. After an engaging seminar Grace presented on chemical bonding the week before, she'd been invited by a group of classmates to join them for a drink. Maggie hoped the invitation indicated that her peers had finally accepted Grace. She supposed it was a woman's burden in life to be continually attempting to fit into places where she wasn't wanted, the perennial square peg in a round hole.

The couple worked in silence as rain fell in sheets against the window. As William sliced the carrots into even rounds, the heavy sound of his knife against the wooden board brought Anne Boleyn to Maggie's mind – another woman's whose life had ended violently at the hand of a man.

Maggie sighed audibly. It seemed impossible to suppress her moroseness. Even the weather spoke of her sadness; it had begun to rain soon after William arrived home.

'What's the matter, lass?' he said, putting down the knife. 'It's more than Briar, isn't it? How'd your interview this morning go?'

Maggie pushed her hair from her eyes.

'Marian was extremely sympathetic. She shared with me her love of George Lewes and the effect his death had her. It prompted me to think about losing Briar ... and how I would feel if I were to lose you,' she explained. 'Our discussion offered me a slightly different perspective of everything.'

William gazed at her with sympathy and interest, and, more noticeably, concern.

'Marian told me she was so intensely stricken with grief when George died, she was incapable of even attending his funeral.'

Maggie stared into William's hazel eyes. The rain falling against the window patterned the wall in shadows behind him. *If something were to happen to him ...* she shook away the thought.

'Marian left it to others to farewell the man she loved. She has regretted it ever since.' Maggie lowered her gaze. 'Briar had no family. The milliner and his wife, who all but raised her, died some years ago. There is no one but us to mourn her.'

Maggie realised she'd felt similarly following Claire Clairmont's death, a loss from which she had not yet fully recovered. *If I am still mourning for Claire now, how long will I mourn for Briar?* she mused sadly. Clearly, Marian was still mourning George. If it was still acceptable to wear her black widow's cap, she believed that the authoress would. Perhaps the mantilla Marian wore in public was less disguise and more a symbol of her widow status ...

Having Clairmont and the journals shipped to Italy had offered Maggie a point of closure, a moment in which to say goodbye. But while Andy Stackhouse continued to investigate Briar's death, that point seemed far in the distance.

William held her close. 'Would you like to give Briar a send-off, lass?'

Maggie hadn't considered the idea, but, as always, William seemed to know just what she needed.

'It's a grand idea,' he went on. 'I'll talk to Doctor Carmichael and Andy. She was only here a short time, but she made quite an impression on everybody. Briar would like that, I reckon.' He smiled.

William had such a unique view of death. Perhaps it came from living in a colliery town where each day death was a real possibility.

'I'll see Reverend Calder—'

'Oh, no!' Maggie cut in, alarmed. 'Briar was an atheist, quite a staunch one, in fact. Would Reverend Calder agree, do you think, to a more non-denominational ceremony? Perhaps outdoors, by the river?' Maggie remembered how fond Briar had grown of the countryside during her time in Durham.

William nodded. 'He will ... if I ask him,' he said, raising an eyebrow before turning back to the vegetables.

Maggie sighed. She was aware she was not Reverend Calder's favourite person. In fact, she was probably his least. He still had not warmed to her idea of a girls' school and made a point of shooting her a disdainful glance every time they passed on the High Street.

'Yes, you have a way of putting people at ease, while all I seem to do is repel them,' she said.

It was an offhand comment, but William ceased his task and turned.

'Do you believe that, Maggie?'

She thought for a moment and nodded. 'I suppose, I do. Here at least.'

A troubled look crossed William's face. She wondered what was going through his mind, but after a moment's rumination, she decided she didn't want to know. Although her words had been careless, they revealed exactly how she felt at that moment. Frustration and anxiety gnawed at her like a rabid dog.

'Mister Cross is an unusual man,' she remarked to steer the conversation.

William raised his eyebrows.

'He walked me to the bridge this morning. He's never done it before. It could be he thought I was fragile after recent events or ...'

'Or?'

'It was as though he was probing for information about the interview. He and I have never discussed George at such length before.'

'Jealous, you think?'

Maggie nodded. 'I believe he was. But of whom, I am not sure.'

***

GRACE HAD NOT RETURNED by the time they retired. William was glad his mam was having some fun with her classmates, although to hear Grace talk of them, they seemed like a serious bunch of lads who'd rather discuss Archimedes than the football scores. He was certain someone would see her safely home. It was the way in Durham to look out for one another.

Although, no one had been looking out for Briar.

He turned his head on the pillow and stared at Maggie's profile. *Perfect*, he mused. *It would make a bonny cameo.* Her straight nose and full lips and her brow, so wonderfully rounded and smooth. He made a noise – part sigh, part yawn. She took his hand.

Knowing the other was awake would usually mean a coming together, but not tonight. Maggie's words hung between them like a heavy pall. Knowing she felt unloved, a pariah, had emptied him out until he was hollow inside, as though she had tipped him upside down and shaken. It wasn't the truth of her words that disturbed him because Maggie did not repel people. She attracted them like ants to a honeypot. They simply couldn't see beyond the aspects of her character that made her different. Yet those aspects were what made her most appealing. Still, he could not deny that some people were fearful of her allure; Maggie wanted change, and she demanded it immediately. The Geordie community had followed the same customs and practices for generations. They were not quite ready for her.

William had discovered over the course of recent days that every person – man and woman – who witnessed the bollocking she gave Reggie Owen on the High Street commended her and supported her actions. He believed that they finally saw the woman Maggie truly was, a woman who would fight tooth and nail against any injustice. Without her realising, opinion was changing towards her. The problem was that change wasn't coming fast enough for her.

He squeezed her hand. *If only she'd have more patience*, he thought.

'What you said before when we were in the kitchen ...'

She turned and looked his way.

'It's not true. So many – Mister Armstrong, Andy, Isla and even Tommy – have mentioned the tongue lashing you gave Reggie Owen the other day. They're all proud of you, Maggie. I'm proud of you. I know it's not in your nature, but try to be patient with them. They'll come around eventually.'

'But how long is eventually, William?' she asked into the dark.

⚜

MAGGIE WORE her sky-blue hat to Briar's ceremony. It looked quite stunning with the charcoal-coloured skirt and coat she wore. Black was out of the question. After all, this wasn't a funeral. It was a ceremony. 'Funeral' was too final a word.

Reverend Calder had allowed Briar to be buried in the graveyard at St Bede's. Unmarried, independent, career-minded ... Briar was not the typical female interred in the hallowed earth of his church. Maggie supposed that William had said a quiet word in Calder's ear.

As she placed the sky-blue toque on her head that morning, Maggie had silently vowed to live by Briar's scripture. She would ensure that every lesson Briar had taught her would stay with her, always. To be courageous and bold, and to act when needed. And to never take no for an answer. Since she had learnt of her friend's death, something deep within Maggie had shifted. The world, now deprived of a woman such as Briar Haines, needed to beware.

Maggie intended to heed Briar's warning and be warrior enough for them both.

To begin the ceremony, Reverend Calder said a few words regarding the fragility of life, especially the tragic loss of one so young. He refrained from mentioning God, as per William's instructions, and Maggie was satisfied. When he finished, he introduced Matthew Drummond. Maggie was not aware he was going to speak. She realised that with most of the townspeople in attendance, he would not have wanted to miss the opportunity to show his solidarity. Over the few months he had been in Durham, he had somehow become the most prominent member of the community.

Matthew dressed in a sombre black suit and top hat. As he readied to speak, Maggie noticed the wash of unspent tears in his blue eyes. Despite what she had learnt about the mine, despite the fact he had sent Briar away, his obvious emotion tugged at her heart. Oh, how she longed for him to be honourable!

'While Miss Haines worked in my employ for such a brief period, she had an impact on all of us at the colliery that was akin to a lightning strike.' He paused, waiting for the quiet laughter to die. 'She not only resurrected my office's décor, which I believed was beyond redemption, she also resurrected my shrivelled old heart. For the first time in many years, I began to feel again.'

Maggie watched him as he spoke. Was it possible Matthew had real affection for Briar? Perhaps, discovering her snooping had truly broken his heart ...

He continued. 'Briar Haines was a valued employee and formidable woman. She became my friend and for that, I will be forever grateful.'

Matthew's eye fell to Maggie. His gaze was hopeful.

'From Briar, I learnt to seize opportunities when they arise. She was a woman of action and not one to ask permission. Her assertiveness and courage were qualities I envied and will always attempt to emulate.'

Maggie started. Matthew's last words mirrored the vow she had made that morning. Confused, she watched him make his way through the crowd. Those gathered patted him on the back, the women grasped his hand, all offered him condolences. In Briar's death, it appeared he had finally gained acceptance.

Maggie moved to the front of the group. It was her time to speak. Mister and Missus Cross were standing to the back, Marian wearing a mourning gown and a black mantilla. Then Maggie spied Jack, standing among those gathered. Dressed in a dark suit and bowler hat, he was less a crow and more a raven. Maggie had never seen him so formally attired. His cheeks were wet with tears. Smiling at him gently, she then braced herself. How could she get through this moment without weeping, too?

Reverend Calder had reluctantly agreed to her speaking. Yet she wasn't quite certain how to begin or how to continue once she had. Maggie could not be truthful about her relationship with Briar. She would have to skirt around the edges of their friendship, and that didn't seem to do her friend justice. Taking a deep breath, she gazed into the sky for an instant. The air was still misted, the weak sun barely touching the mourners.

'I've known Briar Haines for such a short time. But since our first meeting, she had a remarkable effect on me. Briar would often argue how similar we two were. Our ideals and beliefs were most definitely aligned; however, Briar was much braver and bolder than I.

'She liked to describe herself as a simple milliner's girl … and in her heart, she hadn't much changed from the young girl whose creativity and talent was nurtured in the backroom of a London millinery. Yet she was so much more than that. Intuitive, resourceful and so, so amusing, Briar was unique, a work of art.'

Maggie fell silent for a moment, gathering strength before continuing.

'But she was loyal, doggedly so. She would stop at nothing to keep a promise to a friend.'

She met Matthew's gaze in the crowd.

'And in that, we are alike.'

CHAPTER 32

THE DAY BEGAN like any other. Maggie walked William to Prebends Bridge, then they parted. William headed towards the High Street and the offices of the *Durham County Advertiser* and Maggie to Marian Cross's home on the eastern shore of Framwellgate Bridge. Maggie waited for a few minutes until William was out of sight, then she followed his path to the High Street.

Constable Stackhouse was at his desk. He looked up when he heard the heavy oak door push open.

'Miss Almond,' he said, rising. 'Good day to yer.' He gestured towards a chair and Maggie took a seat.

Following an abridged number of pleasantries − for an urgency had overcome Maggie the day before at Briar's ceremony − she got to the point of her visit.

'Have you developed any theories regarding Briar's death, Andy? I mean, it seems highly unlikely that she could have killed Reggie Owen. What's more, it seems near impossible that Reggie could have drowned Briar bearing the injuries he did. Doctor Carmichael believes he was killed with one blow.'

Andy nodded. 'To be truthful with yer, Miss Almond, I

agree with your theory. There must have been a third party present but—'

'Footprints?' Maggie suggested eagerly. 'Surely a footprint must have been captured.'

'Aye, there were many footprints but they became muddied by the fisherman and his son. By the time I arrived, the surrounding area was a literal quagmire. I couldn't tell one boot from t'other.'

Maggie bit her lip. 'You said the men found Briar face down on the bank of the river?'

'Aye. I found Owen's body face down as well. Ten yards from the first victim.'

But Briar drowned. Who took her out of the water, then? Maggie wondered. *And Reggie Owen was no victim ...*

'Have you spoken with Mister Drummond?' she asked. 'Did he tell you anything of Briar's movements that day?'

'Miss Almond, it's not procedure to discuss ...' Andy's words tapered away when he saw Maggie's stricken face. 'Let me see.'

As Andy rummaged through the files and documents on his desk, Maggie considered the physical evidence. Reggie's cart was found on the road, a hundred yards or so from the river. And Briar's bag had been found near Swin Bridge. Had she thrown it from the carriage to leave a clue to her whereabouts or had she lost it in the struggle?

Finally, Andy unearthed the document he was searching for and Maggie watched as his dark eyes moved along the lines like busy ants, searching for the relevant information. He cleared his throat and read.

'Drummond stated that "On the morning of the four-teenth I found Miss Haines attempting to pick the lock of the file cabinet. She gave me no reason for her actions. But she had betrayed my trust. Perhaps I acted recklessly in dismissing her, but for her to remain in my employ was unfeasible. I suggested to her that if she left town, I would refrain from calling the police. She agreed and left to gather her things. I immediately sent Reggie Owen to meet her at her lodgings and escort her to the station."'

Andy handed the statement to Maggie. As she read Matthew's words, she examined each delicate line of ink. It was exactly as he had explained it to her. Except he had not told her he'd asked Briar to leave town, or that he'd sent Reggie Owen to ensure she did. The empathy she had felt for him at the ceremony ebbed away.

What had been the haste? she wondered now. *Why not allow Briar more time to collect her things, to say goodbye? And why did he send a thug like Reggie to take her to the station instead of Jack?*

The constable sighed ruefully. 'Miss Almond, I know as well as you that something is amiss about this entire situation but without evidence ...' he opened his palms, 'there is very little I can do but assume Reggie Owen drove Briar Haines off the road while escorting her to Newcastle Station and attempted to ...' He paused momentarily and cleared his throat again. 'To force himself upon her. She somehow broke away and, in defending herself, fatally injured Owen. Then perhaps Owen still had enough life in him to kill her.'

Maggie looked at him doubtfully.

'Reggie was as thickset as an oak,' he continued. 'It is feasible he had strength enough to drown a poor wee lass like Miss Haines even with a head injury.'

Maggie frowned. 'And then have the energy to stumble ten yards away before collapsing himself?'

They stared at each other for a few minutes, attempting to reason out the conundrum. The scenario made little sense, and they both knew it. William had told her Andy was an honest man. However, without evidence or a witness, or a third party coming forward, there was nothing he could act upon.

As Maggie went to leave, Andy spoke again.

'By the way, I heard back from the Manchester constabulary.'

'Oh, yes?'

'They had nothing to report. As far as they are concerned, the Drummond family is spotless.'

'I see. Thank you, Andy. I appreciate your efforts. We can but hope a piece of evidence presents itself soon.'

They bid each other farewell and Maggie left the station. At a loss, she stood by the entrance for a time, deep in thought. Then she began walking towards the Stanley Pit.

SITTING BEHIND A TREE, concealed from the road, she waited for most of the day until the change of shift. At three o'clock, she finally heard the bell ring. Shortly afterwards, colliers began leaving through the gates, then soon after that, Matthew Drummond walked through the gates as well. Briar told her he always took the thirty minutes between shifts to leave the pit and walk to town. Other times, he'd walk in no particular direction. Briar had tracked his movements and could discern no pattern to them. But he was as regular as military drums, she said, 'as though he was trying to burn off energy'.

When there was no one left in sight, Maggie checked the time on her wristwatch, emerged from her hiding place, then walked along the road and through the gates, straight-backed as though she had business at the colliery. Which she did, she reasoned. A few colliers who were yet to depart hovered at the drinking trough. Maggie wished them a good afternoon as she walked towards the office. When she reached the door, she knocked and waited. After some seconds, she turned the handle. Locked.

Maggie realised she had ignored all her father's advice regarding engagement. She should have scouted the area, researched the enemy's movements before advancing. However, she couldn't wait. She could not wait one more day to discover the truth about Briar's death.

She turned and looked around. The colliers at the trough had departed, but there was another man who seemed to be patrolling the area. Although he had the look of the pit about him, he wore a suit. Better still, he had a healthy cluster of keys hanging from his belt.

'Excuse me,' she called.

He looked her way.

'I was a friend of Miss Haines. Her poor mother sent me a telegram this morning and asked if I might drop by to see if she left anything behind. She's desperate for a keepsake, you understand.'

It was a risk, but one she was willing to take to get inside the office.

Before the man could speak, she continued. 'I'm due home in less than an hour and my husband becomes most concerned when I am late. If you're able, would you mind opening the door for me? I'll only be a minute or two.'

Maggie glanced at her watch. She had less than twenty minutes until Drummond's return.

The man approached warily. He was of a similar build to Tommy Fellowes: slightly hunched, legs bowed. When his eyes alighted on Maggie's beseeching, troubled countenance, he smiled.

'You're Miss Almond, aren't yer?'

'Indeed, Sir. To whom do I have the pleasure of speaking?' His accent told Maggie he was one of the fabled Yorkshire men she and William had tried so hard to spot.

'Well, you'll no believe it, Miss, but me name is Francis Drake.'

Maggie feigned astonishment. 'Surely not! The great explorer and privateer! How did you ever wind up in Durham, Sir Francis?' She had no time for games but realised she must play along with the pantomime to gain his trust.

The man laughed. 'For me sins,' he said. 'For me sins ...' He had clearly introduced himself in this way many times before and enjoyed the shock on people's faces when he revealed his name.

'If you wouldn't mind, Mister Drake ...' Maggie gestured to the door.

Francis Drake approached, removing the keys from his belt. 'I heard about your stoush with Reggie Owen on the High Street. I must commend yer, young lady. He wasn't the most amenable of lads and he gave most folk a hard time. It dinna surprise me in the least that he treated his missus similar. I'm not sorry Reggie Owen has taken his final breath. Although I'm sorry for your friend, Miss Haines ... She was a cheery soul to have around.'

Maggie felt a flush of emotion at the man's words. Briar had touched so many people's hearts, even a burly Yorkshire-man's. *Unlike Reggie Owen*, she mused. *He certainly wasn't liked in Durham. There seems to be any number of people happy to see Reggie six feet under.*

Mister Drake unlocked the door. 'I'll just be here, Miss, on the balcony,' he said, pushing it open for her. 'Call out if yer need anything.'

From the doorway, Maggie scanned the grounds, then checked her watch once more. Fifteen minutes left – ten if she wanted to avoid Matthew Drummond completely. She turned to the room, then looked around to gain her bearings.

Briar had decorated the room in a tasteful manner, and everything was spotless. A vase of violets sat on the window ledge. *Briar's handiwork*, thought Maggie. Their slight droop and faded petals reminded her just how recently Briar had been alive. Less than a week ago, she had picked the flowers and placed them in that spot. Maggie gazed at them for longer than she should.

Averting her eyes, she moved to Briar's desk and checked the drawers. They were empty. Not a pin remained. Then she approached Drummond's desk: gleaming mahogany. She scoured the surface and the drawers, searching every nook and cranny for anything that seemed awry. But nothing did.

Stopping, she took in the room once more, noticing the hangings on the wall. Maggie checked behind them, pressing her cheek to the wall and inching out the frame. Nothing was concealed, no hidden safe. Nothing. Yet something was amiss. Maggie examined the four walls again, then she looked above her at the gas lamp. Finally, she lowered her eyes to the ground.

It was the rug.

Axminster.

It was much too grand for the room, more suited to a manor house than a pitmaster's cottage. Briar would never have chosen that rug. Never.

Stooping to her hands and knees, in an energetic flurry of activity Maggie attempted to shift the thing. She was barely able to lift the corners. It seemed weighted, similar to the expensive carpets and rugs at Chester Square. It took the efforts of both Beatrice and Ada to drag them outside for cleaning. When she was a child, she would join them in the weekly ritual and grip the rug beater in her hands. It was the only time in her life when she'd been given permission to hit out. How she had enjoyed it ...

Now, she hastily checked her watch. There were but a few minutes remaining, yet suddenly, she didn't care about the time or being seen. She was certain the key to Briar's death was at her fingertips.

She was determined to discover just exactly what was hidden under that Axminster.

Maggie examined it again. The legs of Briar's desk were pinning the rug to the ground. Fuelled by frustration and grief, Maggie attempted to push the desk away. As she did, she heard Drummond's voice on the balcony. She stopped, heart pounding, breathless from her exertions.

Time slowed. Maggie stared at the door handle for what seemed like an age. Then Drummond entered.

'Maggie,' he said, cordially. 'It's so lovely to receive you ... but I am disappointed. Mister Drake informs me you're here to collect Miss Haines's belongings. Her mother sent you a telegram, apparently.'

He smiled and closed the door.

'Now, we are both aware Miss Haines had no family to speak of.'

Maggie swallowed. Her heart was beating madly.

'You should have come to me, Maggie. I could have assisted you.'

Maggie tried to remember all she had learnt from her father and Briar about deception. After a moment, she spoke.

'But Matthew, I did drop by to look for something Briar might have left here in her haste to depart. You see, last year, I lost someone extremely dear to me.'

Maggie walked a little closer and showed him her wristwatch.

'She bequeathed this to me and I can't describe how much comfort this small token has offered me in my time of grief.' Maggie looked at the timepiece fondly. 'I was hoping I might find a similar memento with which to remember Briar. I confess,' she smiled, 'to having coloured my appeal to Mister Drake with a white lie or two, so he might allow me entrance. He was most kind once I explained I did not wish to disturb you with such a sentimental mission.'

She attempted to keep her voice level, natural, as though her behaviour was entirely understandable.

'Ah, but we both know that's not the truth, either.'

Drummond approached. Two steps across the Axminster rug. Maggie met his gaze.

'Because surely,' he continued, 'as we are friends, you could have come to me with your request.'

It seemed to Maggie that the most sensible course of action now was to keep silent.

Drummond strolled across the room to the window. Looking out, he waved to a pitman.

'Miss Haines was an exceptionally curious young lady,' he said as he turned back to Maggie. 'But that didn't strike me as unusual, at first. It was when I discovered she was a friend of yours from London, that you had a history together ... I must admit, it alerted my suspicion.'

Maggie gasped. *How did he know?*

'When I found out, I had Reggie follow her. It seems she often visited you at the lovely cottage you share with Mister Dodd and his mother. He followed her everywhere, reporting to me each day just what he had discovered.'

Oh, Briar! Why hadn't you realised?

'It was then that I discovered you two were more than friends. Much more, in fact ...'

Maggie was breathing hard, attempting to remain calm, willing herself not to run. *Had Reggie Owen witnessed our kiss? Had he been spying through the window like a schoolboy?* Maggie imagined Reggie's fury at seeing the woman who took his wife away kissing her employer's assistant. *That's why he hated Briar ...*

'It made me wonder what role Mister Dodd had played in your arrangement,' Drummond said, raising an eyebrow.

Maggie struggled to contain herself. She straightened and lifted her chin.

'Well, I am the one who is disappointed now, Matthew,' she said. 'If you've nothing more mature to say, I must leave. I apologise for the inconvenience my unexpected visit may have caused you.'

Maggie went to collect her bag from Briar's desk but Drummond intercepted her, clutching her arm.

'I don't think so, Maggie Almond.'

CHAPTER 33

MAGGIE HUDDLED against the pillar of Prebends Bridge. The stone was cold but its strength fortifying. Her heart had calmed but she could still feel it pounding in her throat. She couldn't have returned to the cottage; Grace was home. All she could think to do was wait for William, as she always did. She pulled her coat around herself tightly and cried. Until now, she had not allowed herself the luxury of tears.

She had run from Drummond's office and the Stanley Pit, run the long way back to the river so no one would see her. Now that she was settled in a hollow beneath the bridge, hot tears streamed down her cold cheeks. In the waning light, through the blur of her emotions, she saw the river had turned an unusual blend of pink and gold, but she pressed her eyes together, fighting the memory of that afternoon, so recent and raw.

'You're such a fine woman, Maggie,' Drummond had said, moving his hand down her arm. 'I sensed a connection the moment we spoke on the green.'

She felt him twist a lock of her hair around his finger, the press of him against her back. Maggie looked at the door, then to the window, attempting to discern some movement on the balcony. She wondered if Drummond had dismissed Mister Drake. Listening hard at the silence, she willed a noise, any noise that might show she was not alone.

'If you would kindly release me, Matthew,' she said, turning. 'I should get home. I told William my destination and he'll be expecting me.'

He smiled. 'I doubt very much you told Mister Dodd, or anyone, in fact, of your whereabouts. You act on impulse, Maggie, just as I do. Your display at the town hall ... brilliant! And the dressing down you gave Mister Owen? Why, that stirred me to my core. You act best when you are fired up, don't you? That's when you're most exhilarating.'

She forced herself to look him in the eyes. They were arctic.

'I came here to find what Briar couldn't.'

He nodded, stroking her cheek. 'And did you?'

She shook her head. Recalling her father's words about being interrogated by the enemy, she was determined to remain composed and tell as much of the truth as she was able.

He leant in until she could feel his breath on her cheek. 'Then perhaps I'm not the devil you take me for.'

'I'd like you to let me go now, please. You're making me extremely uncomfortable.'

'You're uncomfortable!' he cried, moving away from her.

Maggie rushed to the door and tried the handle. Locked.

'I have done nothing but attempt to fit in here! But you and Dodd and Briar Haines have gone to great lengths to send me packing!'

Send me packing ... Maggie swallowed. It was the same expression Briar had used in her note. She scanned the room for a weapon, but to no avail.

'It seems nothing I do will change your opinion of me. I

confessed I cheated during our chess. I offered you the foundation funds for your school. For Christ's sake, I have given the men of Durham their jobs back! What do I need to do to earn your trust? You have rebuffed all my attempts to prove my good. I feel I might as well be the demon you all believe me to be.'

'Then let the inspectors in!' Maggie shouted, turning her back to the door. His steely eyes flashed and she steadied herself. 'You say you want to be part of the town then there is a very simple solution, Matthew. Let the inspectors into the seams!'

Then in two steps, he was upon her, his grip on her arms vicelike. He pressed his cheek to hers. 'There it is,' he said. 'The fire that stirs me so.'

She attempted to squirm out of his grasp, but he held her firm.

'We have a connection, Maggie. You want to be part of this town as much as I do. And you know what you need to do in order to achieve it, but your ideals prevent you from seeing it through. I know why you haven't married William Dodd – your heart won't allow it.' He put his lips to her ear. 'You're just like me... you want to live life on your own terms,' he whispered.

She jerked her head away. 'So, you're not allowing an inspection of the mine on principle?' Maggie asked, astounded.

He gave her a sly smile. 'Not everyone needs proof of my actions to believe in me, Maggie.'

Pinning her arms to her sides even more tightly, he gazed at her, relishing her discomfort.

'Do you really think anyone would believe *you* if you claimed I ravished you?'

Her heart rose in her throat but she refused to lower her eyes.

'Everyone knows you're a whore. All they need is proof.'

'William would believe me,' she said, struggling to keep her voice from breaking. 'And he's the only person who matters.'

'Even the pure-of-heart Mister Dodd would have doubts, Maggie. Let's face it. How long has he been waiting for you? The man must have the patience of a saint!'

He gazed at her for a moment, searching her eyes. 'You're exactly the same as Irena. She put it about wherever she could, but when I offered her love, a genuine connection, she rebuffed me.'

Irena. The woman to whom Matthew was engaged. He had told her their story when they had played chess.

'But you are more beautiful than Irena,' he whispered close to her cheek. 'I cannot count the number of times I have imagined this—'

'This? Imagined what? There is nothing between us, Matthew!' She refused to accept the situation. She refused to close her eyes or look away. 'Let me go.'

He straightened and stared at her.

'The number of times, Maggie Almond, I have imagined burying myself in your sweet, pink cunny and now, I finally can.'

The moment didn't seem real. Surely, it was a nightmare, a hallucination. He kissed her neck. Her shoulders tensed as though a jar of spiders had been set loose on her skin.

She screamed then. Filling her lungs with air, she released the biggest noise of which her body was capable.

He silenced her with the press of his mouth. She almost choked as his tongue forced entry. Gagging, she struggled to push him away. When he didn't budge, she bit his lip. She tasted his blood, warm and metallic. He broke away and she darted towards the window. He was upon her in an instant, grabbing her by the hair, wrenching her to face him.

'There's no one to hear you, Maggie,' he said, wiping his mouth. 'The pitmen are below ground and I dismissed Mister Drake when I arrived.'

She struggled for release. Tears sprang to her eyes, and terror mounted in her chest like a flame. She kicked and clawed and spat, but he was too strong. With what seemed such a slight effort, he had her on the ground. Her head hit the floor hard and a sharp pain traversed her neck and shoulders. He grabbed her legs and hauled her across the room to the rug. Pinning her shoulders to the floor, he stared down at her like a hungry wolf. She screamed again. He pressed his hand over her mouth and she bit him once more, drawing blood. Pulling his hand away, he examined the injury.

He smirked. 'This is going to be most enjoyable,' he commented calmly, then ripped open her blouse. He stared at the creamy skin above her corset for a moment, almost lovingly.

'You are incredibly delicious, Maggie. I could eat you,' he said, tracing a line with his finger around her throat. 'I almost took you during our chess match. The way you stroked your neck before you made a move and the way in which you licked your lips after each sip of chocolate ... it inflamed me. It was all I could do to hold myself back from throwing you on the ground and fucking you in the drawing room. Andrew has been with me for years. He is extremely discreet. He wouldn't have made a fuss.

'Then when I caught up with you on the bridge and you touched my arm, so casually as though it meant nothing ... But it meant everything, didn't it? And I knew at that moment that you wanted me as much as I wanted you. After I left you, I went back to my house and sat where I had sat during our games. I imagined you opposite me – your buttery skin and the glorious rounds of your breasts – and it gratified me to know you felt as I. Then, when Reggie told me what he'd seen occur between you and Briar Haines, I knew your feelings for Mister Dodd weren't set in stone.'

He's convinced I care for him ... the man is beyond reasoning with, Maggie thought, astounded.

Restraining her arms with his knees, Drummond lifted his shirt over his head.

This will happen if I don't do something ...

She screamed again and he clutched her face tight in a pincer grip, making her jawbone ache. She sobbed in terror and pain.

'Shut up, or I'll have to hit you. And I'd prefer you conscious for this.'

He released her face and began to unbutton his fly.

Her eyes flicked from the floor to the walls and the ceiling. She was trapped. There was no escape. Furious and terrified, her heart pounded a tattoo against her chest. All she could do was writhe and struggle. She squeezed her eyes closed, attempting to reach beyond her present, reaching for an escape. Suddenly, an image entered her mind: Atalanta. Knowing the great huntress had defeated her attackers, Maggie vowed to keep fighting.

She would not allow this to happen.

'It's no wonder Irena left you,' she spat through her tears, 'if this is your idea of seduction.'

He stared at her hard. 'I gave Irena the best of me, but it wasn't enough. I won't let you make the same mistake, Maggie.' He drew up her skirts and she locked her legs tight. 'If it's romance you want, I'm happy to oblige.'

He released her breasts from her corset. She could feel his breath and his lips against her skin. He pinned her arms again with his hands, then slid down her body, kissing and licking, exploring her belly, then her thighs. In his reverie, he seemed to forget himself. His hands left her arms as he attempted to force apart her legs.

Now free, Maggie's hands combed the floor for anything she might use, scratching into the pile of the carpet. *There's nothing. Nothing!* Then she felt it. Turning her head, she saw it was Briar's hat pin, the one her granny had given her. Maggie gripped it in her fist, raised her hand and thrust it into the side of Drummond's head.

He gasped and rolled off her, pressing his hand against his ear. She stumbled to her feet and ran to the window. She threw it open and climbed through the portal to safety.

Now, as she sat beneath the bridge hiding like a hunted rabbit, she murmured to herself, 'I am safe.' But a terror seemed to have engulfed her like a fog. She loathed feeling this way. She could still taste Drummond's blood in her mouth. Closing her eyes, she waited.

Then she heard his footsteps on the bridge and down the stairs to the path beside the river. He was whistling. Had she ever heard him whistle before? Of course she had. When he spotted her, he went to her immediately. He quickly scanned her face and the position of her body. His expression – a dreaded mix of fear and concern – made her sob even more.

'What is it, lass?' William asked, joining her on the ground.

He touched her gently, wondering if she was injured. Her hair was loose and dishevelled, her eyes puffed and red.

'Maggie, tell me,' he said, his voice growing alarmed. He inched opened her coat and stared at her ripped blouse. And the blood. 'Are you hurt?'

All the while she watched him, taking in each reaction, watching his mind make sense of it.

'I went to the colliery this afternoon,' she began.

He gazed at her sorrowfully.

'I needed to act. I went searching for the second set of ledgers, although I hoped not to find them, William. I had so hoped Drummond was an honourable man ...' She let out a sob.

He moved closer and wrapped his arm around her shoulder then pulled her coat across her chest.

'But he found me there and ...'

'What did he do, Maggie?' he said, urging her to continue.

'He wouldn't allow me to leave when I asked.'

'Did he hurt you?'

She nodded.

'How?'

Maggie swallowed.

'Not in that way,' she responded. 'But he was going to.'

William's chest heaved, his body tensed.

'I found this.' Maggie opened her fist.

Briar's hat pin lay in her palm. She'd had it grasped tight since she'd run from the pit. Now her knuckles ached, and the emerald had broken the skin of her palm.

'It's Briar's. She left it behind. It was buried in the pile of the Axminster rug. It was her granny's, and she would never have left it unless there had been a struggle or ...'

'Or?'

'Or she hoped I'd find it.'

୧ଓ

WILLIAM BUTTONED Maggie's coat and walked by her side back to the cottage, her arm looped through his. All the while, anger was building in his chest like a torrent about to break the banks. He glanced at Maggie. Trembling, shaken, terrified. He stopped and removed his coat and wrapped it around her shoulders. He had never seen her so vulnerable. Drummond had made her a different woman. He inhaled deeply, struggling to tamp down the urge to go immediately to the pit. William stared at his boots as they stepped along the path. They didn't feel like his feet or legs. He couldn't feel the ground beneath him. He suddenly thought it might be a dream. Maggie squeezed his hand.

When they arrived at the cottage, William prepared the bath. He helped her undress. She was sore, she said. Her whole body ached. He examined her as she stepped into the tub. There were bruises on her back and arms. And blood. She had bitten him, she said. To William, it looked as though he'd bitten her as well. Her neck and breasts were peppered with welts. As he went to wash her hair, he noticed a cut on her head ... her chestnut locks were matted with blood. The cut was not deep, but a tender, egg-sized lump had formed around it.

'He pushed me to the floor,' she murmured.

She's such a wee lass, he thought, as he rubbed the cloth over her slender back. *What sort of man would force himself upon a woman?*

William lifted her arm and gently rubbed a cloth over it. 'You'd tell me, wouldn't you?'

She turned her face to his, covering her body as best she could with her arms.

'You'd tell me if he ... It would make no difference to the way I feel about you.'

'He didn't,' she said. 'And I would.'

Thank God she fought back. Thank God she is here now, he thought. He ladled the warm water onto her head and she winced.

'My poor lass,' he said. There was a steeliness in his tone he could not control. She turned in the tub and faced him.

'I know what you want to do,' she said. 'But you mustn't.'

He frowned.

'You want to punish Drummond. But he was correct in what he told me.'

William looked at her, astonished. 'Nothing that man said to you was true.'

'I mean, we have no evidence, William. Nothing to prove he is anything other than what he says he is. There may be something in his office, but it is now too dangerous for either of us to go there. All we have is me. And who will believe it when I speak out and inform Constable Stackhouse that Drummond attempted to rape me? Drummond was right when he said I'm viewed as a whore.'

His heart was breaking for her. *How can I ever protect a woman like her?* He had believed that if he could do nothing else in this life, he could protect her. But it seemed he was mistaken.

'And now, he is the injured party,' she continued. 'He gave me a few bruises and a graze on my head. I jammed a hat pin in his ear. He could argue I was trespassing.'

William was fast losing control of the fire in his chest. *How can she be so reasoned?* He could not understand how logic had so quickly replaced the fury and passion that had driven her to go to the Stanley Pit.

'If you were to beat Drummond to a pulp, it would be you who'll end up behind bars. And that I couldn't live with.'

'But how can I look him in the eye?' he said. 'How can I ever be around him without wanting to ...' William clenched his fists.

'You will just have to. The same way as I will.'

CHAPTER 34

MAGGIE SPENT the next two days at home in bed. William visited the Crosses and sent her apologies, citing a cold – a condition, he assured them, that she would recover from quickly. However, Maggie was uncertain how long it would take to recover from her encounter with Drummond. Her body still ached and the lump on her head still smarted. But the pain from her injuries seemed minor compared to the effect his attack had had on her mind. The events of that afternoon haunted her like a fevered nightmare, no matter how hard she attempted to push the man from her thoughts. The feeling of his breath, lips and hands on her skin, the glimmer of salacity and longing in his eyes ... and the smell. He stank of the pit. It was an odour she had grown accustomed to, even welcomed, as the scent of home. But on Drummond, it had made her wretch.

Worse than all was the fear that was now her permanent companion. When she had fled the colliery, it pursued her mercilessly. Now, it lingered like an unwelcome guest. She had been helpless, utterly powerless. No matter how hard she had struggled, he was stronger. Maggie had believed she could overcome any foe; it's what her father had told her. But if she hadn't found the hat pin …

Maggie closed her eyes tight, pushing it all away. Her thoughts drifted and latched onto Briar. Maggie wondered if Briar had endured a similar experience at the hands of Reggie Owen. She pressed her face into the pillow.

William had been wonderful, but she sensed a distance. She could see him wanting to get close to her, to comfort her, yet holding back. She could not bear his unease and resolved to speak with him that evening.

⊙⚜⊚

AFTER DINNER, they bid an early goodnight to Grace and retired to their room. They did not talk as they prepared for bed. Maggie waited until they were both settled under the covers.

'There's something you're not saying.'

There was a long silence. The sound of his light breath told her he was still awake. Their fingers twined. Finally, he spoke.

'Why did you go there, Maggie?'

She turned her head towards him and examined the outline of his profile in the scant light.

'Why did you go to the pit?' he asked again.

She took a deep breath, readying herself to explain. 'I'd seen Andy Stackhouse that morning. He showed me Drummond's statement. The man lied to me, William. He hadn't just let Briar go. He had instructed Reggie to escort Briar out of town.'

She stopped and looked at him again. He was noble, honourable … everything Matthew Drummond could never be.

'I went there to find answers. I needed to act for Briar's sake.'

William released her hand and placed his arms behind his head. Feeling his hurt like a welt to her chest, she reframed her response.

'Without evidence, you can't write about what you witnessed underground, and Andy can't investigate Briar's murder.'

'So, you went to the pit looking for evidence?'

'Yes.'

'Evidence neither I nor Andy could produce?'

'I couldn't wait any longer, William. I had to know.'

William leapt from the bed. Startled, Maggie turned on the lamp. Pacing the room like a tiger, his face was an unrecognisable mix of fury and sorrow. Large tears pooled in his hazel eyes. Finally, unable to keep his fury caged any longer, he slammed his fist against the wall.

Her heart broke at the sight of him.

'I never imagined Drummond would ...' Maggie began, clutching her knees to her chest. 'I believed I'd be able to handle the situation – slip in and out before he returned. Despite your ... *our* suspicions, I didn't take him for a man who would be violent.' She swallowed, slowly realising where her rash actions had led. 'Violent with me, anyway.'

He turned and looked at her. 'You were wrong, weren't you?'

The brutal flatness of his tone struck her into silence.

Drummond had driven a wedge between them. *Was that his purpose?* she wondered. *Divide and conquer?* He had admitted his longing for her, an aspect of their encounter she had not shared with William, fearing such a revelation might drive him to take action.

Maggie had observed William since it happened, since he had found her huddled under the bridge. He had gone about his business as though in a dream, staring through the window towards the dales or gazing into his tea until it was cold and undrinkable.

'Oh, Maggie,' he said finally, desperately. 'I failed you. My only job is to protect you. After I found you, I should have gone to the pit and killed him.'

Alarmed, she straightened and stared at him in the soft glow of the lamp, her heart reaching for him.

'I've never had murder in my heart, but it's there now, like an unrelenting burn.' He placed his hand against his chest. 'To feel this way and not be able to act. It's that what lies between us.' He paused. 'I'm angry with you, Maggie.'

She stared at him, not quite comprehending.

'I'm angry with you for placing yourself in danger. If I can't protect you, who will?'

'I will!'

Doubt was written all over his face. William wore the same expression that she had read on the faces of a hundred men. She threw off the bedclothes and stood before him.

'Be honest! Tell me exactly what is bothering you. Say it!' An anger such as she had never known ignited inside her.

He looked down at her, his mouth clenched tight. He shook his head almost indiscernibly.

'Say it!' she demanded once more, standing in front of him toe-to-toe.

Then he did.

'You truly believe women are equal and capable of doing without a man,' he said with conviction, 'but they are not.'

Before she could stop herself, Maggie raised her arm and slapped his face. Her palm stung when she drew it away. William stared at her for a moment in surprise, then she closed her eyes, attempting to calm herself, struggling to find her way to peace.

'I'm sorry, lass,' William said finally.

She opened her eyes. 'I'm sorry, too.'

He took her in his arms. 'I didn't mean it, Maggie. It's Drummond, not you who I'm angry with. He had no right to do what he did. I saw him today from the office window. He was strolling down the High Street, cool as you like, shaking hands, chatting with the shopkeepers, as though only the day before he hadn't ... He was wearing a bandage over his ear. You hurt him, lass, and that gives me some comfort, but it took every ounce of my self-control to stop from going out onto the road and wringing his neck.'

Maggie pressed her cheek against his chest.

'And I'm angry with myself for doing nothing,' he finished.

'I shouldn't have gone to the pit by myself. That's the truth,' Maggie said. 'I was trespassing. That's the truth as well. But it doesn't give Matthew Drummond the right to attack me. He has stolen something from both of us, William, but I know without a doubt we'll be able to find it again.'

'Together?'

'Together.'

THEY SLEPT LATE the following morning. A sense of understanding had formed between them and the burden Matthew Drummond had laid on their shoulders seemed lighter. The knowledge they were united against their common foe bolstered them both. They woke to the sound of knocking at the door.

'Willie, Mags, are yer awake in there?' It was Jack.

William went to the window and leaned out. 'He's brought the hansom,' he said. 'There's luggage.'

Maggie imagined Briar stepping from the cab as she had

on her arrival in Durham. What Maggie wouldn't give to live that day again ...

'Perhaps it's Papa,' she said, hoping it was. Her father's company would help mend her wounded spirit.

'It's a parent,' William informed her, drawing his head through the window. 'But it's not your father.'

Maggie threw back the covers, clutched at her robe and ran from the room. She flew down the stairs. When she opened the door, Lydia stood on the other side, wearing a breathtaking travelling ensemble. Maggie, still dressed in her shift and dressing gown, seemed dwarfed by the older woman.

'Good morning, darling,' Lydia said and offered her daughter a kind but cautious smile. The sun was rising behind her, bathing her in light, giving her an angelic appearance.

At the sight of her, Maggie burst into tears and fell into her arms.

ॐ

WILLIAM MADE breakfast for them all, Jack included, while Maggie and her mother became reacquainted.

'You know, Maggie, I loathe to admit when I am at fault, but I was and have been for so, so long. My actions were despicable, and I can only hope one day you will forgive me. I have missed you so incredibly much.'

Maggie grasped her mother's hand. Jack viewed the scene as a cautious spectator. William had mentioned the formidable Countess of Wessex on several occasions.

'Thank you, Mister Dodd,' she said when William placed her tea on the table.

'You can call me "William", Ma'am,' he said.

'And you can call me "Lydia".'

Maggie smiled. Briar had vanished from her world and her mother had re-entered. She supposed that was life; a series of exits and entrances. All the world's a stage. *Shakespeare knew the world so well*, she thought.

THE GROUP WENT about the business of breakfast, for it was a business-like activity for men like William and Jack, men who were raised with little and taught to value every morsel God gave them as though it were gold. They ate with a determination and single-mindedness which fascinated Maggie. She imagined that their subconscious told them if they took their eyes off their plate for even a second, someone could snatch it away.

Lydia discussed her journey from London. Jack's hansom impressed her.

'It's far more lovely than any of the cabs on London streets at the moment,' she commented.

Jack's chest puffed with pride as though the Queen herself had complimented him.

Lydia had also brought with her several parcels containing gifts for Maggie. After breakfast, as William and Jack saw to the dishes, the women went upstairs.

'Your father described your lifestyle here in the North East. Although I wanted to gift you all of Madame Tisseur's latest creations, I settled on these.'

Maggie opened the packages. In them were a selection of simple skirts and blouses, a beautiful velvet frock coat coloured a dark chocolate brown, black suede walking shoes and several more personal items, including a silk nightgown and matching slippers.

'Part of your trousseau?' Lydia suggested.

Maggie examined the silk. It was the lightest shade of pink she had ever seen.

'Madame Tisseur calls it "rosewater". Just the merest

blush of colour.'

'It's lovely,' Maggie said, then began to cry again. 'It all is.'

'More tears? Good gracious, Margaret. I wanted my arrival to be an occasion for joy.'

'Oh, it is. Much more than you can know.' She hugged her mother. The gifts were a sign of her mother's acceptance of her choices. 'And William?'

'He is lovely, Maggie. So devoted to you, good-humoured and handsome. What's more, he cooks! I couldn't ask for anything more for my only child.'

Maggie wiped her eyes. Although gaining her mother's approval had never seemed important to her before, now she had it, the feeling was wonderful. To know Lydia supported her was worth more to Maggie than all the gowns in Madame Tisseur's boutique.

'And there's this, my darling,' Lydia said, producing a small package from her purse. It was wrapped in red and gold washi – delicate Japanese paper a friend of Henry's had crafted. 'Your father told me about your plans for a school.'

Maggie unwrapped the parcel. What lay within was a bank cheque for £150.

'I want to play a role in your dream, Maggie. And I won't allow you to refuse my contribution,' Lydia said. 'You can name the library or a wing after me.'

Maggie laughed, wiping the tears from her eyes. 'I'm afraid it won't be that type of school, Mother.'

'It will be one day, darling.'

Maggie kissed her mother's cheek in gratitude and love.

'And Papa?' Maggie asked, carefully putting away her gifts.

Lydia rose and moved to the window. She examined the dales for a time, moving her head as she followed the sway of the grasses and wildflowers.

'When he returned to London from seeing you, he travelled to Hampshire. He has been staying there ever since,' she said without looking at her daughter. Then she sighed and sat down on the bed.

'I was foolish. So foolish,' she said, stroking the velvet of the frock coat. 'For twenty-five years, I was so overcome with guilt, I wasn't capable of loving Henry in the way he deserved. But what I feel for him now is so much greater than what I ever felt for Raymond ... Maggie, I'm afraid I've squandered Henry's love. Now I want him desperately, but I'm concerned it's too late.'

Maggie took her mother's hand. 'Papa adores you. Those types of emotions don't just evaporate.' She thought of Grace. Surely that was merely a passing fancy?

'When Henry returned from seeing you, he had changed. Always so calm, he was frustrated and dispirited. Apart from you, he refused to discuss anything with me. Then, without warning, he packed his bags and left for the country. At this time of year, he left for the country!'

Her father was wrestling with a dilemma, Maggie realised. Was it Grace or Lydia who would make him truly happy? What risk could he live with?

Gathering herself, Lydia fixed her hair. 'By the way, where is Missus Dodd?' she asked. 'I am looking forward to meeting her.'

'She is studying at the university.'

Lydia raised her eyebrows in surprise.

'Grace won't be home until this evening,' Maggie said, suddenly grateful for her absence.

⚜

THE FOLLOWING MORNING, Maggie watched both women carefully, as a scientist might observing the behaviour of animals. As carefully, she imagined, as George Henry Lewes studying his sea creatures. Both women were beautiful and intelligent, forceful and wise. Her father had been wrong, Maggie realised. He hadn't formed an attachment with Grace because she was different to Lydia; it was as though her father had fallen in love twice with the same woman. The only discernible difference was social class.

The two mothers – Henry's women – seemed unusually comfortable in one another's company. Maggie did not believe Lydia suspected Henry and Grace of any wrongdoing. She did not believe her mother would be capable of suspecting her husband of a liaison with a woman of Grace's humble status. The women were extremely gracious to one another, with Lydia thanking Grace many times for her hospitality.

'The more the merrier,' Grace responded. 'I miss having a full house.'

'Tell me about your studies, Grace. Maggie mentioned the sciences, I believe?'

Maggie watched her mother listen to Grace with sincere interest.

'You're extremely fortunate to have this opportunity. I wish I had been permitted to study.'

'It's never too late, as Maggie showed me,' Grace said.

'Yes, mother, you would make a wonderful lawyer,' Maggie said wryly.

Lydia smiled. 'My daughter is mocking me, Grace, by referring to my litigious nature.'

William rose and collected the cups and plates.

'If Maggie had her way, all the women in England would be at university instead of seeing to the comforts of their men …'

Maggie threw her serviette at him and the women laughed.

CHAPTER 35

The Manchester Guardian
Wednesday, November 24, 1880

DEAR READER,

Last week I told you about my gradual and growing affection for George Lewes. After a rocky, volatile beginning, our relationship soared heavenward and my love for him grew exponentially. My relationship with fiction writing was much the same.

You will recall, dear Reader, that I once feared my imagination. But as soon as George and I became one, my love for writing fiction bordered on obsession. I had no time to lose; remember, I began writing novels rather late in life compared to other authors. Therefore, once I lay pen to paper, I took to the art like a duck to water.

For the better part of two decades, I steadily produced and published. After *Adam Bede* came *The Mill on the Floss*, closely followed by *Silas Marner*. In 1863, Blackwood's published *Romola* in three volumes. *Felix Holt: The Radical* came next. All were successful, both financially and critically.

Wedged between these major works were shorter novellas, plays, poems and books of philosophy and ideas. With each new project, George negotiated a more lucrative contract. He relished this process and would talk endlessly about the negotiations, travelling back and forth to London, knowing he possessed all the power in the world, for he was representing George Eliot. I trusted him completely to captain my career, and he steered it to outstanding success.

Finally, *Middlemarch*, the book many consider my tour de force, was born in 1871.

After *Middlemarch* appeared in the world, the adulation I had craved since girlhood became a reality. However, it is not without irony, dear Reader, that I admit to you now that it proved too overwhelming for me. Despite my wealth and fame, I often found myself melancholy.

An author's success can be so fleeting, so George advised I get out more in society and 'be seen'. Readers' tastes are fickle, he informed me, and he insisted it was necessary for me to remain in their line of sight. Yet after an evening mingling with strangers and conversing on minor topics (all so unnatural and forced), even the hint of a headache could turn into a debilitating migraine that would leave me in bed for days. George enjoyed the attention and the company (he had always loved entertaining) yet I preferred limiting my social life to the those I trusted, such as my dear friend Barbara, who you may know now as 'Barbara Bodichon', and Maria Congreve. I was always happiest to remain at home.

The Brays and Sara Hennell eventually forgave me for my secrets and my choices, and they, too, were often by my side. But looking back, most of that time was spent abroad or in Surrey at my suggestion, away from those demanding my attention. When the years became our enemy and illness began intruding on our lives, we took refuge during the winter months at The Priory, our London home in Regent's Park. Our private Sunday salons there became renowned and, like everything else in my life, George managed these as well.

Invitations were sent on a Tuesday to interesting authors and thinkers, people whom I didn't shrink from the prospect of meeting. There were the regular attendees, including Thomas Huxley, Henry James and the Trollopes, and many other creative luminaries. George also received dozens of messages each week from those he referred to as 'lesser mortals'. These were usually younger readers of my work who would nominate themselves to be included in our weekly gatherings. There were so many that George developed a waiting list and would choose two or three each week to attend. And then there were those who arrived on the day and waited on North Bank for permission to enter ...

I realise what you must think of me, dear Reader, for surely, gaining an audience with Queen Victoria would have been a simpler task than attending a George Eliot salon! However, those carefully curated Sunday afternoons were a means of managing my success with which I could cope.

I accepted, somewhat grudgingly, that I could not be a hermit, although my first instinct was (and still is) to hide inside my shell. My success depended, in large, on the expression of my ideas and opinions; it was impossible for me to hide away any longer, no matter how much I desired to do so.

இஜ்ரு

IT HAD BEEN five days since the incident with Drummond and the dreadful event was gradually becoming more distant. Maggie had been strengthened by Lydia's arrival, and William and Grace's constant, yet discreet, care.

To her surprise, Lydia insisted they go for a walk on the dales early each morning, an activity that allowed them time to renew their relationship. On this morning, Maggie had made a point of picking some wildflowers as they had explored the Durham countryside. It was November the 6th, the second anniversary of George Lewes's death, and she intended to visit Marian that afternoon.

Gripped in her hand was a pretty selection of wildflowers: wood cranesbill, rough hawkbit and wild honeysuckle. The names amused Lydia, as did Maggie's intention of assembling the arrangement herself. Maggie wanted to show her mother the beauty of the North East and the delight that came from such a simple activity as picking and arranging wildflowers.

As they were returning to the cottage, it was Lydia who spied the carriage first. Maggie noticed that her mother had looked at the vehicle with hope; she could almost hear her mother's thoughts wishing Henry to be concealed within.

The women walked towards the hansom. It was not Henry, but Missus Cross and her husband.

George Eliot must be as impatient as me, Maggie thought, and glanced at her mother. A small crease marked her otherwise flawless brow. Maggie clutched her hand in sympathy and in an instant Lydia's countenance brightened, her feelings concealed by the mask of the Countess of Wessex.

Maggie made the introductions and Mister Cross bowed low to her mother, as was the privilege of her rank. It was a gesture that amused Jack so much, he had to turn away and pretend he was tending to the horses. Mister Cross's actions surprised Maggie somewhat as well. Such mannered formality seemed out of place in their rural context, and dressed in a simple burgundy walking ensemble, Lydia had lost many of the airs and graces of a countess.

'I apologise for the intrusion,' Marian said. 'But I was concerned for you, Maggie.'

'Thank you, Marian. I am much improved. My mother arrived unexpectedly a few days ago and she has been seeing to my health,' Maggie said. 'After our morning ramble on the dales, I have energy in abundance. If you have time, would you like to chat now?'

Marian nodded, seemingly heartened by seeing Maggie well.

Maggie turned to her mother. 'Would you mind entertaining Mister Cross for an hour or two?'

'Not at all, darling.' During their brief introduction, Lydia discovered she was acquainted with Mister Cross's sisters. She and John adjourned to the sitting room while Maggie and Marian sat at the table in the kitchen.

'I collected these for you,' Maggie said, handing the bouquet to Marian after tying a simple string around the stems. 'This day must be particularly painful ... I find the wildflowers of the dales simply delightful, and I hope that they might bring you a little comfort.'

'Thank you,' said Marian, inspecting the arrangement. 'They are friendly and playful,' she concluded. 'I can see George in them. George was always playful,' she explained. 'He would create the most amusing and animated characters.

He had been an actor, you know,' she added in a low voice. 'The stage had been his first choice of career.'

Maggie reached for her notebook and drew it across the table. 'What do you mean?'

'Oh,' Marian smiled. 'He'd prance around like an old-fashioned French barber or dancing master. Sometimes he would produce his violin and play ...'

'To what end?' Maggie enquired, puzzled.

'I'm none too sure,' she admitted. 'We never talked about his showmanship. It seemed too intimate a topic to discuss, even for us. I believe he was playing the jester to my sibyl. His foolishness cast me in a more pleasing and sombre light.'

Scientist, philosopher and writer, George Lewes had played the fool to promote a certain image of Marian. It was ingenious and selfless, Maggie concluded.

'If that was the case,' she continued, 'You were the oracle, the wise woman whom devotees from all around would come to hear soliloquise.'

Marian had the good grace to blush, albeit slightly. 'In a manner of speaking.'

Maggie hastily scribbled her notes, recalling yet again Dorothea's description of the young woman who had attempted to kiss the authoress's feet.

'But with that role comes a certain distance, doesn't it? I mean, a prophet cannot be intimate. They cannot share everything. We idolise them. Is that what you wanted?'

Marian shifted and looked down at the table. 'This reminds me of the table at Griff House,' she remarked. 'My father crafted it. He was so adept at woodwork; he could make anything. I wonder if it still stands.'

Noticing Marian's reticence, Maggie did not press for a response. Instead, she stared at her shorthand squiggles on the page and attempted to make sense of what Marian had just told her. She craved love and intimacy. Her outpouring to

Herbert Spencer and her willingness to throw away her reputation and live with George Lewes, her one great love, proved that. And she had intimate female friendships that meant a great deal to her. However, she had steadfastly held George's sons at arm's length, admitting she was uncomfortable around them and incapable of showing them a mother's love.

'Children,' Maggie said after a few minutes. 'Why did you and George never have children?'

Marian thought for a considerable amount of time about the question, to the point where Maggie believed the enquiry had offended her. *Yet, surely*, Maggie mused, *someone had asked before now?* The couple lived as husband and wife for twenty-four years. They were inseparable, devoted to each other, not to mention free-thinking. *Wouldn't having their own child only strengthen their union?* she wondered.

'In our early days together, we had no money ... we lived on a shoestring. With the little we had, George needed to support his sons and Agnes, and after Chrissy was widowed, I sent money to her once a month as well. As a result, we never spoke of children; we simply understood that we both had other responsibilities at that time.' Marian paused, remembering. 'Then when I began to write fiction, my books became my babies. I was so invested in them, I don't believe I would have had the emotional energy for human children as well.'

'Is it a regret?' Maggie asked, thinking on her own choices.

Her encounter with Matthew Drummond and the aftermath had only strengthened her relationship with William. If there were any positive aspects of that horrific afternoon, it was that. She imagined that marriage and children would only bring them closer together ... wouldn't they? William would be a wonderful father, and now Lydia was back in Maggie's life, it seemed more important than ever to fortify herself with family ...

Marian nodded. 'Of course. Sometimes. But I enjoyed playing the role of mother to the young men and women who surrounded me. George called them my 'acolytes'. When they'd arrive on a Sunday, George insisted they sit on a footstool by my feet and introduce themselves. He'd watch the exchange and then move them on after a few minutes. Poor things, they were always disappointed. How they hungered for my attention ... Their behaviour reminded me of my own desperate attempts to gain my mother's attention.

'Like me, those young people needed guidance. I suppose that I embodied for them a vision of what women could achieve outside the normal limits and constraints imposed on women's lives.'

'Disciples, if you like.'

Marian nodded.

ON THE DRIVE back to the house, John described his conversation with the countess. He was no stranger to peerage, but he was behaving like an infatuated schoolgirl. Lydia Almond was exquisite, Marian supposed, and she and John were of a similar age. She wondered if there was an attraction there, and, if so, whether it bothered her. She concluded it did not.

It struck her that women like Lydia Almond, her daughter as well, had such an easy way with strangers. Hospitality and attentiveness seemed innate. They made an art of making one feel at ease, perhaps too comfortable. Marian quickly attempted to recall all she had revealed to Maggie during the interview.

She had not mentioned Edith. *Thank goodness. What might Maggie think ...*

Yet it was on Edith that Marian's thoughts alighted now. *Where would I even begin?* she wondered. Their relationship was so complex, so laden with inscrutability. While Marian adored the adulation she received from Edith, she was also embarrassed by it and ashamed of her desperate need for validation from one so young. Marian sighed. At sixty years of age, she still could not fathom the workings of her own psyche.

'We're nearly home, dear,' John advised, assuming his wife was weary from the drive.

Marian closed her eyes and leant her head against the window. Finding comfort in the jolt and rock of the carriage, she drifted into a scrappy sleep.

The Priory
Regent's Park

MARCH 14, 1872

Dearest Barbara,

My dear friend, you will never believe what occurred this afternoon during our salon. I am grateful you were not there to witness it, for you would have surely commented in some way, mockingly or disparagingly, embarrassing both me and the young woman involved in the incident. I know you can never withhold your opinions. However, the odd moment brought you to mind and I considered what sensible advice you might offer.

A young woman, Edith Simcox, who writes anonymously as the critic H. Lawrenny, praised Middlemarch in the Academy some time ago. When I read the review, I believed the author noticed aspects of my novel other critics had failed to. Their insight was quite remark-

able. When George uncovered Lawrenny's identity, I agreed to invite Miss Simcox to the salon. I felt I might have some counsel to offer a young woman who seeks to conceal her true self behind a male pseudonym ... I have an abundance of motherly advice yet so few with whom to share it.

When Miss Simcox arrived, she kissed my hand with some ardour. But later, in front of all the guests, she asked if she might kiss my feet! I was astounded, simply dumbstruck. I sensed the entire room's eyes on me (an occurrence that you know I find intolerable), waiting for my reaction. I sat like a woman on trial. The young lady took my silence for agreement and, as her lips were about to brush the toes of my slipper, I believe I heard the entire party gasp. Coming to my senses, I requested in a whisper that she cease such behaviour. I must have sounded like a stern schoolmistress for when she lifted her eyes to mine, they were awash with tears. Were they tears of rapture? Disappointment? I was unsure.

It is only to you that I can relate these moments of such perplexity. When did I become so adored?

When our guests had departed, George jested that I had become both Messiah and Sappho. Barbara, you must know I do not wish to be either! When I protested, George, barely containing his amusement (the rogue), suggested that perhaps the young woman simply admired my feet! Even in the despondency that the incident had provoked in me, I laughed aloud at his ludicrousness. Then I recalled a distant but distinct memory.

Do you remember when you visited us in Devon? One day at mid-morning, we were sitting by the cliffs as George collected his samples, our feet submerged in a rock pool. 'Yours are beautiful feet,' you commented. Struck by your observation, I examined them closely. To my surprise, I realised they were lily white and soft, absent of callous, corn and bunion. My toenails, I recall, resembled pale pink petals floating in a shallow dish of water.

'If only my feet were on display instead of my face,' I replied. 'Then someone might have loved me before now.'

'Perhaps, next time that you are mocked as "plain" or "ugly" or "horse-faced", you should remove your shoes and stockings and reveal your feet to the harsh critic!' you joked.

Didn't we laugh so! In my aural memory, I can hear the sound distinctly: high and joyous, our merriment resounding from the rock wall behind us.

Now serious young women are brought to tears in my presence. And here I am, sighing, listless and confused. Will I ever be that care-free again?

I wait to receive your counsel as to how I should proceed with this young woman. I give you licence to let loose your opinions like the winds of a hurricane.

Yours in bewilderment,

Marian

CHAPTER 36

BY THE SUNDAY morning of Little Jack's baptism some weeks later, Maggie sensed her spirit had gradually healed. Although she had said nothing to Lydia about the event that haunted her, having her mother close by had been a tremendous comfort. William continued to rage silently as though his veins were flowing with thunder and lightning, both at Drummond's actions and his own inability to defend her. He felt hamstrung, and Maggie knew exactly how frustrating that could be. Yet he continued to stroke her hair as they lay side by side in the dark and whisper reassurances of his devotion in her ear.

Maggie hoped an event such as a baby's baptism would not only help to put the Drummond episode in perspective, but also assist her in viewing life as a series of promising new beginnings rather than violent and abrupt ends.

She had been afforded some distraction by Lydia and Grace. Despite the two getting along so famously, Maggie feared if she left them at close quarters for long enough, Lydia would sense something about her host. Grace had to be commended for giving nothing away. However, Maggie had noticed her looking wonderingly at Lydia, prompting Maggie to muse on Grace's feelings. Without knowing the strength of her attachment to Henry, she could not even guess.

To Maggie, it was a boon that the baptism and following tea would separate the women for a while. Everyone's focus, including her own, would be on the baby and what a charming little man he was. The events would thrust her problems to the periphery, providing her with a little breathing space.

Maggie dressed extremely carefully for the event. She was to be the godmother, after all. It had surprised her when Beth had asked. Beth explained that the way Maggie had championed Lucy Owen's cause in the face of an irate Reggie was not only a lesson to women, but to all men as well. Therefore, Maggie was exactly the breed of godmother she wanted for her son.

Maggie felt honoured to have been chosen, and she was determined to take her new role extremely seriously. She vowed to instil Little Jack with tolerance and respect. He would view girls and women as equals, and realise the world was only made richer through difference and variety.

With these factors in mind, she wore a majestic princess line dress of light green silk embroidered with pale pink orchids. Hemmed in gold brocade, the gown was finished at the cuffs and neckline with handmade Belgian lace.

William admired her appearance as she descended the staircase, staring at her for some time as she stood facing him.

'You look bonny,' he whispered, kissing her cheek. 'Absolutely lovely.'

She sensed William viewed the baptism in the same light as she – a turning point.

They arrived at St Bede's and waited for Beth, Jack and the children to arrive. Leaves crunched beneath their feet as they walked to the steps of the church. A magpie cried a harsh, ascending call and Maggie looked heavenwards. The bird had disappeared, nowhere to be seen, but thin cirrocumulus clouds sheeted the sky. Entranced for a moment by the light grey ripples against the blue, she recalled one of her science lessons at Cheltenham. She had exhibited a distinct lack of prowess when called upon to sketch and label the various clouds that populated the heavens. Then she remembered Briar's rendering of a lone cumulous cloud in the idyll she had painted. Maggie closed her eyes and felt the bite of the crisp morning air on her face and momentarily pined for her friend. *A woman wasted ... talent and intelligence cast aside like rubbish.*

Tears formed behind her eyelids. Briar was everywhere. In the call of a magpie and the folds of a cloud. *And she had been with me in Drummond's office that dreadful afternoon*, she thought. How else could Maggie explain finding the hat pin?

She felt William's hand tighten around her waist and she opened her eyes. Drummond had arrived. She hadn't known Beth and Jack invited him. All the affirming thoughts which she had planted in her mind in the hours leading up to the baptism quickly shrivelled like an autumn leaf.

He was wearing a bandage over his ear and was holding a woman's bag. Maggie looked more closely. It was her purse. She'd left it behind when she'd fled the colliery.

Watching him, seeing him hold her belongings, her chest tightened. It was as if a fracture in the delicate crystal of her being had begun on that afternoon in his office, later splintering into hundreds of tiny, sharp shards. Since then, she had been frantically gluing the pieces back into place. Now, Maggie was afraid any movement, a single gesture, might see her shatter completely.

Drummond was offering his congratulations to Jack. She looked at William and watched his eyes fill with fire. His jaw tensed. She had never seen him look that way before. Maggie gripped his arms and turned him away.

'Don't. Not today. I know exactly what you're feeling, but this day is about Little Jack.'

'The nerve of him,' William seethed. The thunder and lightning that had run through his blood since the attack was now etched on his brow. 'To turn up here today … the bare-faced audacity of the man.'

'He has my bag,' she murmured, fortifying herself. 'I am going to collect it from him.'

Alarmed, he grasped her hand as though she might float away. 'I'll go.'

She shook her head. 'You want to hurt him and you will, given the chance.' Maggie knew it would only take a single misplaced word from Drummond to set the bull free. And misplaced words were an idiosyncrasy of Drummond's character.

'This is something I need to do.'

Maggie squeezed his hand, and he released her. As she approached Drummond, she knew what Lucy Owen must have felt each time Reggie arrived home from the pit. She knew what Briar must have felt in the moments before she died. She knew what millions of women must feel every day – powerless and terrified. Maggie inhaled deeply and straightened, refusing to give Drummond the advantage.

He watched her as she drew closer across the green. She raised her chin and looked at him squarely. Maggie could gauge neither his thoughts nor his feelings by his expression. However, she knew she would be in a much better position if she were to take the initiative. She heard her father's voice in her mind. 'A battle waged from the high ground will always see the army victorious.' Instantly bolstered, she forged on.

'Good day, Mister Drummond,' Maggie said when she reached him.

'No more Matthew?'

Maggie ignored him. 'I believe you have my purse.'

He raised it in front of him as though he wasn't aware it was in his possession and it had somehow, miraculously, appeared in his grasp.

'Thank you for retrieving it for me.' She reached for the handle. In doing so, her hand brushed his and her stomach rolled.

With the purse back in her possession, she was about to move away.

'The doctor said I might be deaf in my left ear forever, Maggie.'

She looked into his eyes. They suddenly appeared soulless to her, empty.

'That damnable hat pin pierced my eardrum.'

She was pleased she had hurt him and that the injury might be irreparable, a constant reminder of his ill deeds. At the moment, it certainly felt as though the wounds Drummond had inflicted upon her would take a lifetime to heal.

'If you desire an apology, Mister Drummond, you are going to be disappointed.'

He moved a step closer and lowered his voice. 'I don't expect a woman like you to apologise.'

I must walk away, Maggie thought. *Let me walk away.* All she wanted was to be back by William's side, yet she refused to allow Drummond the upper hand. She stared at him, ready for the onslaught.

'Whores don't apologise,' he continued. 'They lie and cheat, scratch and bite, but they never apologise. Briar Haines was exactly the same.'

Maggie's heart spasmed in anger at the mention of Briar. She opened her mouth to speak, but Drummond spoke first.

'I'd wager she fought like a Kilkenny cat before she died. I would have liked to have seen that.'

৩৯৯

DURING THE CEREMONY, as Maggie stood at the baptismal font, as she took her seat in the pew and as she followed Jack and Beth down the aisle once the proceedings were over, she was aware of Drummond's eyes on her.

She fought like a Kilkenny cat.

His words kept returning to her. Tumbling around in her mind, disrupting all sensible thought. *Did the vile man play a part in Briar's death? Just what did he pay Reggie to do?*

Once outside and positioned on the green again, she and William stood with Tommy Fellowes.

'Briar told us a man she believed to be an inspector visited the pit some weeks ago. Matthew Drummond rushed him off and Reggie Owen escorted him from the pit. Do you know anything about this?'

Tommy shook his head slowly, as though attempting to remember. 'Not that I can recall ...'

'But surely,' William said, 'an inspector would have to meet with you first? It's a requirement under the act.'

'Not necessarily. Tha's but one inspector for the entire North East. He can't waste time on pleasantries. Besides, you said Miss Haines assumed he was an inspector. Why, the man could have been a salesman, a buyer,' Tommy sighed, exasperated. 'He could have been a man looking to addle a few quid! If he was an inspector, he could be in Northumberland or Yorkshire by now.'

Maggie studied him. William was correct when he had described Tommy Fellowes as a man under pressure. It seemed to Maggie he was close to breaking point. William noticed, too.

'Aareet, Tommy?' he asked his godfather quietly. 'You don't seem yourself.'

Tommy was silent, staring at the fallen leaves on the ground.

'We're concerned,' William went on. 'Briar Haines, Reggie Owen ... Whose death might Matthew Drummond be linked to next? Our miners?'

Tommy instantly looked up.

'Haddaway, man! Leave off,' he cried, drawing the attention of those on the green, including Drummond's. Tommy paused and lowered his voice. 'I'm trying to manage this situation and ... and the more you two sticky beak around, the harder everything becomes,' he said, then stormed away across the green without farewelling Jack and Beth.

CHAPTER 37

The Manchester Guardian
Wednesday, December 1, 1880

DEAR READER,

When George Henry Lewes died in November, 1878, my heart broke into a thousand pieces. George was my entire life. He managed my career, and he managed me. No person before or since has known me so exactly. We both drew heavily on observation in our writing, but I never realised until he left me how carefully and astutely he had been observing me for twenty-four years.

In the weeks following his death, it seemed impossible that I could ever put the pieces of my fractured soul together again, and I did not want to. I avoided his funeral. I spent Christmas alone. Thoughts of Christmas cheer and Yuletide merriment were too arduous to confront, so I hid myself away. How can I put into words how I missed George? His merry laughter, booming voice and physical presence had disappeared in an instant. We had shared a bed for almost a quarter of a century, never spending a single night apart. Then suddenly, in the space of a day, one half of my bed became empty.

One half of me did as well.

Despite my success and the adoration society had shown me, George's death returned me to being nothing more than a hermit crab in a scavenged, thrice-used shell. I spent December at the Heights alone. I would permit no one entrance into my bleak dominion.

Grief overwhelmed me. I cried, I moaned, I wailed.

My poor maids, Brett and Missus Dowling, were kind. They reminded me to bathe and change my clothes. The pair of mother birds would take turns cutting my food into portions, then placing it into my mouth. It was all I could do to chew.

It was not until New Year's Day that I finally ventured from my room and down the stairs. My grief seems unreal to me now, although pangs still reoccur daily as reminders of what I have lost. In all my manifestations – a zealous scholar, an obnoxious evangelical, a jealous and hysterical young woman, a spurned lover and as a writer of great renown – I had never felt so far removed from myself in mind, body and spirit as I had at that time. I suppose this is why, when I finally emerged, that I went into George's study; I was hoping to rediscover myself. After all, who knew me better than George?

Immediately, his unfinished manuscript drew me to it like the moon draws water. He had placed it in the centre of his desk, as though he believed he would return to his work as normal the following day. It was a mahogany partners desk I had gifted George on our twentieth anniversary. I looked at the topmost page, traced his distinctive handwriting with my fingers. He had titled his final work *"Problems of Life and Mind: The Study of Psychology"*.

Although he had no formal warning from our doctor, George knew the end was near. In the weeks leading up to his death, he had been feverishly, desperately attempting to complete the work. He had not shown me the manuscript; sensing the encroaching hand of death, he would not allow me to edit his words as he completed chapters, although it had been our practice up to that point. 'Too slow, too slow ...' he would say, waving me away.

So, when I found the pages there, as if waiting for me, I sat down in his chair and read.

'In every science we define the object and scope of the search, the motive of the search, and the means whereby the aim may be reached,' the book began. 'The purpose of the following pages is to set forth *what* it is we study in Psychology, *why* we study it, and *how* we ought to study it.'

After absorbing those words, I became determined to take up the torch and continue the manuscript on George's behalf. What my beloved had been unable to do, I would do for him – I would complete his final work.

For an entire month, I did nothing but revise and edit his pages. George was not formally educated; he possessed neither a science nor a medical degree. However, his insights into the human mind were well researched, meticulous and expressed in such a way that any Tom, Dick or Harriet might gain an understanding of their own minds.

Deep thinkers, writers and philosophers cram between England's borders, yet only a few have dedicated themselves to the study and observation of the sciences. George began as a philosopher but went on to develop theories regarding an individual's health, specifically their mental health. He used his notes from the specimens we had collected all those years ago on the beaches of Tenby and Ilfracombe to discuss nervous systems and reflexes. The conclusions he reached formed a theory he called 'Scientific Psychology', an idea that combines the objective study of mind practiced in biology and the subjective study of consciousness practiced in philosophy. In other words, George was questioning whether our behaviours stem from our biology or our environment.

I worked day and night on the manuscript. What he had written in his last days made little sense; my darling was in so much pain he could not write a comprehensible sentence. However, by that stage, I had worked my way through his observations and arguments and could carry on in his voice, as it had once been. It was an immense comfort to channel George in this way. It felt as though we were working together once again.

More important to me, dear Reader, than the learnings I was drawing from the manuscript was the healing of my soul that George's words brought about. With each page, each cut, each addition, the tiny pieces of myself that lay scattered like chaff before the wind found their way back together. You can be assured that I am not a sentimental person or a superstitious one. I have never visited a clairvoyant or a mind reader, as is the fashion these days. However, I would swear on any hallowed tome that George placed his manuscript in the centre of his desk with the wish that I find it.

MAGGIE LOOKED up from the page and stretched her fingers. Alone in the cottage, she had taken advantage of the quiet to work on her article. William had escorted Lydia to the cathedral that morning; she had never visited Durham and was keen to see some of its grand buildings. She had, however, mentioned that Edward Maltby, the Bishop of Durham at the time of her marriage to Henry, had attended their wedding.

'From memory,' Lydia informed them at breakfast, 'the

bishop gifted your father and I a Waterford decanter.' She turned to Maggie. 'The one your father keeps in his study.'

Maggie was familiar with the object. How many times had she poured claret from it when she and Henry matched wits over a chessboard?

'The bishop was at your wedding?' Grace asked, astonished.

Lydia nodded, nonplussed. 'He was a dear friend of Henry's father.'

Maggie had watched as a strange expression washed over Grace's face. It was an odd blend of confusion and grief. It appeared that until that point, Grace had not fully comprehended the rank of the Almonds in English society. While Maggie hoped her parents would reunite and enjoy a more honest union in the future, she sympathised with Grace. It was infuriating to discover the happiness one yearned for was entirely out of reach.

It was early afternoon. Maggie glanced out of the window and noticed the mist had not yet lifted over the dales. It hung there idly, refusing to shift. She sighed and returned to her writing.

Grief was the theme coursing through her article. Torpid ... indolent ... grief.

'If you don't mind me saying, and this is merely my observation,' Maggie had said as she interviewed Marian the day before, 'your grief for George was all-consuming. In fact, you allowed it to consume you. And completing George's manuscript assisted you to emerge once more, if you will.'

Marian nodded.

'But what role did John play in your healing process?'

The authoress gazed at Maggie as though from a distance. They had met at Marian's house by Framwellgate Bridge. At Maggie's request, her mother had escorted her to the open-fronted Georgian residence. The thought of meeting

Matthew Drummond on the High Street, or even spying him in the distance, sent a chill through her entire body. After their exchange at Little Jack's christening, Maggie had grown even more wary of the man. He had shown neither remorse nor fear; they seemed alien concepts to him.

'John forced me into the world, I suppose,' Marian responded.

'How did he manage that,' Maggie queried with a smile, 'when you seemed so intent on living the rest of your life as a hermit crab?'

Marian laughed. 'Persistence.' She paused for a moment, allowing her amusement to settle. 'Sheer dogged persistence. He called every day. At first, I refused to see him. Brett and Missus Dowling would open the door to him, and he'd insist on waiting in the library or drawing room. He'd wait for hours. Closeted away upstairs or in George's study, I'd listen to his tread as he roamed the room. Sometimes I instructed them not to allow him into the house at all. Then I would watch him, waiting by the gate, also for hours, smoking his cigarettes ...' Marian's voice trailed away.

Mister Cross was at home. Maggie wondered if the authoress didn't want him to overhear their conversation. Not for the first time, Maggie wondered about Mister Cross's jealous streak. George Lewes possessed none of John Cross's attractiveness or wealth, but he was spectacularly intelligent, a true thinker. The manuscript Marian spoke of had already, in just twelve months since publication, changed the medical profession's opinion regarding the mind and human behavioural development.

'But you eventually saw him.'

'In February of 1879,' Marian said, 'I finally surrendered. Burying myself in George's manuscript had given me the space I needed to discover that I could control my response to my sorrow, even if I had no control over the sorrow itself.

So, one day when Johnny arrived and was waiting in the drawing room, I sent Brett down with a message. I did not want to see him that day, but he could call again the next.'

Marian frowned in thought for a moment. 'His mother had died only a few days after George. In my grief, I had forgotten, never realising that John's persistence to see me may have been driven by the desire for mutual consolation. And he was grieving for George as well. They had been friends – we had been friends. It was heartless of me.'

Maggie nodded and reviewed her notes quickly. *A need to share in grief*, Maggie wondered, *or perhaps a need for another woman in his life to care for?* John Cross had devoted himself to his mother for decades. When she died, there must have been an unexpected and unwanted space in his heart that needed to be filled. Perhaps his romance with Marian was a part of his healing process.

'After his initial visit, he continued to call every day. Before George died, he was Johnny, our "nephew", but in those visits, I sensed he wished to become something different. I had always enjoyed watching him; he has a graceful, athletic body. To me, he was the embodiment of youth. It was somewhat of a comfort as George and I aged to have him in our lives. He is so terribly handsome, don't you think?'

Maggie nodded. 'I suppose there is truth in Menander's words.'

'"Time is the healer of all necessary evils,"' quoted Marian, smiling.

Maggie certainly hoped so.

'During John's visits, I would watch him and note the differences between him and George. John was and still is incredibly dapper while George would wear a suit until holes appeared in the knees and elbows.' Marian glanced at Maggie and they laughed. 'John had received a top-class education at Rugby, but he had spent his career as a banker, arranging figures into columns. In many ways, his mind could not venture outside those neat rows ... While highly intelligent, John is not a curious or creative man; he was simply not educated to be so. But when he retired, he wanted to learn about art, philosophy and literature. He was hungry for it, obsessed with reading the classics.'

Maggie made a note in her book. *Rugby. Drummond.*

'Perhaps ...' Marian went on, then stopped, unable to voice the thought. Maggie noticed a blush rise in her cheeks.

'Perhaps he hoped to be worthy of you?' Maggie suggested.

Marian nodded. 'Is that narcissistic? A woman of my age and appearance thinking that way?'

Maggie placed her pencil and notebook on the floor, then took Marian's hand. 'Of course not,' she replied earnestly. 'It's not ego or obedience and modesty, or a lily-white complexion that makes you beautiful, Marian. It is your mind. That is what John was hungry for.'

Marian squeezed Maggie's hand and smiled. 'Our interviews have nourished my soul.'

'Mine as well.'

Thus reassured, Marian continued. 'So, we began working together on a translation of Dante's *Divina Commedia*. Before long, I began to call Johnny "Dante" and he would call me "Beatrice". But we were play acting ...' she said, lowering her eyes and flattening a fold in her skirt.

Maggie waited for more.

'John admires artists, but despite his eagerness to be learned, he does not possess an imaginative spirit. At times, the project became for me a frustrating chore.'

DID I SAY TOO MUCH? Marian asked herself after Maggie departed. She had not meant to speak of John's failings, if one could consider a poor understanding of Italian and the classics a failing. However, the fact remained that it was a shortcoming among her circle and in her mind. In contrast, Maggie was just so wonderful to converse with, so comfortable to be around. Whenever she spent time with Maggie, it was as though she was seated opposite Barbara or Sara, or even Maria. Maggie's wide brown eyes were so compassionate and inviting.

It was gracious of her to express her desire to read George's book, the one they had discussed during the interview. 'I have an interest in psychology,' Maggie had remarked as Marian searched for the volume among the stacks she had travelled with to Durham. Marian thought she was merely being polite, but Maggie had continued. 'Claire Clairmont sparked my interest. As did Shelley, Mary and Fanny ... and William Godwin, of course. They were such an incredibly complicated bunch. I have read John Stuart Mill, some Wundt and your friend, Herbert Spencer. But now that we have discussed it, I am extremely interested in reading Mister Lewes's book as well.'

When Marian had found her copy, she handed it to Maggie. George would have enjoyed her company, she decided. His antics would not have shocked a young woman such as Maggie Almond. She would laugh and play along, Marian was sure of it.

She sighed, and her thoughts returned to John. She shouldn't have been so cruel. She had eventually accepted his proposal out of loneliness. George had taken care of her for twenty-four years, never leaving her alone, and John seemed willing to assume those responsibilities. Had she loved John then? His attentions certainly flattered her ... Perhaps her ego had taken control. To have the affection of a young, fine-looking man such as Johnny Cross was empowering. In the end, she had given into his pestering and attempted to transform herself from dowager aunt to lover.

The Heights
Witley, Surrey

OCTOBER 16, 1879

My darling Dante,

I am miserable without you, although it has only been three days since we have parted. How I longed to travel with you to London to visit your brother, but you were correct; it is better we tell your siblings of our relationship when we are all together. O, learned one, you are wise in matters of the heart, far wiser than I, who allows my love for you to override my common sense. All I wish is to herald our love to the world! Now, as I cast my gaze through the window here in Surrey, I note the leaves drifting to the ground and cannot but feel my heart growing cold without you by my side. You are my warmth and I am ablaze when you are near.

While I see you strive to improve yourself, I fear you do this for my sake and not your own. You have intelligence of a different kind and you mustn't attempt to mould yourself into a style of man other than what you already are, and particularly not for me. Your attractiveness to me springs from other sources – your kindness and care being two.

I am certain some may view our relationship as strange. Why, to some it may seem that you are only just out of pantaloons! But it is your beauty and consideration that makes me strong. For me, you are hope, you are the future. When we are together, your energy is evident in every word you utter and every movement of your body. How easily you laugh! How enthusiastically you perform even the simplest tasks! With you by my side, I believe I grow younger each day. Perhaps soon our ages will converge and matter no longer.

My thoughts today have ventured to Naples. Do you recall the four of us strolling along the Via Caracciolo e Lungomare? We stopped to admire Vesuvius. The waves broke against the sea wall and the spray tickled our faces. You, Anna and George continued our promenade, but I remained, so enchanted I was by the view. As though by magic, a hawker appeared beside me, selling tiny portraits of the mountain.

'Ti piace? Ti piace?' he shouted at me above the roar of the sea.

'Non sono interessato,' I said in response, again and again.

But I could not deter him. His shouting, combined with the noise of the waves, swarmed my head. Distressed, I turned my back to him, but he gripped my arm and wrenched me to face him. In an instant, you were there, pulling him away and leading him down the promenade.

You rescued me then, and you rescue me now. Sweet John, you are my Hercules. Your strength renews me. Writing this letter, imagining you, has lifted my mood. O, the power you have over my mind, heart and soul ...

I shall not attempt to explain the measure of my love for you here. You are aware of the passion I possess for you, my Dante. The mere thought of you stirs me so. You are the moon and I am a restless sea. To be back in your orbit is all that I desire.

Yours in love and tenderness,

Beatrice

CHAPTER 38

UNDETERRED BY THE MIST, Maggie took a stroll by the river after she finished her article. She contemplated all the writer had revealed to her. *Play acting* ... What had Marian been referring to? Maggie remembered the way the writer had looked down at her skirt, embarrassed. *But by what?* Maggie speculated. *Was it the age difference between her and her husband? Or Mister Cross's intellect?* But Maggie knew that John Cross was not a fool. In fact, he had built an extremely successful career in finance. He did not have the intelligence of the likes of George Henry Lewes, but Lewes was unique – there could be no other like him. His mind was as rare and exotic as one of the sea creatures he discovered in the rock pools at Tenby.

Maggie sighed. Poor Marian. Could it be true that she had given herself to a man who was not her intellectual equal?

Her thoughts turned to William. They had not made love since the attack. While she longed for him, she was afraid, too worried that memories of the vile event would haunt and tarnish her intimate moments with him. Yet sexual intimacy, Maggie believed, was fundamental to their relationship. *What if I am never able to be with William again?* Maggie wondered, suddenly anxious. She shook her head in an effort to thrust the thought from her mind.

It will just take time for me to recover, just as Marian said.

Maggie walked on. Soon, she found herself on the outskirts of the town. She was about to turn back when she noticed a house with a sign nailed to the gate: For Lease. Maggie examined the two-storey building. It was enormous, too large for William and herself alone. *But it would make an extremely adequate school*, she thought. *Not far from the cathedral and the university, abutting the river ...*

She decided it was more than adequate – it would make a wonderful school.

Maggie had safely deposited Briar's money in the bank, along with the £150 Lydia had given her. She and William had agreed the combined funds would be used for nothing else but a school. She looked at the building again. Could this be their future?

Maggie knocked on the door of the residence. An elderly lady opened it and a spark of recognition flashed in her eyes. 'Can I help you, lass?' she asked.

When Maggie explained the nature of her visit, the woman, Missus Mary Merchant, showed her into the sitting room.

'Take a seat and I'll put the kettle on.'

Before Maggie could object, the woman hurried from the room. It was furnished with several chairs – too many, it seemed to Maggie, for a family sitting room – and a lesser number of small tables. A fire blazed in the substantial hearth and shelves heaving with books lined the opposite walls.

'You're Willie Dodd's lass, aren't yer?' Missus Merchant asked on her way back into the room.

Maggie nodded and helped Missus Merchant place the tea tray on a table. The woman sat down heavily in a chair.

'Please, allow me,' Maggie said, offering to pour the tea. 'You seem exhausted.'

'Idleness is going to be the death of me,' she said.

'Oh?' Maggie asked, resuming her seat.

'Until a few weeks ago, I ran a boarding house here for the students,' Missus Merchant explained, gesturing in the university's direction. 'My husband and I opened it in ...' she closed her eyes for an instant, trying to recall the exact year. '1853. Yes. Since then, we haven't been without a full house of young men, eager to make their mark on the world.'

Maggie looked around her, imagining the sitting room occupied by young scholars debating and discussing while Missus Merchant moved between them, seeing to their comfort.

'God chose not to bless Charlie and me with children of our own and inviting these young people into our home was a comfort, of sorts. It made us feel useful in a way we could never have imagined. To say we were lonely before is an understatement.'

Maggie nodded and sipped her tea, wondering where all the young people were now.

'But just a few weeks ago, Mister Drummond bought the premises. He bought my home, then raised the rent. I lost Charlie last year in the collapse, you see. I was managing without his wage, but with the rent rise, I would have to charge the students much more that I could ever be comfortable with.' Missus Merchant shook her head. 'An impossible situation. So, I stopped taking in lodgers and have decided to move to something smaller. I'll be leaving as soon as someone else takes on the lease.'

Maggie frowned. 'Matthew Drummond, the owner of the colliery, bought your home?'

Missus Merchant nodded. 'He's been snapping up properties left, right and centre,' she said ruefully. 'I suppose I shouldn't complain. At least this means he's in Durham for the long haul. That's a good thing, isn't it?'

'Yes, I suppose so,' Maggie agreed doubtfully, a sense of great unease washing over her as she sipped her tea.

***

MARY MERCHANT'S boarding house seemed less ideal as a home for her school once Maggie learnt the identity of the new owner. More concerning was the knowledge Matthew Drummond was buying other properties in Durham as well.

When she returned to the cottage, Lydia, Grace and William were home. As she informed them of Drummond's purchases, worry creased their faces.

'But why? What does he need all that property for?' William asked.

Maggie shrugged, recalling Briar's words. *Clues are everywhere, we just need to find them.* And an entire home was an extremely large clue.

'Property has always been the currency of the aristocracy, I suppose,' Maggie said.

Lydia nodded in agreement, buttoning her gloves. She and Grace were heading out to a string recital at the cathedral, a prospect Maggie found almost as disturbing as Drummond buying up Durham.

'It's power,' Lydia said. 'Most wealthy men love power.' She glanced at Maggie. 'Your father is the exception, of course.'

'Power ... and the colliery is the key to it all. Owning the colliery means Drummond owns most of the male population. If he buys up the town, he will own their homes and lands, too,' William said, rubbing his hand along his forehead.

'Agreed,' Maggie said. 'And as most of the female population are not employed in salaried work ...'

'He will own them as well,' Grace added.

'Is he trying to build an empire?' Maggie speculated.

'It certainly stands to reason,' Lydia agreed. 'And he has chosen a far corner of the country to build it in, where few others will think to look.'

Grace rose from the table and stood, looking through the window at the vastness of the dales. 'Politicians have always only ever seen the North in terms of coal. As long as Drummond keeps their trains and ships running, they'll no' ask any questions about his motives.'

'After Durham, he could move on to Tyne-and-Wear, Northumberland ...' William said.

Maggie nodded, thinking. 'Colonisation of a domestic variety.'

William sighed, then closed his eyes for a moment. Maggie took his face in her hands and kissed him.

'Whatever Drummond is up to, we'll face it together,' she said. 'A man such as he cannot match wits against us.'

'Hear, hear!' Lydia cried heartily, lightening the atmosphere.

A moment later, they heard Jack's hansom on the road. The mothers departed and William and Maggie cast each other a disbelieving glance. They laughed quietly at the absurd situation, listening as the sound of the hansom faded into the distance.

With the house to themselves, William drew Maggie onto his lap and kissed her neck, taking her in, relishing her presence in his life.

'I was discussing Marian's marriage with her yesterday,' she said.

William looked at her, curious. 'Aye?'

'Her second marriage. She and George Lewes came together like a stellar collision. Their union was the convergence of two brilliant and passionate people. Her marriage with John Cross does not seem as ... spectacular.'

'Not every relationship can produce sparks. Marian may have yearned for companionship over fire the second time.' He kissed her neck again.

'Perhaps. But it started me thinking about us.'

A worried look crossed William's face.

'On that afternoon in Drummond's office, he told me that if he were to rape me, no one would believe it wasn't consensual. Not even you.'

Maggie had not told him many details of the attack. William, disgusted anew by Drummond, embraced her even more tightly.

'You know that's not true, don't you?'

'Oh, of course,' she replied. 'That's not what has been troubling me. But rather than divide us, which I believe was his purpose by saying such a thing, he has only driven us closer together. And I wouldn't have believed that was possible.' Maggie stared into his hazel eyes. They were so familiar now. Each fleck, every brushstroke, was a work of art.

'I'm ready to be with you again,' she whispered.

࿇

WILLIAM WAS quiet as they walked into the High Street the following morning. He had expected to sleep like a babe; to be with Maggie again in that way was a relief, both of the physical and mental kind. When Reggie Owen had beaten his younger brother, the lad had been terrified for months. Johnny was small for his age and Reggie had laid into him with all the cruelty of Cain. When William had pulled the brutes off Johnny, he was lying in the dirt, curled like a squirrel in its nest, whimpering and bloody. His restoration had taken time and concentrated care. Maggie's experience was no different.

When Maggie had undressed the evening before, it was the first time he had seen her naked since the attack. She stood before him, no longer ashamed of the now-faded yellow blemishes discolouring her shoulders and thighs. Previously, she had covered her body, mortified by the marks left by the hands of Matthew Drummond.

William had led her to the bed, and, after slipping under the covers, they lay face to face for an age, staring into one another's eyes as the shadows from the hearth danced on their skin like sprites.

When he had wrapped his arm around her waist, noticing the silky coolness of her skin, he'd expected her to shy away from his touch. But she didn't flinch; instead, she drew him closer, allowing her legs to twine with his. They were fastened in such a sweet embrace, William hadn't wanted the moment to end. Their bodies were knotted like snakes. Then they had kissed and, in an instant, the rest of the world fell away and the only people on Earth were he and Maggie, locked for eternity in an Eden of their own making. If he was struck dead at that moment, he wouldn't have cared. When they had finally come together, he noticed a tear on her cheek. Concerned she was pained, he paused, searching her face.

'I'm happy this has finally happened. It feels like home,' she whispered.

Her words had warmed and moved him; he had felt a tear in his own eye then, too.

Later, as he waited for what he hoped would be the deepest, most fathomless sleep he'd experienced in many days, his wandering thoughts had snagged on Matthew Drummond and he felt a hate rise in his chest that was so strong, he feared it would not be tempered easily. Although the idea of pummelling the fiend was attractive, William knew he would have to use his smarts and not his strength in order to defeat the wretched man.

As he moved the various players around in his mind – Drummond, Reggie Owen, Briar Haines – nothing made any sense. But then he added a fourth person to the stage – Tommy Fellowes. Although he didn't want to believe it, he was growing more and more convinced that his godfather was involved in Drummond's machinations.

※

'WHY ARE YOU SO CONTEMPLATIVE TODAY?' Maggie asked as they walked along the river path. 'You're usually so chipper in the morning.'

'I'm just experiencing a taste of what you went through last year with your mother.' He turned to face her. 'It's Tommy. I don't know how he fits into all of this, but I've come to the conclusion he does somehow.'

She took his hand. 'I'm sorry.' Maggie knew how much he cared for his godfather, but was relieved William had realised there was something amiss with the man's recent behaviour.

They stopped for a moment as a family of mallards waddled officiously across the path in front of them, their emerald heads glistening in the morning sun. Maggie and William smiled, the image lifting their spirits.

When the couple reached the High Street, they were greeted by an unexpected visitor. Mister Latey was waiting for them outside the ironmongery.

'Jack said you pass this way each morning.'

William took his hand and greeted him warmly.

'Whatever are you doing here?' Maggie asked as she shook Latey's hand.

'Distance makes it impossible to wine and dine you, so visiting my most popular writer is the least I can do. It's my job to make you feel special. C.P. Scott gave me strict instructions not to let you get away.'

'Really?' Over the preceding weeks, she had allowed Briar's death and Drummond's machinations to consume her. Although she filed her weekly article promptly by each deadline, once the envelope fell into the post box, she rarely gave it a second thought.

'Readers love the series, Almond,' Latey continued, inspecting his cigar. 'Mister Scott wants to place you on retainer.'

'Oh?'

'Good grief, Almond! Is that all you have to say?'

Maggie looked at William and he winked. She winked back. For the first time in many days, a spot of good news had come her way. Light, buoyant, heady ... she sensed she might fly away if someone didn't tether her to the ground.

'Well?'

Of course, both she and William knew she would eventually agree with a jubilant 'Yes!'. However, despite her lack of patience, Maggie hated to be rushed. So instead, she thought of how George Lewes might respond on behalf of his wife.

'I'll give your offer some thought, Mister Latey. If you'd like to get a contract to me, I'll look it over in the next few weeks.'

Latey smiled, rubbing his bald head in exasperation.

'Now, shall we have some tea?' Maggie suggested.

ᘓᘓ

ONCE THE THREE were seated in the tearoom, Latey cleared his throat, produced a folder from his satchel, then pushed it across the table to William and Maggie.

'There is another reason I came here,' he said gravely. 'Matthew Drummond. Watch yourselves. He's a bad egg.'

Maggie opened the folder. She and William scanned the documents as Latey summarised the information.

'Matthew Drummond is a loose cannon, make no mistake. He's the proverbial black sheep of his family, involved in gambling houses, cock fights, prostitution, opium. Trafficking among the workers in the family's cotton mills is just one of his many nefarious pursuits. The worst of it is, a young woman at the family's Oldham mill became pregnant and claimed Drummond had intimidated her into relations. The family attempted to pay her off, but she wouldn't leave him alone. The poor woman wanted a father for her child. Drummond had told her he loved her, apparently.' Latey paused. His voice lowered. 'According to my source, she disappeared.'

Maggie felt the blood drain from her face. In an instant, she became aware how fortunate she had been to escape the man. She felt William grip her arm, steadying her. Maggie recalled Drummond's story of Irena, his lost love. Could this woman be Irena? If so, he was more deluded than she ever imagined. Much more so.

'The girl? The baby?' William asked.

Latey shook his head. 'No one knows.'

'But the pregnancy would have been the final straw,' Maggie said. 'There is nothing more frustrating for a monied family than an unexpected and unwanted heir. They are sure to have covered it up and then sent him away.'

'Sent packing,' William said, wryly.

'Indeed.'

William and Maggie shot each other a glance. Each knew what the other was thinking. That poor girl and infant. What had Drummond's family done to protect their delinquent son?

'And the police?' William asked.

Latey shrugged. 'Unfortunately, she was a single girl in the family way. Poor and uneducated, it's not likely the constabulary would have given her a second thought, even if someone had bothered to report her missing.'

Maggie felt the heat rise in her chest. 'And Drummond's other crimes?'

Latey took a sip of his tea. 'Rumour has it, the constabulary in Manchester are in the family's back pocket.'

'That's why Briar's contact in Manchester couldn't provide Andy with any information,' said William, shaking his head. 'And she had thought he was an honest copper ...'

After finishing their tea, the couple farewelled Mister Latey. He was bound for Edinburgh. While William enquired about his trip, Maggie felt tears form behind her eyes. She thought of the poor young girl, pregnant and alone. Drummond was nothing more than a monster, a privileged madman. Maggie regretted ever attempting to befriend him.

'Did his family truly believe his behaviour would change once they removed him from Manchester?' she asked William when they were alone. 'They've made their problem ours, and without evidence of his wrongdoing, there's not a thing we can do about it!'

'What could he planning here, Maggie? Cock fights, prostitution, and opium dens ... Is Durham to be Sodom or Gomorrah?'

They walked to the river, both silent and contemplative. A fisherman arrived with a satchel and rod, wading in the shallows on the opposite shore. It would not be long before the river would freeze over and the fishermen of Durham would take a hiatus. A thin layer of ice was already forming near the bank. The couple watched the angler's gentle movements. After a while, Maggie broke the silence that had settled between them.

'I've not told you much about Drummond's attack,' she began hesitantly. 'At first, I didn't want to recall it, and I knew if you were aware of the details, you wouldn't be able to control your anger, even if I begged you.'

William inhaled deeply, still clearly frustrated by his perceived inactivity.

'When he forced me to the floor, I looked into his eyes. I saw lust and fury, but there was something else.'

William turned and looked at her, the barely contained anger in his belly twisting at Maggie's words.

'Longing.'

He frowned, sickened. 'Are you saying he loves you? The man's got a very strange way of showing it.'

'I believe Drummond yearns for acceptance and friendship, maybe even love.'

William, forgetting his own feelings for a moment, looked at her in astonishment. She shrugged.

'I believe he saw Briar as a friend, perhaps something more. When he discovered her "betrayal", he sent her away knowing Reggie would vent his fury on her. Or perhaps he instructed Reggie to ...' Maggie couldn't say the words. She lowered her gaze to the ground for an instant. 'And I think Drummond did genuinely want my friendship, just as I had wanted his. But when he learnt of my connection to Briar – and when Reggie told him of our kiss – it was the final straw, a betrayal so absolute, he needed to punish me, too. His frustration with me manifested as sexual violence—'

'Please, stop.' William could bear it no longer. He placed his hand over hers.

'I've been reading George Lewes's book, you see.'

They were silent again for a time. In a flurry of activity, the fisherman they had been observing lifted a trout from a section of fast-flowing water.

'Briar told us Drummond admitted the other boys brutalised him at school in Rugby. Shelley was treated similarly at Eton and it is what Miss Clairmont credited for his rebellious, volatile and erratic nature.'

William gazed at her in amazement. He yearned to beat Drummond to a pulp yet Maggie was able to view her experience rationally. She was searching for a reason for the attack; it was her way of making sense of what happened. He shook his head in awe of her strength.

'I'm not suggesting Drummond should be forgiven or pardoned for his crimes,' Maggie continued. 'However, I believe he is a product of his environment. William, we had suspected he was complicated, but I believe he is a far more complex man than we ever imagined.'

CHAPTER 39

'WHAT AN UNEXPECTED PLEASURE,' John Cross said as he entered the drawing room, 'to have both of you here together.' He was clearly confused by their unannounced presence, but he remained impossibly gracious.

Marian was already seated in her usual chair by the hearth. She seemed pained, her face pale. Maggie and William positioned themselves by the bookcase.

'Missus Cross has been ill,' Mister Cross went on, placing his hand gently on his wife's shoulder. 'Although the presence of your company is always a pleasure, we should postpone this interview.'

'This isn't a *Guardian* interview,' Maggie assured the host. 'William and I are here to speak to both of you actually, regarding a separate matter entirely.'

Mister Cross made a sound. It was a throaty noise, almost a grunt. His head turned sharply towards his wife for a moment before he regained himself. 'A social call?'

Maggie nodded.

'Splendid! I'll ask Julia to make tea.' He hurried from the

room and Marian smiled in that gentle way she had, both apologetic and forbearing.

Mister Cross soon returned with Julia, who was bearing a tray laden with tea and scones.

When each of the party was seated and equipped with teacups, Mister Cross continued.

'Now, how can we help you?'

Maggie and William glanced at each other before Maggie began.

'We were wondering if you might be familiar with a mutual acquaintance, Matthew Drummond, the colliery owner. It seems you both attended Rugby School.'

Marian turned her head slowly towards her husband. Her movements were liquid, as though she were moving through water.

'Yes, that's correct. He was in the year below me.'

'It's odd you've not mentioned that before, dear.' Marian put in. 'Considering the impact Mister Drummond is having on the Durham community.'

Maggie and William glanced at each other again. Marian's tone was hostile, yet the addition of the endearment immediately diffused the observation. Maggie had to agree with Marian. It was unusual for Old Boys not to acknowledge each other.

Mister Cross seemed unperturbed. 'We never mixed in the same circles. He was reserved to the point of remote. In fact, it would seem odd if I had made myself known to him, as though I was scratching for a connection that never existed.'

Maggie understood what he meant. John Cross was his own man, successful and wealthy. He had no need for connections.

'He claims the lads harassed him at school,' William said. 'That he was beaten and tormented by the other boys.'

'That could well be, Mister Dodd. Quiet boys, small boys, boys who were different or eccentric were all put upon or persecuted in one way or another.'

'Goodness,' Marian said. 'You speak as though this behaviour was acceptable.'

'Not by any means, dear. It was simply the custom, deplorable as it was. Every boy at Rugby is forced to be someone they're not in order to fit in. No mercy is shown to those who refuse.'

'Custom ...' Maggie repeated.

All eyes looked her way. Maggie placed her teacup on the tray.

'I have been reading Mister Lewes's book, the one you loaned to me Marian,' she explained. 'Early psychologists differed in their ideas of how the mind worked, but they all considered the mind as something static, unchanging. Mister Lewes's theory considered consciousness as a series of ever-changing relations between body and mind, feeling and thought. In his way of thinking, a person's environment is crucial to their psychological development. He goes on to suggest that the psychological traits an individual develops throughout their lifetime can be internalised so deeply that they can even be passed on to their offspring.'

'Hereditary of a different kind,' William said.

'Exactly, Mister Dodd,' Marian said.

'Mister Lewes concluded that the individual develops idiosyncrasies and patterns of behaviour through their social customs, education and personal experiences.'

At Maggie's words, Marian nodded. 'I have applied George's theories in my own work, you know. *Middlemarch*, more than any other of my novels, I consider to be a novel of the mind.'

'Lydgate believes "a medical man likes to make psycholog-ical observation",' William commented.

Maggie raised an eyebrow. He shrugged. She touched his hand lightly.

'Indeed, Mister Dodd,' the authoress said. 'However, Lydgate is deluded, as we all are. He makes a monumental misjudgement when he marries Rosamond.' Marian sighed. 'But haven't we all been deluded, misguided or mistaken at one time or another?'

Maggie remembered her own missteps during the summer of 1879. Her mother and Briar had deceived her. And she had deceived herself when she believed she could not fulfil her purpose with William by her side. More recently, she had mistakenly believed the community would accept her even though distrust of outsiders such as herself had been bred into them through custom and belief for centuries. And then there was Drummond ...

'At the beginning of the novel, Dorothea is almost too perfect, but she evolves from her flawless state after she marries Edward Casaubon,' Maggie said after a moment, thinking aloud. 'She misperceives Casaubon because of her determination to idealise him. And, by the end, she has learnt to follow her heart even though this means she must relinquish her fortune.'

Just as I had hoped Matthew Drummond to be honourable because I longed for a friend, Maggie thought.

'Bravo, Miss Almond,' Mister Cross applauded, as though he had read her mind. 'You are quite the scholar.'

Maggie smiled, taking in Mister Cross's countenance. Was he Marian's Rosamond? She wondered what missteps Marian may have made in the twilight of her life.

WHEN THEY BID the Crosses farewell, Maggie and William began their walk back to the cottage.

'Perhaps, Matthew Drummond was bullied at school due to his Mancunian background,' Maggie conjectured. 'Maybe his own father harassed him as Sir Timothy had harassed Shelley? Then Drummond interpreted those harsh lessons as meaning that to get on in the world, he needed to become the tormentor himself. He chooses to be a tyrant, subconsciously or consciously, to either make people fear him enough to leave him alone or befriend him.'

Once they were by the riverbank, William stopped and embraced her. 'I'm not deceived in thinking you're the most brilliant woman in England.'

'Only in England?'

He smiled, then went quiet. He took her hands. 'You could do anything you wish. You could do great things ...'

'What is greater than discussing psychology and novel writing with George Eliot?' she retorted. 'I am writing, gaining an audience and the series had been exceptionally well-received, according to Mister Latey. I now have the funds to begin a school. I will make change, fundamental change in the way we educate girls. And one day in the future, the changes I have prompted here will mean women won't need to descend into the mines in order to feed their children, or to succumb to the desires of a lecher like Matthew Drummond. They will vote and have a voice in how they are governed ...'

William watched as Maggie gained momentum, her mind flooding with possibilities for the future. She was speaking with such clarity that her words had gained power.

'And, I could argue, you are the one short-changing yourself by remaining in Durham. You're a talented and courageous writer, William Dodd. But you don't write for renown. You write to make people aware of the injustices occurring in Britain, and that takes immeasurable courage. You could write for any newspaper in the world!'

She paused, remembering what Briar had spoken about on the day they had shared a kiss.

'Some may believe we are living in a small way here in Durham, but we're not. The fire of change we ignite here, in this little place, will catch hold and become very, very dangerous.'

Filled with a fire of a different kind, William kissed her deeply. When their lips parted, he was certain of what he needed to do.

WHEN WILLIAM RETURNED to the *Durham County Advertiser*, he walked immediately to Mister Armstrong's office. The editor never closed his door. He welcomed his journalists coming to him with ideas or complaints. Armstrong looked up from his desk.

'Aareet, Will? What can I do for yer?'

'I want to write about the Stanley Pit.'

Armstrong gestured to a seat.

'Drummond has instituted none of the improvements the union recommended.'

'Do yer have proof?'

'I went down a disused shaft, the one in Shield Row.'

Armstrong nodded. He, too, had grown up among the colliers of County Durham.

'I followed the seam until I reached the Stanley Pit.'

'Tha's trespassing, yer now,' he said as a matter of procedure.

William was certain Armstrong had engaged in similar unlawful acts in the guise of a journalist seeking the truth, but he nodded gravely.

'I found nothing to show that Drummond has improved the mine, Harry. The man is lying. And I know he's behind what happened to Briar Haines and probably Reggie Owen, too.'

Armstrong raised his chin. 'How?'

It was impossible for William to reveal how he knew. He could not tell his editor that Drummond had attacked Maggie, or their suspicion of his involvement in Briar's death. While he had no proof on the latter, after his conversations about the man with Latey, the Crosses and Maggie, he knew it to be as true as gold.

'I have a source at the *Manchester Guardian*.'

'Is there anyone who can corroborate what you're accusing Drummond of?'

'The *Manchester Guardian* has confirmed Drummond's family sent him to Durham. They were tired of covering up his ... indiscretions.'

'It's still sounds like conjecture and, to be honest with yer, Will, a little like sour grapes,' Armstrong said, rising and straightening his waistcoat. 'Come on, man! You know as well as I that without evidence and corroborating witness statements we can't publish. And if we did, Drummond could sue the newspaper.' Armstrong rubbed his head in vexation. 'William, I don't trust him anymore than you do. If you can get one statement, lad, one witness who'll speak to either the failure of Drummond to improve the shaft, or his involvement in Briar Haines's murder, then you can have your story.'

Armstrong's words sparked an idea in William's mind. There *was* one person he could interview. Rising, satisfied, he shook his editor's hand, then headed immediately to the office of the Miner's Union.

CHAPTER 40

'TOMMY,' William pleaded. 'You've got to give me something. You know as well as I that Drummond's as rotten as dirt.'

Tommy Fellowes lowered his head into his hands.

'You do know something,' William said. 'I can see you do.'

The older man rose and walked to the window. He stared through the murky pane at the High Street for some minutes, silent, contemplative.

William examined Tommy's physique, hunched and hobbled by a life spent underground; the man had first descended into the dark when he was but eight years old. William could sense his anguish now. Rising, he placed his broad hand on his godfather's shoulder.

'Tommy, you can tell me. Whatever it is, you can tell me.'

Tommy groaned. He leant his forehead against the window. When he eventually straightened and turned, it was with an expression of such utter defeat that William was suddenly uncertain whether he wanted to hear what Tommy was readying to tell him.

'A year ago, I visited Deborah in Manchester.'

Deborah was the youngest of Tommy's girls and the pair

had always shared a close bond. She was only three when her mother had died, and Tommy became both father and mother to her. But when she met a brewer from Boddingtons, she married him and moved from Durham to be with her Mancunian.

'It was not long after the collapse. The colliers were demanding the pit reopen, but without an owner, my hands were tied. I just needed ...' Tommy's thoughts seemed to drift.

'A little breathing space?' William suggested, remembering a phrase Maggie used.

Tommy nodded. 'Exactly. A little breathing space,' he echoed. 'One evening, late, Deb's husband Billy took me to a gentleman's club ...'

William sighed, knowing where this revelation was heading. Billy Shard wasn't just a brewer, he was one of the chief brewers at Boddingtons. He was a self-made man, part of the new aristocracy in Manchester.

'I lost a ... I lost a fortune to Matthew Drummond, although I didn't know who he was then. He was just another man at the hazard table. I settled the debts as best I could, promising to repay the rest within the month. Drummond accepted my proposal. He shook my hand, Will. The man shook my hand.' Tommy held out his hand and looked at it in amazement. In Tommy's world, a man never reneged on a handshake. 'But then before I knew it, he had bought the mine and arrived in Durham seeking what I owed him. It was over £100, Willie.'

'Why didn't you tell Deb? Billy could have settled your debts in a heartbeat.'

Shame swept across Tommy's face and he seemed to shrink, collapse in on himself.

'Deb is the only one of the girls who'll have a bar of me. The older two remember my gambling from back when

Audrey was alive. They've never forgiven me for making Aud's life a misery. Why do you think they moved away as quick as they could? I couldn't have Deborah hate me, too.'

William ran his fingers through his hair. He knew a man like Tommy Fellowes could never raise £100 except by returning to the gambling table.

'So instead of paying him what you owed, you promised to look the other way when he bought the pit.'

Tommy nodded regretfully. 'I know it was wrong, worse than wrong. Yer own fatha, my best friend, died in the pit only a year before ... but I couldn't see a way out.'

'You could have told someone, Tommy,' William replied flatly. 'You could have discussed it with me. I would have helped you.'

'But I'm sick with shame over it. Disgusted at meself for gambling, for helping Drummond with his schemes. I never thought I was capable of such deviousness. I betrayed the same men I've advocated for over twenty years. How can I ever put that right?'

There were tears in Tommy's eyes. William took him by the shoulders.

'There's one thing you could do.'

Tommy wiped his eyes.

'Go on record, Tommy. I want to write about it for the *Advertiser*.'

Tommy thought for what seemed, to William, like an age. The man finally nodded, as though relieved.

❧

THAT EVENING, William wrote the article. Maggie approached the writing desk in the sitting room and squeezed his shoulder, reading his words.

'Poor Tommy,' she remarked. 'What a dreadful situation he has found himself in.'

William placed his pen on its stand and turned. The hearth fire flickered in his hazel eyes.

'I agree, but it's all his doing. If he'd just told someone. Better still if he'd not gone to the gentleman's club in the first place. Gambling is to him like nectar to a bee.'

Maggie was aware very few gentlemen ever attended gentleman's clubs. Raymond had described to her how sordid such establishments were following a stag engagement he had attended. He told her florid stories of excessive drinking, gambling and, when Maggie had wrung the information from him, he revealed a female performer had danced naked on their table. While Maggie was no prude, she certainly did not support the degrading practice of women revealing their bodies for payment, especially for the enjoyment of males.

Now they knew the depths of his vagaries, Maggie realised a gentleman's club was just the sort of establishment a loathsome fiend such as Drummond would frequent.

'It's a dreadful confession to have revealed publicly in print,' Maggie said.

'Especially when all and sundry believe he triumphed over his gambling habit when his wife died.'

'For a seasoned collier, he strikes me as a gentle soul at heart.' Maggie frowned, thinking. 'Would it not make more sense to reveal my secret, rather than Tommy's?'

William placed his hands on her hips and stared at her, disbelieving.

'Well,' she went on. 'Mister Armstrong said you need only one corroborating statement. If the statement came from me ...'

Maggie was aware of the enormity of her offer. To share her story of Drummond's attack with the whole county would likely ignite an entirely new wave of public opinion against her. Since she had upbraided Reggie Owen, she believed she was making some headway with the community, albeit slow. To reveal her experience on that afternoon in Drummond's office could possibly move her cause backward. There was no doubt many would view her as a harlot, for surely that was how Drummond would paint her in response to the article. But it would plant the seed of a suspicion in the reader's mind, and in Maggie's experience, suspicion very quickly matured into mistrust.

'You'd do that for Tommy?' he asked, amazed.

'I'd do it for you,' she replied, love filling her heart. 'I can see how painful it is airing your godfather's dirty linen. If I can ease even some of your burden, the sense of my benevolence would be protection enough from the slurs I would incur.'

Maggie immediately thought of the two heroines in *Middlemarch*. Dorothea Brooke was self-sacrificing and altruistic; she relinquished her own happiness for her husband's intellectual satisfaction. Rosamond Vincy was the antithesis. She refused to sacrifice any of her material comforts to support her husband, who only wanted to improve the community. While Maggie realised she would never be as noble as Dorothea, nor as self-seeking as Rosamond, she believed her actions would place her somewhere in between.

'Your selflessness astounds me, but I'd never do that to you.' He rose and took her face in his hands. 'I could never bring that sort of trouble on you. Tommy is my godfather, but you're my life.'

Maggie kissed him, deeply, passionately. Neither of Eliot's female characters could boast a partner as wonderful as William Dodd.

ONCE WILLIAM HAD RETURNED to his article and Maggie to her sewing (she had successfully graduated to a pretty cross-stitch of tulips and jasmine), Grace entered the sitting room and stood expectantly in the doorway. Both Maggie and William looked up from their various pursuits and noticed her manner. It was both eager and regretful.

'I'm going on a trip,' she said.

Surprised, Maggie and William glanced at each other before turning their attention back to Grace.

'May is poorly. She's asked if I wouldn't mind staying with her, just until she's feeling better.'

'May?' Maggie asked.

'My younger sister. She lives in Carlisle. She's expecting and the doctor's told her she needs rest for a while. Meanwhile, she's got a husband and three more bairns to care for.'

'What about your studies?' William asked. 'You've been working so hard of late.'

'It's almost Christmas break,' she explained, moving further into the sitting room and examining the fire. 'If I return in the new year, I'll only miss a week or so.' Grace took the poker in her hand and shifted the billets, provoking a healthier blaze.

'You'll be in Carlisle for Christmas, then?' William asked.

'Aye. You'll manage here with Beth and Jack. I'll warrant you'll enjoy having the place to yourselves for a wee spell. And it will be nice for Lydia to have you all to herself.'

Grace outlined her plans and itinerary to the both of them. When she left the sitting room, Maggie laid down her cross-stitch and followed close behind.

'Is it Lydia being here?' Maggie asked, taking her arm. 'If it is, I can ask her to move to town. The request would not slight her, and she would probably enjoy finding an elegant home by the river. She's hit it off very well with Mister Cross. They share a fondness for whist. It's a game I never learnt and she'll be glad of a companion close by. I'm positive she would appreciate being in town.'

Before Grace could respond, Maggie guided her into the kitchen and closed the door.

'I know you formed an attachment with my father while he was here, and it cannot be easy living under the same roof as Lydia if you still have feelings for him.'

Maggie had driven onto a bumpy road of enquiry, but she hated the thought Grace might feel uncomfortable in her own home.

Grace patted her hand. 'Don't be daft, lass,' she said, taking a seat. 'I admire Lydia very much. We've hit it off surprisingly well, considering ...' She lowered her eyes for a moment. '... we are so different. I won't deny the affection between Henry and me, but it's as I said, May needs my help.

'Besides, I've not left Durham since the pit collapse. Everything around me is a reminder of Archie and the boys. While it has been a blessing having Willie and you here, I've realised I still have some healing to do. Your father helped me realise it, in fact.' She paused, smiling in fondness at a memory. 'Tha's no more to it than that,' Grace said, kissing Maggie on the cheek. 'Now, I'm heading upstairs to pack. You continue on with your sewing. You're making a fine job of it, lass! I'll see you on the morrow.'

THE NEXT MORNING, Maggie was still thinking on their conversation when Jack arrived to take Grace to Newcastle station. Fond farewells were shared, but Maggie could not shake the sense there was more to Grace's departure than she was revealing.

Soon after, William headed off to work and Maggie began her own. The events of recent days had shifted her perspective somewhat. As she considered her article, she realised that she now felt her school was less a selfish desire on her part or a statement of her principles, and more an absolute necessity for the community.

To believe the theories of George Henry Lewes, theories exposed by George Eliot herself in her novels, a child's environment had as much to do with shaping their character as their biology, perhaps more. To Maggie's mind, there were two significant environments in a child's life: home and school. If a child might be influenced by teachers modelling decency, equality and respect, if they could be educated on an equal footing in a safe and caring environment, free from taunts and bullying, then, Maggie reasoned, men like Drummond might become extinct eventually, as extinct as Darwin's giant ground sloth.

This is what she told herself as she penned her next instalment. She also kept in mind the words William had said to her as he departed for the *Advertiser*, clutching his article. 'The moment of truth!' he had called as he walked through the gate.

Maggie sincerely hoped so.

Truth.

Marian Cross had adopted many identities throughout the course of her life. Now she was finally ready to disclose the truth about the woman she actually was, or so she had led Maggie to believe.

Maggie stared down at her shorthand scribble and frowned. She knew Grace was hiding something about why she was travelling to Carlisle, and she knew Marian was not being entirely honest with her either. There was something the authoress was omitting about her life. During their last interview, it had hung between them like an invisible temptation. Maggie could sense it, almost taste it, then Marian had snatched it away.

Unlike Claire Clairmont, Marian would not leave journals from which Maggie might discover the truth one day, no matter how confronting it might be. She would need to extract the truth from her subject, carefully and with precision, like a surgeon. She even sensed Marian wanted it so. The truth was a splinter embedded deeply under the skin. Although it caused her pain, there would be no better treatment than to dig it out.

Reading Lewes's book on psychology had made Maggie aware of the capabilities of the human mind. All at once, it could be one's best friend and one's worst enemy. The problem was that for her to find the blossom of truth among the vast valleys and dales of Marian's mind, Maggie had to be cleverer than her subject.

She closed her notebook and looked through the window to the horizon. Having grown familiar with the authoress's mind and intellect over the preceding weeks, being smarter than George Eliot seemed to Maggie an impossibility.

CHAPTER 41

The Manchester Guardian
Wednesday, December 1, 1880

DEAR READER,

Over the years, I have become, quite unwittingly, a symbol of the women's movement. My choice to remain unwed, my fierce independence and my friendships with women involved in the suffragette movement have led the public to believe I am an advocate for gender equality.

However, while this may be so, I have always remained quiet on the 'woman question'. I am constantly afraid that people will misconstrue my words as advice, not to mention (heaven forbid) base a militant action on something I have uttered.

Like most women, society forced me to overcome a plethora of obstacles before I was able to find my way out of the labyrinth and reach the heady heights of fame where I find myself now. I have had to overcome the various statuses my birth, environment and education have attributed to me. You see, when I was studying in the 1830s, education in England was the preserve of well-born men. In fact, it remains so to this day.

While I treasured my education at Miss Wallington's School, it was rigid, based on a set of unwavering and outdated beliefs. It was an education much like the one I envisaged for Rosamond Vincy. She is a genteel product of a girl's school. She is the perfect showpiece of Missus Lemon's Finishing School. However, in many ways, Missus Lemon finished her off!

Any spark of creativity or original thought poor Rosamond might have had was crushed by her education. She was forced to believe the most vital piece of knowledge a woman should learn is the correct way of stepping from a carriage. Such vile dogmas urge schoolgirls to interpret ambition as egotism, something to be subdued, and to cultivate proper modesty by channelling their passions into obedience to God.

This was not only Rosamond's education, but mine. We were educated to be wives.

Yet where did that place me? Unlike the delicate Miss Vincy, I was neither attractive nor amenable. A middle-class gentleman in the mould of my father or brother would never have given me a second glance. Therefore, while this type of education may appear harmless to some, for me, it never rang true.

Instead, I took the example of my favourite female authors – Jane Austen, the Brontës and Mary Shelley. Even then, I believed for a time that female writers had to be the daughters of educated men. It is the reason it took me so many years to turn my pen to fiction. Jane Austen's upbringing always destined her to write such a wonderfully cutting line as 'Mr Collins was not a sensible man', but mine had not. Mary Shelley had the fame and learning of her mother and father to drive her to greatness, but I had not.

Therefore, dear Reader, it was not until I read the work of Mary Shelley's mother, the great Mary Wollstonecraft, that I discovered the truth. It was she who taught me what a girl's education should be, and what an educated woman can achieve.

Yet many women, my friends included, have argued that my writing does not reflect Wollstonecraft's doctrines. They believe it suggests a woman's place is in the home. They cite Dorothea Brooke, and contend that her epic and intense vision at the beginning of *Middlemarch* transforms into nothing more than a romantic marriage to Will Ladislaw. To their minds, falling in love with Will causes her desire for learning, for education, to evaporate instantly, like dew on a summer morning!

Perhaps it's time, then, for me to reveal a secret to you.

Originally, I had imagined Dorothea form a romantic partnership with Doctor Lydgate, for with their grand passions and dreams of doing good, surely these two would be perfectly suited. But as I wrote, I found that it was not Lydgate to whom Dorothea was attracted. And I ask you, is it not a realistic weakness to have such a righteous man of medicine as Tertius Lydgate fall under the spell of the vacuous Rosamond? Is it not true that life rarely turns out the way we think it will or wish it to? And so it has for my characters.

Given the opportunity, I would have married George Lewes in a heartbeat. I can guarantee that a wedding band would have made no difference to our work, success or friendship, or how we viewed each other. We were equals, first and foremost, and had been from the moment we began to share ideas in a London bookshop.

Therefore, I argue that we should not see marriage as an end to a woman's fight for education and independence, and neither should it be the termination of a woman's dreams for balance between the sexes. I certainly don't believe that it was for Dorothea Brooke! And I know from personal experience that marriage between two like minds, between equals, can be a step forward for both women and men.

'In schools such as the one I went to, the uninformed mind is shut down, forced to wither. It is not encouraged to expand. Instead, it grows smaller.'

Maggie nodded in agreement. This meeting, she realised as she was writing her questions, would be part interview and part research. Marian had been silent on Maggie's idea of a girl's school in Durham, even though at the now infamous Town Hall meeting she had suggested they discuss the 'woman question'. Over the course of the interviews, Maggie had learnt that her subject was ever guarded; sensitive information needed to be wrested from her like a toy from a child.

'Rather than formulating my own ideas about literature and science, school taught me to quote others who came before. During my days of evangelicalism, I did little more than spout quotations from the Bible and Christian theorists.'

They had met again in the Wolsey Room. With the Christmas break approaching and exams a distant memory, the students' dedication to their studies had waned, making it a peaceful location. Maggie's footsteps had echoed as she walked through the library, attracting the attention of one lone scholar who seemed pleased to see another fellow human in his deserted surrounds. A grateful smile had passed across his lips.

'When did you realise your education had been lacking?' Maggie asked, looking up from her notes.

'My job at the *Westminster Review* opened my eyes in more ways than one,' she said, raising an eyebrow, clearly referring in part to her relationship with John Chapman. 'But it wasn't until I met Herbert Spencer and then George that my eyes were fully opened. Both were self-educated – their minds were intensely curious. If they could not find the answers they sought in books, they conducted the research themselves. Curiosity is one of the first natural instincts to be destroyed during the process of formal education, especially in girls. In girls, we view it as downright seditious.'

'Are you against university education?' Maggie asked. 'After all, we could view it as doctrinal as well.'

'Not at all!' she replied. 'I'm simply suggesting it is often unnecessary. And people should not be judged by a degree hung on a wall. You are an excellent example of a woman forging a highly successful career without the help of a university education.'

Following her disappointments of the previous year, Maggie had not seen herself as a woman 'forging a highly successful career' but, given Latey's feedback and his updates regarding readership, she supposed she was.

'Mister Latey and C.P. Scott have done nothing but sing your praises. What's more, £100 for a few months' work is nothing to sneeze at. And I believe they have offered you a retainer?'

Maggie looked at her in surprise then nodded. She hadn't mentioned anything of her conversation with Latey to Marian.

'Mister Latey told me about his offer,' Marian said, noticing her bewilderment. 'You were wise not to jump at it immediately. They will always come back with something more attractive when great talent is on the line.'

She appreciated Marian's openness and business sense. Discussing money was taboo among Maggie's 'people', especially the women. She recalled the distaste she evoked at one of Lydia's formal dinners by mentioning the wage she earnt at the *Illustrated London News*.

'When I was seventeen,' Marian continued, 'my father took me away from school to become his housekeeper. Chrissy had just married and moved away. As you know, Maggie, I fed chickens, churned butter and pickled vegetables. But at the same time, I taught myself Latin and Greek. I paved my own pathway for learning, as you are doing here in Durham. Even if I had wanted to further my education more formally, there were no colleges that accepted women at that time.'

Maggie nodded. Like Marian had in her youth, she, too, was learning something new every day, especially regarding human nature.

'But it was George who suggested I read *Vindication*.'

Maggie looked at her, astonished. George Eliot, a figure so strongly associated with the women's movement, had not read *A Vindication of the Rights of Woman* until she was in her thirties. It seemed impossible.

'By the 1850s, most suffragettes wished to distance themselves from Wollstonecraft. They wished to disassociate themselves from her ideas because of the slurs on her private life, slurs that were no different to those cast against me. In fact, her books were extremely difficult to hunt out. Yet the same women who separated themselves from her forgot she had been a woman of great dignity, who had impressed men such as Samuel Johnson and William Godwin with her intellect and wit. It only took William Pitt's propaganda juggernaut to label her a whore and the entire women's movement turned their back on her.'

Maggie had not heard Marian use a word such as 'whore' before. She was clearly passionate about the work of Wollstonecraft.

'What did you learn from her?' Maggie asked.

'Wollstonecraft wished both women and men would gain knowledge to bring about the growth of character. She, too, despised women like Rosamond Vincy. Readers believe Rosamond is a caricature of a wife. She is not. Women do not wish to see themselves in Rosamond, so they label her grotesque, although it is a reality that many gifted men waste their ambitions attempting to maintain a certain lifestyle for a wife who is fit for nothing but to sit in a drawing room like a china doll.' Marian's words had taken on a new energy. She paused. 'Men and women should make each other better, Maggie. Husbands and wives should be friends, and we should educate them at school and at home to be so.'

Maggie's observation had taught her that women surrendered their power to their husband once they were married. However, listening to Marian, who clearly believed it could be a partnership of equals, suggested to her that perhaps it didn't have to be that way. It certainly hadn't been so for Marian and George. And for Marian and John? Perhaps the pendulum had swung a little the other way ...

The interview ended shortly afterwards when the Wolsey grew dark. A librarian entered and informed the women there had been a snowfall, the first of the season. The library was closing early as a result.

When the women exited the building, they stood silently for a time in wonder, examining the lacy quilt spanning the lawn and the white flakes that still floated from the heavens. They smiled at one another. Although the winter would draw on, the first snow of the season was always as marvellous as a dream.

Breaking the quiet, John Cross came hurrying across the green. When he met them, he wrapped a heavy cloak around his wife's shoulders and squeezed her tight.

'Would you like a ride home?' he asked Maggie. 'I have a carriage.'

Maggie looked to the road. Jack gave her a friendly wave.

'No, thank you, Mister Cross. I'd like to walk in the snow for a while.'

He nodded. The women made a hurried goodbye. Marian seemed disappointed as her husband bustled her into the carriage.

Maggie buttoned her coat, pulled up the collar and began her walk back to the cottage. Before she had gone too far, she paused and closed her eyes, sensing the snowflakes softly kiss her face. When she opened them again, the snow was falling more abundantly. Although in the half light of the late afternoon she could barely see two feet ahead of her, Maggie realised Marian had gifted her a sudden and remarkable clarity.

☙❧

ONCE THEY RETURNED to the warmth of their home, John hurriedly relieved Marian of her cloak, coat and boots. Julia stood by, not quite knowing what to do. After all, such tasks were a maid's job. When she realised she would not be needed, Julia absented herself and headed towards the kitchen. Mister Cross always called for tea when Missus Cross returned, or when Miss Almond departed.

John settled his wife into her chair and poked at the fire.

'Where a weakness is not controlled, it will govern,' she murmured.

'Excuse me, dear?' John asked, looking up from his position at the hearth.

She shook her head. 'It is something a teacher once told me.'

John made a noise. *John makes so many unusual noises,* Marian thought. *What does this one mean?* She wondered if it was a display of his consternation, his interest or perhaps the opposite ... How she wished he would just use words to express his feelings. It was a foible she hadn't noticed until they were married. When Johnny was 'nephew' and not 'husband', she was certain he made no noises at all. She and George had enjoyed his company because of his silence. No one could compete with George in the loquaciousness stakes.

She sighed. Loquacious, from the Latin *loquax*, meaning talkative.

Piazza Farnese
Roma

MAY 5, 1860

Dearest Maria,

You once said to the girls in your charge, 'Where a weakness is not controlled, it will govern.' It has taken me almost thirty years to discover you were quoting Mary Wollstonecraft. Did you realise it at the time? Had you read Vindication?

I know you have not been sympathetic to my current circumstances. Bitterness took hold of my heart for a time, but I have come to understand that what you taught me at Missus Wallington's (and what still influences your own thoughts on the matter) was not reality. While I mean no disrespect to you, your teaching did not support my idea of womanhood. But I have found it now, in my life with George.

Since we have been in Rome, he and I have taken to enjoying our morning coffee in our room overlooking the piazza. Here, we sit, we watch and we observe. For me, observation is a reward: an unseen gesture, an unheard comment, a sniff of disregard; they all contain truth. It is this truth that I attempt to live, and to bring to my fiction.

During my time with you, nothing exceptional was ever expected of me apart from what was considered a woman's duty. Later, I spent many years mulling over what a woman should be, then George taught me that humans – male and female – constantly evolve if they allow it to be so. Our capacity for intellectual and moral expansion is enormous.

From my observations and personal experience, I've concluded that freedom and equality are necessary to the common human pursuit of intellectual and moral excellence. Therefore, I suggest to you that boys and girls should be educated together. Before you protest, let me assure you that I am aware they can corrupt each other – but I believe they can also improve each other. After all, they live in the same society. Should our future men and women not have the opportunity to build friendships on equal ground? Might not such solid foundations grow respect and understanding between the sexes?

To me, dearest Maria, that would be a weakness controlled and vanquished.

It has been six years since you have written, but I live in hope.

Yours ever optimistically,

Marian Lewes

CHAPTER 42

MAGGIE and her mother prepared tea. It was the first time they had ever done so together. Maggie believed, in fact, that it may have been the first time Lydia had ever lifted a colander from the sink or held a saucepan over a stove.

On the walk from Marian's home, Maggie had thought a great deal about the authoress's views on education. Just as girls should be taught Latin (as Maggie herself had been at her progressive school), boys would benefit from being instructed in the domestic subjects; only then would there be true equality in society. But would a community such as Durham accept a coeducational school with a balanced curriculum?

'Mother?' she began as the pair prepared the vegetables at the table.

Lydia took her eyes off the turnips for a moment and looked at her daughter. She had been concentrating stringently on the knobbled purple vegetable in her grasp.

'Were you in agreement when Papa suggested he enrol me in Cheltenham?'

Lydia placed the knife on the chopping board and wiped her hands on the apron she was wearing.

'To be honest, I did not have a great deal of say in the matter. Henry was determined we would not educate you to be a wife.' She raised a wry eyebrow. 'And he certainly succeeded in that regard.'

Maggie grinned.

'However,' Lydia continued. 'I believe everything Dorothea Beale instilled in you was excellent. I don't just mean the knowledge you possess. You have the confidence to pursue whatever it is you desire, be it a career or a family, or possibly both. You have your own mind and you're not afraid to use it.' She sighed then and touched the edge of the table, running her fingers along the oak. 'I wonder how my own life might have differed if I had received a similar education to you.'

Lydia had been educated in the style of a Rosamond Vincy. Maggie ceased her labours and looked into her mother's blue eyes. 'Do you mean Raymond?'

Lydia nodded. While her mother had travelled to Durham and apologised for her behaviour of the previous year, Maggie realised they had never discussed her history with Raymond Turner.

'What a terrible mess I made of things,' Lydia confessed. 'If I had been educated to be a woman rather than an ornament, I might have had greater courage in my convictions when my father suggested a match between myself and Henry. School taught me to obey my father, despite the unhappiness it caused myself and poor Raymond. I repressed my natural defiance.'

Maggie recalled a conversation she had last year with her father.

'Do you realise Papa fell in love with you because of your fire and your rebellious ways?'

Lydia raised her eyebrows. 'Really?'

Maggie nodded. 'Did you love him, Mama?'

'Not at first.' Lydia replied honestly. 'In fact, I was furious with him, although I didn't show it. That would have been unladylike.'

Maggie laughed.

'My anger seethed within me like a viper, and he sensed it. On the eve of our wedding day, he broke with tradition and came to see me. Aware my parents would not permit him into the house, he climbed onto the eave and tapped on my window. It must have been at least midnight, but I wasn't asleep. I was bristling with anxiety.

'When I opened the window, he was balanced so precari-ously, I feared he would fall and come to harm.' She paused and smiled. It was a gentle parting of her lips. 'He told me if I was unsure of our nuptials the following day, I should say so. I was not to concern myself with rumours or gossip or the reputations of our families. He wanted only for my happiness, and if that wasn't to be found as the wife of Henry Almond, he would readily agree to a separation, although it would pain him to do so.'

Maggie had never heard the story before. She attempted to picture her father perched on an eave like a starling. 'How did you reply?'

'I must admit to considering his proposal, but then I looked into his earnest brown eyes and saw the expectant hope contained within ... and I kissed him. I told him it was a silly suggestion and I would never think of abandoning our plans. There was nothing else I could do, you see, for it was in that moment that I fell in love with him.'

Maggie smiled then embraced her mother tightly, taking in her familiar scent. Lydia had worn the same perfume for as long as Maggie could recall. She wondered if it was the same hint of gardenia and jasmine Henry had detected when he had kissed his betrothed at her bedroom window all those years ago. When the women broke apart, Lydia pressed her lips to her daughter's cheek. Then mother and daughter returned to their tasks.

෨෨

ARMSTRONG HAD BEEN PLEASED with the article and the quotes from Tommy Fellowes, suggesting only a few tweaks and tucks. William had to admit that the language he'd chosen to use in the piece carried with it the potent whiff of emotion.

Armstrong advised him the article would be published, but Drummond had to have the right of reply. Without a quote from the head of the colliery, it would appear as though the *Advertiser* was 'trying to stitch him up', Armstrong said. William agreed, although his first instinct was to deny Drummond the courtesy.

He hadn't sent word he would call, but when he approached the colliery office, Drummond opened the door and walked out to meet him.

'Mister Dodd,' he said. 'What a pleasure.'

Drummond held out his hand. After a second's hesitation, William shook it.

'I'd like a comment from you for an article I'm writing, if you wouldn't mind.'

Drummond agreed affably and led William into the office. William's eyes danced from the rug to the door and then to the window. He couldn't stop himself from imagining what Maggie had suffered in the room. His mouth grew dry.

'What would you like me to comment on, Mister Dodd?' Drummond asked, taking a seat behind his desk.

'First, a claim you have implemented none of the

improvements the union advised. Second, another that you have bribed a union official to ignore the wrongdoing.'

Drummond stared at him for some time. William watched his pale blue eyes grow colder by the second. 'Union official?'

'I'm not at liberty to disclose any names.'

Drummond turned his left ear towards William. 'I apologise, Mister Dodd. Would you mind speaking up? I've recently incurred an injury and the hearing in my right ear is yet to return.'

William repeated his words as calmly as he was able.

Drummond rose and walked to the window. He stared through the pane at the pitmen going about their work. 'All I have done is put the colliers of Durham back to work, yet you seem intent on punishing me for it.'

'Not at all, Mister Drummond,' William responded. 'But it is in the best interests of the community to learn the truth. As you know, everyone is thrilled to have the colliery open once more, but if they were to know of the alleged oversights, the same oversights that led to the collapse last year, they might have a different opinion.'

'Why have you taken such a grand dislike to me, Mister Dodd?' Drummond asked, turning to him.

William shook his head, then glanced at his notes. 'I really don't know—'

'Is it because of the attraction between myself and Maggie?'

William breathed in deeply and clenched his jaw.

How dare you call her 'Maggie'?

'I do not believe Miss Almond holds any affection towards you at all, Mister Drummond. In fact, I would characterise her feelings for you as quite the opposite.' He was struggling to remain composed, yet he could not help a steely edge creep into his tone.

'Did she share what went on here, in this very room?' Drummond went on. 'She told me once you two shared everything.'

Although aware he was being baited, William was fighting his own will to prevent himself from leaping up and hitting the man. Drummond gazed at him, confused.

'I suppose she did not, being a moment of such passion and your relationship being so ... undefined.'

It was all William could do to remain seated. Fury welled in his chest and the murderous rage that had overtaken him when he discovered Maggie huddling like a foundling beneath the bridge was rising in him once more.

'Maggie told me exactly what occurred. I saw her injuries. There was no passion on her part, only cold and petrifying fear.'

'Then we'll have to agree to disagree on that point,' Drummond concluded amiably.

William looked at his notes, waiting for the fire to pass. 'Do you have a comment for me or not?'

Drummond took his seat again, tapping two fingers on his desk. 'Only to say, I have put Durham back to work. This is my home now and I intend to remain here for a very, very long time.'

William looked up and their eyes locked. He snapped his notebook closed and stood.

'You're not only a deluded brute, but you're a fool as well. Maggie offered you friendship, genuine and honest friendship, and you attacked her for her troubles. She was willing to give you what only some of us are fortunate enough to have earned: her trust.'

He left the office without saying goodbye. When he was through the gates and on the road, he ran.

CHAPTER 43

WILLIAM DID NOT TELL Maggie about his meeting with Drummond. Even two days later, when Armstrong published his article in the *Advertiser*, he still did not tell her. He had not been able quell the anger within himself following their exchange.

He named Tommy Fellowes as the source. Remembering Tommy's past failings, the community were disappointed but not surprised at his actions. Nevertheless, they offered him sympathy and support, as they also recalled the passion with which he had advocated for miners in the past. Meanwhile, Drummond went to immediate lengths to quash any suggestion their dealings with one another had been corrupt. He addressed the colliers at the pit, then he addressed community concerns at a meeting he organised at St Bede's.

William had wanted Drummond on the back foot when the article appeared in the newspaper. Instead, by requesting a comment, he had alerted Drummond to danger. He was ready with excuses and promises as soon as the publication rolled off the press. Presented with the truth of William's article and the lies that spouted from

Drummond's nefarious mouth, the community chose to believe the latter, reluctant to live through another mine closure.

Maggie rubbed William's shoulders sympathetically as he read, then reread, his article.

'I know you feel like it was a complete waste of time, but you're wrong. You've got some people doubting Drummond. As they say, there's no smoke without fire. We'll get him one day. Maybe not today, but soon.'

He frowned, unconvinced. 'Drummond's going to get off scot-free while Tommy's reputation is in tatters. He made pointed comments during his address at St Bede's about Tommy's gambling habit, and even suggested Tommy's been stealing from the union dues ...' William shook his head in disgust. 'The poor man will be forced to resign. There's nowt else for him to do.'

'His downfall is Shakespearean in magnitude,' Lydia said. Maggie and William agreed. To Maggie's surprise, Lydia had been following the proceedings avidly.

'Tommy knew the risks when he spoke to you,' Maggie said, taking a place by William's side. 'I believe going on the record was his way of making amends with himself and his family, not to mention the colliers he represents. As you said, he is a good man. Colluding with Drummond must have been a terrible experience for him ... The guilt and angst ... I can't even imagine.'

William took her hand and smiled. 'I'm so very glad we have each other.'

'As am I—'

There was a knock at the door. Maggie rose and opened it. Standing on the other side were Lucy Owen and her children. She was dressed in a pretty emerald cloak, and her cheeks were plump and rosy. It seemed that out of Reggie's reach, she had thrived.

Lucy and the children brushed themselves of snow before entering.

'Oh, gracious,' Maggie cried. 'Did you walk all the way from town in this snow?'

The children nodded, grinning. They had clearly delighted in the experience.

William went about making refreshments for them all as Maggie introduced her mother.

'Tell me, Lucy,' Maggie said excitedly. Although their time as compatriots had been brief, Maggie had felt a certain affinity with the young woman. 'What are you doing back in Durham?'

William drew the children towards the pantry to help him find the shortbread Maggie and Lydia had baked the day before.

'I canna guarantee the quality, mind. The bakers, you see, aren't from around here.' He glanced at Maggie and her mother mischievously.

When they were out of sight, Lucy answered Maggie's question.

'When I heard what happened to Reggie, I was numb for weeks. I knew I was supposed to be grieving, sorrowful and lonely. But I felt nothing of that.'

Maggie nodded sympathetically.

'While I knew it would devastate the children, I only felt elation.'

Maggie clutched her hand. 'That's entirely understand-able. He brutalised you for so many years. Of course you would be happy, knowing you could now live in peace.'

Lucy nodded.

'Then, once the children had overcome the initial shock of the news, we decided to come home. Without Reggie, I think I can make a very happy life for us here.'

'Bravo, Lucy!' Maggie said. 'I am thrilled you have returned.'

'As am I,' Lydia put in as she prepared the teapot. 'Marriage must be an honest and open partnership. Otherwise, it can never be a happy union.'

Maggie looked at her mother as she warmed the pot in the way Grace had shown her. It seemed there were quite a few lessons her mother had learnt recently.

Refreshments and shortbread were consumed with gusto. The presence of the children seemed to distract William from thoughts of Drummond, Tommy and the article. Maggie watched him entertain them for a time; he had such a natural way with youngsters. Then she and the women discussed how Lucy might support her family now she was alone.

'It's the only aspect of my return that concerns me,' she admitted. 'My brother would happily have kept us with him in Bristol, but ...' Lucy shrugged.

'Durham is your home,' Maggie finished. 'Obviously, you can't find work at the colliery. Since your departure, I have discovered that Drummond is a despicable man, even more brutal than your late husband. Beth might need help at the store ...' Then Maggie frowned, deep in thought. A minute later, a smile spread across her face.

'What is it?' Lucy asked, curious.

'What are your interests, Lucy? What are you good at?'

Lucy looked at her, puzzled. 'How do you mean?'

'In what subject would you be confident to instruct children?'

'Numbers,' she replied without a second's hesitation. 'I was always quite gifted with numbers.'

WILLIAM INSISTED he drive Lucy and the children into town. As they were readying to depart, donning coats, scarves and boots, there was yet another knock at the door. It was Constable Stackhouse. He briefly took in the scene – Maggie and William, then the children who crowded near the entrance and, finally, Lucy. His eyes stopped on her momentarily. Maggie noticed the constable blush. His cheeks became the colour of a robin redbreast. Andy removed his hat and slotted it under his arm, then pushed his hair from his brow.

'Good morning, to yer all.'

'What can I do for you, Constable?' Maggie asked.

'It's William I need to speak to, Miss Almond.'

William walked outside with Andy. Maggie watched the snow silver William's dark hair and his face become grave as Andy told him the news.

ANDY OPENED the cell door and William entered. He had seen the inside of a cell occasionally when he had written for the *Courant* in Newcastle. He could recall each visit he made to Newcastle Gaol. He had always been fearful the gaolers would mistake him for an inmate and lock him inside. The place was cold and damp and rancid with the smell of piss and shit. But it was the echoing screams of the men that William remembered most. They would have done anything not to be there. William would have done anything, too. If not for his career as a journalist, he would happily have avoided the dreadful place altogether. The prisoners and gaolers treated each other like animals.

The lone cell in the constable's office was smaller than those in Newcastle, but it was clean and warm. It was rarely called into use in a county such as Durham. Most of the crimes were so minor as to be considered sins; the offenders were usually penalised with a strict talking to by the constable, or a meagre fine they could afford. Tommy sat on a narrow bunk with his head in his hands.

'What's the matter with you, man?' William asked, removing his cap. 'To confess to two murders I know you did not commit ... It's madness!'

Tommy lifted his face and took William in. 'There's nothing else for me to do. Matthew Drummond paid me a visit last night. He threatened Deborah, Willie ... he threatened to hurt my girl if—'

'If you didn't confess to the murders of Briar Haines and Reggie Owen?'

Tommy nodded glumly. 'I dinna kill the girl. I would never harm an innocent lass. I want yer to know that, Willie.'

'I know, Tommy,' William murmured, his heart sinking. 'Tell me exactly what happened.'

Once Tommy began, William sat by his side on the bunk and listened carefully to his godfather's words, contemplating each one, sifting through the facts, hoping to find a clue that would prove the man's innocence. William heard how he was summoned to the colliery by Drummond on the late afternoon of Briar's disappearance. Drummond explained he was sending Briar away. Reggie was escorting her to the station to make sure she was on the ten o'clock train to London.

'Yer see, Willie,' Tommy almost whispered. 'I told Drummond that Briar was a friend of yours and Maggie's.'

William's shoulders tensed. 'When?'

'Not long after he employed her.'

William sighed and rubbed his forehead. *That poor lass*, William thought. *No wonder he had Reggie follow her.* William was unsure how he would ever be able to divulge this to Maggie, or the part he had played in it.

'Oh, Tommy,' William said, heaving another sigh.

'If I knew where it would lead,' the older man said. 'I swear, Willie ...'

Disappointment swept over William's face like a sullying cloud and prompted Tommy's tears. William was incapable of offering comfort. The image of Tommy Fellowes, his own godfather, as the voice of the colliers, as his father's best friend, was in pieces on the cold stone floor of the gaol cell.

'Just tell me what happened next.'

Tommy wiped his eyes on the heels of his hands and breathed deeply for a moment while he calmed.

'I followed them.'

'Why?'

'I knew Reggie was a demon. I wasn't privy to Drummond's orders, but I knew Reggie would be up to no good. Sure enough, on the road out of town, after they had stopped at Miss Haines's lodgings, Reggie turned south instead of north. The lass sensed something was wrong immediately. When I saw her drop her bag near Swin Bridge, I knew she was trying to lay a trail. Then after another mile or so, she called for him to stop. I was at least a mile behind Reggie's cart, but I heard her cry out. Reggie pulled the horses up.'

William wondered what excuse Briar had given. She was a creative lass and not reluctant to make a scene.

'Before the cart was entirely still, she leapt from the seat and took off at a sprint into the woods. She was fast, but Reggie followed. I drove my cart up to Reggie's and went into the woods myself. By the time I reached the trees, I could hear her screams and the shouts and grunts of Reggie. She was fighting hard to get away from him. I walked towards the sounds as quick as I could, but these legs ...' he paused and looked forlornly down at his bowed limbs. 'When I got to them, Reggie was already holding her head under the water. She was still fighting, though; I could see her arms flailing. Only a man of Reggie's strength could have held her down.

'I looked about me for a weapon – yer know I could never take Reggie in a fight – and I found a rock. I bashed him on the back of the head with it. He never saw it coming. But he straightened and turned, and looked at me in surprise. His hand went to his head, and he saw the blood. Then he stumbled a few yards away and collapsed. I ran to the girl and heaved her from the water, but it was too late.'

William felt sick in the stomach, not only because of Reggie's actions, but because of Tommy's deception. 'And you left them there for the animals to find,' he said in disgust.

Tommy did not respond.

William rose and walked the length of the small cell. It was only two steps for a man of his size. He tried to think.

'Do you believe Drummond directed Reggie to murder Briar, or did he kill her for another reason?'

Tommy shrugged. 'I don't know, Willie. Drummond is a devil, but Reggie was a thug. You know how he treated his wife ...'

And I know how Drummond treated Maggie, William thought.

❦

MAGGIE SAT by the hearth as William told her what Tommy had confessed to him. Lydia was present, too.

'It beggars belief. The tale is worthy of Dickens,' Lydia said, ashen faced when William had finished.

Maggie's complexion had grown even paler than her mother's. She was silent, staring into the flames. William went to her and knelt down, taking her hands.

'Maggie, there's something else.' He took a deep breath. Knowing Maggie's feelings towards Briar, he hoped she could find it in her heart to forgive him.

'Drummond knew Briar was a friend of ours from London. He must have suspected she was working with us.'

Maggie's wide brown eyes met William's. They swam with tears, waiting for release.

'How? We were always so careful. All he witnessed was an acquaintance forming after she had arrived. It was only natural she would make friends. Even with what Reggie would have seen ... It was still no proof she was a spy. How could he have known we were friends?'

'Because I told Tommy.'

CHAPTER 44

The Manchester Guardian
Wednesday, December 15, 1880

DEAR READER,

Forgiveness is possibly the most difficult of all human behaviours. Throughout my life there have been many people whom I have had to forgive in order to grow. Anger is such a destructive emotion; it devastates the way forward like a flash of lightning. To grow, we must forgive. I learnt that from George, of course. He could so readily and effortlessly forgive. George forgave slights against his appearance and manners; he forgave his wife for locking him into a marriage and a financial predicament that, for many years, was crippling; he forgave me for my haughtiness during our first meetings. Finally, he forgave himself for all his failings as a man. This made him an even nobler one. Well, in my eyes, at least.

George would often chide me. After an insult or negative review, I would take to my bed for days. I could not eat or sleep. Writing was impossible. George would burst into the room and throw open the curtains. 'Polly!' he would say, because that was his favourite name for me (although for what reason I am still unsure; he did like to amuse himself). 'You are atrophying in here. Your ego is as fragile as Baccarat crystal! You must learn to forgive and forget.' During these episodes, he would liken me to one of the plants for which he cared; George liked to consider maladies of the psyche from a scientific – occasionally botanical – perspective. 'You are destined to thrive! Forgive whoever it was for the affront and grow.'

I am now sixty years old. Over my long life, I have been maligned, defamed and rebuffed. More, I would wager, than most women of my advanced years. My appearance, lifestyle, values and opinions have all suffered criticism. As a public figure of some renown, I have finally accepted this is my lot. However, I have forgiven most people who have wounded me. I have even forgiven the great American author (although he prefers to believe he is an Englishman) Henry James for slandering me in public as a 'horsed-face bluestocking'. That particular comment had me in bed for a week! I now take it as a badge of honour. Horse-faced? I cannot deny my similarity to the equine species when I gaze into the looking glass each day. And bluestocking? I am proudly so.

When we embark on any new relationship, we do so with a certain level of trust, whether it be with a lover, a friend, a spouse or even the coal man. I believe trust is as valuable as a facetted gem and when it is broken, the pain seems irreparable. However, we must find it in our hearts to blast through the boulder of anger that blocks our way and forge a path to forgiveness.

⚜

HER FEET WERE FROZEN when she reached Marian's home. Water soaked her boots through and the hem of her skirt was dripping. There had been a heavy snowfall overnight; departing the cottage in a rush, citing her appointment with Marian as an excuse, she had worn the wrong boots, coat and hat. William had run after her, offering to drive her into town, but she had declined. She could barely look at him and she certainly did not wish to speak to him. She feared if they were to discuss his error in judgement, she would voice feelings impossible to rescind.

She was being foolish and stubborn, she knew, but at present, forgiveness seemed impossible. They had promised one another they would not divulge their relationship with

Briar to anyone. She had trusted him to honour that promise. Yet he had confided in Tommy.

The previous night, seeing his pain, his absolute anguish at not only discovering Tommy's betrayal but also the role (albeit unintentional) he had played in Briar's death had almost softened her. But then she remembered. Briar had lost her life to Reggie Owen. With flashes of her own attack by Drummond plaguing her mind, Maggie could not stop herself from imagining what her friend might have endured. At the hands of a man like Reggie, death might have been welcome.

She pushed her thoughts aside and knocked on the door. Julia answered promptly and took her wet cloak and hat. 'I'll put these near the fire, Miss,' she said. 'They'll be dry in a jiffy.'

Maggie slid her feet out of her sodden boots and placed them together by the door. When she turned, Mister Cross was making his way down the stairs. They bid one another good morning.

'You are early, Miss Almond. Marian isn't feeling quite herself today. I'm afraid her lower back is aflame with pain from her kidneys. I had intended to send word to you, but although I have counselled against it, Marion wishes to proceed with your meeting.'

'I'm so sorry to hear it. Please, she need not feel obliged. I can come back tomorrow,' Maggie said, remembering the journey she had so stubbornly taken through the snow to get here. Mister Cross seemed pained himself. Clearly, he did not wish to defy his wife's instructions by sending Maggie away.

'I hope to get her back to London by the end of the week ...'

'I see. Perhaps we should go ahead then,' Maggie said, growing frustrated. 'I will stop if she becomes very uncomfortable.'

Mister Cross reluctantly nodded then led Maggie up the

staircase. She had never ventured upstairs before. In keeping with the sitting room, the furnishings were understated and elegant. She could see exactly why Mister and Missus Cross had chosen the home.

Before they entered Marian's bedroom, Mister Cross stopped her.

'I have given my wife a small dose of laudanum,' he whispered. 'It should ease the pain she is experiencing. If she seems not entirely lucid, you will consider this when writing your article. Missus Cross trusts you, Miss Almond.'

'Of course,' Maggie answered.

Marian rested in her bed, propped up by a great number of pillows. A chair was already waiting by the bedside. She held out her hand and gripped Maggie's.

'I'm so glad you came. I was watching the snow fall last night, and I feared it would hinder your journey here this morning.'

Marian had not been quite so warm during their previous meetings. Maggie recalled Claire Clairmont describing the effects of laudanum on herself and Shelley. She had remarked that it was 'warm and numbing'.

Maggie sat. 'This is our final interview, Marian. Neither snow, nor rain, nor heat, nor gloom of night stays this journalist from the swift completion of her appointed rounds.'

Marian laughed. 'You've adapted Herodotus. You are very clever.'

Feeling as she did, Maggie could only muster a half smile at the compliment. 'I know Mister Cross wishes to take you home to London. I am determined not to delay your departure.'

Marian patted Maggie's hand then examined her for a moment. 'You are a devoted friend, Maggie. But I am concerned ... You do not seem yourself today. Your stockinged feet, sodden hem and damp hair ... You did not dress for the weather. While I've noticed this is a minor fault in your character, today your oversights are profound.'

It seemed to Maggie that Marian could see everything, such was her power of observation.

'I had a disagreement with William last night and hastened from the cottage early this morning, forgetting more suitable attire,' she said, looking down at her sodden dress.

Marian leant her head back onto a downy pillow. 'Friends will always have disagreements. They will always unintentionally hurt one another in their efforts to improve the other. There will always be misunderstandings and missteps. That is the risk we take when we begin to trust in people, when we begin to care. It is how we grow, Maggie.'

The younger woman nodded. She remembered having a similar conversation with her father last year in his conservatory, after she had pushed William away.

'Where would you like to begin today?' Marian asked.

'Mister Cross,' Maggie said, opening her notebook. 'We have discussed Mister Lewes at such length. As I looked over my notes this morning, I realise our discussions about him go for pages. He was your teacher and husband, manager, lover and, most importantly, your friend. But I want to learn more about your relationship with Mister Cross. As I'm certain both men would agree, your first husband was an extremely hard act to follow.'

Marian smiled slowly.

'You mentioned during our very first meeting on the Palace Green that your honeymoon was difficult. One reason you offered was your level of fame. You could venture nowhere without being harassed by admirers. But surely Mister Cross was aware of this? He had been in your life for some time before you married. You had travelled with him before. For a time, he was your and Mister Lewes's closest confidante and—'

'Being husband to me changed a great deal in our relationship.'

Maggie looked up.

'It was easy to ignore the attention before Johnny was my husband because it was not directed at him. It did not affect him then. George adored the attention, and I tolerated it for him. He could listen for hours to my praises; in fact, he took great pleasure in encouraging them. John is different.'

Maggie waited for elaboration, but the authoress remained silent for some time. Maggie searched Marian's face for some indication of what she was thinking. Eventually, she decided it was now or never – she had to find out what Marian was keeping from her.

'Why did you marry Mister Cross?' Maggie asked. 'You were a spinster for nearly a lifetime. Why did you choose to marry John Cross at sixty? It seems ... out of character.'

Marian shifted on her pillow. Her eyes grew heavy. Maggie could see she was uncomfortable.

'Laudanum doesn't remove the pain,' she said quietly. 'It merely distances it, as though what I'm experiencing is the memory of pain.'

'Marian,' Maggie said, determined to persist. 'Why did you marry John?'

The older woman sighed. 'I believed it would make us closer friends. You see, Maggie, what I had lost in George was my best friend. He and I shared everything ... When he died, I found I could barely live without him. I hoped that John might go some way to making life tolerable again ...'

Marian's voice drifted away.

'And did he?'

When no answer came, Maggie looked up from her notes.

Marian was asleep, the laudanum claiming her unspoken answer.

Maggie rose and walked to the window. The snow had begun to fall again.

☙❧

MAGGIE LEFT THE HOUSE, closing the door quietly behind her. She didn't want to speak to Mister Cross, so she crept down the hall to the kitchen and grabbed her coat and hat. They were draped over a chair near the range. Julia had been correct; they had dried in a jiffy. Then she slipped her feet into her wet shoes and tiptoed through the door.

The snow had recently ceased and the river path was white. Not a single footprint sullied the image. *Crunch*, she stepped forward, *crunch* again. Such a satisfying sound. She imagined herself a pioneer, forging onwards, ever onwards into the wild.

Marian had spoken of forgiveness and trust, as though she sensed Maggie's dilemma. Such a keen observer. Even in her laudanum fog, she had noticed Maggie's physical and spiritual disarray.

When she approached Prebends Bridge, she saw William waiting for her in their spot. Snow dusted his cap and coat. She wondered how long he had been waiting for her.

'Hello,' she said quietly when she drew near to him.

She had startled him. He spun to face her. 'You were a long time.'

'Marian was not well and fell asleep. I sat by her side for a while, thinking. Looking at her and thinking.'

She edged nearer, closing the gap.

'About?' His tone was tentative.

'Marian seemed so young when she was asleep. Apart from her greying hair, she might have been a young woman again. I am sure her condition is more serious than she told me, or even her husband is aware. William, I don't think she will last out the year ...' Tears began forming in her eyes. 'But I don't think she is concerned. She had loved George for a quarter of a century ... She had loved him with everything she possessed, every ounce of her being. Her mind and body, her spirit and soul, were so firmly twined with his that I believe she began dying the moment he left her. A small part of her began drifting away each day.'

William wrapped his arm around her; their familiar warmth buoyed her spirit.

'It's exactly how I feel about you. I refuse to spend one moment away from you, and I refuse to be angry with you any longer.'

He pulled her closer into an embrace.

'You trusted Tommy. It was a mistake but entirely understandable, just as I wanted to believe Matthew Drummond was an honourable man. All they can accuse us of is naivete and the desire to believe people are better than they actually are.'

She sighed, resting her head against William's shoulder.

'Drummond fooled us, William. He is much more cunning than we could have ever imagined. He would have discovered Briar's true purpose without Tommy. But I know that whatever Drummond has in store for this town we can face together. And together we will stop him. He has no power over us and never will.'

They took one another's hand and began their walk back to the cottage through the freshly fallen snow.

CHAPTER 45

TWO DAYS LATER, as Maggie was wrestling with the final article, she received a message from John Cross notifying her they would leave the following day. Marian was well enough to travel, and she longed to return to London in order to begin on a new work of fiction. The message finished with 'My wife has requested the pleasure of your company for tea this afternoon at three o'clock.'

When Maggie read the note, she couldn't help but smile. Marian never asked or negotiated; George Eliot was queenlier than the Queen. Still, Maggie was grateful for the interruption to her work. The idea of ending the series was daunting, and she still didn't know how Marian's story should conclude. In a way, her marriage to John Cross signalled the beginning of new life for Marian, yet it seemed the great writer couldn't see her future in that light.

Promptly at three, Maggie knocked on the Cross's front door and was shown into the sitting room by Julia. The couple were waiting for her. Marian was standing at the window, hands clutched behind her back, gazing at the cathedral. So slender, she had the lithe form of a much younger woman.

'The cathedral would be such a wonderful setting for a novel,' said Marian, turning.

She glanced at her husband and Mister Cross excused himself, referring to their belongings that remained unpacked.

'Oh, indeed,' Maggie agreed, eagerly. 'Is it what you have in mind for your next work? A novel set in Durham?'

Marian stared at her, bewildered, then she slowly shook her head. 'You should write that story, Maggie. Observation is a gift which you possess. For over a year, you have watched your neighbours as an outsider, seeing what they can't see themselves. It would be a masterpiece.'

Maggie laughed. 'I believe I am more afraid of writing fiction than you were, Marian.'

Marian took a seat and gestured to the other chair for Maggie. 'Then perhaps I will have to speak to Mister Dodd ...' she said, raising an eyebrow.

'I think we will leave the fiction writing to you, Marian,' replied Maggie, amused.

As Marian settled into her chair, her demeaner grew more serious.

'Maggie, I do not intend to write anything else. My well is finally empty. I am handing you the torch.'

Maggie's stomach sank. The thought that there would be no further tales from her hero completely astonished her.

'But—'

'A story centred around the Stanley Pit collapse would make a gripping work of fiction. I will even make an intro-duction for you at Blackwood's. You're an extremely fine writer and, with your imagination and determination, you could easily move into fiction.'

Maggie could not quite believe what she was hearing ...

she longed for the ability to capture the moment forever. For her writing to be praised by George Eliot was a joy she had only ever dreamt of before now ... The author of *Middlemarch* suggesting she write a novel? Maggie's heart lifted. Then she felt the sudden prick of tears behind her eyes as she remembered that Briar had once counselled the same.

Marian folded her hands in her lap as though the matter had been settled. Their conversation was soon interrupted by Julia, who arrived to serve them tea. Once she had departed, Marian produced an envelope from her pocket then, after staring at it gravely for a moment, she handed it to Maggie.

'I have written you a letter. Once you read what it contains, I trust you will know what to do with it.'

Maggie went to tear open the envelope with the energy with which she performed every task.

'Stop!' Marian said sharply. 'Not now ... Good gracious, girl, it isn't a letter from the Million lottery!'

Maggie looked abashed and she placed the envelope in her bag.

'It is for when you are alone.'

Maggie nodded contritely, as though rebuked by Queen Victoria herself, then lifted her teacup to her lips.

Durham County
Great Britain

December 1, 1880

Dearest Maggie,

John's first proposal came when we were reading Dante together. It was so unexpected, so out of the blue, that I asked him to repeat himself. And he did. He claimed he wanted to take care of me as George had. I must admit, the thought was tempting and John was so attractive ... How I adored looking at him. Michelangelo could not have chiselled a finer specimen. However, I informed him it was an utterly ridiculous notion and he should never mention the subject of marriage again.

He wasn't deterred and continued to visit me daily. We would read Dante and he would stay for supper. Eventually, he asked me to marry him once more. He was so earnest in his request, I could not help but take it seriously the second time. However, I dismissed him again, reminding him of our age difference and the fact he could marry any woman in England. I reminded him that he was a relatively young man who might want a family, and I was incapable of giving him children.

Yet he persisted. What made me relent? I can hear that question issue from your lips in that soft, honeyed way you have of asking troublesome questions.

I met with my dear friend Barbara. She guessed something was on my mind and I confided in her. Barbara advised me that if he made me happy, I should marry him. She had offered me the same advice regarding George all those years ago.

Johnny did make me happy. It was in a different way to George, but his kindness and gentleness were restorative for me. My physician believed marriage was an excellent idea as well. Even though I was old and ill, he informed me a partnership with Johnny Cross was just the thing to put me right. As for my concerns regarding the physical aspects of marriage, he said there was nothing stopping a woman of sixty from having an entirely satisfactory sexual relationship.

It was a matter I had discussed with Johnny. He was delighted by the doctor's assessment, but suggested we wait until our wedding night to consummate our marriage; despite my intense desire for him, I assented, consumed as I was by the romance of his suggestion.

Based on those two counsels, I finally agreed to Johnny's proposal and we were married at St George's in Hanover Square on May 6th. John made all the arrangements. I wore a lavender silk gown trimmed in navy lace, and he wore an exquisite burgundy frock coat with turquoise trousers. In my eyes, the groom was far more glamorous than the bride.

We spent our wedding night on the ship ferrying us to Calais. John had seen to organising our honeymoon as well, and he had reserved a lovely cabin on deck. Dressed in my silk nightgown, anointed with perfume, I waited nervously (and rather excitedly) in our bed until he had finished his whiskey. Listening closely, I heard the glass placed on the shelf. Then I heard the cabin door open and close, and the sound of his footsteps on deck.

Confused, I continued to wait for some time, imagining he would return shortly. But he did not. Eventually, I fell asleep.

I could not help but wonder if he was even more nervous than I. Although he was a grown man when we had met, since George and I had known him, we had never seen him with a young woman on his arm. But we had assumed there must have been women … I can still recall there had been a rumour of an Hungarian princess at one time. But Johnny was always so discreet, we were never sure.

Following that evening, we continued our travels through France and Germany. At every stop along the way, he had reserved apartments with two chambers. We would bid each other goodnight and go our separate ways. Arriving at each new destination, my anxiety rose. In Paris, I was mistaken for John's mother, and in Munich, during a day of sightseeing, I was forced to stop. My legs would not keep pace with his; they had finally worn out.

I became more and more obsessed with our age difference and, to make matters worse, oh, how I longed for George … Every location we visited reminded me of being there with him and of our intimacies. We had always had a strong physical connection, in addition to our intellectual one.

Eventually, we reached Venice. Once again, John had reserved an apartment with two chambers. He had also purchased tickets for the theatre that night – Mendelssohn's Italian Symphony. I did not share with Johnny my first experience with that particular symphony, how I had grown hysterical with jealousy and contempt; however, I felt just as anxious that night in Venice as I had as a young woman in Birmingham. You see, I was intending to broach the subject of our sleeping arrangements after the performance.

I wore an emerald gown John's sister had helped me choose as part of my trousseau. I powdered my face to hide the lines and rouged my cheeks, hoping I might gain a youthful glow. Finally, I asked the maid to fix my hair in a different way to the simple bun that was my preferred style. I had hoped it would make me appear more alluring.

The opera was wonderful, although my experience was sullied by the conversation I knew I must have with Johnny. On the gondola ride back to the Hotel Europa, I broached the subject of physical intimacy. He listened closely. When I finished, he apologised for being so remiss, assuring me he loved me in every way. It was the memory of George that was holding him back, he claimed. He told me that having seen our love firsthand, he was hesitant and nervous, fearing he would never measure up to George in that regard. I assured him that was nonsense.

That night, he came to me in my chamber. Although we had shared kisses before, when his lips met mine, they felt alien, and the touch of his hands were foreign to me. While the experience was not unpleasant, it was nothing like the charged intimacies I had shared with George, and I could sense John's apprehension. I attempted to reassure him, but it only made matters worse.

After that evening, what had been an enjoyable honeymoon of companions became fraught. We could not agree on anything. We bickered and our tolerance for each other became strained. The heat only made the situation more impossible. And he absolutely hated the mantilla I wore.

'You are not a widow anymore,' he cried on one occasion. 'You are a bride.'

But I did not feel that way. I was still grieving for George, but I was also experiencing a new grief at the sudden death of my marriage to John. For apart from that first night together, he did not come to me again. It appeared that my reassurances had not been enough.

The tension between us increased. Finally, as though to exclaim to the world how dissatisfied with me he was, he leapt from the balcony of our apartment and into the Grand Canal. I heard the splash, then the uproar that came soon after. I rushed to the window and saw John floundering in the murky depths of a Venice canal. He went under and I screamed. A gondolier dived from his vessel and saved him, dragging him out of the water with some difficulty. It was as though my new husband's body was weighted with lead.

We returned to England immediately. I hired a nurse to accompany us. For most of the trip, John was sedated. I was in constant fear he would attempt to take his own life again and I simply could not imagine losing him as well.

However, the worst of it was that it was not only for him that I was concerned. For what did it say about me that my husband attempted to kill himself on our honeymoon? Did he not love me? Did he find me so physically repulsive that death was preferable to sharing my bed? Or was it his own inadequacy that had forced him to take such drastic action? I had so many questions, yet no way to find answers for any of them.

At least, back at the Heights we would be concealed.

Concealment. Once we were home I slowly came to realise that in his life, John, Johnny, 'nephew' and Mister Cross had worn almost as many masks as had I in mine. He had hidden his true nature so expertly from both George and me that we never guessed his secret ... You see, Maggie, John was not made to love women in the way that George was.

At first, my disappointment knew no bounds. But after much consideration, I realised that John wished the best for me. I know if George had suspected John could not love me wholly, he would never have suggested that he look on me as a potential wife. Yet John concealed his nature in order to do so, because he does love me – fervently, as you have seen – in his own way. Now that I understand him more clearly, our relationship has evolved and, while not entirely satisfactory, it is greater than tolerable. He attempts to please me and I pretend I am satisfied with all aspects of our marriage.

However, we have not shared a bed since that night in Venice. It is difficult for me to admit that he has made no further attempt at such an encounter ... and neither have I. You see, once I came to know John better, I realised that on the night we finally came together, he sacrificed a part of himself in an attempt to fulfil my needs. To go against his true self, so much so that he tried to end his life after the fact ... I am sure you will understand that I simply could not – will not – ask it of him again.

To my great relief, John has much improved since our return to England. We now live companionably and equally as friends, although to the world, we are husband and wife.

I could sense you trying to pry this information from me, to have a fuller understanding of my marriage. I have accepted that John and I will never have the physical and intellectual relationship I had hoped for – a meeting of the body and mind in the way that I had with George. In retrospect, I admit that was an unreasonable expectation to have of a man so different from my true love.

Oh, how I longed to tell you the truth! Yet despite my desire to tell my story honestly, I have no wish to betray John. He does so much for me, and in such good faith. He has love in his heart for me; I can see that through his every action. And, while it may surprise you to know this, I still live in fear of being laughed at, particularly as I have worked so hard throughout my life to be revered.

I trust you, dear Maggie, to do with this information what you will. You have lived a similar life to me and so I feel you are the best judge of what is newsworthy.

Although Doctor Paget assures me my illness is not life threatening, I sense it is. I hear George calling to me in the depths of night and occasionally in the day. He would have enjoyed Durham and relished the myriad of life-and-death dramas that seem to characterise the place. 'It is far, far better than fiction, Polly!' I can hear him exclaiming joyfully. Be assured that I do not wish to minimise your pain; however, George partook in all aspects of life (even death) like a glutton. He thrilled in meeting people, and I think he would have liked you very much indeed ... as do I.

Good luck to you, dear girl, with your writing and your school. You deserve every success. You have given me faith that when I leave this world, I leave it in expert hands.

Yours contentedly,
Marian Evans Lewes Cross

CHAPTER 46

The Manchester Guardian
Wednesday, December 22, 1880

DEAR READER,

I know how your imagination must be churning. For a woman of my advanced years to be married to a man twenty years her junior is scandalous, is it not? But, as you must have discovered from reading these missives, I am no stranger to scandal.

In truth, I never imagined I would fall in love again. At three score years of age, I considered myself well past my prime. However, when John Cross proposed to me, I decided – after some understandable hesitation on my part – to accept. Wholeheartedly. Unreservedly. Delightedly.

Johnny yearned for a large wedding at St. George's in Hanover Place, where all the fashionable weddings take place. He demanded guests by the thousand! In my insecurities over our marriage, it comforted me that Johnny longed to make a great show of the day. However, I pressed for a more modest ceremony with only close friends and family present.

For twenty-four years, I had considered myself a married woman. While I had never experienced the pleasure of being a bride, I was, to my mind, Missus George Lewes. Following George's death, I was also a widow, an aspect of my character I did not wish to deny. Therefore, I chose lavender for my marriage to John and decided I should have black lace around the neckline and sleeves of my gown. In retrospect, I must thank Mary and Eleanor, Johnny's sisters, for persuading me navy blue was quite enough to show my widowhood – it was much less sombre. And I admit I took some pleasure in being escorted around London by Johnny's sisters as they helped me assemble my trousseau, choosing flowers for my bouquet and deciding on my wardrobe for the honeymoon.

It was Charley, George's eldest son, who walked me down the aisle. As he did, I could feel George around me everywhere. He sat in every pew and his beaming smile shot waves of good wishes towards me. George would have wanted me to be happy. He told me many times that his role in life was to protect me and keep me warm. I believed it vexed him that he could not see the job done to its end.

I kept our wedding a secret from you at the time, dear Reader, for while I knew I would receive the best wishes of some, I was certain there would also be slurs and criticism flung at me for wedding a man twenty years my junior. It was not until we were aboard the ship and sailing across the English Channel en route to France that Willie, John's brother, was instructed to send our wedding notice to the *Times*. Although I have been toughened like old leather from the insults and attacks on my character over the past forty years, I did not wish the first days of our marriage to be sullied by abuse. Prior to marrying me, my husband had led a quiet life far away from the spotlight, and he did not relish the attention our union would bring.

Dear Reader, John and I have been married for only six months, but we have enjoyed peace and contentedness during that time. Johnny has lived out what was once George's duty: he has taken care of me very well. He is currently seeing to the renovations of our new home in Cheyne Walk, where my study overlooks the river. When I begin my work in the wee hours of the morning, before the hammer, thump and thwack of the tradesmen disturbs my peace, I can hear the cry of golden plovers as they congregate on the shore. I am reminded of Warwickshire and Old Griff, and that life is a cycle of beginnings and endings. I find myself at the start once more, enjoying the light of a new day dawning.

Merry Christmas one and all,

Yours contentedly,

Missus Marian Cross

MAGGIE PLACED her pen on its stand. She removed Marian's letter from the envelope and read the words once more. It was clear to her that Marian had been wanting to share this truth with her for some time but had been reluctant to until the very last moment; the letter was dated early December. Since receiving the confession – for that's what Maggie considered it to be – she must have read the words a thousand times. Each time, she would be overcome by a different emotion: grief, sadness, shock, compassion. She did not believe Marian wanted her to use the information in her final article. In fact, she had trusted Maggie not to, just as Claire Clairmont had trusted her to tell her story. Yet Marian had needed to confide in someone who would not judge her or attempt to remedy the situation. Mary Anne Evans had evolved into so many women; Missus John Cross was her last manifestation, and she wanted Maggie to know the truth of it.

Maggie knew it was not a satisfactory way to live and certainly one Marian had not expected when she had agreed to marry John Cross. However, she had companionship and John was a caring and doting partner, even if he could not be a husband in every way that mattered. Maggie was certain the final article would satisfy both Marian and John. While she had revealed the truth of Marian's life, she felt sure that leaving this final veil in place was what Marian wished her to do.

There was a knock on the door and William poked his head into the room.

'Finished yet?'

Maggie nodded as she blotted the pages.

'I've got something to show you.'

By the time she entered the kitchen, William was waiting by the door with her coat, hat and boots. He was as excited as a schoolboy.

'Hurry, lass. You're as slow as cold treacle.'

Maggie rolled her eyes. William's expressions never ceased to amuse her.

'Where are we going?' she asked as she tied her laces.

He remained silent, grinning like a lunatic.

They walked through the snow to the river, then along the path until they reached the old mill house at the spot where they went swimming last summer. Perched on the river's edge, the two-storey structure had been abandoned for years. Maggie looked at William and raised an eyebrow. She wondered why he had brought her to the place in the dead of winter.

'It's for sale,' he said, snatching her hand. 'Come inside.'

He led her through the door and into an open space where the grain would have once been stored.

'This would make a bonny school room, wouldn't it?'

Maggie looked around her. An image struck her in an instant: the room lined with tables and children – dozens of children, both girls and boys.

'Upstairs, the miller's residence is a grand place. We could live there. And there's room enough for Mam if she gets lonely at the cottage. But to my mind—'

'She could teach here alongside Lucy and me.'

William nodded. Clutching her hand, he led her upstairs to a glorious room at the front of the house, overlooking the river.

'This would be our room.'

Maggie imagined waking there. She looked out the window at the river, then below at the grounds. They were large enough for the students to play in. It would be a perfect place to work and live.

'You could teach the children to fish,' Maggie suggested.

William nodded. 'A place this size is not cheap, but with

the money from your article and future series, Briar's funds, your mother's contribution and with what we've saved ...'

Maggie looked around her for a moment, then left the room and inspected the others. Four bedrooms, an expansive sitting room and a kitchen. The residence also seemed to possess a plethora of nooks and crannies; in these, Maggie instantly pictured bookshelves, writing desks and armchairs for reading. When William caught up to her, he informed her they were once used as storage spaces for grain sacks. *Grain sacks, indeed!* Maggie thought. The home was almost as grand as Chester Square, although it would require repair and renovation.

Descending the stairs, she examined the schoolroom once more. Finally, she walked out into the garden and looked back at the house. William followed.

'You're killing me, lass. What do you think?'

'It's a wonderful idea, William. It will be perfect for ...' Maggie looked at him expectantly, her eyes light and hopeful.

'Miss Almond's Preparatory School?' William suggested.

'The Briar Haines School for Girls and Boys,' Maggie corrected.

William nodded and pulled her into his arms.

As she gazed up at him, Maggie saw him anew. He was her partner, her support, her love ... and her best friend. They were their truest selves when with each other. She knew she would find no other to better match her and she didn't want to.

William watched as a different light appeared in her eyes.

He waited, gazing at her, searching her face, unsure what was coming. Finally, she let him go and took a step back. She took his hands and looked into his eyes.

'William, would you—'

Then he realised. 'Hush! You know I support equal rights, but this is my part.'

He quickly lowered to one knee and produced his mother's ring from his pocket. He'd been carrying it for weeks.

'Maggie Almond, would you do me the honour, the absolute pleasure ...' he paused, offering an opportunity for her to object. When she didn't, he continued with renewed vigour.

'Would you do me the honour of becoming my wife?'

She wasn't certain why this was the moment, but it was as though a switch had been flicked on in her mind. Everything that had happened over the last few months and all she had learnt from writing Marian's tale had led her to this end.

'Yes!' she cried into the sky, pulling him to his feet. He slipped the ring on her finger.

He took her in his arms and spun her in the air. When they kissed, Durham instantly felt like home. But it wasn't Durham that was home, it was William. He was her home and her heart. She never wanted to be separated from this man.

'We will make a wonderful life here together, William,' she said, kissing him again.

ENJOYED MAGGIE ALMOND AND THE MASKED WOMAN?

Thanks for reading *Maggie Almond and the Masked Woman*. If you enjoyed the story, sign up for my newsletter at www.jennybondbooks.com. You'll be notified of giveaways, new releases and receive updates of my author journey.

And share a review where you bought the book, on Goodreads, or contact me at www.jennybondboooks.com and share your thoughts.

Book 1

ALSO BY JENNY BOND
THE DAWNLAND CHRONICLES

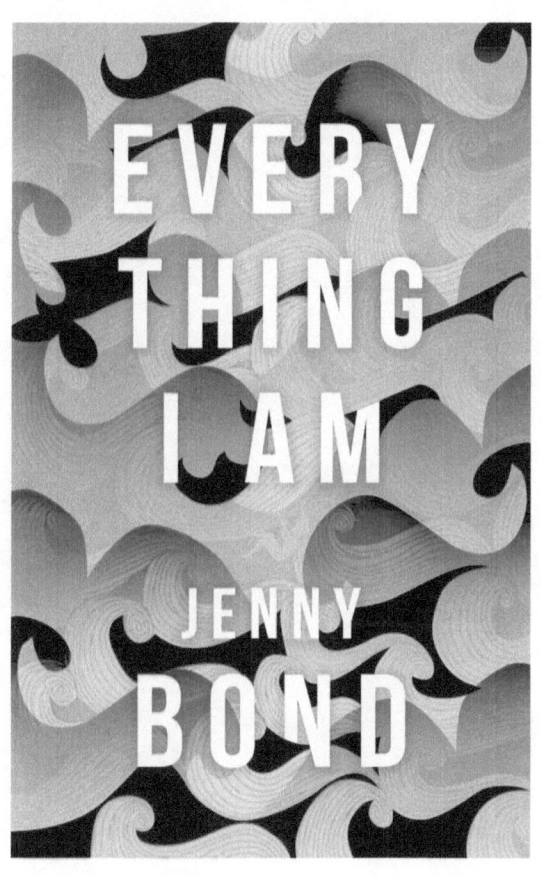

AFTERWORD

Why George Eliot? In Book 1 of the series - *Maggie Almond and the Scandalous Sister* - Maggie keeps a framed portrait of the authoress on her nightstand. Eliot is Maggie's literary hero and *Middlemarch*, her favourite book. Independent, talented, outspoken and unconventional, Eliot is the woman on whom Maggie has modelled her life. So, when Eliot arrives in Durham, requesting Maggie write her story, Maggie simply can't say no.

Maggie Almond and the Masked Woman came together quickly. George Eliot, aka Mary Ann Evans, Marian Evans, Marian Evans Lewes and (finally) Marian Cross, was a complicated woman. As I researched her life, I realised Eliot's challenges, hardships and triumphs would provide perfect lessons for Maggie as she navigates her new life and burgeoning career in Durham. Likewise, Eliot's characters in *Middlemarch* inform Maggie's choices and experiences as well.

I enjoyed bringing Durham to life in the novel. My mother's family hails from the county. Until recently, the clan lived in a small hamlet called Windynook. Growing up, I was swept up in the romance of the quirky name. I vividly remember posting my grandmother's letters to her cousins who lived in the village, in awe of the length of the address.

When I lived in England in the early 2000s, I visited Windynook and it was not as romantic or quirky as I had imagined. The neighbourhood was working class and rough around the edges. But the historical centre of Durham - the castle, cathedral, university and the river that winds through its centre were beautiful.

My grandmother and her siblings migrated to Australia in the early 1920s. Her brothers were colliers, and my grandmother, Elizabeth, was just 17 or 18 years old. They found a home in Newcastle in NSW, another mining community. Within a few months, my grandmother moved to Sydney to find work.

Even though she left Durham when she was a teenager, Elizabeth would often use words – such as *nowt* and *daft* – and she would often omit *the* from sentences. *Put it on table* was an instruction I received frequently. More importantly, she described to me the dangers of a pitman's life and the sense of dread that rose in her chest when her father and brothers walked to the pit each morning to begin their gruelling and perilous occupation.

As well as countless websites and journal articles I scoured during the research process, three books helped me immensely:

1. *George Eliot* by Jenny Uglow (1987)

2. *Road to Middlemarch: My Life with George Eliot* by Rebecca Mead (2014)

3. *The Journals of George Eliot* edited by Margaret Harris and Judith Johnston (1998)

Of course, I re-read *Middlemarch* as well as *Adam Bede* and *Scenes of Clerical Life* to reacquaint myself with the author's style and themes.

Finally, I drew a great deal of inspiration from the journals and letters written by Eliot. Although I have attempted to use my own words in *Maggie Almond and the Masked Woman*, I hope I have imbued Marian's correspondence with her voice and a sense of her hopes, challenges and values.

STRIDE FURTHER INTO
MAGGIE'S WORLD

Check out my Pinterest board for the novel - images that provided inspiration and information during the writing process.

Listen to the Spotify playlist of the series. Music, past and present, aimed to reflect the themes and atmosphere of the story.

To access either of the above, on the relevant platform search 'jennybondbooks'.

ACKNOWLEDGMENTS

Thank you for reading *Maggie Almond and the Masked Woman*. I hope you found the experiences of Maggie and Marian moving and inspiring.

Women throughout history have had to fight so hard to have their views taken seriously and to live in the manner they wish. I would like to say thank you to those advocates of equal rights - past and present, men and women.

As always, I would like to express my gratitude to my editor Sylvia Balog. Her appreciation of words and her affinity with historical fiction make my stories so much better.

Likewise, without Jo Egan's eye for detail and knowledge of all things grammar - and spelling - related, readers could not enjoy the polished and professional product that they do. It is an absolute pleasure to work with both these amazing women.

ABOUT THE AUTHOR

I'm an author of contemporary fiction, historical fiction and non-fiction. I have published my books in Australia, New Zealand, USA and Europe.

I'm also an English teacher and I've been lucky enough to introduce the love of language to many students around the world.

I guess this also planted the seed of an idea that I should give writing a go myself

Sydney, Australia, is where I was born and raised, but prior to my reinvention as a writer (which had something to do with a friendly argument with my husband!), I held the position of Head of English at Eaton House The Manor in London's Clapham Common. I also taught English and Drama for eight years at a selective high school in Sydney, and for five years at a private girls' college in Canberra.

Whether I've been at home, living and working in another country, or travelling for the sake of adventure, I have never spent a single day without a book by my side. This meant slipping from the act of reading into the act of writing didn't actually seem that much of a change.

I've long been a fan of great historical fiction writers such as Hilary Mantel, but I also spend quality time with books by authors from other genres, such as Margaret Atwood, Kate Atkinson, Karen Brooks, Tim Winton, Ian McEwan, Jane Austen, John Irving and E. Annie Proulx.

I live in Canberra, Australia with my husband, two sons, and a lively Staffordshire Bull Terrier named Mick.

I enjoy running, swimming and yoga daily, as I believe staying active is an integral component of a happy writing life. You can visit me at www.jennybondbooks.com.au.

As well as historical fiction, I have a passion for really big donuts.

www.ingramcontent.com/pod-product-compliance
Lightning Source LLC
Chambersburg PA
CBHW050105120726
47904CB00004B/1224